Breathred leaned back, satisfied with his handiwork. The spell had worked just like the handbook said it would. He didn't have long to dwell on his success. A prickling dappled his spine. A weighty pressure fell on the base of his neck. The prickling rapidly became a cold sweat. He was too late. His stupidity had let him become entrapped in the vampire's grip.

He tried not to move, even though the smell his own fear filled the recesses of his quivering nose hair. He forced his hand to reach for a stake, but found he was immobilized with fright. He tried not to dwell on the fact vampire hunters did not freeze up when faced with a vampire. It was just so unseemly.

The vampire nuzzled his neck. The soft hair of its mustache sent goose pimples over the soft flesh. Breathred's right eye slowly moved to his side. Hoping for a glimpse of his captor, all he could see was the monster's shadow frosting the left side of his face.

Then the beast struck. Four missiles of agony coursed through his neck. Breathred let fly an anguished squeal sounding like a cross between a game show contestant and an inebriated wildebeest. The sound seemed to weaken the vampire's hold on his brain. Breathred shot from the floor like a monkey on fire, but the vamp refused to relinquish his bite. Streaking from one end of the kitchen to the other, he tried to dislodge the bloodsucker to no avail. The vampire wouldn't let go.

Breathred would have thought his girlish whimpering would have 'caused the monster to release him, if for no other reason than to laugh at his hapless victim, but no such luck. A mad dash into the aging stove sent the old lady's supper flying into the air. Luckily, for the floor, the majority of it landed on Breathred, scalding those areas not encased in leather and superheating those that were.

Another round of shrieks filled the air. This time they were of a higher octave, but no less annoying in timbre. Amid the howling, Breathred decided he had had enough. He was a vampire slayer, by Gumby.

Champagne Books Presents

Mis-Staked

By

J. Morgan

This is a work of fiction. The characters, incidents and dialogues in this book are of the author's imagination and are not to be construed as real. Any resemblance to actual events or persons, living or dead, is completely coincidental.

No part of this book may be reproduced or transmitted in any form or by any means, electronic or mechanical, including photocopying, recording, or by any information storage and retrieval system, without permission in writing from the publisher.

Champagne Books
www.champagnebooks.com
Copyright © 2007 by J. Morgan
ISBN 978-1-897445-74-7
April 2008
Cover Art © Christopher Butts
Produced in Canada

Champagne Books
#35069-4604 37 ST SW
Calgary, AB T3E 7C7
Canada

Dedication

This book is for my Dad. I may not be living in his basement, but I ain't far from it. And for Rochelle for helping me get it together when it was all over the place.

Prologue

Don't be alarmed. Let me get this out of the way, so you faint at hearts don't go all postal before I get this story going. This tale is purely fictional in nature, except for those parts which are unfortunately real. It is even more tragic to note the parts you think are made-up are those are in fact the unabashed truth. To those readers who feel better sleeping at night thinking nothing is real, feel free to keep thinking so. I have never been a primate to deny the delusions of the delusional.

First off let me assure you, I have endeavored in no way to attain this position of being the sole chronicler of the imbecilic hero, whom you will shortly meet. Like life itself, the odious task was thrust unwilling upon me. Through circumstances beyond my control I came into the service of one Breathred E. Petrifunck. I do not wish to go into the particulars of the sad event. Let us just simply say it was the best thing that ever happened to him.

Before I go any further, let me tell you, I am not human, nor do I quest for such an unsavory burden. I am simply content to be a citizen of simian descent, a chimpanzee to be more precise. A sight more intelligent than one Mr. Petrifunck, I have no modesty in assuring you.

Which explains his choice of a name for me, Stud Lee Monkey. Like I stated earlier in this preface—humanity is a burden to those of you who wear it. I have overcome this painful moniker, nonetheless. Through considerable tribulation on my part, I am the chimpanzee you see before you today. The evidence of this is the lengthy tome you now hold in your hands.

As I said before, my main purpose in this dreadful melodrama was to assist Mr. Petrifunck. For those of you who consider yourselves well versed in the occult, you may wrongly name me a *familiar*. Through another failed attempt at rising above mediocrity, I rose above my birth to become so much more. Perhaps if time allows, or readership demands the tale, I will go into that debacle at a later date. Considering the readership of these penny dreadfuls a sequel is a distinct possibility, but I digress.

This is tale, however, tells the story of how my erstwhile master came to fame, or infamy depending on how history chooses to record it. It all started with an ad in the back of a comic book. You know the kind: "See the mysteries of the unknown in seven easy steps." It might have worked out differently if the moron hadn't been more than a little bit inclined toward that brand of science, or if this hadn't been his first foray into the field. This was just another in a long line of attempts to become something more than a drain on society, and his father.

Once the packet arrived from—forgive me—The Boffrend School of Vampire Slaying and On-line Technical Support, there was no stopping him. Believe me when I say this is something I would never try to make up. It is just so bizarre it had to be true. In no time he devoured the flimsy tome, using his well-chewed highlighter to single out those sections of particular interest. The fact he came to excel in this his chosen profession was no surprise to me. Despite his ingrained naiveté, he was somewhat of a genius in his own demented way. It was just the rudiments of common sense that seemed to elude him.

I watched all this with silent bemusement. I gave the whole thing a month before he switched to something less trying on his fragile mentality. It wasn't until after the second and third crates arrived I began to worry. By then it was too late. Our road was set to my ultimate humiliation.

Author Notes.

* To help finance this manuscript, each chapter heading will contain a snippet of wisdom from Dr. William Wainsboro, author of the Boffrend School of Vampire Slaying Handbook, Volumes One through Thirty-Seven.

** Being a chimpanzee doesn't mean I'm willing to work for bananas and humorous outfits. Those I get for free.

One

When dealing with the undead, the best course of action is to run like hell.

It was raining. It was always raining. If you find yourself living in Seattle for more than a week, you become used to it, or you move somewhere slightly drier, like in the middle of a rain forest. That isn't to say it doesn't have its perks. You never had to wake up and ask yourself: *Is it going to rain today?* Because ninety-percent of the time the answer is yes. The other ten percent you dress for rain just in case. Tonight was no exception to the rule. The rain started as a slow drizzle and pretty much continued along the same vein through the day and into the night.

To the man dressed in black, it was nothing new. Breathred had suffered these slings and arrows for most of his life and was accustomed to the weather and to the numerous other little things existing solely to make his life miserable.

Case in point. Leather did not coexist well with water. It tended to shrink in the most uncomfortable of places, but what was he to do? Vampire slayers had to wear black leather body suits. It said so right on page thirteen of the handbook. So once again, he found himself damned by the very thing he strived to become.

The longer he waded through the wet night, the more the leather shrank to his body, like a painful second skin. He dealt with pinched genitalia and cramped calves in the only way he knew how: he sweated, which only aggravated the condition. Even that simple sentence was not adequate to describe the situation. Unfortunately for him, his body produced enough sweat that an entirely new ecosystem popped into existence to handle the runoff.

Breathred couldn't help himself. He came from a long line of sweaty people. He swore somewhere along the line someone would have figured out a way to breed the condition out of the gene pool. As of yet, no one had the foresight to do so. Long ago he had formed the opinion the condition resulted from the fact that his family only had two branches, and they went up and down in a single line.

Finally, the ceaseless squish-squish-pinch of the leather was more than he could bear. He had to do something, no matter how unbecoming it might look. Breathred hazarded a peek to see if anyone was looking. Once satisfied no one was giving him a second glance, he reached down and pulled at the crotch of his body suit. Sweet relief flooded his face. Then the leather slipped from his wet fingers and slammed the suit once more back into its former position. The effect was like a gunshot through his prostate. He immediately doubled over and gasped in unrestrained agony. Needless to say, he fell writhing to the rain-washed street.

After executing several gyrations defying modern science, he lay limp and panting on the rain-soaked sidewalk. His face rested slackly amid the pooling water. Once assured he was still whole, he allowed his eyes to roll back to their proper position. He watched the procession of passing ankles for a few minutes more before attempting the more arduous task of sitting up.

Except for a momentary spike of pain riding his spine straight to his brain, Breathred found he could indeed still move without the use of functional testicles. Just a theory, mind you, because he had never put the functional part of that statement to use before. There had been this one time at fat camp, but he wasn't sure if he could consider it an actual test, or even if he wanted to. Lord knows he had spent enough time suppressing the memory to be bringing it up now.

Deciding vampire slayers didn't squat on rain drenched sidewalks he stumbled to his wobbly feet. The exercise left him winded, but otherwise unhurt, except for the obvious—the throbbing groin. Against his better judgment, he ran his hand over the damaged body part. Despite what Father Benedict had warned him about, he found he did not go blind from doing so, nor did he come to find the sensation pleasurable like Father Sebastian had tried to convince him it would.

After the systems check was finished, he was happy to discover despite the soaking, he was remarkably dry after the unfortunate experience. Besides, luck seemed to be with him for the moment, the leather had worked its way loose from its previous fit. Feeling better, he let his gawky frame prance down the sidewalk undisturbed by the stares his leather-clad form was beginning to draw.

To say Breathred Petrifunck was geeky would be putting the case mildly. He stood six four in bare feet. Most of it comprised of jutting bones with very little muscle poking out in any way, shape, or form. The only part of his body that had any definition was his stomach and the only definition befitting this body part was pudgy. Over the years he had tried to work on it, but never seemed to get past slightly pudgy before deeming himself fit enough to wear shorts and an oversized tank top to hide the fact his workouts had been less than successful.

He hadn't had to endure the perils of teen acne, so his face was clear of blemishes; his only redeeming characteristic. His eyes never could seem to settle on a color preference, so they shifted from blue to green before finally affixing themselves to gray. His nose was a little too pointy but otherwise defined his face quite well. He also allowed himself a makeshift mustache and beard, though the hair couldn't seem to grow in the places he wanted it to and flourished in the areas that didn't need the excess. He tried to totally forget the unruly mop of black hair all together.

In spite of all these flaws, both those named here, and those left out for the pacing of the story, Breathred saw himself as quite a dashing figure, which was all that mattered, anyway. It wasn't too much of a stretch of the imagination to see him in the same light as he saw himself, unless you were within twenty feet of him. From a distance he had a mysterious Johnny Depp quality that made people take notice. Up close was a different story.

His legs once again responded to nerve impulses, other than pain that is. Breathred found he was able to make good time to the distant corner of the street. At his destination, Breathred reached into his pocket, extracting a soggy piece of paper. Through the smudges he was able to discern the address leading to the eventual end to his quest. Looking at the street sign, he judged he was, indeed, on the right track and promptly turned down the next blind alley he came to.

The alley ended abruptly against a brick wall, which he would have seen if he had not still been reading the now-useless piece of paper. The impact was neither loud, nor was it painful when compared to the leather-wrenching groin injury of the earlier paragraph.

Still, the skull-jarring hit did give him one brief moment of conscious-altering euphoria enabling him to transcend his usual state of being. In that instant he saw answers to questions he had never even considered. As it is with such things, the feeling passed all too soon, but it did leave him with enough insight to realize he had made a wrong turn.

While not as intelligent as a moment ago, he was able to safely stagger back onto the sidewalk without further injury. From there he had little trouble accessing his meager mental database, ticking through the rough-hewn collection of numbers until finally settling on the newest in the collection. With the address firmly affixed in his mind's-eye Breathred headed in the proper direction, more or less.

After half an hour more, his search came to an abrupt end. In truth it wasn't all that abrupt, but for the purposes of story direction we'll say it was. As incredible as it is to believe, he had circled his destination four times without noticing it. On the fifth circuit, Breathred found the object of his search—102 Carrington Ave—nestled amongst the weeping buildings.

From the exterior the place looked homey. Its decor was from somewhere in the fifties. In the intervening years the city had grown up around it, giving the place the appearance of a willow among redwoods. An iron fence bordered the house, casting flickering daggers on the wet sidewalk. The ancient structure was broken apart by age and abuse. It was almost undetectable by the raging river of ivy that had already taken over the yard, with sights on the street beyond.

Breathred took a deep breath, idly fingering the signet ring on his right hand, as he always did at times of self-induced stress. This was no time to be nervous, but he couldn't help himself. Everything he had ever done in his sad, pathetic life led up to this moment. The ring was part of his journey, but he didn't like to think about it. Some things were best left forgotten, like he could ever be fortunate enough to become a victim of selective amnesia.

This adventure was to be his *trial by fire*. All the hours of study were finally going to pay off. He patted the handbook where it was situated right next to his heart beneath his black duster. It was his own private talisman. He wouldn't be able to whip the book out in front of his client, but he felt better knowing it was there. He pushed those fleeting thoughts of failure from his mind. A new life started for him at this exact moment.

He ran down his mental checklist and judged that he was as ready as he would ever be. He pushed the rusty gate until it whined in protest. It lodged against a mass of ivy and came to a screeching halt, leaving Breathred with less than twenty inches of space in which to squeeze his lanky frame through.

Drawing a deep breath, his oversized chest popped up, allowing a mountain of pudge to suck in. Rising up on his tiptoes, no easy thing to do with wet leather grabbing at hair and other assorted epidermal extremities, Breathred slid between the two rusted gateposts.

At the last minute a bulge (his modesty prevents me from revealing which bulge) caught on the gate's heavy iron latch. He tugged and slipped free, throwing him clear of the confining opening. After his own momentum took over, Breathred spiraled down the cobbled walk. He was able to regain his balance just as he slammed into the peeling paint of the front door.

Thankfully the brass door knocker dominating the thirty-six by eighty inch panel stopped his headlong advance. It rang with a muted thump, as it struck the middle of his forehead. The sound was followed by dull echo Breathred was sure came from a back molar he had been meaning to see a dentist about.

The throbbing ring subsided just as the door creaked open. A chain stopped the door an inch from the frame. Breathred bent down to peer through the meager sliver. A cobwebbed eye glared back at him. It unnerved him somewhat, but being in the profession he was, he decided it was best to become accustomed to disembodied eyes.

"What'd ya want?" a voice croaked.

"Oh great floating eye, there are many things I want, but I guess world peace would be a good start," Breathred answered in a clear and distinct voice. He hoped he had chosen wisely. It was so hard to know for sure in these situations.

"Dumb-ass," the voice stated, before slamming the door, which added a new crease to the tip of his nose.

Rubbing yet another damaged piece of anatomy, it dawned on him the floating eye must have an owner. This epiphany was indeed a jump for his beleaguered mind. In someone else, it might be a breakthrough. In Breathred, it amounted to a blank spot in need of filling. Giving his nose a final twist, he decided to take a different approach to this turn at knocking on the door.

"If you're a Moonie, I have mace," the muffled voice shouted through the door.

"No, madam. It is I, Breathred Petrifunck, fearless vampire slayer," Breathed announced, deciding to overwhelm her with his magnetic personality.

"Vacuum salesman. Already have a vacuum. A Eureka, which is better than the swill you're probably hawking."

"No ma'am. Vampire slayer!" Breathred shouted through the keyhole. "You answered my advertisement."

He listened to the sliding of locks and assorted other attachments. This went on for several seconds before the door finally creaked open again. This time the floating eye was joined by another eye to match it, as well as a face and a body.

"Well, come on in, but don't try any funny business. I won't stand for any funny business, do you hear me?"

Breathred nodded and moved past the woman who looked about eighty (a hundred and seventy-five might have been closer to the truth) standing framed in the pale light filtering from the pasty interior. A flashing blue wig sat cocked on the left side of her chubby head. If you crossed a shar-pei with a spoiled lemon, you would come close to describing the look of the woman's face. The rest of her enormous form was covered in what could have been a tent if not for the stylized flower patterns that gave her the appearance of a Rose Parade float.

Noting the presence of an aged and cracked Louisville Slugger gripped in her left hand, Breathred thought it best to set the woman's mind at ease. How to accomplish the feat was the problem. Despite her gruff exterior, she was obviously a haunted woman. Otherwise, she wouldn't have called him in the first place.

"Okay, dingleberry, you have five seconds to explain yourself before I start swinging," she said, testing the air with a sharp swing that belied her age-worn appearance.

"As I explained outside, you rang me this afternoon in answer to my advertisement in the *Weekly Probe*," Breathred said, deciding caution was the best course to follow.

"You bastards aren't getting another penny out of me until Elvis sends me my child support check," she screamed, brandishing the bat viciously.

"No, My Lady. I am here for your vampire." Breathred rose up to his full height, but was more than ready to run for the door.

Two

Don't worry, no one hits a home-run their first time out. The secret is not to look like a fool while doing it

"You're here for Bruiser." The old woman let the bat drop to her side. Breathred couldn't help but notice her grip on the bat had in no way lessened, in spite of it dropping.

"I guess I am, Ma'am," Breathred said, nervously moving out of swinging range. "Before I get started, what was the first clue letting you know Bruiser was one of the undead?"

"It was your ad. He had every symptom you listed—bad breath, fangs, the whole works." She shuffled over to an ancient armchair. With an immense sigh, she let her massive bulk plop onto the protesting Lazy Boy.

"How long has he been acting like this?" Breathred asked, wishing he had brought a notepad to make him appear more official.

"Well, a week I reckon. He likes to go out just after Jeopardy for his constitutional. Normally, he's home in time for the late news. This one night he never came home. How I fretted over him being out there all alone! He's such a delicate soul. Then, the next night he came strolling in like nothing happened," she explained, mopping a strangled tear from her cheek with a dingy washcloth she pulled from the folds of her muumuu.

"Did he act strangely when he returned?" Breathred inquired, making mental notes.

"Well, he just curled up on the couch and started licking himself, as pretty as you please. I let it slide, seeing as how grateful I was to have the dear home again. So, right before Jeopardy—he never misses his Jeopardy—I brought him his dinner, like usual. He wouldn't touch it. I fixed his favorite, and the ungrateful little shit wouldn't even nibble it!" she screamed at the swinging door behind her.

"And you found that odd?"

"Usually, he gulps it down and whines for more. So, when I went over to get his plate, he tried to bite me!" She slapped the arm of the chair in disgusted fury.

"What did you do then?" Breathred felt the excitement of the hunt taking over.

"I kicked the little fucker. Try to bite me and I'll give you the same," she warned, cocking a painted-on eyebrow toward him, just in case Breathred felt froggy.

"Well, yes Ma'am. I don't think that'll be necessary. Back to the vampire—where is he now?" Breathred hoped to change the subject. The thought of another assault on his person might diminish his credibility as a vampire slayer.

She motioned behind her. "He's in the kitchen. Last time I went in there he was sitting on top of the freezer, hissing at the light bulb."

"I'd advise you to vacate the house until I've dealt with the vampire," Breathred stated, eyeing the door he assumed led to the kitchen.

"Bullshit! *Storm Stories* is coming on. That Jim Cantore sho' butters my muffin. Do what you got to do, but my butt ain't moving." She ended her statement by grabbing the remote and flicking on the TV.

Breathred thought about forcing her to leave. That thought lasted about as long as it took to think it before evaporating from his mind. It wasn't that he thought she could take him. Well, probably couldn't take him. If it wasn't for the bat, he might have given it a harder try. She was a civilian and, as such, deserved his respect. If she wanted to stay here and see to it he did the job correctly, he couldn't stop her. She was footing the bill after all.

He slapped his forehead. He forgot to mention his fee. According to the handbook, fees should be discussed up front. The possibility of not surviving an encounter with the undead also increased the possibility of the client not paying death benefits to the slayer's family.

It was too late now. Surely, the vampire couldn't be too powerful. Otherwise, the old lady would have been running and screaming from the house. Then again, considering the woman in question, the direct opposite might be true, which would have the vampire running for his life. His fears aside, this was going to be a cakewalk. He had the handbook, the garlic, the holy water, and enough silver-tipped stakes to throw the Dow Jones into a recession. Breathred steeled his resolve. It was time to get down to business.

His hand roamed under his duster until it settled over the crucifix he had specially blessed for tonight. It felt warm to the touch. Strange, it had to be about nineteen degrees outside. The old lady had the small house set at about ten thousand degrees below freezing. He dragged the golden crucifix from the heavy covering of his jacket, allowing a soft glow to shine in the dim light. In the end he decided its warmth comforted him. As well it should, he had bought it from the EBAY window at the Papal web page after all.

Taking a deep breath, he pushed in on the kitchen door. It swung in, tossing him off balance. He tumbled into an avocado-green fragment loosed from the very bowels of hell. Yellow-ochre floor tiles swam up to meet his collapsing body. His cheek skidded across the cracked tile, soon followed by the rest of his lanky form.

"Keep it down, Dipshit. Jim's trying to explain about cumulus clouds," the old woman shouted from the living room. "Hey, check my Hamburger Helper, while you're in there. If it burns, it's your ass."

Breathred groaned. This was not going well. He rolled onto his back. A shiver of pain ran up his spine. Fate picked that exact instant to throw a shadow over him. The vampire!

He jumped to a crouch, trying to catch a glimpse of the undead specter. His head snapped to and fro. It would have swiveled, if he could have managed it. He could find no sign of his quarry. The foul spirit must be in his gaseous form. That was the only explanation he could think of that made sense.

Again, the shadow flitted across his upturned face. If the vampire assumed solid form while he was unprepared, he was as good as dead. Breathred scoured his mind for the answer to his dilemma. The handbook had mentioned something about forcing a vampire to come forward. Then, it hit him. The proper mixture of holy water and garlic extract would form a mist he could use to ensnare the most devious of vampires.

Breathred thrust his hands in the deep pockets of his duster, releasing a barrage of vials from the lint-choked depths. He almost cried as bottles flew everywhere. He hastily reached out to gather them up. His hands flew around the uneven floor, as the small bottles rolled down the sloping floor toward the back door.

With one eye watching for the vampire, he finally retrieved the last of the vials. Thankfully, he was able to accomplish this without losing any more of his precious tools. He had at least had the foresight to pad his pockets with tissue. Otherwise, they would not have survived the trip here in the first place.

He rummaged through the glass menagerie, locating the two bottles he needed. He scooped the rest up and threw them back in his pockets. He then turned to his outside pocket and pulled out a miniature Bunsen burner, which he set on the floor in front of him.

"Don't forget about my Hamburger Helper, Pretty Boy," the old woman snarled, sending Breathred's hands to shaking.

On the third try, the burner ignited. A thin blue flame licked the underside of the brass bowl Breathred held over it. He allowed two drops of holy water to hit the sizzling brass. He quickly added three dollops of garlic extract to the mix. In no time a fine green mist rose from the brazier.

Breathred leaned back, satisfied with his handiwork. The spell had worked just like the handbook said it would. He didn't have long to dwell on his success. A prickling dappled his spine. A weighty pressure fell on the base of his neck. The prickling rapidly became a cold sweat. He was too late. His stupidity had let him become entrapped in the vampire's grip.

He tried not to move, even though the smell his own fear filled the recesses of his quivering nose hair. He forced his hand to reach for a stake, but found he was immobilized with fright. He tried not to dwell on the fact vampire hunters did not freeze up when faced with a vampire. It was just so unseemly.

The vampire nuzzled his neck. The soft hair of its mustache sent goose pimples over the soft flesh. Breathred's right eye slowly moved to his side. Hoping for a glimpse of his captor, all he could see was the monster's shadow frosting the left side of his face.

Then the beast struck. Four missiles of agony coursed through his neck. Breathred let fly an anguished squeal sounding like a cross between a game show contestant and an inebriated wildebeest. The sound seemed to weaken the vampire's hold on his brain. Breathred shot from the floor like a monkey on fire, but the vamp refused to relinquish his bite. Streaking from one end of the kitchen to the other, he tried to dislodge the bloodsucker to no avail. The vampire wouldn't let go.

Breathred would have thought his girlish whimpering would have 'caused the monster to release him, if for no other reason than to laugh at his hapless victim, but no such luck. A mad dash into the aging stove sent the old lady's supper flying into the air. Luckily, for the floor, the majority of it landed on Breathred, scalding those areas not encased in leather and superheating those that were.

Another round of shrieks filled the air. This time they were of a higher octave, but no less annoying in timbre. Amid the howling, Breathred decided he had had enough. He was a vampire slayer, by Gumby.

He swung around, throwing his back against the wall. He smiled, when he heard a bone-curdling crunch on impact. It took him several seconds to realize the sound originated from his own fractured spine, and not from any damaged he'd managed to inflict upon the vampire, which was absolutely none. For the second time in the span of an hour, Breathred's eyes took a first hand perusal of his brain, as he slid limply to the cold floor of the kitchen.

He lay there, trying his best to ignore the pain. It seemed inconsequential to worry about mere physical pain. He had suffered the vampire's kiss. Any minute now his body would change and he would become that which he hunted. How ignominious to fail on his first mission.

Being one of the undead wouldn't be so bad. He rarely left his father's basement during the day, anyway. If he could stomach sushi, blood should be no problem. It would be like salty ketchup. Now that he thought about it, there were a number of people he wouldn't mind putting the bite on—that smelly Mr. Callabash, for one. Breathred had never forgiven him for an erroneous graded D-minus in the fifth grade. Smelly old fart always had it in for him. Yes, this could work out for the best, he thought with a devilish grin.

A weight fell on his chest, which could only be the vampire's hand. This was it, the coup de grace. Breathred squinched his eyes tight, not wanting to see his final moments at the vampire's hands, or fangs—whatever the case may be.

The undead beast's tongue flicked over the flesh of his neck. It felt like raw, wet sandpaper against his skin. Breathred felt the soft purr of its breath tickling his nose hairs. A river of sweat swam over his forehead in expectation of his immediate demise.

Breathred silently clicked off the seconds until his life ended. He was hesitant to state the obvious, his life was meaningless, but it was close to being so. He had never amounted to anything. There was so much more he could have done with the life he'd been dealt. Heck, he never even left his father's house, unless moving into the basement counted, which he was sure didn't. If this was to be his end, then he would face it like a man, or like a mewling coward who was able to at least open his eyes to witness it. It was the least he could do, considering how badly he had screwed everything else up.

On the count of three his eyes flew open. A pair of slotted eyes greeted him. They were framed by a face of gray fur. He noticed none of those details. The one thing he did take note of was the fact the vampire's long white whiskers tickled his cheek.

Realization hit him like a soon-to-be-ex-wife with a summons in one hand and a ball peen hammer in the other. The vampire was a cat. Incredulous to be sure. Vampire cats simply were unheard of. Could this be a new breed sent by the undead hierarchy to ensnare People for the Ethical Treatment of Animals for its own foul devises? It was too dastardly to consider.

To his ultimate horror the ca-mpire, as Breathred decided to call it, licked him and proceeded to situate itself on his face. Breathred was content to let his captor do as he pleased, as long as it continued his existence. It was when the ca-mpire lifted his leg and started licking regions best left unnamed when Breathred had finally had enough. He could take being transformed into one of the walking dead, but being the receptacle for said feline's nether juices was where he drew the proverbial line.

The main problem, as Breathred saw it: how did one remove a ca-mpire from one's face? He gently raised his hands until they were even with his cheek. The cat stopped its bath and glanced over incredulously. It offered Breathred a disgruntled meow as if to say, do you really think that is such a good idea? Truthfully, Breathred wasn't so sure, but the fact a pair of semi-attached hairballs now dangled precariously over his pursed lips gave him very little choice.

Throwing caution to the wind, he slapped his hands together. The cat, being slightly smarter and quicker, saw the move coming. Defying gravity as only a cat can, it leapt into the air, performed a perfect back flip and came right back down onto Breathred's shocked face seconds after the two hands had slammed together.

Breathred let out an unholy scream, which galvanized the cat into action. The cat let out its own howl before sinking all four sets of claws into the side of Breathred's head. The action sent the slayer flying to his feet. After that, instinct took over. His arms flailing Breathred soared around the kitchen. He tried every possible tactic he could think of to remove the hysterical feline. His attempts only drove its claws deeper into his thrashing head.

From the corner of his eye, he spotted a spatula hanging from a rack next to the stove. Angling his body, he swung toward it. He snagged the utensil on the first try. Using one hand, he was able to pry the cat's tail up. He deftly inserted the spatula under the upturned appendage.

This only served to drive the animal mad. Its claws dragged inward, sending tendrils of pain throughout Breathred's aching cranium. Breathred fell against the kitchen door, flipping back first into the living room. His twirling flight took him directly into the path of his irate client. The sight of him and the howling cat drew her away from her show. She shot him a perturbed glare, but made no move to aid him in his plight. With no other opinions in sight he fell to the floor at her feet.

"Boy, what the hell is wrong with you? Are you on the crank? Have you been snorting jungle weed in my kitchen? My God, what'll the neighbors think?"

"Mabam, wub you tindly remube dis rrussy fub my race," Breathred croaked from under the cat's gyrating body.

"Here now! I am not paying you to play with my Bruiser! I'm paying you to kill the vampiric beast. Get busy with your job and let me finish watching my story," she wobbled to her feet and ripped the cat from his bleeding face. She snorted with an upturned glare. "Is that my Hamburger Helper on your clothes?"

The cat took that moment to decide it was his job to clean Breathred off and jumped from the woman's clawed hand to Breathred's heaving chest. After getting over the initial shock of the cat, Breathred allowed himself to breathe again.

He pointed at the cat. "Is this the vampire, ma'am?"

The cat took exception to this and slashed his hand with his claws. He purred and continued to eat the congealed tomato sauce and burnt hamburger off the side of Breathred's face.

"Yes, you fool. Can't you tell he has fallen under some demonic spell? Are you blind as well as stupid?" She turned to the TV suddenly and let out an aggravated howl. "Will you look at that? You made me miss the end of my show. Jim always winks at me just before he signs off." She clasped her hands together, turning her attention back to Breathred. "Well, are you going to get rid of the vampire or are you just going to lay there, bleeding all night?"

"Madam, you have my word there is no vampire here." He answered her. He had begun to rethink his whole ca-mpire theory. The cat backed up this notion by licking an unsavory section of his anatomy and throwing Breathred a superior-sounding snort to confirm this suspicion.

"Good job, then." She dragged her purse from the folds of her muumuu. He started to stop her, but she pulled out a ten and handed it to him before he could say anything. "You should know that I took out for the cost of the Hamburger Helper. After all the mess you made you should go down to the Chinese takeaway and get me some supper. My blood sugar's a bit low after all this excitement," she sniffed.

"I will be more than happy to." Breathred replied, silently hoping she would beg off. "Do you wish to give me the money?"

"I just gave you a ten, didn't I, Dumb-ass? You better be glad I'm letting you keep the damn change and aren't charging you for having to clean up the kitchen. Tell Wang that Polly sent you. He knows what I like." She flopped back down in her chair and waved her hand at him, letting him know the discussion was at an end.

Breathred shrugged and headed for the door. Bruiser looked up from his continuing bath and gave a growl sounding a little too amorous for Breathred's liking. He didn't even look back as the door closed behind him. He just hoped no one from Boffrends heard about this. Somehow he doubted vampire slayers were supposed to get their heads handed to them by a cat or be stiffed by little old ladies. Then again how was he to know? This was his first night on the job, after all.

Three

The main thing to remember is this—no matter what you think, the undead are not *more afraid of you than you are of them.*

The place had been boarded up for some time. That suited Leopold just fine when it was theoretically going to be his house. Now that he was in residence, the matter was a totally different story. The advertisement listed the dwelling as having Old World charm. True, he had not specified exactly what he wanted when he phoned his solicitor about acquiring property in the Seattle area. Next time he would not make the same mistake. He had an image to uphold and a boarded up derelict was not the image he wanted to project. He had yet to find any Old World charm in the musty ruins—another bone of contention he felt the need to bring to the attention of his solicitor at the earliest opportunity.

Then again, he had not come to Seattle to entertain. This was business, pure and simple. Maybe when he was done with this undertaking there would be time to call in a decorator and, let's not forget, a fumigator. Leopold swore he had seen things shoved in the back of the closets to make even a vampire prince of his nature call out for his mommy in stark terror. Not that he had, but he was just saying that roaches should never be the size of Pomeranians. The place had potential, but whoever had it last had let it fall to shite. What did you expect, when one was dealing with these colonials?

He stopped in front of the picture window dominating the second story sitting room. Even from behind its smeared and streaked surface, the city looked breathtaking. How gay the city looked all decked out with its blinking lights and garish marquees. Even the night couldn't hide the opulence this new world offered. It was so different from the world he had been born into.

Bloated, plague-ridden bodies and noxious gas lamps were no substitute for what lay before him. He shuddered at the images the thought invoked. So much had changed since the dark and stormy night so long ago. It really had been a dark and story night, but these novels just scream for a dark and stormy night to be inserted somewhere. The memory of it still lingered in his mind like an unwanted friend.

He didn't ask for what happened to him. This half-life had been thrust upon him. His wants and desires had taken no precedence in the decision whatsoever. Even now, the fate-filled moment controlled him. Soon, that would not be the case.

It had taken him a long time to discover his destiny. In the course of his dire existence, he had lived many lives—some grander than others. The others had been so putrid he tried not to dwell over-much on them. Despite their diversity, they all shared one thing: each was dictated by his unnatural existence. Well, no longer.

Leopold du Chambris Portus now knew who he was. He was more than the Belgian noble struck down in his youth by some vampiric specter. He was more than the undead prince who feasted on the lives of the wicked. Lewis had shown him this long ago, but he had been too blind to notice until now.

How much he owed sweet Lewis. To think he had lived for so long without his stalwart companion by his side. Looking back, Leopold marvel at how easily the years of loneliness had been swept away by the man's introduction into his life. For the first time in his long life he felt whole. It wasn't luck that brought the mulatto lad to his notice. It was fate. Just like fate had brought him to Seattle. Well, maybe not fate exactly, but it did involve at least one layover in Atlanta.

He turned away from the window. His maudlin thoughts were getting him nowhere. He had decided to think happy thoughts from now on. It was a strange concept to be sure. A vampire with happy thoughts—who ever heard of such? Despite the absurdity of his unspoken statement, it was all true.

He had Lewis to thank for it all. Who knew a reject from the seventies could awaken so much within him? Feelings he had long suppressed had come to the forefront. Leopold let a muffled whimper escape his puckered lips.

Leopold instantly stopped in mid-whiffle. He had to watch these melodramatic outbursts, but he had become so emotional as of late. It seemed like he was always either on the verge of tears or hysterical laughter. Lewis had said it was a natural reaction after coming to grips with the truth about oneself.

Leopold removed a pastel violet handkerchief from his jacket pocket. He gently dabbed the blood-red tears from his cheek. Yes, he must rein in these all-too-human emotions. It would not help for his enemies to learn the condition he was in. Only Lewis knew, and for now that was quite enough.

He plopped into the red velvet chair set beside the empty fireplace. Smoothing his pink frock coat, he let his mind drift to the reason he had come to Seattle. The Mother was waking. He, and the rest of the unholy court, had felt the shivers of her stirring through the veil.

While his role as her consort was now out of the question, Leopold still sought to ingratiate himself into her good graces. If he could somehow accomplish the feat, he would still have a foothold in the new regime he would soon bring about. How nice it would be to sit at the Mother's right hand when she again came to power. Perhaps she could get him into those exclusive shops that had long been denied him, like the Pier One. Damn them and their wicker delights.

But that time had yet come. The Mother was still far from waking. Only the slight tremors of foreboding announced her coming. The Bleeding Moon must rise before she reached her full strength and there was the problem of her sacrifice to be solved.

All the scrolls said the same thing: a virgin's newly-spilt blood must be presented to the Mother at the exact time of her awakening, or the waiting would continue for another millennia. Not just any blood would do. Oh no, the texts were quite clear on what type to use.

The question was—where was he going to find the blood of a thirty-five year old virgin who was pure of heart and not someone just too ugly to get laid? If the virgin hiccup wasn't enough, the sacrifice had to be a knight of the old order, a slayer of monsters. The impossibility of the task sent a migraine flowing to the pit of Leopold's brain. Lewis would know what to do. The young vampire had got him this far.

Leopold looked up at the dusty clock hanging limply on the faded wall. It was time to go. He could feel the hunger beginning to take root in his stomach. The stale want was driving him mad. Rising, he took one last look at the Seattle skyline. The newborn city called to him. He must dance among its varied people. The nightlife called, and he wanted to boogie.

~ * ~

Breathred emptied the change from his pocket. $1.76 was all he had to show for his night's work. Who knew one old lady could eat so much Chinese takeout? The number of egg rolls she ate alone, boggled the mind.

At least he was able to slink pass the hawk-like gaze of his stepmother without her noticing him. He couldn't take her snickering. It was bad enough having to live directly beneath her and his father. He was thirty-five years old and she was almost half his age. His father was twice her age plus eighteen years. Eeuw.

If the age difference wasn't bad enough, the noises the two of them created at all hours of the day and night were most unseemly. After six months of being forced to overhear them he wasn't entirely sure the sounds were altogether legal, either. Until he found out for sure, he intended to stay in the basement. He was just grateful they had moved into the upstairs bedroom, and there was no way he'd ever eat off the kitchen counter again.

Right now, all he cared about was a hot shower and enough Gold Bond Medicated to sooth his burning parts. He definitely had to rethink the leather. If nothing else, a body suit made of natural fibers underneath might help. He'd have to think on it some more.

"So, did you bag the big bad vampire?" a voice called mockingly as he reached the bottom of the stairs.

Breathred whipped around to find his chimp glaring at him from the bed. Breathred shook his head. He had entirely forgotten about Stud, something he thought he'd never be able to do. Wouldn't you know the only spell he ever had work for him was the one that gave his familiar the power of speech?

"No, it turned out to be a cat," Breathred mumbled, slipping into the bathroom.

"It was a what? Did you say cat?" Stud howled from the bed.

"Yes, Stud. It was a cat, but it was a big cat."

"I told you I wished to be called Reginald," Stud snorted.

"Nothing doing. I named you Stud before you could talk, so you're stuck with it," Breathred retorted, a little angrier than he should have been. But the chimp was provoking him.

"Whatever. Did you at least kick the cat's ass?"

"Well, as I said, it was a big cat," Breathred hoped the sound of the shower would drown out his answer. There was no way he could live with the monkey now. He slipped into the shower before he could hear Stud's response. The hot water felt good. He could almost ignore the places where the leather had rubbed him raw, except for when the spray of water chose to coat those areas. He bit down on his facecloth, so Stud wouldn't hear him whimpering. There was no way he would give the chimp any more fodder for his verbal abuse. Stud already had enough without him adding anything else to his already-scathing repartee.

Breathred let the steaming water soak his bunched neck. The muscles instantly relaxed. Who knew vampire slaying could be such a stressful endeavor? He chalked it up to first night jitters. Tomorrow would be better. If he ever got another client, that was. The handbook had said nothing about how long it took for vampires to surface. He had been surprised when the first call came in. He knew vampires liked to keep a low profile, otherwise they wouldn't have remained so well hidden for as long as they had.

The human race was just lucky they had people like him to watch out for them. He reached down and shut the water off. He had hidden from the monkey as long as he could. The last thing Breathred wanted was for the little poo-thrower to come in and tell him to stop playing with it, again.

He waded through the wall of steam and grabbed his towel from its hook. It seemed best to dab the tender parts first, then rub the rest as vigorously as possible to make up for the less than adequate drying delivered to those other parts. He knew it made no sense, but it made him feel better about neglecting them.

He draped the towel over his shoulder and turned to the mirror. He stroked his hand over the surface, wiping off the condensation. Man, he looked old. Whoever said clean living made you younger lied. He had more crow's feet than a Kansas farm. He definitely needed to talk to the Avon lady about some age-defying cream.

Mis Staked

A rustling to his left snapped his attention away from the mirror. A vision of crazed, amorous felines flooded his brain. He slowly cocked his head to the left. Through the steam, a form took shape. Glowering eyes stared up at him from the commode.

"Got a shrinkage problem there don't you, Big Boy," a decidedly feminine voice said.

Breathred bent forward for a better look at his stalker. Hazel eyes peered over a wilting comic book and recognition slammed home.

"Luna, what are you doing in my bathroom?"

"Number one, I swear," Luna answered, putting the book on the floor beside the commode.

"That's not what I mean. What are you doing in here at the same time as me?" Breathred hid himself as best he could behind his soaking hand towel wishing he hadn't slung the big fluffy one back over the shower rod.

"Reginald said it would be all right." She reached for the toilet paper.

Breathred turned his head. "Do you think you could wait until I leave the room before you do that?"

"Don't be so uptight. You're one to talk. Don't you think you'd better cover Mr. Happy before Seattle gets a new space needle?" She laughed, snapping her fingers at his groin.

Breathred did the only thing he could do in such a situation. He ran from the room like a scared little girl.

Four

The female of the species is oft time the most dangerous to handle.

Breathred did his utmost to ignore the chimp, but found it increasingly hard as the evening wore on. Everything would have been fine if it wasn't for the fact the chimpanzee was ignoring him, a preposterous thing for it to do in the first place. How dare Stud ignore him when it was his place to ignore the chimp?

This whole embarrassing situation was all Stud's fault, anyway. After all, the chimp had been the one who let the girl into the bathroom. Women and male nudity had no place in the same apartment, let alone the same room. He was still reeling from the encounter. He doubted even therapy would erase the incident from his mind. The very idea that Luna had seen his Mr. Wigglesworm was damaging enough without the little monster shooting him obscene winks every few seconds.

Luna gave him a sly smile from where she sat across the room. His hand fell to his lap. It was a reflex action. He didn't do it because he thought she had some kind of x-ray vision, but why take chances? Women were mysterious creatures. Who knew what secret powers they could be hiding?

Breathred scratched his head and gave the girl an appraising glance, trying not to appear to be looking at her. Yes, he would have to remember to look into getting some lead-lined boxer briefs online once she left, just in case. Maybe, he could check on EBAY. Perhaps they had something there he could buy. If not, he could start wrapping his personality in aluminum foil.

Through his fog of paranoia, he heard Luna laugh; her soft giggle always distracted him. Breathred looked up. From the expression on Stud's face, he had just said something extremely witty. They both looked at him and burst into a roaring fit of laughter. Whatever it had been, it was obviously about him. It always was.

Luna gave him a warm smile. The world around him fell silent as he fell into her. Her soft hazel eyes twinkled back, when she caught his glazed eyes staring at her. Her full lips upturned at their corners ever so slightly, drawing a thin sheen of sweat across his brow.

She always made him melt like a warm bowl of Rocky Road. Normally it was only when he was in her company, but lately it had been happening when he wasn't even around her. The odd thing was, she had the opposite effect on other parts of his anatomy he'd rather not mention, propriety being what it was.

It was totally ridiculous for him to feel this way. He had only known the girl for six months. It was silly to think she could have such a profound effect on him in such a short period of time, but she had. If he had been a tad bit wiser on such matters, it wouldn't have been a mystery to him at all. Instead, he looked for answers to fit into his logical world.

After numerous attempts at reasoning it out, he settled on the most plausible of his irrational explanations for his condition. It had to be an allergic reaction. His condition had to be purely medical in nature. It was the only answer to fit all his symptoms. Unfortunately, his bevy of doctors had, as of yet, found no visible cure for his unique dilemma.

Breathred found his mind drifting back to that singular moment six months ago. He had gone to the Java Jumper, a place similar to a well-known coffee establishment based in the Seattle area. (I should point out said company refused to allow the author the use of their much-publicized name in this manuscript due to a contractual dispute or, in other words, the money grubbing sum-bitches wouldn't cough up the cash for the endorsement.)

The day, like any other day, had been wet. His only thoughts were on getting a warm cup of coffee into him and escaping the downpour. He made it inside just before the bottom fell out.

Upon entering he was just wet enough to appear pitiful without looking totally destitute. He hurriedly sat in his accustomed seat. The place was not yet full but he anticipated the evening rush. Once seated, he waited for Mabel to work her way over. Mabel was a rotund lady of about forty-eight. She had a motherly quality Breathred found reassuring, so he made a point of sitting in her section whenever possible.

That day had been different. It was the start of his bright new life. He had received his new correspondence course in the morning post. He had been too busy running some errands for his father, to open it and decided to wait for his evening coffee to peruse the package. The idea gave him a Christmassy feeling about the whole thing.

By the time he'd reached the Jumper, Breathred was absolutely giddy with the thought of what the package contained. He held the plain, brown envelope before him. *Boffrend Academy* was emblazoned in gold letters in the upper right corner. He could hardly believe it had finally arrived. Before the end of the day he was going to be on his way to becoming the greatest vampire slayer of all time.

He was so engrossed in the handbook he didn't even look up when Mabel finally got around to him. He blindly ordered his decaf latte and went on reading. He hoped she would understand his rudeness, but this was important.

In short order the coffee appeared, but without the accustomed

Mabel behind the cup. In her place stood a vision in waitress-blue. Breathred was dumbstruck. The waitress was the most beautiful creature he had ever seen. His throat closed up just thinking about being this close to her.

She was a bronze goddess of the highest order. Her long black hair was tied back into a ponytail. Her lips were full and formed into an eternal smile that lit up the entire room. But it was her eyes that trapped him. He had never thought of brown as an attractive color for eyes, but on her it was a masterful stroke from the maker's hand. She had a sultry gypsy quality, like Marlene Dietrich in *Golden Earrings* with Ray Milland.

Through the course of the evening, he learned she was a Native American, not a gypsy as he first thought. She was finishing her graduate work in anthropology. Working at the Java Jumper helped pay for her textbooks and lab fees. In spite of the grant and scholarships, she still had trouble making ends meet. She had been forced to take a job just so she could eat.

Breathred remembered every detail of their first meeting. As he fell into bed that night, it struck him he hadn't even gotten her name. He didn't think the fact strange. He often forgot such things. His mind worked on a different plane at odd times.

It took a week before he finally worked up the courage to go back and ask her name. He made it a point to seat himself outside her section. It would be no small lie to say he was shaking when the time came.

She instantly set him at ease. She even remembered him by sight. That had never happened to him before without a restraining order coming into play. After some shameless flirtation, she relinquished the prize. Her name was Luna Walking Batch.

The name soared through him like a bolt from above. He could imagine no other appellation could possibly have suited her any better. He found it fitted nicely into every Barry Manilow song he knew. This was fortunate for those around him, because he only knew two. They were also much nicer, in his opinion, than the one Stud constantly harangued him with, which involved him "…sitting in a tree, k-i-s-s-i-n-g," of all things.

Why he would want to do such a thing, he had no idea. He was simply content to enjoy her company, as he hoped she was in his. She had to feel the same, otherwise why was she always popping up at his place?

His dreamy-eyed countenance cleared. Someone was shouting his name, repeatedly. They sounded most urgent. Since he smelled no fire, he saw no need to rush into anything. He shook his head, dropping most of the cobwebs littering his drowsy mind. It wasn't until a hairy knuckle-slap to the side of the head, he responded.

"Breathy are you all right? You look like you swallowed a Sasquatch!" Luna said.

"I must have dozed off."

"Are you sure the cat hasn't got your tongue, Bad-Ass?" Stud smirked.

"Behave, Stud." Luna scolded.

"That's all right, I'm used to it by now." Breathred moaned.

"Well, get dressed. We're going out," she announced, choosing to ignore his melodramatic response. "You, too, Monkey Boy. We're making a night of it. All three of us."

"You can't be serious!" Breathred exclaimed. The thought of going anywhere with the demented beast was more than he could bear.

"You heard her," Stud said. "Even though she may have insulted me, I'm willing to forgive her since I get to put on my dancing shoes."

"Of course he's going with us. It's unfair to keep him cooped up in this dreary basement all the time. He needs fresh air and frankly, so do you," she preached to the unrepentant choir. "Besides, he'll be good. Won't you Stud?" Luna asked turning to the cornered chimp.

"When am I anything but the picture of refinement?" Stud gave her his best hurt face.

"Then it's settled."

Breathred watched as she crossed her arms. He knew her well enough to know that meant she would hear no more on the subject. As much as he would have liked to, he knew better than to fight her.

He sighed and gave in to the inevitable. He never questioned the strange relationship that existed between the girl and Stud. He just knew the chimp was the one subject not to cross her on. The fact his stalwart simian milked it for all it was worth was disheartening in itself, but Breathred had learned it was a battle he couldn't win.

Since he had missed the bulk of their conversation, Breathred had no clue even where he'd agreed to go. With Luna it could be anywhere from Burger Town to gay Paree. He rifled through his closet for something to work for any occasion. He finally decided on his all-purpose outfit he wore to everything. You couldn't go wrong with a white shirt and black pants.

Once dressed, he was ready for the worst. When dealing with Luna and her schemes, it was best to start at the worst. At least that way you could always work your way up, but you never went down any further than the worst possible scenario. He tried not to imagine apocalypse as an optional ending for tonight, but with Luna you couldn't count it out.

~ * ~

Lewis was tired of being wet and cold. He was used to the slow, sultry heat and sunshine of New Orleans. Seattle was none of those things. He had long ago stopped believing the myths about vampires. Being immune to the weather was just one of many. Vampires felt the heat and cold—perhaps not to the extent of a living human—but they were still affected by it.

Ever since he and Leopold set foot in Seattle, he felt like he was in a soggy, damp grave. Not a sensation he wished to revisit, thank you very much. Once was enough. He could hardly wait until this whole crazy scheme was over with, so they could get the hell outta Dodge.

With the way Leopold was acting, it could take forever. Who knew a three-hundred-year old vampire could have a mid-death crisis? White folks, go figure.

Lewis should be with his master. There was no telling what Leopold was up to by now. After the fifth stanza of *I Gotta Be Free*, he just had to get the hell away. It was just so depressing. Finally, he slinked out while the old fool went looking for his copy of *Hello Dolly*.

So for the better part of the night, he just prowled the streets, looking for anything to take his mind off of his troubles. Thanks to the two hookers a couple of blocks over, he was full as a tick. What he needed now was a little distraction to take the edge off going home.

Ahead the vampire spotted a nightclub that looked to be the ticket for his woes. The main thing it had going for it was the place wasn't a vampire dive. Before his turning, he never realized how boring a club could be. Leopold had taken him to his first vamp club, and boy did he learn different. The old ghouls sat around all night in one big bitch-fest. It wasn't even a good one where everybody slammed each other. They always said the same thing. No matter where it was or who was there, they all said the exact same fucking thing. Five or six hours of hearing "in my day" over and over again was more than any man could take, whether he was a vampire or not.

Unlike those old fops, he knew the truth. In my day you couldn't tell the living from the dead, because they both smelled the same. Well, screw that! He liked his victims a little more on the clean side. Don't even get him started on dental hygiene. Just thinking about it was enough to make him want to gag, and *he* drank *blood* to survive.

But, Lewis wasn't here to dwell on the boring side of un-life. He was here to party. The place was jumping. It was no mean feat for a Tuesday night. He bet you couldn't even get in here on a Friday or Saturday night, not that he'd have any trouble in that department.

A floating waitress swam past him. From her tray, he snagged a drink he would not drink. With well-trained ease Lewis shifted into the crowd before she noticed the drink missing from her tray. The surging mass of people closed up behind him, erasing any sign of his passage.

The vampire let his eyes wash over the room in hopes of finding a midnight snack. Most of them were too drunk or stoned. One bite and he'd stagger all the way home. From experience, Lewis had found it best to take only sober victims. A hangover on a dead brain was a bitch. Alcohol killed brain cells, even undead ones.

He'd have to pick something up on the way home. If luck was with him, he'd run across an early-rising jogger. The health conscious offered such sweet tasting Chablis.

Lewis angled toward the DJ. The rapid-fire beat blaring from the loudspeaker drew him onward. Unlike his confused master, he understood the value of a well shaped female form and stopped to appreciate several on the way to the dance floor surrounding the DJ booth. As he stepped on the rotating disk, an intoxicating scent flooded into him. The smell of blood so pure and untainted Lewis scarcely believe it existed, hit him right between the eyes. The odor was so sweet the impact threatened to send him sprawling to the floor.

Not giving a flip about being seen, Lewis jumped from the dance floor with a superhuman bound. His nostrils flaring as they fought to trace the scent to its source, he hit the dance floor running. The place was just too crowded. Without a better plan, Lewis decided to mingle and hope he ran across its owner before they left. He set up a nonchalant search pattern taking him through the entire club without missing a single part of it. After thirty minutes, Lewis feared he had imagined the entire episode.

The vampire stopped suddenly in the midst of a growing mosh pit. His head pivoted to the left. There it was again. It was close, no more than ten or twelve feet away. He narrowed it down to an open booth in the corner. Through the haze of smoke he saw the source. A man and a woman sat in hushed conversation. Young lovers, how sweet. A third shape jumped between the two. At first Lewis thought it was a small child, but no. It was a monkey dressed in a gold lamé leisure suit.

Lewis had to laugh. These mortals and their idiosyncrasies were a constant amazement.

It didn't matter how weird the couple was. He had to get a taste of that blood. The question was which of the trio owned the delightful blood? Lewis let his power flow out to them and wash over each of them in turn. Common sense ruled out the monkey. He didn't drink out of his species, if he could help it.

His senses hit the woman first. A blackness surged from her that was almost frightening. No, she wasn't the source. Discounting her left the man. A second ping revealed it to be true. How bizarre.

Edging closer to the couple, he hadn't taken more than a few steps when the girl turned to look him straight in the eye. Even across the crowded room, her gaze bored into him. A river of fear ran down his back. What was this girl?

"I know what you are," a voice whispered in his mind, and he knew it belonged to her.

Lewis stumbled back onto the crowded dance floor. One thought held his panic in check: get the hell out of here. He had to get away from her. Against his own volition, the vamp spun around upsetting a trio of dancers. They screamed in protest. He didn't care.

Streaking from the dance floor, he cautiously hazarded a glance back to the trio. She still sat at the table, but her eyes never left him. She tipped her head toward him. A scream strangled itself in his throat, and he fled through the door and out into the night.

Five

The hours between daybreak and nightfall may seem safe, but don't be fooled. Not all bloodsuckers have fangs. Take lawyers for just one example.

Breathred was not in the mood to wake up. He wasn't even in the mood to be alive at this moment. Luna had kept him out until right before dawn. He wasn't sure, but thought someone must have slipped something into his milk at the last bar they stumbled into. He had a funny taste in his mouth and, for some reason, a pair of strange underwear hung around his neck.

Rolling over, while doing his best not to think about whose underwear they might be, a shaft of filtered of sunlight struck him between the eyes. The sudden burst of radiance sent him scrambling back the way he'd come. Definitely in no shape to face the day, Breathred jerked his pillow over his head, doing a passable impression of a turtle. Waiting patiently for death to claim him, he lay in bed for another fifteen minutes staring out with one shadowed eye.

His mind dredged through the facts about last night. Halfway into their night on the town Luna began acting strange. Not exactly sure what happened but something set her off at the first club they'd gone to. At one point the girl looked visibly shaken, making them leave in a hurry.

She spent all night looking over her shoulder. Luna didn't think he noticed, but it was hard not to. He suggested they make an early night of it. Not that he was tired. He'd been just a little on the sore side. The cat-inflicted wounds had been giving him fits. He wouldn't have admitted such a thing to her though.

For some reason he got the feeling she didn't want to let him out of her sight. Stud even commented as much when she left them to use the facilities. Of course the diminutive demon termed it differently. Breathred couldn't see how he could get any luckier than he already was, and what did cards have to do with anything? They weren't even playing cards. The chimp could be strange at times.

The telephone rang, driving a spike into his already aching head. Breathred glanced over at the clock. Who would be calling at 11:57 in the

33

morning? Oh crap! He had overslept.

Breathred jumped out of bed to find his legs were in no shape for such an endeavor. He tripped over his clothes in his hurry to stop the pounding. Breathred barely missed colliding with the couch. An impromptu spin saved him from anything worse than bruised pride.

The phone kept up its incessant ringing. He plunged through the remainder of the makeshift living room to where the phone normally rested. In its place Stud lay sleeping in nothing but his "The King Lives" boxers. Breathred skidded to a stop in front of him. The underwear was in an unseemly position. He shook his head in disgust. The little pervert was having the Estelle Getty dream again.

Picking up a stick he kept around for these occasions, Breathred jabbed the stick into his side, flipping the creature off of the phone. Stud landed with a wet thump and emitted a noxious explosion that sent Breathred gasping for breath, but made no sign of waking. Just as well. Breathred couldn't stand the idea of dealing with him just yet. The underwear would have to come off before he even thought about waking the chimp.

He eyed the phone suspiciously. Grabbing his ever-ready bottle of Lysol from the bookshelf beside the phone, Breathred gave it a healthy dose and gave Stud a shot for good measure. Satisfied the phone was now safe to touch, he picked up the receiver.

"Hello," he grumbled.

"Is this Mr. Breathred Petrifunck?" a husky female voice asked.

"You're not a telemarketer are you?" he asked back, ready to slam the phone down.

"No, my name is Professor D. L. Grayson. I'm calling in response to your ad."

"Well, in that case you have reached the offices of *Petrifunck Paranormal*. How may I be of service?"

"Now that I have you on the line, I'm really not sure," Dr. Grayson admitted.

Breathred answered in his best businesslike tone, "Please be assured I will hold this conversation in the strictest of confidence. Feel free to discuss your situation."

"This is not something I wish to discuss over the phone. Is there any way we can meet later today?"

"My calendar is free any time this afternoon, I can meet you then, if it's convenient," Breathred said, giving himself a gold star for his professionalism.

"I have a free hour after five before my evening class starts at six. Can we possibly meet then?"

"Of course. I and my associate would be more than happy to meet you then."

"Good. I'll be in the Science building at the college. Do you know where it's located?"

"Yes, I am familiar with the campus." Breathred said, not wanting her to know he had no idea where it was, but Luna did.

"You will find me in room 507. I guess I'll see you then, Mr. Petrifunck. If possible, I'd like for you to keep this between you and me for the moment," Professor Grayson repeated.

"You have my word this will go no further than my ears," Breathred reassured her.

"Till then, Mr. Petrifunck," she said, and hung up.

Breathred fell back into his chair. This was all just too much. Two clients in two days! That had to be some kind of record. True he had only made a buck and some change on the first one, but this one would be different. She was a professor. Professors never cheated anybody, like mean old ladies did.

This would be a good day. Wait a minute. Today was Wednesday. What did Wednesday mean? Comic book day! A client and comic book day, what more could a man ask for?

For those of you who have no concept what all the hoopla is all about, it's quite simple. Every comic book company ships their comics to a main distributor. Then the distributor sends the comic books to select dealers on Wednesday. To any most right-thinking people, this has no bearing whatsoever on their lives. Not so the comic book fan. In expectation of said event every Tuesday, a massive gathering is planned by the comic-buying community to go to their own private Mecca.

This event doesn't happen once a year or even once every month. No, every week. That's fifty-two times a year and happens as regular as clockwork, barring national holidays. To a geek like Breathred, it was like having Christmas fifty-two times a year. No other day invigorated him like Wednesdays. Birthdays didn't even come close.

But today was even more special. The latest issue of *Tales of the Undead* hit the shelves today. Of the multitude of titles populating the comic shelf, not to mention his floor, closet and bed, this was the only one that mattered. Aside from the Boffrend handbook, all 178 issues of the hallowed magazine taught Breathred everything he knew about vampire slaying.

He checked his alarm clock. Its red numbers proclaimed 12:32 pm. His late start didn't give him much time to get everything done by six. Planned just right, he might be able to squeeze it all in. The big thing was to get hold of Luna. She had morning classes and one overlapping the dinner rush at the Jumper.

To have any hope of catching her meant getting Stud up and running. He tossed the remote toward the sleeping monkey. It cracked the animal in the gut and sent him flying into the air. The chimp came down in his typical ninja stance. A disturbing thing to witness, especially since it was evident the Estelle Getty dream had yet to run its course.

"What in the bloody hell are you thinking?" Stud growled. "I could have Chimp Fu-ed the crap out of you."

"Stow it. We have to go." Breathred shouted from the closet.

Stud crossed his hairy arms. "You may have to go, but this primate ain't going nowhere."

"We're going to the Jumper." Breathred teased, pulling the underwear over his head.

"So, what? Unlike you, I have no interest in mooning over Luna."

"Edith might be working." Breathred smirked.

Stud rushed to his own closet. "Why didn't you say so, you dumb homosapien?"

~ * ~

Forty-five minutes later the pair walked into the Java Jumper. The place sat devoid of the majority of its lunch crowd. There were enough bodies to make Breathred feel self-conscious of the leering eyes as he and Stud plopped down at the counter. On general principles, the slayer dismissed the majority of the stares.

Stud was more of a regular than most of the people in here. Breathred had been bringing the chimp in here for as long as he owned him, if anyone could be said to own the chimp. Sometimes Breathred got the distinct impression Stud saw the situation totally reversed.

Scanning the room, he saw no sign of Luna, but caught a glimpse of Edith roaming the far end of the counter. In the entire world, aside from Luna and Stud, she was the only person he willingly called his friend. Edith presented an imposing figure with skin the color of rich milk chocolate and a tall voluptuous figure, reminding Breathred of an Amazon, only one dressed in a blue waitress uniform.

"Hey sugah, be right with ya," she yelled seeing him, her thick Southern accent floating across the room.

Breathred waved an enthusiastic hello, earning him a warm smile from the woman. His happiness at seeing his friend proved short lived. The smell of axel grease wafted across his nose. Rubbing the throbbing vein in his forehead, he looked over to see Stud running a comb through his pompadour with the look of lechery in the first degree on the chimp's face. Breathred felt the embolism coming at any minute. The chimp would be the death of him.

"You had better behave," Breathred warned him.

"Like I would act otherwise around the delightful Miss Edith," Stud whispered.

Breathred glanced around the room to make sure no one was listening to their conversation. "And remember, try not to talk too loud. We don't want you snapped up by some science freako."

Stud gave a silent shudder. Ever since they got the Discovery Science Channel, the chimp had developed a profound fear of scientists in general, which Breathred had found quite useful when dealing with Stud in social situations. By the time Breathred finished his warning, Edith had made her way over. He gave Stud a last eye twitch to reinforce the threat before turning to her.

"Well, boys what'll it be? The usual?" Edith asked.

"Nothing, I'm sorry to say. I was looking for Luna," he mumbled, feeling bad about not ordering anything.

"She hasn't made it in, yet," she answered, as she turned to Stud. "What about you, little man?"

"You know what I want, Hot Stuff."

"Monkey Boy, you couldn't handle what you want." She shot him a disapproving look belying the laughter in her eyes.

"You know what they say…" Stud jumped up on the counter.

"And what would that be?" Edith asked, warily.

"Once you go chimp, everyone else seems limp." He cocked his eyebrow.

"You know what sugah? That's the exact same thing I told my ex-husband right before I peeled his nut sack off with a spork," Edith growled. "And if you don't get yo' monkey ass off my counter, you'll find out about it firsthand." To illustrate her point she pulled a cellophane-wrapped piece of plastic from her overflowing cleavage.

"Well of course propriety and all that," Stud stammered, as he slid off the stained counter top.

"Do you want me to give her a message, Breathred?" she asked, clearly in no mood to put up with either of them for much longer.

"Yeah, tell her it's really important she gets a hold of me before five." Breathred said, emphasizing the "really" and "important".

"Should I have her call your cell phone?" Edith asked, jotting down the message.

Breathred shot the chimp an angry glare. "No, have her call Stud's."

The woman let out a chuckle. "Lost yours again?"

"No, someone ran up my bill by calling 1-900-Hot Monkey Love."

Raising an eyebrow, Edith tapped the note before placing it in her apron pocket. "I'll be sure to give her the message as soon as she gets here."

Breathred swung his leg off the stool. "Well, we'd better get going."

Edith reached over and cupped his head back to hers before he could get up. "I know people who could put that monkey straight, if you know what I mean." With a wicked smile she drew a line across her neck with her thumb.

"I'll keep it in mind," he answered.

"You do that. Baby. Now, get," she cackled, pushing him from the counter and toward the door.

~ * ~

Stud could tell Breathred felt better after leaving the coffee shop, in spite of not catching Luna at the Jumper. With Edith on the case the chimp couldn't very well see what they had to worry about, not that he was concerned to begin with. Breathred was doing enough stressing for the both of them. So all he had to do was survive a trip to Clint's Comic Emporium and, hopefully, they'd be home in time for *American Idol*.

He made it a point to stick close to his master on these little excursions. The chimp had no love for crowds. Unbeknownst to humans, they stink. They didn't just stink. They stank. The whole stinking lot of them smelled like a week-old burrito fart.

If the smell wasn't bad enough, they had the bad habit of patting him on the head and he hated it. He wasn't some dog. He was simian supreme, the height of the evolutionary scale. Until he learned differently, Stud would continue to consider humans a little above cattle, but not as low as insurance underwriters.

Avoiding a group of head patters if he ever saw one, Stud spotted the comic store before Breathred, which was a wonder. The boy definitely had it bad not to have spotted his own personal wet dream. The thought gave Stud pause.

What if his big buddy was growing up? The concept was disturbing. For the past three years he had been the only grownup in this relationship. A change in the status quo would be quite unsettling.

"Come on, Stud. The comics are in. The comics are in!" Breathred screamed with glee before taking off at a dead run toward the little shop.

Stud breathed a sigh of relief. All his worrying was for nothing. His little man-boy wasn't going anywhere just yet. Stud wobbled after him, content the world had not tilted on its axis for the foreseeable future.

Stud sauntered into the shop a full five minutes after Breathred. He was immediately assaulted by a wall of quivering flesh. It stopped him cold in his tracks.

A dead silence loomed over the shop's narrow confines. A few hushed conversations invaded the lull, but otherwise the room was void of sound. The shuffling of comics by the shop's owner was the only sound dominating the place.

Stud scrambled up to a wooden rack full of bargain discount back issues. This drew a sharp intake of breath from those closest to him. Bared teeth and an upturned middle digit silenced them.

Once atop his tower of periodicals, Stud had a full view of the shop. He caught sight of Breathred edging close to the sales desk. *Go get 'em, boy, but I'm staying put*, Stud thought.

Breathred saw his bid for comic heaven dashed, as a pair of Goth twins pushed him to the back of the line. He knew from experience you didn't mess with those two. It wasn't that they were dangerous. They weren't, on the whole. It was just too hard to clean white-face and mascara out of your clothes once they touched you.

Breathred decided a few minute's wait wouldn't kill him. It would damage him mentally, but not kill him. He checked his watch. It was 2:57, three hours until his meeting with Dr. Grayson. How long could this realistically take?

An hour and a half later, Breathred saw the daylight at the end of the tunnel. After the Goth kids, came the Marvel junkies, then a horde of Gathering players descended in full regalia. Breathred knew when to back away, and this was the time to back away.

When the store finally emptied, Breathred emerged from the back issues and made his way to the counter. Clint, the store owner, gave him a tired smile. Exhaustion peppered his weary face. Despite the tired look, he happily retrieved Breathred's books from their cubical.

Clint placed the books in front of him. "Big stack for you this week, man."

Breathred scrunched up his face, looking shamefully toward the floor. "I can't get everything this week. My fundage is running a little short."

"That's cool. Get what you can and the rest'll be here." Clint slid the books toward him. "Say how's the new job going?"

"Rough, but I just got a new client," Breathred flipped through the stack. He pulled two titles he couldn't live without then pulled the Holy Grail from the bottom of the stack, *Tales of The Undead*.

"Sounds cool. This it?" Clint asked before ringing him up.

"Yeah, I'll be in as soon as I get paid," Breathred assured him.

"No problem. I know you're good for it."

"You haven't seen Luna today have you?"

"No, her manga won't be in till the end of the month," Clint said.

Breathred picked up his books and change. He headed for the door then stopped. "Say, if you see her, tell her to call me."

"Sure thing. Have a good week, man," Clint called out.

"You too."

This was not good. He had wasted way too much time. It was after four and he didn't have the time to go back to the Jumper to find out from Luna where the stinking science building was. Without her, he could spend half the night wandering the campus and still not find the right building. He could get lost going to the bathroom, and he knew it.

~ * ~

Stud knew something was wrong with his master. Behind the childlike exterior, Breathred was a troubled man. This was one case where tough love wasn't going to help solve the problem. Even though it was breaking character, Stud would now have to be caring and helpful.

Stud pulled him down on the nearest bus-stop bench. "Breathred, mind telling me what's wrong?"

"I'm hopeless." Breathred dropped his head into his cupped hands.

"In what way besides the obvious?" Stud regretting saying it before it left his mouth.

"You see? That's what I mean. If my own chimp doesn't respect me, how can I respect myself?" Breathred moaned.

Stud placed a tiny hand on the man-child's shoulder. "You're being too hard on yourself. I know I give you a hard time, but it doesn't mean I don't respect you."

"You mean it?"

"Of course I do. You may have your little foibles, but you pretty much have everything in hand. You keep *me* in line; don't you?"

"Yeah, I guess so," Breathred agreed, reluctantly.

"See, there you go. Now, tell me what's really troubling you."

"I have to meet the new client at the college, and I have no idea where to go. I've been trying to find Luna so she could help, but I don't have the time to look for her anymore. I wasted all afternoon at Clint's when I should have been out trying to find her. If that wasn't bad enough, my goolies are still itching from last night." The words flew from him in a sobbing stream.

Stud slumped down. This was worse than he thought. Breathred was losing what little confidence he'd managed to build up over the years, and what made matter's worse, he didn't have all that much to begin with. The problem was he'd begun to depend on Luna. Breathred had never depended on anybody before and had done all right for himself. Since his unrequited paramour stepped into the picture, Breathred looked to the girl for all the answers.

True, she did have most of them. Her omnipresence wasn't the point. Breathred was smart in an academic type of way. Everything else he tended to be clueless about. For him to foist all this on Luna was unfair—to both him and her. Well, his co-dependence had to stop, and now was as good a time as any.

"Snap out of it, Butt-Brain. We don't need her. We're the team here. You're the one with the degree from Boffrend's, not her." Stud had to suppress a chuckle when he said it. "Between the two of us, there's nothing we can't do. Now, where are we supposed to meet this client?"

"At the science building." Breathred sniffled.

"No problem. We go to the college. We can check the school index and find it ourselves. It can't be that damn hard. Co-eds do it all the time." Stud rose to his feet.

"Yeah, we can, can't we?" Breathred half-heartedly grinned back.

"You bet your ass we can." Stud slapped him across the back.

Breathred stood up with renewed vigor. Stud smiled as he fell in step behind him. All the boy needed was a little push. The good thing about dealing with the simple-minded, they never realized behind every mediocre man was an above-average chimpanzee.

Six

From Dusk to Dawn isn't just a movie—it's the vampire way of life.

True to his word, Stud had little trouble finding the Science building, once reaching the college campus. After a fifteen-minute tour of the grounds they found themselves on the steps leading up to the William Gates Memorial Science Complex.

They had made it with minutes to spare, which was good for them. Breathred had an unnatural fear of elevators to go along with the other long list of phobias dominating his feeble psyche. He appreciated the fact Stud had learned to cope with them over the years, but wished the chimp wouldn't keep throwing them in his face at every opportunity. It didn't make the chimpanzee any easier to deal with, but it did make things quite interesting for those around him.

Room 507 thankfully sat right across from the stairwell exit. After the walk across the city to get here in the first place, he could tell Stud was about as tired as a primate could be. Breathred, on the other hand, had caught his second wind somewhere in the stairwell. The excitement was carrying him long after sanity should have told him to fall flat on his face.

Breathred straightened his black duster. He had opted to forego the leather body suit in favor of a more comfortable outfit, though remained dressed in all black, as befitted his occupation. The fabric was just not as stressful against his tender flesh as leather would have been. He was still chafing from last night, but didn't want to bring the fact to anyone's attention by walking all funny. Smelling like baby powder was bad enough without anyone knowing the reason why.

Once Breathred was sure the outfit presented the proper image, he knocked on the classroom door. No one answered. Backing up a step, Breathred wondered if he had the right room. Maybe, they'd come to the wrong room. It wouldn't be the first time that mistake had popped up. Being half asleep when he took the call probably could explain the confusion if the room number was indeed wrong. Looking down to Stud for moral support, the chimp shrugged, which was really no help at all.

Breathred was about to knock again when Stud reached up and opened the door. Not to be outdone by his companion, Breathred eased in front of him and entered the room. It took him a minute to see the shape of a woman at the far end of the room who was almost invisible among the scattered desks and failing fluorescent lights lighting the cramped space.

Breathred guessed the woman must be Dr. Grayson. Truthfully, she looked nothing like he had imagined her to be. She was sitting atop her desk going over a file with a pen tucked into the corner of her mouth, her auburn hair pulled back into an unruly bun, held together by crisscrossed pencils. Totally engrossed in her work, she didn't notice them until Stud let out a none-too-subtle grunt.

"May I help you?" she asked, obviously startled by the strange-looking pair.

Breathred fell into his slayer mode. "Breathred Petrifunck of *Petrifunck Paranormal* at your service. We spoke this afternoon."

"Ah, yes. Thank you so much for coming," she said with a hint of doubt in her voice, which raised a notch when Stud eased his head around Breathred's side. "Excuse me but is that a chimpanzee behind you?"

Breathred shoved Stud back behind him. "Pay him no mind. He's my assistant."

"Mr. Petrifunck, I think I may have made a mistake in calling you. I hate to have wasted your time." The professor stood up from the desk and began ushering them back toward the door.

"I don't think so ma'am. You're obviously in need, otherwise you wouldn't have called." Breathred stuck his hand against the doorframe to halt his untimely expulsion.

"You silly button. She called you because I told her to do it," Luna snorted, ducking under Breathred's outstretched arm to enter the room.

"Luna?" Breathred's jaw dropped a full five inches at the sound of her voice.

Luna gave him a peck on his confused cheek. "Who else, Sweetie?"

"Ms. Walking Batch, as I told Mr. Petrifunck, this was a mistake."

"Wrong, Doc. You showed me the ancient tablet. I guarantee Breathy here is the only one who can help you figure it out," Luna said, folding her arms.

"Well, I'm already here after all," Breathred interjected. Normally, he wouldn't come between Luna and her folded arms, but this was a special occasion. "You have absolutely nothing to lose by explaining the situation now, do you?"

The professor threw her hands up in resignation. "All right, come back in."

"Hold everything, Toots. We ain't doing nothing until we discuss our fee. We have expenses to think of," Stud jumped in.

"The monkey talks!" Dr. Grayson shouted, stumbling back to her desk in shock.

"Course I do. And it's a chimpanzee, if you please, Hot Stuff.

Otherwise the human there wouldn't know his head from his ass." Stud pointed back to Breathred.

"B-but monkeys don't talk."

"Look, we've already been over that. I talk. I walk. Hey, hey I'm the monkey. Get over it so we can get to the good part," Stud said, sounding frustrated by the whole thing.

Breathred finally found his voice. "Stud, shut up!"

"That's right, Honey. Let us humans figure this out," Luna said in her best schoolmarm impression.

"Doctor Grayson, I'm truly sorry, but you have to understand. You called *Petrifunck Paranormal*, not the police or even a private detective. We operate outside the bounds of human understanding. It'd be best if you realize we don't conform to the way the world normally operates or we'll never be able to help you." Breathred hoped he didn't sound like a total dufus, but if he didn't say something, this thing was going to just get worse.

~ * ~

Dr. Grayson sat on the desk and looked over the unlikely trio. This was all so bizarre. She had figured from Luna's recommendation the man might be a little eccentric, but talking chimps were a bit much. God knows what else he had scurrying around in his duster. He looked like a reject from a Bon Jovi video. Had she sunk as low as this?

The bad thing was, she needed his help. The stone tablet was so unlike anything she had ever seen before. Dr. Grayson had been able to decipher the text. The hard part had been, actually believing what the tablet had said once she finished. If she tried to show it to her colleagues, they would more than likely laugh her butt straight off campus.

Desperation led her to take the girl's advice. The tablet spoke of things she always assumed were nothing more than popular fiction and myth. Carbon-dating the tablet had placed its age on the order ten thousand years, way before the birth of Christ, before history was even documented. The facts boggled the mind. If the tests were correct, then how could this tablet possibly exist?

She looked again at the motley crew. She had to go to somebody. Why not a rock star, and an Indian with a talking monkey thrown in to sweeten the nuthatch? Nobody else would be willing to believe her.

"Okay, you're hired." Grayson sighed, truly at the end of her thin grip on sanity.

"Then let's discuss our fee," Stud interjected before the moment passed. "If this is purely on a consultant basis, we get fifty dollars an hour, plus expenses. On the chance this involves any monster slaying or any contact with the undead in any form or fashion, our fee is tripled."

"You are a blood-thirsty little creature. Aren't you?" Dr. Grayson noted, dryly. "In any case I can't pay anything close to such a large amount. You'll have to abide by the restrictions lain down by the university."

"And they are?" Stud asked. "Quite frankly, what you're saying smacks of communism."

She stopped, letting his words sink in before ignoring them completely in favor of retaining her sanity. "Since this course of action is not fully sanctioned by the college board of deans, I'm going to have to treat this as if you are laborers for one of my archeological digs."

"Which pays what?" Stud shot back.

"Forty dollars a day each, excluding the chimp." Dr. Grayson felt an aneurism building in the back of her brain.

"Why not the chimp? I have the same rights as any other citizen of this great country." Stud rose to his full height—a good four foot-three. It wasn't imposing, but she hoped it made him feel better because the sight was giving her a case of the giggles.

"Because for me to pay you, you have to have a social security card," she smirked, thinking she had finally tripped him up.

"Here you go. Now, sign me up," Stud said smugly, pulling the card from his wallet and handing it to her.

"How does a monk..." She paused as he gave her a dirty look. "Excuse me—chimpanzee—get a social security card?" She stared at the social security card in her hand with disbelief.

"The internet, baby," he answered with a slick smile.

"Look, can we get down to business, please?" Breathred begged before things could deteriorate any worse than they already had.

"Come with me." Dr. Grayson turned her back to them not waiting for the rebuke she knew the chimp had boiling in his throat.

She led them to the back of the classroom where a set of double doors led to her private office. The office was separated into two parts. A small desk and filing cabinet sat to one side. The other side of the room was dominated by a long table full of artifacts obviously from her various digs. Grayson immediately led the trio to the far end of the table, stopping in front of a broken slab of stone.

Once they were settled, she started, "Two years ago, while on a dig in Canada, I unearthed the tablet I'm about to show you. While this is commonplace on most digs, this particular tablet proved older than anything ever found in the northern hemisphere of the Americas. It even predates the pyramids.

"My team and I were excavating an isolated region located in Alberta. We thought we had stumbled onto an ordinary village site. For the most part, that was true. It wasn't until we excavated one of the outbuildings we unearthed, for the lack of a better term—a temple.

"The temple was simple in construction, like others associated with the Inuit tribes who populate the Northern Americas, except for one thing. The others were dominated by animal totems, but the central god of this particular structure was humanoid in form. The wooden totems we unearthed were carved in the shape of a female. My first guess was they represented a new earth mother, or rather an old one as yet unknown to the archeological record. Some of the inscriptions seemed to back this hypothesis.

"In the center of the main room sat a wooden altar about the size of a man. At first I thought it was a solid piece of redwood, possibly an ancient sarcophagus. On closer examination it turned out to be a collection of blocks fitted so perfectly together, you could barely detect the seams. The altar was looped in two places by huge bands of rope, about as thick as my arm in diameter on either end.

"My crew tried unsuccessfully to move the altar. It proved too heavy to so much as budge. When we examined it closer, we found the rope to be interwoven with strands taken from the garlic plant and even had clumps of the root inside of it. At the time I didn't find this strange. It was common practice in earth mother worship to have vegetables and fruit as offerings on their altars, which this obviously must have been.

"In the middle of the altar's top we found a recessed panel. Doing our best not to damage the structure, we carefully removed the panel. Tucked beneath the six-inch block of wood, we found the stone tablet.

"Unfortunately, our dig was cut short. The dig began in early winter and the weather became too volatile for us to remain in the area. We brought the tablet back with us for further examination. After securing the funds to finance another dig, we went back the following year, but storms had erased any sign of the site. So, we were left with the tablet without anything else substantial to back up our findings." Dr. Grayson leaned against the table as she finished her explanation.

"So, what did the tablet say?" Breathred asked, his face scrunched up, clearly trying to make sense of her story.

"That's the strange part. For one thing it was not written in any form of pictogram one would associate with the American Indians, which forced us to look elsewhere for our Rosetta Stone. The closest thing to it was Ancient Sumerian, but even saying that is a stretch. It took me two long years to finally translate the text. This is what it said." She opened a notebook lying on the table. In a low voice she began to read, *"'The Mother wakes to darkness. Her light the only radiance we need. She hungers, so we hunger. The moon is her lover. In the hours of night she walks. Let every man know that she will walk again at the dawning of each turn of the world a thousand ages from the first. The world will tremble and the children shall rise from their homes to conquer that which is ours by right.'"*

Breathred looked at the woman. He wanted more. There had to be more to it than a weird obtuse poem. He could tell Dr. Grayson thought so too.

"I know what you're thinking." She gave Breathred a wry smile. "There was more but unfortunately, the tablet had deteriorated to such a state it was impossible for me to decipher anything else."

"Interesting, as histories go, but what makes you think we can help you?" Stud asked, reading her notes over her shoulder.

"By itself the text is like you said—nothing to draw any real conclusion from. But if you add the stills we took of the temple's interior, it paints a different story. See for yourself." From inside the notebook she pulled a series of eight-by-tens and laid them on the table.

All three friends hunkered over the photos. They were of two huge totems. The monstrous structures must have been at least forty feet tall and ten to fifteen feet wide at the base, if the perspective between the statues and the people standing at their bases was correct.

Breathred followed the totems from their bases upward. Carved at each statue's top was the face of a woman. The detail in the ancient sculptures was spectacular. It was as if the wooden statues were living and breathing before him. Then, it stuck him. The woman's canines were protruding past her lips. They were sharp and came to a point just below the thin, bottom lip. The lips themselves were curled into an evil smile.

He looked over to Stud to see if the chimp was seeing the same thing. The shocked look on the simian's face told him all he needed to know. They were looking at the oldest evidence of vampires ever recorded. The concept was just fantastic.

"That's a Vampire," Luna said, finally catching on.

"Exactly my point. If the temple totems belong to a vampire goddess, then the text belongs to a vampire prophecy. The discrepancy is this—the temple dates to somewhere around five hundred B.C., and the tablet is so much older the two can't possibly be related. But here they are in the same place," Dr. Grayson said, drawing blank stares from the companions.

"It would also explain why whoever put the tablet inside the altar used garlic-laced ropes to bind it in place. They didn't want the tablet to fall into vampiric hands." Breathred rubbed his jaw, thoughtfully before finally asking. "Doctor Grayson, what is it you want from us?"

"After some serious work I've secured a grant to return to the site. This time the money is through a fund granted to the college by a corporate sponsor. The ceiling—while limited—is enough to see us through to the end of this semester. What I want is for you to come along as my private advisor. If there is something to this vampire business, I want someone along who knows what's going on."

"So you expect some kind of vampire interference?" Luna asked.

"Not really, but truthfully I don't know what to expect. Until a few months ago I would have laughed at the idea of vampires existing as anything more than a myth. Now, I'm not sure what to think."

"I can't speak for the others, but I'm in," Breathred announced, to no one's surprise.

"Me too," Luna and Stud answered in unison.

"Thank you. As strange as it sounds, your help to help makes me feel better." Dr. Grayson smiled.

"When do we leave?" Breathred asked.

"The expedition leaves at the beginning of next week. I know this is short notice, but until Miss Walking Batch mentioned you, I had no idea of what to do. If I can get you to fill out these forms, I should have your paperwork ready to submit by tomorrow morning. Look, I may have been a little rough on you at the beginning, but I think we understand each other now. If you can come by after noon tomorrow, I'll have everything ready. Luna, you can sign the paperwork after class. Okay?" Grayson turned to the girl.

"Sure thing, Doctor Grayson," Luna said, overjoyed to be included.

"Unfortunately, you will not get paid for this, since you're enrolled in the university, but it will count for credit toward your degree," the professor sounded sorry to say.

Luna didn't look entirely happy about the fact, but said, "Cool."

"I can put the monkey on the payroll, but I'd rather he didn't come with you tomorrow, Mr. Petrifunck. It might be kind of hard to explain his rather unique appearance if someone saw him." Not to mention how hard it would be on her already frazzled nerves; but she kept that to herself.

"That's right, discriminate against the chimp. Another case of the man trying to keep the ape down," Stud howled.

"Shut up and be glad she didn't dissect you." Luna grimaced at the chimp. He shut up but continued to sulk.

"If that's everything, I think we're done until tomorrow." Dr. Grayson walked them to the door.

Breathred was unusually quiet. It didn't mean he wasn't excited. His mind was already at work on the most pressing problem ahead of them. Who would pick up his comics while they were gone?

Seven

A vampire court consists of a master and at least one subordinate. Where do you think Lucas got the idea?

Lewis yawned. He hated waking up. Being dead hadn't cured him of such a mortal foible. Only one thing made the whole enterprise worthwhile, he had news for Leopold. Depending on the old hag's mood, Leopold might even listen.

He stretched the last of the undead rest from his bones, as he entered the master's chambers. His back was killing him. He really had to get a new mattress for his coffin. The old one was slap worn out. Maybe, one of those sleep-number jobs. If it was good enough for the Bionic Woman, it was good enough for him.

Lewis found Leopold staring out the window. The elder vampire was dressed in a paisley frock-coat with matching pantaloons that must have come from Prince's closet, circa 1986. The man seriously needed to get a total makeover expert on his case or at the very least a straight guy with some Dockers.

"Leo, my man. You, all right?" Lewis asked, falling into a chair.

"Yes, Lewis, I am fine. I was just looking at the city. Soon, the Mother will rise and all this will be ours. It is a lofty thing, is it not?"

"If you say so," Lewis answered, more than a little bored by the subject.

"I didn't hear you come in this morning. I trust you had a productive night?" The question had become a nightly ritual between the two and meant nothing. Lewis knew by now Leopold asked to be civil, but could care less how the younger vampire spent his nights, as long as he was around when the older vamp needed him.

"Kinda what I need to talk to you about. I think I found your sacrifice." Lewis grinned.

"You jest. How could you find the impossible? I have had agents scouring the globe in search of this myth for decades, and you sit there and tell me in the span of a single night you have done what they have been unable to do." Leopold twisted in his chair, letting out an amused chuckle.

"What can I say? It's a black thing," Lewis said, idly cleaning his fingernails.

"Pray, tell me of this apparition," Leopold demanded, "and it better not be you snacking on another crack-head and having visions of the Virgin Mary again."

"You're not going to let that go, are you?" Lewis snarled.

"Of course not. Tell me about your mystery virgin before I grow bored with the whole affair."

Lewis had to fight the instinct to bitch-slap the vampire. He counted to ten, then began to speak, "I saw this cat at this little club up on the east side. He smelled so pure I though I was going cheese myself."

"Then, why is he not laying at my feet?"

"He had some muscle with him. He was protected," Lewis explained. "It was some chick, but she was not some chick, if you know what I mean."

"No, I don't know what you mean. Please feel free to explain to me how some 'chick' stopped you from getting me what I want." Leopold bared his fangs and approached the younger vampire.

"She had the power, man. The crazy chick smelled all wrong, like a wet dog or something. I swear she knew what I was. I could hear her talking to me, in here." Lewis pointed to his head. "She warned me to back off. Take it from me. The chick is bad mojo, Boss Man."

"Bad mojo? Did you just say bad mojo? Is this some bad movie? Did you at least have the sense to track them down?" Leopold yelled, throwing a spray of spittle into Lewis' face.

"Man, you better tone yo' freak down, before I throw down on yo' ass." Lewis jumped up into Leopold's face. "Ain't no honky gonna get in my face talking shit, and in case you're wondering, honky includes you."

Leopold backed away. Lewis was right. The elder vampire was losing his cool but contributed it all the pressure he'd been under. The Mother's awakening was so close, but without the sacrifice it meant nothing. Besides Lewis was his friend, his only friend. Perhaps the time had come to stalk a psychiatrist. A little Prozac in his diet might be just the thing to calm his frazzled nerves.

"I apologize, my friend. It's just, we're so close," Leopold said, softly.

"S' alright, Man. We all gotta blow off steam every once in awhile, but watch it next time."

"Let me start this again. Do you think you can find this man again?"

"Man, he smells so good it'd be hard for him to hide in this city. All I need is to catch the scent, and then I'm on him like white on rice," Lewis assured the old vampire.

"Good. My other plan is going into action on Monday as scheduled." Leopold beamed.

"So, the doc went for it, huh?" Lewis said, knowing nobody would pass up a hundred grand.

"Yes. Little does she know she has uncovered something so important, the world will tremble when its origin is revealed." Leopold sounded like a cartoon villain, but Lewis didn't want to say so.

"So, she heads out and gets the Mother, but how do we get it once she's got it?" Lewis still hadn't figured out how Leopold planned to pull the trick off.

"I have an idea or two on the subject, but if they don't work out, I can send two of my thralls with the expedition. I'll simply allow her to think they're nothing more than representatives of the parent company who's sponsoring her expedition. When the Mother is uncovered, they'll contact me," Leopold explained.

"What if they open it?" Lewis found himself asking. The old man was actually getting him involved in this madness.

"The Mother will not allow it. Only one born of the blood can open the casket, and even then they must have the sacrifice," Leopold assured him with an evil wink.

"Then we're sitting pretty."

"Now that that's settled, did you find the article I wanted?" Leopold asked greedily.

"Course I did, man," Lewis groaned, pulling a CD from his jacket.

"*Pure Funk*! Get me the Victrola." Leopold swooned, as he cradled the jewel case in his shaking hands.

"It's called a CD player, man. Get it right." Lewis snatched the CD from Leopold's trembling hands.

He snapped the boom box's lid and inserted the disc. He pushed Play and turned to leave, as Wild Cherry began blaring from the speakers. He wasn't about to watch this. There was nothing worse than a white boy trying to get his groove on.

~ * ~

The trio left the college too excited to head home. Instead, they decided to celebrate the coming adventure with a late-night dinner on the town. So, they headed toward Ivar's for a steaming bowl of chowder—Luna's treat due to the fact Breathred had blown his last ten dollars on comics, and Stud made it a point to never leave the basement with money on comic book day. Breathred would bum you to death, if you let him, when it came to comics.

The wind blowing in from the docks was cool without the bite of the cold the later months would bring. Breathred, after a lifetime living in Seattle, was use to the permeating smell of fish around the docks. Luna, on the other hand, found herself overwhelmed by it. She had been to Ivar's a couple of times before with Breathred, and the effect was always the same. But they did have the best damn clams she had ever tasted.

Luna had made it a point to stay as far from the docks as she could, but tonight was special. Breathred was in such a good mood. How could she say no, after offering to take him wherever he wanted to go to celebrate?

She did make an effort to make them rush past Pike Place Market. The row after row of fresh fish was more than she could take. Her nose filled with the smell of brine and decaying flesh. Those around her might not have smelled it, but she could. Luna fought back the sickness swelling in the back of her throat and pushed on.

Regaining her composure, she looked over to Breathred. He was so caught up in his own world he failed to notice her discomfort. Stud gave her a worried look. Luna offered a weak smile that seemed to satisfy him. Thankfully, neither one questioned her about it.

The restaurant was packed, as usual. That was the bad thing about the good places to eat. The tourists always seemed to know about them, making it hard for the locals to enjoy them anytime they wanted. Damn Rachel Ray and her forty dollars a day.

Luna spotted a table near the ferry side and pushed the money for their supper into Breathred's hand. She and Stud made a beeline for the seats, leaving him standing in a very long line.

The fresh breeze blowing off the water erased most of Luna's queasiness. The urge to projectile vomit was still lurking on the fringe of her mind, but she could deal with it. Watching the seagulls play helped to take her mind off of the feeling. A boy of about six was throwing fries into the air. The birds deftly dived to catch the food before it fell to the ground.

She never got tired of watching the gulls' antics. Sometimes she felt like those birds. They were trapped by their nature. They were wild, but learned to adapt to the humans surrounding them. Luna wished it were so easy for her. This place was so far removed from the world she knew. Sometimes she wondered why she had ever left her home in the first place.

She missed the rolling hills and forest-covered mountains. Luna wasn't the first member of the tribe to leave her reservation, nor would she be the last, the girl thought happily. Luna would, one day, return—of that she was certain. The only thing making her time away worthwhile was the fact her studies would strengthen her tribe. When she graduated, Luna could protect their heritage. The government tried, but you had to be of the tribe to understand its history. It took being of the blood to see what the outside world couldn't.

After meeting Breathred she wondered how he would fit into her world. She knew what he was. Hell, she couldn't even think of how to describe what he was. That was what made Breathred, Breathred. The unknown quality defined him, if nothing else.

Luna knew for certain Breathred had feelings for her. What exactly those feelings were she didn't know. Her only consolation, she wasn't even sure he did. In fact, she knew he was clueless. Her mother once told her the wolf knows its mate on sight and once recognition is made nothing can separate them. She felt that way about Breathred, sometimes. She knew one thing for certain: the only one who really knew what was going on was the chimp, and he was enjoying the show too much to tell.

Breathred showed up with their three steaming bowls of soup a short while later. He nearly tripped over the boy running to get more fries for his new pets and narrowly missed tipping their drinks all over a pair of purple-haired old ladies in the process. He mumbled a meek apology before turning back to their table.

Without a word they dug in. The creamy white chowder was enough to end any thoughts of conversation. A ship's bell chimed in the distance. Soon, it was joined by another. Tourists streamed by as they ate. By mutual consent they took no notice of these things.

When the last drop was scraped from the bowls, they leaned back with satisfied grunts. Breathred slurped the remainder of his soda before speaking.

Breathred spoke up breaking the silence. "Look, Luna, I'm sorry about the pay thing."

"It's all right. I can use the credit anyway." She swirled a piece of bread around the rim of her bowl, hoping he'd drop the matter, but knowing he wouldn't.

"No, it isn't! You got us this job, you deserve something." Breathred paused. "So, when the job's over and we get paid, I'm going to give you a twenty-five percent finder's fee."

"No, you're not. You need this money more than I do. I'm really okay with this. Okay?" she said. "You don't have to do that and I mean it."

"If you won't take the percentage, then I'm making you a full partner of *Petrifunck Paranormal*, and that's final." Breathred turned to Stud for his agreement.

"He's right, Sweetheart. Without you we're an idiot and a chimp," Stud piped in.

"Hey!" Breathred yelled.

"Okay." Luna threw back her head and laughed. "You guys make a girl feel all fuzzy. Do you know that?"

Before they could object she reached over and gave them both a big hug. Luna gave Breathred a kiss on the cheek to seal the deal. He turned five shades of red by the time she pulled away.

"I can't pay much, but I, uh." Breathred stuttered. "What I mean is we, uh, we just want you to know how we feel."

"So, now that that's out of the way—what do you think about what the doc had to say?" Stud gave Luna a nudge at Breathred's embarrassment.

"If the tablet is real, it could be trouble. The vamps would kill to get their hands on a relic from their past," Luna mused.

"I'm more worried about the prophecy the tablet spoke about. If this queen was to come back, the whole world could be overrun by blood-suckers," Breathred was quick to add.

Stud put in his two cents worth. "Get real. This queen or whatsit is ten thousand years old. She could have already taken over the world by now if she wanted to. It's a myth. I say we wait until we see this temple before we start worrying about something like vampire myths."

"I think Stud's right. More than likely the village was dominated by a vampire who set herself up as a goddess. Wouldn't be the first time something along those lines happened," Luna said as she watched the young boy launch a plateful of fries into the air.

"Still, I'm sure whatever the case, we need to be on guard. Who knows what could happen?" Breathred worried.

Stud threw up his hands. "You're paranoid. The occasional vamp, I can believe. But this story is out there even for you."

"Okay boys," Luna said, "settle down before you scare the norms. We need to get our stuff together for this trip. From the looks of you two, you haven't been camping in your entire lives. We need to get you some supplies."

"With what? I'm tapped. I suppose I could hit Dad up for a loan till I get paid," Breathred speculated. He could just hear the old man, now. He shook his head, knowing he wouldn't be asking his dad for anything.

"Hell, when you tell him you're getting your ass out of his basement he'll probably give you the keys to his car." Stud laughed.

"Shut up," Breathred gave the monkey a nudge with his elbow.

"What say we meet at the mall after my last class tomorrow? We'll pick up what we can. Is that all right with you?" Luna asked, clearly not taking no for an answer.

"Sounds good to me. If nothing else I have some back issues I can sell to get some money together," Breathred said. Luna could tell he hated the idea.

"You'll come up with something. Now, let's get out of here. All this salty air is killing my skin." Luna jumped to her feet. "Give me your arm, Hot Stuff, and walk me home."

Breathred glowed red, but did as she asked. He was a gentleman after all. Arm in arm they waded through the tourists.

~ * ~

Lewis waited until they were out of sight before detaching himself from the shadow of the building and following them. The vamp knew he would run across the pure soul, sooner or later. He just hadn't figured it would happen this quickly. He could try and take him now, but the girl still had him worried.

The fear was enough to give him pause. They planned to meet at the mall tomorrow night. Tomorrow was soon enough for him to throw something together, one sure to put him as far from harm's way as possible. He had already decided not to tell Leopold anything until after it was all over. The older vampire would just screw up the whole thing, anyway. No,

Lewis would handle this himself.

He knew a couple of newbies who were aching to get in his good graces. Let them run interference with the girl while he swooped in to take the pure one. If they couldn't handle her, he didn't need them around, not that he did in the first place. Either way it went, he would be in the clear.

Smiling Lewis sauntered down the boardwalk. This was gonna be sweet. A little taste might be in order before turning the guy over to Leopold. Why should his master get all the good stuff?

Eight

Make your plans by the light of day, for the night belongs to them.

Oversleeping was becoming Breathred's new hobby. He woke up just in time to get to the college fashionably late. He would have got there sooner, but having to wait for Stud to finish his morning constitutional, only gave him about thirty minutes to get ready after the chimp extricated himself from his labors.

Dr. Grayson's eleven o'clock class was filling the hallway, as he made it to the fifth floor. He was washed back against the wall and forced to wait until the tidal wave of students passed by.

The time allowed him to ponder just what he had gotten them into. This would not be easy. The idea of Stud being in the Canadian wilderness was so frightening he considered calling the whole thing off.

Luna was the sole reason he didn't just march in there and quit. She really went out on a limb to get him this job. In spite of all his fears, Breathred wasn't about to let her down. He could deal with Stud. Sooner or later the chimp had to learn who the boss was in this relationship. Yeah, right. Then again, it would help if Breathred knew who the boss was. Sometimes the line blurred and he wasn't all too sure himself.

When the hallway cleared he peeled himself from the wall. Breathred ran his sweaty hands down the seams of his pants. A pair of tardy students rushed past. He was barely able to dodge out of their way. By the time he finished his spin, the slayer was standing in front of Dr. Grayson's door.

Entering the room, he found her sitting at her desk, going over a stack of papers. Breathred felt like an intruder. His college days were far behind him. Just being back on a college campus unloosed a wave of emotions. Fear, guilt, and the ecstasy that came from learning—all these and some just plain peculiar to any situation whirled through his mind. Choking them back to a manageable dose, Breathred walked into the room.

The sound of his footsteps brought the professor's head up from her work. She offered him a smile in greeting and waved him forward. The gesture wasn't menacing, but for some reason he felt a second or two of fear. Memories of nuns and fifty-foot rulers sprang to mind. Suppressing an involuntary shudder, he reluctantly walked over to her.

"Mr. Petrifunck, I'm glad to see you. My assistant just brought over your paperwork." Dr. Grayson rose to shake his hand. "You'll be glad to know I was able to make an addendum to our agreement."

"How so?" Breathred asked, foregoing a greeting of his own, the addendum throwing him momentarily from his normally good manners.

"It seems you forgot to tell me you have a doctorate in ancient civilizations from Oxford. Don't be shocked. I make it a point to check out those who I'm about to bet my entire career on," she said without an ounce of regret or apology. She motioned for him to take the seat next to her desk. "You don't mind I checked up on you, I hope."

"Not at all," he answered. He silently wondered just how thorough her search had been.

"A doctorate from Oxford. Color me impressed. Why aren't you teaching, or at the very least, on a dig of your own?"

The answer caught in Breathred's throat. The question was so leading he didn't know where to begin, or if he even wanted to. Brushing a hand through his ruffled hair, Breathred peered at the woman with a strange look on his face. Above his left temple his pinky caressed the scar lying hidden just under the hairline. Some things are best forgotten.

"Personal reasons," he said finally, hoping she'd accept the answer.

Her mouth snapped shut before Grayson could say anything. He could tell the woman didn't seem to be satisfied with his answer. Breathred held his breath waiting for her to fold and question him further on it. Finally, her eyes cut away, telling him the moment had passed. The knot in his stomach relaxed.

"Well in light of your degree I was able to give you a pay raise. You'll be getting the same salary a visiting professor would get. I know it isn't a lot for your qualifications, but it's more than you'd have gotten otherwise." Her smile did little to ease the uneasiness he felt.

"Professor Grayson, I would appreciate it if you would keep the tidbit to yourself." Breathred captured her gaze with a cold stare. "My past is not something I wish to have bandied about, especially in front of my partners."

"You have my word, D…uh, Mr. Petrifunck. Now, if you can sign these for me, we'll get the ball rolling, so to speak. I hope you can sign for your, uh, chimpanzee. He isn't with you by any chance?" she asked, her cheek ticking nervously.

"No, he's at home." He wanted to add, "for the moment," but didn't want to frighten her with the truth. Instead, he quickly signed the papers to avoid just such an occurrence. When he was done, he slid the paperwork across the desk.

"With the formalities out of the way, this Saturday we're having a little get-together so the team can get to know each other before we head out. I do hope you can make it," she took the papers and glanced over them.

"I'll be there. It'll give me a chance to see if any of your team has been infiltrated by the undead," Breathred told her.

Grayson looked shocked by his statement. "You can't be serious. I know every one of them. I handpicked them myself. I've seen over half of them this morning. I expect to meet the rest this afternoon to sign their paperwork."

"If someone doesn't show, let me know." Breathred hoped she believed him. The professor hired him for his expertise and this was part of it. If she chose to disregard his advice now, he might as well tell her to forget the entire thing.

"If they all show up, what then? Vampires aren't supposed to be able to stand the light of day. Even I know that much."

"Vampires can't, but their thralls can. All it would take is one bite and any member of your team—and I include you in that—would be completely theirs," he warned.

"And you can tell if someone is a—what did you call it? A thrall?" She didn't believe any of this.

"Not directly, but evil has its own unique scent. I should have little trouble finding them, if anyone is tainted," Breathred answered, hoping it was true. He would make sure to reread the chapter on thralls in the handbook before Saturday.

"You paint an interesting picture for Saturday night. I only hope your worries are unfounded. In any case I am looking forward to seeing you there." Dr. Grayson chuckled. "Make sure you bring the chimpanzee. Why not make a circus out of it?"

"I planned to." Scratching his head, Breathred wondered if she was serious about the circus. If there were clowns, he wasn't coming. He hated clowns. They gave him the willies.

Against his better judgment Breathred knew he would have to bite the bullet and ask his father for the money he needed for the trip. As the manager of the Circle Your Wagons convenience store there wasn't anybody who didn't owe his father a dollar or two. R.J. Petrifunck was always willing to lend a helping hand when someone was short for a gallon of gas or needed a gallon of milk when their money was a week away from coming in. Breathred was banking on his father being in one of his charitable moods when his son came calling. He doubted it would happen, but you never knew. Heck had been known to freeze over every one once in a while.

~ * ~

R. J. Petrifunck saw his son ambling up the parking lot and immediately hid his checkbook. It wasn't that he saw Breathred's visit as an excuse for bumming money. It was just he'd come to know his son over the past thirty some-odd years. Hell, you couldn't even go to Wal-Mart with the boy without having to give him the money to finish out his purchase. His son's skewed thinking on the value of money had cost him over a thousand dollars in loose change over the years. He'd added it up.

"Hey, Dad." Breathred yelled, as he entered the Quick Stop.

"Isn't it a bit early for you to be out of your basement?" R. J. quipped, looking at the calendar sitting beside the register. "Nope, it ain't funny book day, so what do you want?"

"Can't I come by to see you without wanting anything?" Breathred asked.

"Not that I know of, but there's a first time for anything. At least you didn't bring the stinking-ass monkey with you."

"Stud doesn't stink. He's very hygienic."

"If hygienic means smells like a French *hoor* then that's him to a tee." R. J. drawled. "And tell him to stop looking at me when I'm on the pot. My shit time isn't a spectator sport."

"Sure thing, Dad." Breathred groaned, knowing he was losing the battle before it even started.

"Hold on a minute," his father said, and strode around the counter and threw open the door. A woman tried vainly to pump gas into a new-model Lexus. She was frantically waving at the surveillance camera sitting atop the pumps.

"Lift the handle you dumb sum-bitch!" R. J. screamed from the door. He turned about sharply, nearly knocking Breathred to the ground. "You'd think anybody with enough money to buy one of those high-priced ass-warmers would have the money to buy brains enough to know how to pump frigging gas."

"Uh, Dad, I got a job." Breathred said out of the blue.

"Wait a minute." R. J came to a screeching halt at the end of the counter. "Did you just say you got a job?"

"Yes, sir." Breathred beamed.

R. J cocked his brow dubiously. "This isn't like the time you opened a lemonade stand in the front yard, cuz ain't nothing worse than watching a thirty-year-old man trying to sell gourmet Kool-Aid."

"No, I'm going to be working for the university. And the Kool-Aid idea would have worked if Stud hadn't spiked the stuff with Ny-Tol."

"Well, it looks like those five-hundred years of college I paid for are finally paying off. So, what're ya gonna be teaching?" his father asked, mentally counting the days until he'd finally get his basement back.

"I won't be teaching. I'm vampire slaying for them," Breathred answered with a wince.

"Shit fire, and save the matches. Just when I think you got a lick o' sense you go and screw it up. I shoulda slapped your momma when I had the chance," R. J said, rubbing his temples.

"But it pays money, which brings me to—"

R.J. scowled. "How much do you need, Buffy?"

"A couple hundred. It's just till we get paid. Then I can pay you back," Breathred promised.

"You know what? If you didn't waste your money on that super-hero toilet paper, you'd have some fucking cash. Instead you mooch off me and your poor stepmother, and her with a little sister on the way. Do you ever think about us when you go off half-cocked?" his father asked, his neck turning a bright shade of red.

Breathred waited for him to turn around to preach to the beer cooler about dumb-ass children before slipping out the door, barely avoiding a collision with the woman from the Lexus. It had gone better than he thought. He had expected the full treatment. He was walking past the gas pumps when the woman came running from the store. Breathred looked back to see his father jumping up and down on the cola display, and hurried his steps.

The sound of his father's tirade carried to end of the block. Far from disillusioned, Breathred fled before his father could get around to mentioning his son's overflowing collection of beanie babies. This left only two options. After careful consideration he dismissed the first one out of hand. At the most Stud wouldn't bring in more than $62.50, if he decided to throw in the Mini Me costume. Option one painfully shelved, Breathred turned to the most dreaded of money-making ventures.

Two hours later and his comic collection twenty some odd issues lighter, Breathred left Clint's with a little over two hundred and fifty dollars to his name. In spite of his sacrifice, Breathred wasn't even sure it was enough to outfit both him and Stud. Luna would make it work, though. Of that he was more than confident.

With a couple of hours until he had to meet Luna at the Great Northwestern, Breathred, not feeling like going home, decided to walk around for a while. Things were moving so fast he didn't know what to think anymore. After the cat incident, he had thought seriously about forgetting the whole vampire-slaying gig. Then Luna stepped in and changed things. She always seemed to put a spin on his perspective.

Now, he was going to Canada on the greatest vampire hunt of all. Even old snooty Van Helsing couldn't say he'd found the true origin of vampires. Not to say, he didn't have worries. Dr. Grayson was the biggest.

The fact she decided to check up on him set his teeth to rattling. The chance she might discover his true secret was more than an enough to make him want to run to Mexico. Breathred hadn't been joking when he had told her the reason was personal. It was his shame, not hers. Why couldn't she leave it alone?

He absently kicked a can blocking his path. The can skipped across the sidewalk until it clanged into a trashcan sitting close to where he was standing. It was too late to go back on his word, anyway. After signing the papers, the only thing left to do was suck it up and dive in. If Luna and Stud found out, they found out. There was nothing he could do to change it if they did, except for a killing spree.

A look at his watch, told him he had better get going, or there wouldn't be time to grab Stud before getting to the mall. Luna would kill him if they were late. Stud would kill him if he didn't bring him along. The way Breathred saw it—either way it went, he was dead. So he might as well go into it with both barrels cocked and loaded. What was the worst that could happen?

~ * ~

Lewis awoke with the coming dusk. The steady rhythm of Leopold's sleeping came from the casket next to him. The old poof sure liked his beauty rest, Lewis thought as he climbed from the satin-lined tomb. That was for the best, as far as he was concerned. It meant he would be able to slip from the house without Leopold noticing.

It was nearly party time. All he had to do was go pick up the guest of honor. Lewis had been able to follow them long enough to find out they were meeting at the Great Northwestern Shopping Mall, sometime around eight o'clock. The girl had class until seven. That gave him about an hour to round up his muscle.

Lewis had made it a point to talk to them just before dawn. The wannabee toughs were all for it. From the looks of them they had never been in anything close to a rumble, unless you counted Mortal Combat for the Xbox 360. The newbies were nothing more than cannon fodder, anyway. Hell, the damn monkey could probably take them out. Lewis just needed them to distract the girl long enough for him to grab the virgin.

Leopold started mumbling in his sleep. Time to scoot. He wanted no part of having to help his master pick out his ensemble for the night. The last time he stuck around, Leopold gave him an all night dissertation on the finer points of Italian tailoring. That, my friends, was just too much information for a Naw-'leans boy to have to assimilate on an empty stomach.

Nine

If you have only ordered the first half of this course, you can kiss your ass good-bye.

To call the Great Northwestern a mall should be enough to earn whoever called it such, a nice libel suit for even daring to utter such a blasphemy against the shopping industry in general. It wasn't that the place hadn't had at one time earned the right to be called a mall, but those days were long past. Now, it existed as the sole providence of speed walking grandmothers and Goth kids, who saw the G. W. as a rebellion against the establishment of the larger and newer malls represented.

The place was still a great place to shop far from the hassle of large unruly crowds. It had all the prerequisite stores that made the act of shopping worthwhile. The mall had a Sears & Roebuck, a J. C. Penney and a Starbucks. It even had a newly-opened Gap now catering to the neighborhoods surrounding the shopping complex. Despite its seeming prosperity, the Northwestern was dying a slow death. It was just that the place had little to sway shoppers away from the flashier places across town.

To Breathred though, it was heaven—pure and simple. The mall was less than two blocks from his house, which only reinforced this notion in his mind. Despite his undying love, mall security saw him in a different light or rather they saw Stud in an unsavory light. This was due in part to Stud's first visit there.

Before the incident that forever changed the young simian, Breathred had decided to show off his new acquisition. What better place to do this than his home away from home? He really just wanted a corndog, and was afraid to leave the monkey on his own with the poo-throwing and all. So, he bundled up his new friend and headed off.

Looking back, Breathred wished he could change almost everything about the long ago day, beginning with going to the joke store. It had just opened, which instantly drew Breathred's attention. The window promised everything from gag gifts to magics fresh from the Orient. How could he resist?

Stud was a perfect gentleman until he saw the animatronics ape. Then, it was on. Stud broke free from his grasp and went berserk. Breathred tried frantically to grab the little ape, as he jumped from display to display, taunting the inanimate gorilla. The gorilla's refusal to respond to Stud's badgering only seemed to inflame the chimpanzee. Before Breathred knew what was happening, Stud had jumped on top of the gorilla's back.

Crazed and foaming at the mouth, Stud tore into the polyester fur. From amid the rows of fake dog vomit and floating handkerchiefs, Breathred and the store manager advanced on the rampaging primate. Stud saw them coming and was ready for them. For his trouble the manager received a face full of something better left unmentioned. Breathred, a little quicker than the other man, ducked, avoiding the steaming missile meant for him. After the first salvo Breathred hugged the carpet and inched forward on his elbows.

A group of wandering geeks let out a startled scream as they entered the store. Stud's head popped up at their cries. He bared his teeth in their direction, warning them away from his prey. It was the opening Breathred was looking for.

He jumped toward his hysterical monkey. Getting one hand on its neck, Breathred ripped Stud free from the mechanical gorilla. He fell to the floor with the writhing chimpanzee in tow. Stud moved in a thousand different directions at once. It took everything Breathred had to keep him captive.

Once Stud had worn himself out, Breathred took in the carnage. Gondolas were overturned. The floor was littered with merchandise. In the background Breathred heard a babble of Aramaic coming from the manager. Breathred couldn't understand what he was saying, but it couldn't be good.

Then, he turned his eyes to the source of Stud's rampage. It was much too late for the great ape. Aside from the obvious de-furring, it had also suffered a most emasculating violation by the maddened chimpanzee somewhere in the middle of the one-monkey melee.

Needless to say, Stud was banished from the mall immediately, along with Breathred. There was also some talk of ritual castration by the storeowner, but after Breathred reimbursed the man for the cost of the gorilla, all was forgiven. Forgiven but not forgotten was the motto of mall security, whenever the pair walked through the mall's glass doors.

It was still the case, as they entered the mall just as dusk was falling. Two guards started dogging their steps almost within seconds of them entering the food court. Breathred chose to ignore them while Stud made imaginary grabs for his butt whenever they got too close. Breathred knew better than to try to stop him.

Breathred scanned the empty food court for Luna. He spotted her near the Corn Dog Cavalcade. She waved a foot long corn-wrapped weenie, when she caught sight of him. Breathred grabbed Stud by the hand and made for her.

"Hey, guys." Luna chirped through a mouth full of the corndog. "I thought you weren't gonna make it."

"I had to run some errands and got a late start," Breathred explained, the thought of his missing comics bringing a tremble to his voice.

"That's okay. I needed a bite before we headed out, anyway," she mumbled between bites of corn meal and pig by-products. "There's a couple more coming up for you two. I figured you'd be ravenous."

"You guessed right, Toots." Stud gave Breathred a dirty look. "Lame brain wouldn't let me eat before we left. Gave me some bull crap about it violating my parole."

"I did not. He wouldn't get out of the bathroom." Breathred hastened to explain.

"Come on guys, cool it. We're here to have some fun and do some shopping. If you can't behave, you can just go home," Luna warned them with a shake of her corn dog.

"Yes, ma'am," they answered in unison.

"Now, we should get you both some hard-wearing outfits. You want something that won't tear easily, and some good boots. They're a must."

Breathred tuned her out. Not to say her voice wasn't especially pleasant this evening, but he had no interest in clothes. To him clothes were a t-shirt and a pair of jeans and nothing more. He would follow her lead. He could walk behind her without having to listen to the running discourse. He was a man, after all.

Over the span of the next three hours they hit every clothing store the feeble mall contained. He couldn't be sure, but he thought some of them were more for her benefit than his. No matter how nice they looked, Breathred could see no possible way Luna could think she was going to be able to wear a wedding dress in the forests of Canada.

~ * ~

Lewis was growing bored. He had been following the trio all night. They were making him sick with their honey-coated relationship. The boy was whipped. The way he let a slip of a girl lead him around like a sick puppy, made Lewis glad he was a vampire and beyond all that bullshit. He was beginning to think he was going to go crazy before his lunkheaded associates got their asses in gear.

Oh my God, not another shoe store. Pick out a pair already. Lewis plopped down on a bench. This was not worth the aggravation. He should have let Leo handle this. Where were those idiots? On cue they saddled up behind them.

"What took you so long?" Lewis demanded, sensing them behind him.

"We got lost." The top dog smarted off.

"Make sure that condition doesn't become permanent," Lewis hissed. "Now get to work, before I get to work on you."

Lewis sat back without giving them a second glance. The young vamps blended into the crowd, such as it was. Lewis watched with satisfaction. If the young vamps lived through this, they might be of use to him later.

Once they were nearly to the shoe store, Lewis got up. He had his own part to play in this little charade. The vampire slid past a gaggle of grannies with relative ease, making it a point to tip his hat, as he passed. No sense in antagonizing the old biddies. He didn't want them following him around later.

He took up point, just beyond Shoes-N-More. His newbies advanced to the right of the store. Lewis shuffled behind a floating jewelry booth. From his new position he could see his prey while still keeping an eye on his men.

~ * ~

Luna looked up from an incredible pair of pumps to see some youths stagger into the shoe store. Instantly, something about them didn't feel right. Darkness surrounded them. She sensed it close enough to touch. The presence of it hit her like a fist to the gut. Breathred was rubbing his temples, but didn't seem to know why. He was feeling it too, she was glad to see. There was hope for him yet.

They looked a few years younger than her, but Luna knew looks could be deceiving. They were the undead. She could smell the grave all over them. Even the rip-off Polo they had bathed themselves in couldn't hide the scent.

The losers tried to look nonchalant, but from the way they kept peeping at her and Breathred, they weren't here looking for a pair of open-toed sandals. They were after Breathred, just like the vamp from the night before last. But why? Surely, he wasn't a real threat to them yet. Maybe they were trying to eliminate him before he became a threat. Luna blanched at the possibility of her Breathy-poo at the hands of killer vamps.

Either way, she had to get them out of here before things got nasty. Luna gave the store a quick once-over. Three customers were grouped around the cross-trainers. Behind the sale's counter the cashier was popping her bubble gum, trying not to fall asleep. So, all Luna had to do was get the customers and the girl out of the way. The girl was easy.

Luna held a purple sneaker aloft. "Hey, miss. Do you have these in a size eight?"

"I'll have to check in the back." The cashier yawned before slipping through the curtain that separated the showroom floor from the back.

One down, three to go.

"You know Barclay's is having a fifty percent off sale. Maybe we should try there next," she said loud enough for the other customers to hear.

The customers looked around to make sure they heard right. Slapping down their choices, they headed for the door. Luna smiled. Now, it was just them and the vamps.

Sizing them up, Luna had them pegged from the start. They were good—not quite pros, but a few more years should give them the edge they needed. If she let them leave here alive, that was. She was in a good mood, so a few broken bones should be enough to get her point across.

The thought hadn't left her brain when the vamps made their move. The taller of the two sailed over the discount table, his leather jacket flapping like bat wings. Why did they always go for the Fonzi on acid look? In one smooth kick, Luna upended the table directly into the vamp's path. The vampire made a dull thud, as he slammed into the particleboard tabletop. His impact sent a shower of cut-rate Nikes into the air.

Luna didn't have time to think. Things were going full tilt. The second vamp skirted the table, going straight for Breathred and Stud. Before she could move to intercept him, Breathred whirled around.

~ * ~

Breathred turned just as the vamp slammed into his body. The impact tossed him into the wall with a bone rattling bang. Sliding down the wall, the air rushed out of him like a tidal wave. His vision turned to black as he hit the floor, but Breathred held onto consciousness, barely. Through the sprinkling of stars that populated his vision, he saw Luna battling with another attacker. What was going on?

His head was killing him. Some freak was trying to take him out in a run-down Foot Locker and if he wasn't mistaken a pair of Nikes had just violated him. This was not the shopping trip he'd planned on. All he wanted was to buy a pair of shoes and get the heck home before the ten o'clock news came on. Was that too much to ask?

The vamp made another lunge for him. Breathred deftly moved to his left, dodging the attack. Anticipating the vamp's next move, he fell to the ground and swept his foot under his attacker's leading leg. The vampire pitched forward, its arms flailing in an attempt to keep itself upright. Breathred pressed his advantage. Before the vamp could regain his balance, he kicked up, nailing it in the solar plexus. The undead fiend went back into the air, doing an unintentional back-flip in the process. It landed amid the wreckage of the shoe-strewn floor.

Breathred smiled smugly. He offered a silent thanks to the *Ti Beau Correspondence School of Kung Fu and Aerobic Fitness. Lesson Eight*, for those who want to learn it for themselves.

A flash of agony shot through his chest. He doubled over, falling to the floor. Breathred's fingers brushed against his pounding chest. Fire raced through his hand. He drew back singed fingers. Sweat poured from his forehead. He was dying. This was the end.

Despite the pain, he grabbed his chest and pulled out the source of the heat. It was his crucifix—the one he picked up online at the Vatican rummage sale on EBAY. The normally-pale gold was aflame. From the looks of it, the sight didn't mean the cross was reflecting the light around it. The holy relic was actually on fire. Amber flames were licking off its surface.

Confused, he looked up. Through the orange haze surrounding the crucifix, he saw Stud pounding his former attacker in the head. The chimp's furry little arms were a brown blur, as they slammed into the kid. When the boy opened his mouth to scream, Breathred saw inch long canines protruding from the screeching maw.

Vampire! The word hung in his throat. They were not human, not even a big scary cat for that matter. The crucifix was burning because of them. Breathred thought back. His head didn't start hurting until they walked in. The crucifix hadn't started burning until he got close to the one who had come after him. Everything suddenly fell into place. The lessons were coming true. Once you attuned yourself to the unbelievable, it became believable.

The sound of Luna howling, forced Breathred's attention away from Stud onto her. She was backed against the wall by the other vamp. The creature was sliding her up the wall by the neck. The vampire had her dangling about a foot above the floor. Her eyes pleaded with Breathred for help.

Without thinking, he drove his foot into the shoebox shaped rack behind him. An explosion of plywood and splintered two by fours showered over him. From the waterfall of debris, he snagged a ragged piece of wood out of the air.

He shot a quick look to make sure Stud was still okay. The monkey had the vampire's head pulled back and was riding the undead creature around the store like a horse. An idea formed in Breathred's head.

"Stud!" He smiled when he saw the chimp's head snap up. "Bring him over here."

When Stud nodded, Breathred got ready. He watched as the chimp hooked an opposable thumb/toe in the vampire's ear, and with a devious twist he jerked down on the vamp's pointed ear, turning the vamp right straight for him. Breathred muttered a prayer hoping this would work.

He held his breath and slowly counted to three. At three he leapt. Ripping the crucifix from his neck, he planted the golden icon in the vampire's face. Stud jumped from his perch, as the undead flesh began to smolder and burst into flame. Breathred kept his momentum going. He pushed off from the writhing vamp somersaulting toward Luna.

Breathred hit the ground running. Not missing a beat, he slammed into the vampire holding Luna aloft. The thug dropped the girl, and turned to face Breathred with an evil hiss. Breathred didn't give him a chance to strike. In one smooth motion he flipped the makeshift stake into the air. The movement distracted the vamp long enough for Breathred to catch it and shove the foot-long sliver of wood through its chest.

~ * ~

The vampire gasped in disbelief. This was not what was supposed to happen. Lewis hadn't said anything about it being dangerous. It was a cakewalk. That was what the older vampire had said. Distract the girl, and Lewis would handle the rest. So, where was Lewis?

A fountain of black blood flowed from its mouth. It stared blankly toward the plate-glass storefront. A shadow shook its head before hurrying on its way. The dying vampire stared after the shadow in disbelief.

He was immortal. How could he be dying? He was to live forever, not die in some low-rate shopping center. Who was this human to kill him?

The vampire stared defiantly into Breathred's face, searching for the answer. Cold fire met his gaze. The vampire flinched, trying to tear his eyes away. Something lurked within those eyes, a thing that did not belong to a human soul.

A flickering shade crossed the human's pupil. At first the vampire thought he must be imagining it, but the dark thing returned his glare from the recesses of the man's eye. In the blackness, the shade smiled back at the vamp. Too late he saw his doom for what it was, and was afraid. The dying vampire screamed, as it evaporated into a whirlwind of ash, his fate painted on the stagnant air.

~ * ~

Breathred barely even noticed. His concern was wrapped up in Luna. She lay deathly still on the floor. He fell to her side. She couldn't be dead. He needed her. More than that, he couldn't make it without her. Breathred sensed the other vampire flee through the door, but didn't care. All that mattered was Luna.

"Come on, Luna. You gotta be all right. I don't know what I'd do, if you weren't," Breathred said, as he brushed the hair from her face. Then, in a whisper so low even he couldn't hear it, he said, "I think I love you."

Her eyelids flickered open. The panic left him, and he let out a sigh of relief. She looked up at him and smiled. Breathred melted in her gaze. Sensing his revealing expression, he pulled back into himself. His emotions no longer painted his face, yet the feeling still welled within his heart. She was all right.

"Can't take it back now, Sweetie," Luna said, leaning up and planting a kiss on his confused lips.

~ * ~

Stud fell back against a cardboard cutout of some basketball player or another. A huge grin spread across his face. If he'd known all it took was a vampire attack to get things moving along, he would've hired them himself.

Ten

Due to financial constraints, your introductory bottle of holy water will be sent to you in five to six weeks or after your check clears, whichever comes first.

Edith wasn't one to eavesdrop. Not if she was going to get caught at it, that is. She didn't have to worry as she brought Breathred and Luna their drinks. Thanks to the ape of his, the entire restaurant was getting an ear full of their business. The woman saw it as her duty, as both a friend and a manager of good standing in the food industry, to quiet them down. If her decision enabled her to get a closer listen, so be it.

"You kids stow it. You're scaring the norms," Edith pushed Breathred over to sit beside him. "Now, what's all this fuss about?"

Stud smirked from behind a steaming mocha latte. "Luna gave Breathred a big wet one right on the lips."

"She did not. It was reverse mouth to mouth. How many times do I have to tell you that?" Breathred exclaimed to his shame.

"He said he loved her too," Stud added, just to see his master turn a particular shade of purple you could never find in a Crayola box.

"*I did not!*" Breathred screamed.

"Yes, you did, Honey Bunch. Try to deny it and I'll take you to court," Luna said with a devilish wink.

"About time you got around to it. I was beginning to think about hitting you over the head and making an honest man out of you." Edith gave him a sharp nudge to the ribs.

Breathred growled. They chose to ignore him and continue the conversation without his input. Fine with him. If he'd known she was listening, he would've kept his fool mouth shut. Then again, she might not have kissed him otherwise. He rather liked the kissing part.

He cocked a half-opened eye toward Luna. As if on cue, she looked up. Before he could look away, she gave him another wink. He blushed three different ways, all of them more embarrassing than the last. At least Stud was ogling Edith, freeing him from any ridicule from the chimp's corner.

Now, the only problem was how to deal with a girlfriend. Breathred knew people of his sex did so every day but could he? What did one do with a girl? He knew for a fact shopping was involved, as were romantic dinners at restaurants with names like the Chateau. From watching soap operas, Breathred knew the score. He was already used to shopping with Luna, so that wouldn't be a problem. Managing a dinner or two wouldn't be so bad—as long as she paid, of course. He could do this.

Breathred wasn't up for all that funny stuff though. A polite kiss would be okay within reason. Holding hands would be fine. He could even help her pick out clothes. But, he drew the line at purchasing any form of hygiene products with their blue and pink wrapped wings. Oh no, not him. Lead lined bags weren't enough for him to go near those.

As long as he knew where to draw the line, things should be all right. Somehow, Breathred got the idea Luna would be the one to draw the lines. The thought scared him. Women had funny ideas about lines and where they should go. Later, he would ask Stud to explain it all to him. Until then, the best thing to do was to nod his head and look stupid. Daddy always said women knew how to deal with stupid, but if you showed them how smart you really were, they'd cut you off at the balls.

Luna patted his hand gently. "Breathred, can you snap out of it? We have some things we need to discuss."

"You got to get his attention. Like this." To illustrate his point Stud whacked Breathred across the nose with a rolled up newspaper.

"Hey!"

"See? Works every time. How do you think I taught him to take the trash out?" Stud said, as he sat back down.

"Look, those vamps—" Luna started to say.

"Do you think we should be talking about this in front of the bit of fluff?" Stud interrupted.

"He's right. No need to involve noncombatants in this," Breathred added.

"Look here, seeing as this is my place, unless you plan to settle your tabs right now and move this little confab somewhere else, I'm staying." Edith announced, giving each of them a harsh look.

"I guess it'll be alright." Breathred conceded, not wanting to upset her, or pay his tab if the truth be told. He wasn't sure how much it was, but after five years it had to be up there. "We just didn't want to scare you. This type of business isn't for the weak at heart."

"Honey Child, I've got two ex-husbands and three kids. You ain't got nothing that can scare me." Edith laughed.

"If that's settled, can we get this over with? I need my beauty sleep," Stud piped in.

"Like I was trying to say before the buttinsky convention. Those vampires weren't there by chance; they were looking for us," Luna said slowly, making sure they understood her. "Or rather they were looking for you, Breathred."

"Why would they be looking for me?" Breathred asked.

"Maybe, because you're the only vampire slayer listed in the yellow pages," Stud said, drolly.

"And you said it was wasted money." Breathred grinned.

"Yeah, instead of people hiring you to slay vampires, you got vampires trying to slay you. Smart move, Einstein," Stud shot back.

"Shut up. You're nothing but overgrown children," Luna snapped.

"Yes, Ma'am," they said in unison.

"This is serious. I can't have strange minions of the undead trying to kill my Sweetums," Luna said.

"Let them. It'll serve him right for being a smeg-head," Stud snapped.

"Good. Once he's dead, I'm sure Breathred's dad won't sell you to Jerry Springer," Luna fumed. "Or Martha Stewart. You know how he loves her."

"Yeah, yeah, we got to keep the smeg-head alive," Stud agreed, reluctantly.

"Be nice, or I'll throw your *Red Dwarf* DVDs away." Luna shook her finger in warning.

Breathred chose to ignore Stud. "So what should we do?"

"I don't know. I think it's curious they start coming around just as we start working for Doctor Grayson."

"You think they know about the tablet?" Breathred asked.

"It's a distinct possibility. That means Dr. Grayson has a mole in her team leaking information to the vampires."

"That's it. I'm out. Screw the money," Stud said, climbing over the back of the booth.

"Sit back down. Even if you stay here, the vamps know you're with Breathred, and they'll come after you anyway. The best place for you is with us, where we can watch out for each other." Luna patted Stud's hand.

"Seems to me, you kids've bought more trouble than you can pay for," Edith added.

"Well, I'm not backing down. I gave Doctor Grayson my word I'd help her, and I'm not going to let her down. It wouldn't be honorable," Breathred said, firmly.

"He's right. We gave our word, so we're in it up to our necks. That said, we need to come up with some kind of plan to keep us alive until we leave on Monday," Luna said, agreeing with Breathred.

"Ya'll just need to worry about night time. Vampires can't get you during the day. Plus, it appears to me if they knew who you were, they'd have tried to get you at your house, Breathred, instead of at the mall," Edith stated.

"She's right. We can all bunk at your house during the night. If we each take a watch, nobody can get in without us knowing about it," Luna said excitedly.

"You mean, like me and you asleep in the same room, together?" Breathred asked, shooting up from his seat.

"Calm down, Hot Stuff. Just because we're going steady, doesn't mean you get the Grand Tour." Luna gave him a wink that made the red come rushing back.

"Well, I didn't...uh, that is to say..." Breathred finally just shut up. He was afraid someone would explain what the Grand Tour was, and he wasn't sure if he could handle the truth.

"Don't tease him like that, Luna. He'd go blind, just trying to find it." Stud laughed.

"I would not. I know where to—" Breathred began.

Luna and Edith turned to look at him, each of the women giving him the evil eye. Breathred closed his mouth and sat back down. This girlfriend business was harder than it looked.

"Anyway, the first thing to do is get to your place before anybody else decides to come after us," Luna said. Breathred was grateful for her interruption and didn't mind the fact it took the heat off him.

"How do we know those pointed-tooth freaks aren't outside waiting? I for one ain't in the mood to be some vampire's midnight snack," Stud snapped.

"He's got a good point." Breathred hated to agree.

"Look, if they're out there, it means they saw you come in. So, all we have to do is get you out of here without them seeing you," Edith advised.

"Look, Toots. Unless you got Houdini up your skirt, that ain't gonna happen," Stud snickered.

"Smart-ass monkeys ought to keep their mouths shut, before I add chilled monkey brains to the menu," Edith snarled. "You can go out the back way."

"That won't do any good, they'll be watching that way too," Breathred offered.

"Not if I park my Lettus GT by the back door," Edith said, letting out a cackle.

"Excuse me, but what's a Lettus GT?" Breathred asked.

"An Escort with delusions of grandeur," Edith wheezed through another round of laughter.

"Be that as it may, she's right. If she parks right by the back door, we can get in with nobody seeing us," Luna said.

"Let's do it. My ass is itching for some attention, if you know what I mean," Stud said, jumping on top of the table.

"Luna, take them through the back, while I get Cindy to take the rest of my shift," Edith said, as she pushed away from the table.

Luna led them through the swinging door into the kitchen. She heard

Edith's booming voice telling Cindy to close out. She looked over at Breathred. The big lug just blushed and pushed ahead of her. She had to take it easy on him. The poor confused dear was so fragile it hurt.

That was okay. As soon as this business was over, she'd set him to rights. Momma always said if you couldn't break them in the first month, they were too stupid to keep.

~ * ~

Leopold was waiting. Lewis knew it as soon as he walked through the door. Waiting was bad. It meant his master knew everything. So, he missed bagging the prize. Tough shit. It wasn't like the fruit cup was going anywhere. He'd try again…with better help.

"Lewis, come here," Leopold said in a cold voice.

Now, this wasn't good. Leo never pulled the dead voice unless he was pissed. He could run and come back later, when Leo had a chance to cool down. On second thought, he had better face the music now. No sense in letting it get any worse than it had to be.

"Yo, Leopold, what ya need?"

"You went out to play and didn't tell me. I had to hear about your escapade from the vermin you run with. How do you think this makes me feel?" The vampire lord's voice droned from the shadows.

"I don't know. Glad I put forth a little initiative?" Lewis quipped.

"No, hurt. That's how I feel. Hurt someone I trust could leave me out of the loop. What's worse, this little piece of street trash tells me you failed." Leopold emerged from the darkness.

"Look, Leo. He had muscle I didn't know about."

"Yes, let me see. What was it? Oh, yes. A girl and a monkey. You got your ass handed to you by a virgin, a girl and a monkey. Do you care to tell me just how that happened?"

Lewis tried to explain. "He had these freaky powers."

"Of course he did. If you had taken the time to listen to me, you would have known he would be protected. But the big bad pimp daddy had to know best. Didn't you?" Leopold screamed.

"Yes, sir," Lewis whimpered.

"But I forgive you. Do you know why?"

"No, Leopold."

"Because, now I know he's here. I can track him. Your little playmate gave me this before he reached his final reward." Leopold held up a bloody glove. "I won't ask you if you know what it is. Instead, I'll tell you. It's his blood. Even diluted as it is, I can smell its purity. With this, there is no place he can hide from me."

"That's good, right?"

"Very good. We're beyond this other mess, so we'll forget it. It never happened. Are we clear?" Leopold asked.

Lewis knew better than to speak. This was Leopold's show now.

"Now, Lewis I have another question that needs answering. You'll tell me the truth won't you?"

Lewis squirmed afraid to say anything. In this mood Leopold was liable to do anything. He hadn't seen him like this before. In the end he decided to play along.

"Sure, man. You know me. Always willing to help."

"Do you think this coat goes with this shirt?"

Eleven

Freshly turned earth is the first sign something might not be quite right.

Breathred hadn't slept all night. It wasn't that he wasn't sleepy, because he was. The thought of sleeping in the same room, let alone at the exact same time as Luna, was so frightening he considered locking himself in the bathroom until morning. Breathred dismissed the idea early on. From the bathroom it would be impossible to watch for vampires.

So, for the entire night Breathred sat in his chair and stared at the six-by-eighteen-inch window that filtered light into his humble abode. Except for three dogs and countless hookers, no one bothered their rest. Dawn shifted wordlessly into the room, ending his lonely vigil.

Breathred yawned, but made no move to rise. He wanted to go to sleep, wanted it more than anything else, more than the most vaulted *Spider-Man Issue #129*. The exhausted slayer knew he wouldn't be reaching any level of sleep today. There was just too much to do, starting with getting the rest of their stuff together.

Through sleep-clouded eyes he looked over to where Luna lay sleeping. Her hair was unfurled about her head. The frugal sunlight from the slender basement window washed across her face. Breathred smiled. Something about the way she looked made her appear almost angelic.

This wasn't the first time Breathred had noticed that about her. All through the night he took the time to watch her. Not to say he was stalking her. He just wanted to make sure she was still breathing. You never knew when something as simple as a hangnail could bloom into a full blown sporadic coma. You read about it all the time in the *Daily Globe*. Being a boyfriend was so new to him Breathred didn't want to take the chance of her expiring before he became whipped. Stud seemed to think whippedness was the most important part of being a boyfriend, so Breathred was willing to give it his all.

With sleep far behind him Breathred got up. Scratching those parts that needed scratching, he headed toward the bathroom. Maybe a shower would heal his aching head. Lord knows, it couldn't hurt.

He eased the door shut behind him, not wanting to wake his friends.

Breathred winced at the ghost that greeted him in the mirror. One should never look at oneself, until after nine o'clock. Reflections did funny things to a person before that all-important hour.

Hastily averting his eyes, Breathred shambled over to the commode. This was the tricky part of his morning regime. Normally, it was the easiest, but not today. With Luna in the next room those parts usually operating at peak efficiency rebelled.

He couldn't blame them. There was a girl in the next room—not just any girl, but *the* girl. In his mind he knew she, too, had bodily functions she tended to. She busted in on him enough to know it to be bona fide fact, but Breathred didn't want her to know he did those functions, as well. Somehow it pained his sensibilities for her to know those intimate things about him.

At the point of bursting, he reached over and turned on the shower. Hopefully the sound would camouflage whatever his body might toss out. Once relieved of at least one bodily burden, he turned his attention to a quick shower.

Ten minutes of steam did much to clear his mind. The pounding had reduced itself to a dull throb. He could deal with a throb. His mind again focused, he saw his way through the day. The slamming of the basement door ended his moment of clarity. Draping the towel over his nude chest, he exploded through the bathroom door. Visions of day-walkers and zombies filled his fractured brain. Instead a sight worse than his worst nightmare awaited him.

His father, sans shirt—like a shirt could contain those raging man-breasts in the first place—stood at the bottom of the stairs. The remains of powdered donuts freckled his chin and chest hair. A look of bemused spite sat upon his face, like a stale pickle. Upon seeing Breathred, the look turned ugly.

"Boy, am I blind or is that a girl in your bed?" His father asked loud enough to scare Stud from his sleep.

"Yes, sir," Breathred mumbled meekly.

"Shit fire, and save the matches. Thank God, I was beginning to think I had a fruit roll-up for a son," R.J. howled.

"Dad, it's not what you think."

"She's with the monkey? Don't tell me she's with the monkey. If you tell me she's with the monkey, I may have to shoot you myself."

"No, I'm all Breathy's, Big Daddy," Luna unrolled herself from the bed.

R.J. raised an eyebrow. She looked normal, but looks could be deceiving. He let his eyes stay on her for a little bit longer. She was a man. She had to be. No, those were definitely breasts. At least they looked like breasts. These days you couldn't be too careful, what with all them transcombobulators, running around.

Short of asking outright, he wasn't going to be sure. The best thing to do was run upstairs and send the old lady down to ask. Damned if he would. What if the whatsit said she was one?

He would hide in his bedroom until she, or it whatever the case may be, left. Then, he would change all the locks. His idiot son could go live with his ex-wife. She was crazy as a Bessie bug, anyway. Let her deal with their son and his whatsit. Thirty-five years of dealing with him was quite enough for R.J. It was her turn. With any luck he'd be dead before she kicked Breathred out.

"Look, I gotta go," R.J. said, twisting to mount the stairs.

"Dad, did you want anything?" Breathred asked. His father never came down here, so for him to be here something had to provoke it.

"Ah, yeah. There's another one upstairs," his father yelled from the top of the stairs.

"Another what?"

"Another whatsit. I mean another woman," R.J. slammed the basement door shut.

"Would you like to explain to me why there's a woman upstairs?" Luna asked in a feral growl.

"Yeah, Muttly. Is there something you need to tell us?" Stud piped in, as he plopped himself in Luna's lap.

A rapping on the basement door saved him. He'd hoped the noise would distract them from him. The looks on their faces told him no such luck. With twin sets of eyes boring into him, Breathred beat a hasty retreat to the safety of the basement door.

Breathred opened the door, half hoping for a creature of the undead to end his soon-to-be suffering. It wasn't a vampire waiting on the other side of the door, but his visitor did end his suffering.

"Mr. Petrifunck, I'm sorry to disturb you at home, but I couldn't get hold of Ms. Walking Batch, and you weren't answering your phone." Professor Grayson poked her head through the door. "I hope I didn't catch you at a bad time."

"No, please come in," Breathred said, swinging the door wide so she could enter.

"Your father is quite the character. Do you know why he would have that girl ask me if I was a whatsit?" She squeezed past him.

"No, I wouldn't." Breathred shot a stinging look back toward the door, as he started down after her. That old man was just asking to be put in a home.

"Oh, Ms. Walking Batch," Dr. Grayson said, when she caught sight of the girl. She turned to Breathred. "Are you sure I didn't come at an inopportune moment?"

"No, ma'am. It's not what you think." Breathred blushed.

Her eye brow rose up her forehead. "Frankly, it does look like what I think."

"No, it's the truth; we were attacked by vampires at the mall last night. Breathred thought it best if we all stayed in one place in case they came after us," Luna said, the look on her face saying she didn't like the conclusion the professor jumping to.

"My word! You don't think it's because of the dig, do you?" Dr. Grayson asked, shocked by the news. Really, she couldn't believe she was in a stranger's basement actually discussing vampires as if she was discussing the evening news.

"You bet your ass it was, Sweetcakes," Stud said before anyone could stop him.

"It is rather suspicious they chose to attack us right after you hired us." Breathred let the implications hang in the air.

Grayson seemed confused by his statement. "But only you and I know you're even a part of the team."

"Someone had to give the okay for us to be added to the team. It could mean someone in the main office could have leaked the information. From there any number of people could have found out," Luna theorized.

"I guess you're right," the professor responded. "Which might help explain the reason I dropped by."

"Do you want to clarify that for us," Stud snorted, untangling himself from Luna.

"I received a letter from the man funding the dig late last night. It seems a snafu in his office resulted in an error in our departure time. Instead of leaving on Monday, we are leaving on Sunday."

"But how does that connect to the vampires from last night?" Breathred pondered aloud.

"If I hadn't verified the information myself over a month ago, I'd say nothing. Something fishy is going on here," Grayson stated.

"Do you think the guy funding this is in league with the vamps?" Stud stopped scratching his ass to ask.

"I don't know what to think, but I can't dismiss the possibility." She didn't know how to answer the question. A week ago she wouldn't have even considered the possibility, but now she just wasn't sure of what she believed.

"Then, as far as I'm concerned this trip is over. Cancel my reservation, 'cause this chimp's momma didn't raise no fools." Stud pushed past the professor in a huff.

"Stop it right there, King Dong." Luna grabbed him by the back of his shirt. "If the vamps are behind this, it's even more important for us to go."

"How do you figure that?" Stud tried to pry her fingers loose.

"Because if the vampires know about the tablet. That means they know about the Mother. We can't let them reawaken her. That's why we are going to do just what we said we were going to do," Breathred said, bringing them all to silence.

"He's right," Luna said.

"Of course he is. Don't expect it to make me feel any better about it," Stud said. He stopped struggling.

Dr. Grayson obviously didn't like the way this conversation was headed. "So, what are we going to do, now?"

"Just what I said we were going to do. We have the most dangerous weapon of all in our hands—knowledge. We know they're onto us, but do they know that we know? I don't think so," Breathred answered.

"This is just too unbelievable. How do expect me to act normal with all this rolling around in my head?"

"You have to otherwise they'll know we're on to them. The only chance we've got is to keep them in the dark for as long as we can, so we can have time to figure all this out. Can you do this, doctor?" Breathred asked, wanting to see how far the doctor was willing to go to see this through.

"When you put it like that, I have to, don't I?"

"We all have to. If anyone here doesn't have the stuff to do that, say so now," Breathred said, turning to Stud and Luna. He wanted them to understand just how serious this truly was. "Because, if you can't, then you need to stay in Seattle."

They all turned to him. The face that greeted them was far from the giddy schoolboy they were used to seeing. Breathred's face was cold and hard. No trace of give was painted in the lines weathering his face. He looked older and wiser for some reason. It was almost like there was an entirely different person staring out at them from the face they all knew so well.

"I'm coming," Luna said without an ounce of fear.

"Count me in too. Can't have you two lovebirds spooning when there's work to be done." Stud smirked.

Breathred looked her square in the eye. "Doctor Grayson?"

"I started this, so count me in. What's the worst that can happen?"

"We can all die," Stud shot before he thought about it.

"No, that's not the worst," Breathred said ominously.

All three looked at him. It took them a minute to figure out what he was talking about. When they finally did, three sets of hands went reflexively to their necks. Leaving them to their thoughts, Breathred went into the bathroom. He noticed all he had on was a pair of tighty-whities and a hand towel. Somehow, he didn't think his almost nudity was the proper attire for mixed company.

Twelve

I don't want to discourage any of you future slayers, but most insurance companies refuse to pay death benefits to those in our profession.

Before leaving, Dr. Grayson had one more bomb to drop on the friends. The faculty mixer had been moved up to tonight. The trio's already frazzled nerves were in no way prepared to deal with the hazards of meeting potential vamp sympathizers in a social setting. The volatility of the situation was not lost on any of them, Breathred most of all. Just thinking about Stud around normal people was enough to send him running back to his basement for good.

With little else to do but muddle through it, they set about making plans. Breathred and Stud would gather as much knowledge as they could over the course of the day. Research was the best way to help them recognize any sign of either infected team members or vampires who might be lurking on the fringe of the group.

Luna, on the other hand, would get a list from Dr. Grayson of those attending the meeting, right down to the janitors cleaning up afterward. Then, she would use her contacts in the computer lab to do background checks on each and every one of them. All the way back to their grandmothers' babysitters, if need be.

When they finished their assignments, they'd meet back up at the Jumper an hour before the meeting. With Edith as their unofficial fourth Beatle, they would then make a plan of attack. Breathred figured Edith was far enough removed from the situation she should be able to give them the insight they might have overlooked. At least he hoped so.

With a plan firmly in place, Luna headed out. This was the only part of the plan Breathred had a problem with. Luna was going to be the most open to attack. While it didn't worry her, it worried Breathred. Even though it was his plan, he had to fight the urge to tell her to stay. The only thing stopping him was the fact he knew little to nothing about the college. Despite his reservations, she was the only person for the job.

Breathred threw himself into the stacks of books that sat on his shelves. Stud started on his own investigations using the internet. After two hours of futile searching they had all but decided that it was impossible.

Every single passage they read all basically said the exact same thing—vampires inherently revealed themselves before the need for such a device was required.

To Breathred, that smacked of lazy research by somebody. The time to strike was before the undead got a foothold in your community. If you waited for them to reveal themselves it only meant somebody wasn't doing their job.

In the end, Breathred decided to improvise. Combining all the elements vampires were (for lack of a better term) allergic to, Breathred came up with a concoction he hoped would put a crimp in a vamp's digestive system. He began by using a dollop of silver nitrate, a healthy dose of garlic concentrate and a generous amount of holy water, just to be on the safe side. He came up with a cocktail when mixed with whatever punch they were serving should indicate if there was a vampire present and prove non-fatal to normal humans.

Breathred had his doubts the makeshift Mickey would work, but Stud seemed satisfied, which startled him. For the chimp to think it would work, gave Breathred a peace of mind he hadn't enjoyed since this whole mess started.

~ * ~

Luna had a lot to think about after she left Breathred's place, the problem at hand being the least of it. The truth was she never intended to rope Breathred into a relationship. It just sort of happened. Not complaining, mind you. She had known it would happen sooner or later. The fact it had happened this quickly was what her confused.

She had to wonder if he would have come to that particular decision on his own. It might have taken a few years, but Luna was sure Breathy would have come to accept the inevitable. Now things were strained. Neither of them needed the complication right now.

This thing with Dr. Grayson should be the only thing on their minds. The only sensible thing for her to do was to cool it. When this mission was over, then she'd start Breathred's training up. Boy, he needed it.

Just like Breathred, most of her day was spent trying to do the impossible. From the list Dr. Grayson gave her she learned twenty-seven people comprised the team. Most of them she knew from her classes, as either fellow students or professors. They were relatively easy to cross off her suspect list.

Seven of the team members came from other universities. Using the computer lab, she accessed a font of information about each one. She couldn't really tell anything from the data, except their names and their list of qualifications. She'd have to go under the assumption they were clean. Breathred might not feel the same, but he'd have to live with it.

Luna then turned her attention to the staff working the function. As far as she could tell, the second list was clean too. Frustration became her sole companion. If none of the lists contained any clue to the vamps' mole, Luna and her friends were left no better off than they were before she started.

Her temples throbbed. With only an hour and a half until she was supposed to meet the guys, if Luna didn't come up with something soon, she would have to give up.

Luna picked up the list the professor had given her. There had to be someone she missed. Nope, each name had a neat little check by it. She had almost put it down, when something caught her eye.

In the upper right corner of the sheet was. The logo LCP, Incorporated, glared at her from the white surface. They must be the ones financing the dig. She had never heard of them before. Maybe they were listed somewhere on the internet.

Her fingers flew across the keyboard. Within seconds Google had pulled up all the information she needed.

LCP, Incorporated was founded twenty-five years ago. For the most part, it was a medical research company. She scanned the available files. Since its formation, the company primarily dealt with finding cures for diseases attacking the blood. Over the years they had made some minor breakthroughs. Those breakthroughs rocketed the company into the Fortune Five-Hundred.

Luna sat back. Diseases of the blood were a little too close to a home run to be coincidental. What was vampirism, if it wasn't a disease of the blood? Plus, a company who worked with blood research would have plenty of the stuff on hand, giving a vampire a steady supply of the rich stuff.

This had to be it, but she needed something more—a name. Somebody had to be behind all this. Digging back into the site, she came up with it. Leopold du Chambris Portus, the company's founder, as well as its chief researcher. There was no picture available, but there was a bio.

Leopold du Chambris Portus was the son of Belgian immigrants, who had come to this country after World War II. He had attended the Sorbonne for his medical degree, and then returned to America and founded LCP after his mother died of a rare blood disease. The bio said he wouldn't stop until he defeated all such afflictions.

The bio was so sickeningly sweet she wanted to gag. He had to be the one behind the attack. Too many things fell into place for him not to be. Proof was the one thing she didn't have, though, and the one thing she needed before making any accusations.

At least they had a name to watch for. If anyone connected with LCP showed up, they'd know to watch out for them. Luna didn't know how Breathred was making out, but for the first time today she was batting a thousand.

Luna turned off the computer. It was time to get going. Finding the last piece of the puzzle was going to make her late. She would have to make sure to call Breathred when she got home, so he wouldn't worry. He was such a worrywart. He'd just have to deal with her tardiness. She still had to get ready and she needed to pack some stuff to bring over to Breathred's house. She checked her watch. There was less than an hour until sundown. Still plenty of time to get to the Jumper.

The girl smiled. Breathred was probably worrying about her and she wasn't even due yet. It comforted her to see her chosen had finally seen the light. It had been a long time since someone had worried about her. The feeling was kinda nice.

~ * ~

The Java Jumper was crowded. Breathred had a big problem with the packed house. He wasn't able to watch the door. His usual seat was taken, so he had to grab a seat far in the back. Normally, he would have been okay with a change in his seating. Of course that was before vampires started jumping out of the woodwork, and Luna decided today was the perfect time to be fifteen minutes late. She was never late.

Stud wasn't as worried as he was, but the chimp didn't look exactly calm either. Even though Stud was trying to hide it, Breathred saw him watching the sidewalk through the window. The nervous twitch was the giveaway.

If she didn't show soon, Stud was liable to go look for her. He had that way about him. Breathred had to give the chimp his due. He may be a Smart Alec and sawed-off, but he was loyal. When it came to Luna, the monkey was downright parental in a funny, you-Jane-me-Cheeta sort of way.

Breathred flicked at a drop of latte in his saucer. Ten more minutes, then he'd get her himself. It was close to dusk. That left her open to just about anything.

Now, who was going all parental? No, he was going all boyfriendal, if there was even such a word. The way Breathred saw it, it was his responsibility to look after her. Not exactly a modern way to view things, but he couldn't help himself. That was just the way he was. Breathred looked toward the door, thinking he heard it open. It was just another customer looking for a respite from the rain. Where was she?

The opening of the door brought a hush to the friends. Luna stood haloed by the dying sunlight. The door slid shut behind her, diffusing the radiance. Breathred rose to go to her. As the light dwindled away, he stopped short. She was…she was beautiful.

Luna wore a black dress slit up the side revealing a shapely leg. Breathred blushed at the sight. Her normally-straight hair hung in flowing curls that looped around her perfect face and shoulders. A silver and turquoise necklace was nestled above her well-rounded breasts that bloomed from the top of the black dress. A plain old Nike bag thrown across her shoulder was the only indication she was the same girl he knew.

Breathred was rooted to the floor. It was his standby reaction when confronted by a beautiful woman. It had served him well over the years.

Never once had he been rebuked when using it. It was almost like a survival instinct.

But, how did it apply to one's own girlfriend? This was a question worth considering. He thought back to all the movies he had watched over years. To stand agog was good for only so long. Sooner or later, he had to do something. What would John Cusack do in this situation?

"Uh huh uh brubba dok goob," was the best he could manage to say.

"Oh, Breathy you say the sweetest things," Luna gushed.

"You understood that pile of drivel?" Stud poked his head around the dumbfounded slayer.

"Of course. He said I look lovely tonight. Didn't you, Sweetie?" She turned toward Breathred. Before he had a chance to answer, she planted a kiss on his quivering lips.

Slipping past him, she sat down in the booth. Luna motioned for her friends to return to their seats. Stud shrugged and hopped into the booth beside her. Breathred, on the other hand, was still immobilized by the sight of her.

It took Edith to get his butt moving toward the table. "Girl, do you know how much you had us worried. What took you so long?"

"Yeah, my boy Breathred was damn near pissing himself waiting for you," Stud added, giving her a sly wink.

"I was not. I went before we left the house," Breathred said, breaking his silence.

"Look, I'm sorry, but I ran late at the college."

"Don't you know how to use a phone?" Stud snapped.

"I called. Honest I did. Your father said you were already gone, so I got here as fast as I could."

"I believe you," Breathred said softly. "But you shouldn't worry us like that."

"I won't do it again," Luna answered. She patted his hand. "You big lug. You're going to make me go all sappy, if you don't watch out."

"Look, if all this mushy crap is over, can we get down to business?" Stud croaked, wiping a tear from his eye. Damned, if they weren't making him go all sappy.*

*Those of you who remember back to the front of the book, I am the one writing this damn book. If I want to get all sappy, a chimp's got as much right to as anybody. Now, leave me alone and get back to the fecking book.

Edith gave him a dirty look. He dismissed it and turned back to the lovebirds. They were both giving him a hurt look. He was glad to see the mood was adequately broken. That was good. They needed their heads screwed on straight.

For some reason, for just one instant, Breathred had the impurest of thoughts. For one brief second, he actually thought about kissing her with his tongue. The idea both sickened and excited him at the same time. The whole thing made him want to wash his mind with holy water.

"Did you find anything at the college?" Breathred asked, glad to be free from the moment.

"Oh, yeah. I think we have our vampire." She dug in her purse. They waited until she finally looked up, shaking a sheet of paper in her slender fingers. "Here it is. Vampire of the month goes to Leopold du Chambris Portus."

"Did you just say Chambris Portus?" Stud asked, not quite believing his ears.

"Sure did, short stuff. If this guy ain't a vampire, I'll eat your shorts," Luna said, hotly.

"Hey, I believe you, but come on. What kind of name is Chambris Portus? It sounds like something you throw out of a window during the middle-ages."

"What makes you think this is our guy?" Breathred asked, not wanting to give Stud a chance to give voice to his next thought.

She handed him the paper. "Here, check this out."

Breathred took a few minutes to read through the bio. After letting the information sink in, he slid the sheet over to Stud. She was right. This guy had vamp written all over him. Worst of all, the sucker was dogging their back yard. By now, he probably had everything about them sitting in front him.

His first impulse was to back out. When this was a nice little game, it might have been different. This was shaping up to be too dangerous. A member of the team he could deal with, but this guy—he had all the cards. Was Breathred willing to risk Stud and Luna's life on the chance she was wrong?

"I know what you're thinking, Big Daddy, so stop it. We can handle this joker," Stud said without a trace of doubt in his voice.

"Stud, this isn't some video game. You and Luna could get hurt. We aren't doing this," Breathred announced, crossing his arms.

"No, you look. The arm crossing thing only works when I do it. We're a team. You may be our leader, but we all have a say in this," Luna blurted out.

"I won't put you at risk. This is too much for us. This character's been around since the forties. For all we know he could be older than dirt. What are we to him? Jeez, we're a monkey, a girl, and an idiot. We can't make this work," Breathred moaned.

"Breathred E. Petrifunck, you may be goofy. You might even be a little off in the head, but the one thing I never thought you were, was a quitter," Luna groused.

"No, I'm a realist. Luna, if anything happened to you, I couldn't forgive myself." Breathred reached for her hand.

She pulled his head up until his eyes met hers. "I'm a big girl. Plus, I believe in you. Do you think I'd go into this, if I didn't think you could do this? That we could do this? So, put those silly thoughts out of your head. We're going to do this, because there ain't nobody else. Do you get me?"

"You tell him, girl," Edith chimed in.

Breathred didn't answer. He just looked at the faces around him. Each one said the same thing—Luna's right. Doggone it, she was. The last time Breathred checked the yellow pages, he was the only vampire slayer listed. Unless somebody else stepped up, the vampires would win. The Mother would rise and the world, as they knew it, would end. How could he back away from that?

"Okay, we do it," Breathred whispered. "But each one of you will do what I say. If it gets too rough, we get out of there. There's no discussion. It's my decision, not yours. As long as you agree to it, we're on," he said, looking each in the eye in turn.

"Deal," Luna said, glad to see the fire back in his eye.

Stud wouldn't be the odd man out. "Hey, I'm the monkey. I do what you say."

"I think you're all crazy. That's why white people don't make it out of a horror movie alive. Y'all are just too stupid to know when to run." Edith jumped to her feet and pointed one long finger at Breathred. "You make damn sure you bring my girl home safe. The monkey, too, as long as you're at it."

"I didn't know you cared, Toots." Stud winked at her.

Edith gave him a good-natured slap on the back. "I don't. I just don't want yo' monkey ass coming back and biting me on the neck."

"You have my word," Breathred said, wrapping her in a bear hug.

"Now, get out of here, before somebody starts talking smack," Edith snorted.

"Okay, guys. You heard the lady, let's head 'em up and move 'em out. We got a job to do," Breathred ordered. Whatever happened tonight, one thing was for sure; it wouldn't be dull.

Thirteen

When witches gather, they call it a coven. When vampires gather, they call it a massacre.

Leopold looked down on the filling banquet room. The two-way mirror afforded the vampire a clear view of the entire room. He could even see that luscious waiter with the oh-so-tight buns snitching a shrimp from an appetizer cart. They didn't grow them like that when he came from. If they had, he hadn't noticed for damn sure.

He tore himself away from the sight. This was business. Pleasure could come later. Where the hell was Lewis? His companion should be here by now. Lewis knew how to talk to these people. He could but chose not to. It was just his apprentice knew the lingo. One of the reasons Leopold kept the young vampire around. It sure wasn't for his fashion sense. The boy wouldn't know a cummerbund from a cucumber.

Leopold turned away from the mirror. This night had been over twenty years in the making. He had heard rumors of the Mother for years. Almost since his first night as a lord of the undead, the whispers from the old ones danced through the air. Off and on for centuries, Leopold looked for some trace of her beyond the myths that circulated through his world.

His first bit of concrete evidence came over a century ago in the jungles of the Amazon. It was just a fragment of a name carved in a mountainside, but it was enough to further fuel his obsession. Since then, he had stumbled across other arcane references, but nothing like this tablet of Grayson's.

He might have missed it all together if Lewis hadn't set his computer to scan for such things. The professor had posted her findings on the university's web site. The fool woman didn't even know what she had found. Leopold did not suffer from such misconceptions. She had found the Mother's tomb. With everything he had learned from her, he would soon have both the Mother and the power she represented.

Leopold had even gone so far as to buy this hotel to help insure everything would proceed as planned. This game would start on his playing ground. As long as he controlled the setting, he controlled the game. Dr. Grayson would bring her motley crew to him and he would see the one who was to be his agent—his eyes among them.

Badly as he wanted to, Leopold could not join them in this venture. He would not be blind in this. He planned to be close, but not so close as to give himself away. To accomplish that, he needed someone on the inside; someone who could serve him without drawing attention to his true purpose. This get-together's sole purpose was to bring him just such an agent.

The door clicked open behind him. Good, Lewis was here. Leopold looked at his servant. The younger vampire was so subdued in his dress, Leopold almost didn't recognize him. Instead of his usual flamboyant outfits, Lewis was dressed in a conservative suit, Armani or some other bourgeois designer who these fickle moderns sought after so earnestly.

"You are late," Leopold hissed.

"Man, it takes time to look this square," Lewis snarled, pulling at his collar.

"Are you a reject from *Happy Days* that I have to hear the word square uttered in my presence?"

"Chill man."

"Now, you give me Huggy Bear. If I wanted to revisit the seventies, I'd watch Nick at Nite. You'd better shape up or by God I'll shove the stake in you myself!" Leopold shouted.

"Leo, you need to calm down. We still have plenty of time before this thing kicks off. You seriously need to find some bitch on Prozac and take a tug, 'cause this shit ain't cool. Dig?" This honky was getting on his nerves. Leopold had better watch it or he'd show him what black power was all about.

Leopold waved a lace-gloved hand in Lewis' face. "I will calm down, when I see fit to do so. Until then, you will do what I say. Do we understand each other?"

"Whatever. So what do you want?" Lewis asked, not really giving a rat's ass anymore. This suit was itchy. As soon as this was over, it was straight back to some good old polyester.

"I want you to get down there and find me a thrall amid those lackluster academicians. Try to find someone who has at least a modicum of style. I will not be represented by a dud, and I am unanimous in that," Leopold stated with a mad gesture to illustrate his point.

Lewis gave him a thumbs-up. "You got it, Big Cheese."

"Do you have the speech I prepared for you?" Leopold inquired, nervousness overriding his anger.

Maybe Lewis was right. He was feeling a little high-strung at the moment. A little chilling out might do him some good. Now, wasn't the time though. He had to see this to the end. Then, he would cool out. Perhaps with the dishy waiter-boy.

"I got it right here." Lewis tapped the side of his head. "Hey, Man. Are you even listening to me?"

"Of course I am, Cretin. You just do your job." Leopold walked back to the mirror.

Lewis joined him. The room below them had filled as they had talked. Lewis watched the humans mill around like cattle. Cattle he couldn't touch, he reminded himself. Something about all that forbidden fruit called to him, despite the fact he had fed before arriving.

He chanced to look through the two-way mirror toward the door, as it popped open. The sight that greeted him had him hugging the glass. Coming through the door was the virgin. And he had the monkey and the girl with him. What were they doing here? Wait a minute. Dr. Grayson was walking up to them. They were part of the team!

How lucky could they get? This little soiree would kill two birds in one stroke. The best part was he would dump the whole thing in Leopold's lap. He was pretty sure the girl could recognize him. So, that zeroed him out of Leo's mission impossible. The old man would have to handle this one all by himself.

"Leopold, look over by the good professor," Lewis advised.

"What is it now?"

Then, it hit him. The scent was as rich as he had ever smelled. Purity was so strong in the air it hurt to even contemplate it. He followed Lewis' finger. At first thought he thought it was the girl, but he was mistaken. It was the man. How could a man get that old and not—well you know?

"Lewis you were right. He will do magnificently." Leopold gasped.

"Good news, bad news. They know me by sight, so you'll have to handle the party, Boss." Lewis loved dropping that bomb.

"Are you sure?" Leopold asked with a hint of fear in his voice.

"The girl made me at the mall. If I go down there, the jig is up, my friend," Lewis said, deciding it was best not to remind Leopold about the fiasco at the nightclub. The time for fun and games was over, if he ever wanted to hear about something other than the Mother for the rest of his unnatural life.

"Well, damn. You know how I feel about meeting new people," Leopold whined.

"You meet new people every night. So, don't try to cop out with that one."

"No, I meet supper every night. These..." Leopold gestured to the mirror, "people are different. They might want to, heaven forbid, talk to me. They might even try to touch me. I can't be touched by anyone who would wear denim. That's a denim crowd, if I ever saw one."

"Get a grip, Man. They're just people. God, you'd think a vampire would be less of a psycho," Lewis cried in frustration.

"I am not psycho. I may be a little co-dependant, but that is as far as I'm willing to admit to."

"Whatever, you're going to have to get yo' white ass down there and do the do."

"Do you really think I can do it?" Leopold asked, his eyes burning with the need for assurance.

"Man, you got this covered. You're the baddest mo fo on the planet. These humans'll be putty in your hands," Lewis told him, hoping his old charm was working.

"You're right. What do I have to be afraid of? I'm the lord of the undead, not them. I'll do it!" Leopold shouted, his hand pumping vigorously in the air before him. He strode toward the door confidently. He stopped just short of the door and turned back to Lewis. "You'll be watching in case I need you, right?"

"You got it, Boss Man." Lewis shook his head in disgust.

If Leopold made it through this, it would be a miracle. If Lewis still drank, he'd be on his second fifth by now. Turning away from the door, he went back to the mirror. If nothing else, this ought to be interesting.

~ * ~

Breathred was avoiding the shrimp. Anything that pink couldn't be good for you. If one more waiter tried to foist one of the little pukers on him, he looked like he would scream. He also appeared to be having serious doubts about the pigs in a blanket.

Luna saw the snarl cross Breathred's face as a waiter sauntered past him. This was not going well at all. Until this moment she never realized just how far his phobias went. Agoraphobia seemed to be the latest in the string, if you didn't count the shrimp.

Stud, on the other hand, reveled in the whole thing. After working his way through the buffet table, he hit the bar. She watched him slip the Mickey into the punch bowl before moving onto the Daiquiri machine. Luna wasn't sure if the combination was such a good idea, but was growing tired of playing nursemaid over the pair.

Given half a chance, Luna might have to rethink this whole girlfriend job. No chance of that happening. She had worked too hard to snag him in the first place, to allow him to get her goat so readily. Letting a few eccentricities get in the way wasn't her style. Breathred would just have to change, and that was that.

Breathred was talking to, what was his name again? Edmund Truehart. He was the anthropologist from Cambridge. Aboriginal culture was his specialty. He had some experience in Canadian digs. Dr. Grayson had made it a point to introduce him to Breathred.

Now, as she thought about it, it was kind of strange. It was almost like she expected them to have something in common. Breathred mumbled under his breath and walked away, as soon as he could. Luna had never known him to act like so weird. Sure you might have to listen to a two-hour discourse on Ewok culture, but he had never just walked away without even a little mention of *Star Wars* in general. She smelled a mystery.

Playing Velma would have to wait. Some blond floosie was angling right for him. Luna knew the type too, all boobs and mind-if-I-butt-in? Well, she wasn't having a bit of it.

"Breathred, is that you?" Luna heard the woman say from across the crowded floor.

This thing knew Breathred. Oh yes! She would look into this, and if she didn't get the right answers, somebody was going home in a body bag.

Luna cut through the crowd like a hot knife. A few of the bystanders looked at her strangely, but none were brave enough to say anything about her rudeness. College-bred people were smarter than she thought; the crowd knew a predatory woman when they saw one.

Luna snuck up behind Breathred. She came in low and slid her arm into his before he knew what was happening. Her unsuspecting boyfriend jumped at her touch. Good, let him be afraid, very afraid, she thought devilishly. The blonde raised an eyebrow but gave no other indication of her own surprise. Cold fish.

Luna gritted her teeth. "Breathy, dear. Care to introduce me to your friend?"

"Oh, Luna this is…" Breathred stumbled for a few seconds. Luna saw the confusion on his face. He kept mouthing the letter C, no J as if trying to wrap his mind around a name.

"Jessica Easily," the blonde offered, when it became evident Breathred had forgotten his own name, as well as hers.

"I'm sure you are," Luna hissed under her breath.

"Excuse me?" Ms. Easily asked.

Luna extended her hand. "My name is Luna Walking Batch."

"I'm sure you are."

"What the hell did you say?" This witch was one step away from one hard-assed point of no return.

"Luna! Ladies do not use that kind of language," Breathred gasped in shock and horror.

"I'm sorry. It just, kind of slipped out," Luna apologized, but finished to herself: like my hand is going to slip into her face.

"Well, see that it doesn't happen again."

"It won't," she groused.

"What a delightful creature you've found yourself, Breathred," Ms. Easily said, her voice a honey-coated indictment sent Luna seething.

"She is one of a kind. Isn't she?"

"So, how do you two know each other?" Luna asked, ready to get to the bottom of this.

"Oh, we go back, ages. Don't we, Dear?" Jessica's fake voice drove daggers through Luna's eyes.

Middle ages, Luna thought.

"If you say so," Breathred mumbled, suddenly wanting to go home.

"We went to school together. Class of '92, rah, rah, rah." Jessica broke into the lamest cheer Luna had ever heard.

Wait a minute. Breathred graduated in '87. What was this bitch babbling about? Luna had to get Breathred alone. He'd crack on his own, or by God she would crack him—slowly and painfully. Now, the important thing to do was to get him away from this barracuda.

Thankfully, Dr. Grayson helped her accomplish the feat by calling the crowd to order. Luna was able to lose Ms. Easily in the stampede to the raised dais that sat in the center of the ballroom. Luna gave her a snide smile as she and Breathred slid to the front of the crowd.

Dr. Grayson spoke over the hum of the assembled group. "Okay, people. It's time to meet the man responsible for all this."

"Bring him out. We need some more shrimp cocktail!" someone yelled.

"Somebody, get Rudy some coffee. I think he's had enough for the night." Dr. Grayson laughed. "But seriously, let me hear a round of applause for the man of the hour, Leopold du Chambris Portus."

Leopold wasn't surprised to see his quarry close to the podium. He had been calling to him, since Lewis pointed the man out to him. He flashed a moderate smile to the assembly, not enough to reveal his true nature, but quite enough to endear him to them. It was the vampire's way.

He settled behind the podium, allowing time for the applause to die down to a dull whimper. Leopold realized for the most part it was forced, but accepted it all the same. After all they had come to see him.

Now as he thought about it, maybe it was a good thing Lewis hadn't done this. The last thing the young vampire needed was to think he was in charge. Lewis was in danger of assuming as much already without an audience convincing him of the fact.

Leopold paused before speaking. There was someone whispering in the back. He couldn't abide whispering. It bespoke of a poor upbringing. Worse than that, it meant someone didn't want to listen to him. To Leopold's thinking that was the most egregious of social misbehaviors to commit. He had to remember to give him a bite of his mind after tonight's proceedings.

"Well, if that wasn't the best reception I've had since the stock market shot up last quarter," Leopold joked, waiting for the expected response.

The only thing the quip earned him was a twitter. *A twitter—these philistines had no sense of humor whatsoever*, Leopold thought. If he didn't need them, he'd kill the whole lot of them and toss them into the nearest dustbin. Teach them to not appreciate a good joke when they heard one. He'd personally stolen that one from the Trump. Bet they would have laughed, if *he'd* told it. Everyone laughed at The Donald, the bloated bastard. Apprentice this, you overblown peasant. But, he was getting off track.

"As Doctor Grayson may have told you, I was only too happy to finance this venture. I feel only by understanding our past can we hope to build our future."

This time the crowd did explode with genuine applause. Perhaps they weren't as bad as he first thought. In any case it bought them a reprieve. No one would die tonight, except for the damned whisperer, if he didn't shush it.

"Thank you, but my speech is far from over," Leopold said to quiet them again. "As I said, it is a pleasure to find myself associated with someone of Dr. Grayson's renown in the academic community, as well as yourselves, whose own qualifications mark you as experts in your own rights. I hope this expedition will, at last, shed a glimmer of light on a past we can only imagine. I think you will agree this is as good a place as any to quit running off at the mouth. So, Doctor Grayson, if you will," Leopold ended, motioning for her to take the podium.

Breathred didn't listen to what the professor had to say. He was too intent on watching Leopold. It was a dull murmur in the background. He flicked his eyes away from the vampire long enough to see Stud dumping his vamp Mickey into the punch while everyone was watching the stage. When the professor finished, Luna would call for a toast to the expedition. If Leopold was a vampire, they'd have him.

He turned back to the stage. Leopold was smiling and nodding as Dr. Grayson spoke. To Breathred he didn't look like a vampire, but he could be wrong. Breathred wished he'd remembered to put on his crucifix. Then he would have known for sure, but in the rush to leave, he had forgotten it.

"Okay, guys. Mr. Chambris Portus will be available to answer a few questions, so don't run off," Dr. Grayson yelled, drawing a shocked stare from the man.

"I don't think I can do that," Leopold stuttered.

"Sure, you can. I promise they don't bite." She grinned.

But I might. Egad, there was a man in denim angling right for him. What if he somehow touched it? It led to an even bigger question. What if denim was catchy? He could see himself now, buying a pair of Calvin Klein's at some out-of-the-way outlet mall for less than retail, so that no one could see him. He shuddered. Oh no, this would not work.

He turned to make a hasty retreat. Instead, he ran straight into the virgin and his bit of fluff.

"Mr. Chambris Portus." Breathred extended his hand. "I believe we have a lot to talk about."

Fourteen

Never confront a vampire on his home turf. He knows where the bodies are buried and where yours is going next.

Leopold drew back. This was new. Usually, he was the one saying shit like that, to coin a phrase from Lewis' lengthy tome of colorful colloquialisms. Who was this person to talk to him in such a manner? Wait a minute, it was the lushy virgin. How nice. It was a pleasant change to have one's dinner come to him.

"Excuse me," Leopold said, deciding to play it cool. There was no sense in showing anything more than he had to. He didn't want to see the man running across the floor. Did he?

"I'm a member of Doctor Grayson's team, and I was just wondering about a few things. I was hoping you might clarify a few points for me before we left," Breathred said. He was hoping the dirty vamp would slip up somehow and give him a chance to take the undead fiend down right here and now. Breathred didn't think the vamp would, but you never could tell.

"It's a pleasure to meet you, uh Mr.—" Leopold was at a loss at what to do with this virgin. His instinct was to bite first and ask questions later.

He hated meeting people. They all felt you should know their names, even if you hadn't met them yet. It was as though being rich gave you omnipotence or something. If he had learned one thing over the years, it was poor people always responded favorably to the rich, unless you were taking their money. This big lug would be no different.

"Breathred Petrifunck at your service." Breathred took his hand back after it was evident Leopold wasn't about to shake it.

"And your delightful companion?" Leopold turned toward Luna. It was best not to let him think he was the object of interest.

"Allow me to introduce Miss Luna Walking Batch."

"Ah, one of the true Americans. I have long wanted the chance to talk with one of you glorious people," Leopold responded, enthusiastically.

"What the hell do you mean by that?" Luna snapped.

"I meant no disrespect. It is just that your culture has long been a study of mine—particularly, the medicinal practices of your shaman. It has long been a theory of mine that their so-called home remedies could hold the cure of many diseases that stump us modern scientists," Leopold explained. The fact was he was really dying to ask her if she had ever taken a scalp, but under the circumstances it didn't seem too prudent. Maybe, right before he sacrificed her boyfriend, would be a good time.

"See, Luna. What have I told you about rush judgments? I believe you owe Mr. Leopold an apology," Breathred lectured, like that was bloody likely.

"I'm sorry," Luna whined, causing Breathred to raise an eyebrow. *This stuffed shirt wasn't fooling anybody. He was about to ask me if I had ever taken a scalp. It was written all over his face. The French prick!*

"No, the fault was all mine. You wished to ask me something, Mr. Petmyskunk?" Leopold said, turning back to Breathred. The woman was making him nervous. He couldn't help but notice the girl was still giving him the evil eye.

"That's Petrifunck," Breathred corrected him.

"Of course it is. Now, you had some questions," Leopold said, growing tired of this inane discourse. He could be home watching reruns of *Solid Gold*.

"Yes. I couldn't help but wonder why a noted doctor like yourself would be interested in an archeological dig in the middle of Canada," Breathred stated. Let him answer that one.

"As I just said, my interest is purely scientific. Quite frankly, Doctor Grayson's paper fascinated me. I could say there was a medicinal side to this obsession, but there isn't. The chance to actually be a part of something this unusual was too tempting to pass up," Leopold said. Now, the dweeb wanted to play twenty questions. He was over three hundreds years old; he shouldn't have to put up with this crap.

"So, you believe the tablet is correct?" Luna asked.

"Ms. Walking Batch, do you take me for a fool? Vampire queens are the stuff of popular fiction. They have no place in science, but the fact the myth presented on the tablet is so old is startling, don't you think?" Leopold asked. Now, the girl was getting in on the action. That's all he needed, a woman with an attitude.

"I find it hard to believe a man in your power bracket would risk money on something this speculative, if he couldn't see a payoff in it somewhere," Luna stated, firmly.

"Of course there's a payoff. My stockholder's would flay me alive if there wasn't. The publicity alone will bring in millions, plus if the dig is indeed successful, I own the rights. I have already brokered several deals, including one with the Discovery Channel. So, as you see, it's a win/win situation." Leopold smiled. That was it. If he didn't get the hell away from them, somebody was going to die, sacrifice or not. "Now, if you'll excuse me, I must have a word with Doctor Grayson."

They watched him leave. Luna found it funny Jessica Easily

intercepted the vampire before he had a chance to make it to the professor. No doubt she would try to monopolize the rest of his evening. She looked the type to hone in on the slightest hint of fresh money, or old money, for that matter.

"So, what do you think? Is he a vamp?" Luna asked, turning back to Breathred.

Dr. Truehart angled past them. "I wouldn't bet against him being one, if that tells you anything," Breathred whispered. He watched the man squeeze himself between Jessica and Leopold. *Good luck, buddy,* Breathred thought without a trace of humor. "I think you should make the toast, just to be sure."

"Too late," she said, pointing to the banquet table.

Breathred looked up to see a wobbly Stud flitting across the table a bowl full of shrimp cocktail perched gaily atop his furry head. If Breathred wasn't mistaken, he was singing the chorus from *I'm Henry the Eight, I Am*. Doggone it, he should have been watching the chimp. No, that wasn't right either, he should have left him at the house, preferably with a straitjacket wrapped around his furry little body. Breathred should have known an open bar was an invitation for disaster.

Breathred dashed toward Stud. He hadn't made it three steps when Stud toppled over—as luck would have it—right into the punch bowl. A tidal wave of red rain with assorted fruit chunks flew into the air. Breathred stopped in his tracks. Luna slammed into him, but he didn't even notice.

How could he be so stupid as too actually think the monkey could be trusted to behave like a...a human? Now, all their carefully laid plans were ruined. All because Stud couldn't handle a few dozen banana daiquiris. Well, you'd better believe he could kiss watching *Animal Planet* good-bye when they got home.

People massed around the table. Breathred had to push his way past them to get to Stud. Everyone loves an accident, he reckoned as he at last made it through the gawkers. By that time, the punch had soaked into the carpet, leaving one drenched monkey in its wake. As close to swearing as he had ever been, Breathred sank to the floor in disgust well short of the wreckage. What were they going to do now?

Luna made it to the table, soon after. She ruffled Breathred's hair and kept on walking. She didn't stop until she stood directly in front of Stud. Stud wiggled his nose and gave her a drunken grin. Her pinched look sobered the grin straight from his face. He reached up and removed the crown of shrimp from his head.

"Uh, hey Luna," he sputtered.

"Don't hey me, Mister. I swear if all these people weren't here, I'd strip you naked, and feed you to a rabid squirrel. And you'd better believe I know where I can get my hands on one."

"So, I'm sorry isn't gonna work," Stud joked. The grimace on her face instantly shut down his next outbreak of smartass.

"What do you think?" she screamed into his twisted face.

Stud jumped up and ran for the door. "I think I'd better go wait in the car."

Luna made a halfhearted grab for him. In the end she let him slip away. It wasn't like she could kill him. There were too many witnesses for her to get away with it.

Watching him go, she caught sight of Leopold and Jessica walking through the exit to the left. Great. Now they had lost their chance to prove Leopold was the head vampire. The bright side was they probably wouldn't be seeing Ms. Easily, again. That was some small comfort.

Luna turned around and helped Breathred up from the floor. He grudgingly took her hand. Stud's performance had effectively put an end to the party. Most of the people beat a hasty retreat when Luna started her tirade. The rest followed Leopold's example, taking a powder when the smoke cleared.

Breathred looked around for Dr. Grayson. Thankfully, she had stuck around. He needed to tell her about his suspicions. He couldn't let her head out without knowing the truth about their benefactor. Breathred only prayed she believed him.

Luna's hand on his shoulder stopped him. "Whatya doing, Boss Man?" Apparently her anger had found a new victim.

"I have to tell the professor about Leopold."

"I wouldn't do that."

"Why not? She needs to know who's behind this," Breathred said, not believing what he was hearing.

"Wrong. For one thing we're not even sure he's a vampire. Thanks to your dirty little pet we lost the only chance we had to out his bloodsucking butt. We can't just accuse him of being a vampire without the proof to back it up. Two. If she knows, then she's in as much danger as us. I, for one, don't want to put her in that situation. Do you?" Luna asked.

"No, you're right, but what are we gonna do?" He was out of ideas.

"He still doesn't know we know, so we go ahead as planned, and leave the day after tomorrow. So, we go get what we need first thing in the morning. Get a few rosaries blessed, and whittle us some stakes. In short," she brushed a lock of hair from her face, "we do whatever it takes to get the job done."

Breathred gave her a smile. What would he do without her? He'd probably be sitting in his basement playing cards with Stud. On the whole this was much better.

"Come on, Breathy. I got a monkey to skin." Luna grinned and led him toward the door.

~ * ~

Lewis watched them leave. He'd heard everything. So, they knew about Leopold. That was an interesting development, for all it mattered. Leopold had been at this long enough to take them down whether they knew about him or not.

He toyed with the idea of keeping that tidbit to himself, but figured if by some chance they took the big man out, he'd be next on their list. He was all about self-preservation.

Lewis hadn't failed to notice who Leo had left with, either. So they had their mole. Well, not yet, but by morning they would. She was a nice bit of fluff, too. A little waspish for him, but as long as she got the job done, he wouldn't complain.

He waited for the room to clear. When the last person had at last wandered through the door, the vamp stepped into the ballroom. It was still early enough for a snack before he had to meet Leopold back at the crib. Who knew, he might even bring something back for the old poof.

Fifteen

So you finished Lesson One and you think you're ready to fight vampires. Go ahead. We got our check.

Luna tucked Stud into bed fighting the urge to strangle him. Figuring how much he vomited on the ride home, the chimp had been punished enough. That didn't mean he wouldn't be cleaning her car out first thing in the morning, because he was. Even if she had to use him as a scrub brush, her car would not smell like tequila and shrimp. She was adamant about that.

She had to admit the chimp was kinda cute when he was all passed out like that. He looked almost human, not necessarily in a good way. She knew plenty of so-called humans who weren't half as human as him. At least he was asleep. And, it gave her some alone time with Breathred.

She looked over at her reluctant paramour. His nose was buried in the Boffrend handbook. Now that's what she called cute. She fought the urge to rush over and jump in his lap. Breathred wouldn't respond well to any form of emotional outburst, though. In fact he might drop dead from the shock.

What Breathred needed now was a break. He was driving himself too hard over this. Sure, they were depending on him, but if he worried himself sick over everything, it wasn't going to do them any good. The question was how did one calm down a paranoid, delusional, anal-retentive vampire slayer? It was important not to leave out the anal-retentive part. While endearing, it would be the hardest part to overcome.

"Hey Breathred, got a minute?" she asked in her cheery voice. It wasn't one she used all that much, but figured she needed to keep in practice.

"Can't it wait a minute? I really want to finish this," he said without looking up.

This would not do. They had only been together a day—not even a day—and she was getting the ten-years-of-marriage answer. Oh no, he didn't. Luna had hoped to wait before she began his training, but this was a clear sign it was past time to start. Nip it in the bud, as her mother used to say. Or was that Barney Fife? She always seemed to get those two confused.

The secret was to keep it simple. The male mind responded well to simple. Don't try to saturate them with logic. That just confused them. Go with the basics—a touch here, a touch there, sort of like Pavlov's dog. Once you trained them to a certain point, the rest was a cakewalk.

Luna moved up behind him. Breathred was gently sucking his thumb, as he read. She was not surprised to notice he hadn't even acknowledged her presence. That was all right, he'd notice this.

She began slow, running her fingers across the back of his neck. Luna watched a ripple shot through him, but he still gave no sign she was there. Time to pull out the big guns. She kneaded the bunched muscles of his shoulders and neck. She laughed. He was actually getting more tense the longer she did it.

"Luna, are you aware that you're touching me?" Breathred asked, breathlessly.

"Of course I am, Sweetums. I *am* the one who's doing it, after all." Luna laughed. Score one for the visiting team.

"Do you think you could stop? For some reason, I think I forgot how to read." He gasped as her fingers stroked the tip of his ear.

"I think you should put that book down for a minute. All those words can't be good for you. You've had a long day, and need to rest those big ol' eyes of yours," Luna purred into his ear. She couldn't help but notice his foot was twitching. If she wasn't mistaken, foot twitching counted as an inside-the-park home run, wherever you played the game.

"But I really—"

"Didn't I say you should put the book down?" she whispered, nibbling her way down the side of his ear.

"Yes." He moaned and the book slipped from his trembling fingertips.

Luna smiled to herself. Game over. She expected more of a fight. Maybe he was just a quick study. Whatever the case, it was time to wrap this up. Breathred wasn't quite ready to go into extra innings quite yet.

"Breathred, Darling, I think it's time for us to go bed," she let her voice go up an octave. No sense blinding him for life.

"What? Together!" He exclaimed, leaping from the chair.

"How could you think such a thing? I'm not that type of girl," she answered, giving him her best hurt expression. Always leave them thinking they were in the wrong. It was easier than coming right out and saying so. It tended to piss them off.

"Oh, Luna. I'm sorry. I would never impugn your character like that. It was just, you know. You were…" He thought for a minute. "I don't know what you were doing, but it felt…"

"Good. Good is the word you're looking for," she said, batting her eyes. God, he was making this too easy.

"Yes. No! Well, I mean…not that it didn't feel good, b-but I think you're right. It's time to go to bed," he finally managed to spit out.

"If you really think so. I wouldn't want to force you to do anything you didn't want to do." Luna almost cracked up, but held it in. She really ought to write this stuff down. There were women out there who could use this.

"I'm really tired." Luna stifled a giggle as he did his best to invoke a yawn. All he managed was a sneeze. "I just need to take a shower first. You go ahead and go to sleep. I may be in there for a while. At least until you're asleep. I may even sleep in the tub, so I won't wake you up when I get done. That's what I'll do. I'll sleep in the tub. So, good night. See ya tomorrow."

This time she did burst out laughing. Luna hid it behind her hand until he slammed the bathroom door behind his fleeing body. Then, it just exploded all over the place. Her sides hurt from holding it in so long. His face, oh God, it was almost too funny to believe.

Well, her little scheme solved one problem, which only left the big one to worry about. There wasn't anything she could do about that one. Her mother had done her best to solve that problem for her long ago, much to Luna's displeasure.

Fingering the pouch hanging around her neck, Luna pulled it out from under her sweater. The rawhide bag sat there at the end of its braided necklace, accusing her silently with its presence. She remembered the day her mother first placed it around her neck. Luna had been ten, a woman in everything but years. Her time had come, and with it, her heritage. As a daughter of Coyote, Luna knew what was to come and was ready for it. Her spirit burned with the desire to assume the role heritage promised.

Her mother saw it differently. She had the foresight to know Luna was for the white man's world. Only in their world could her daughter gain the things she needed to make their tribe whole. To do that, she would need the protection of the trickster.

For three days and nights her mother gathered the necessary power from the spirit lands. The two of them had sat alone against the mountain they called home. With simple things taken from the land surrounding their home she wove the power into a talisman. When that was done, she laid it across Luna's breast. That one act enabled her to walk in both worlds. How she cried to be denied what was by rights hers.

Thinking back, Luna missed the freedom of her youth. She missed her people and her mother most of all. She had very few regrets about leaving them, but now they swelled inside of her. Luna knew why. The cycle of the moon was calling. The knowledge didn't make her feel any better.

The sound of Breathred turning on the shower brought a smile to her face. If she'd stayed with her people, Luna never would have met him. She'd have led a half-life, because she would have never found her life mate. Yes, her mother had been right to cage her spirit. Soon though, it would be free again.

Luna glanced toward the bathroom door. How would Breathred feel if he knew the truth? Would he still feel the same? Yes, he would. His love for her was painted on his heart, just like her heart was painted with his.

Breathred let out a yelp that cut through the thick basement walls. She started giggling. She had to wonder just how cold the water could get in the middle of a Seattle winter.

~ * ~

The house was dark…darker than it usually was. Lewis fought the temptation to turn on a light. There were still a couple of hours until dawn, and it wasn't like he needed the light, but was just used to having it. An old human habit, he guessed. Lewis had broken many of those old habits, but some were so ingrained he had trouble breaking them. Even after thirty years, it was hard.

Lewis walked through the blackened halls and paused outside the drawing room door, hearing Leopold talking to someone inside. He was in no hurry so waited outside the door. It wasn't like he had anywhere better to go. Besides he loved hearing the old boy reel them in.

"So, you find my proposal to your liking?" Leopold asked in the seductive vampire voice no human could resist.

"Let's say, I find it quite intriguing. But how do I know when this is done you'll come through on your end?" Leopold's companion asked.

"I am a Lord of the Vampiric Host. My word is my bond. Do as I ask, and all I promised will be yours and more. All it takes is for you to agree."

"Why don't you just bite me, then take what you want? I thought that was what your kind did?" the voice asked.

"You watch too many movies. I want your service to be by your choice. A reluctant servant offers nothing but grief," Leopold answered.

"Okay, you got me. I'm in," the voice answered in return.

"I am pleased to hear you say so. Unfortunately, I can't trust you at your word. I need something more concrete to seal the bargain. A pledge if you will." Lewis could just about see the grin on the old man's face now.

"You're not going to bite me, are you?" the voice trembled.

"Yes, but it won't hurt. I promise. All I need is but a taste to bind you to me," Leopold's voice was as dark as the room.

"What if I say no?"

"Believe me. You don't want to say no."

Lewis heard Leopold take the mole. The vampire was true to his word. All he took was a taste. Lewis could feel the want for more coming from Leopold, but the elder vampire restrained himself and took just what he needed. Nothing more.

Lewis waited until he heard the door on the opposite side of the room open and close before going in. It was best not to disturb a newly bonded thrall. It might upset the process. Leopold needed to form a symbiotic relationship with his subject.

"So, we got our mole, I see," Lewis said. He dropped his jacket on the table and went to stand beside his master.

"Yes, a most interesting one too. One not easy to succumb to the usual temptations," Leopold mused.

"You mean the mortal didn't want eternal life?" Lewis was shocked.

"Of course the mortal did. Humans all want eternal life, but it wasn't the only condition of the mortal's service," Leopold replied.

"Then what else did the human want? A new car, a condo, and a subscription to *USA Today*? Shit, man, after eternal life what else is there?"

"No, my friend, this human wanted knowledge of the most mundane sort. It seems our little virgin has an enemy. It was only after I agreed to get the thrall all the information needed to ruin this man, the mortal agreed to my demands."

"You mean, you didn't tell the fool what we had planned for Mr. Petrifunck?"

"I saw no reason to. After all, that is my business."

"You growing shifty in your old age," Lewis joked.

"No, dear Lewis. Do not let this pitiful shell fool you. I was born shifty," Leopold said, as he turned and walked from the room.

Sixteen

Any morning you can wake up to, is a good one in our line of work.

    The first thing Breathred noticed when he awoke was he was wet. Well, not all of him was wet, just his lower half. The top half seemed not wet, if there was such a thing. The second thing Breathred noticed was he was in his own bathtub, holding a toilet brush.
    Breathred would have found all that strange if he hadn't remembered going to sleep there the night before. What did worry him was the toilet brush. He remembered everything but the toilet brush. Even the fact his nether regions were now puckered into the drain did not worry him half as much as that toilet brush.
    The main reason for his concern was his tongue felt blue. Breathred knew there was no way he could feel the color blue on his tongue, but it was there nonetheless. He just knew without a doubt his tongue was blue.
    Eyeing the door suspiciously, Breathred put his fingers to his lips. Maybe, he shouldn't do this. Did he really want to know if his tongue was blue? Of course he did. You didn't want to walk around with a blue tongue. People would call you weird, not that they didn't already. Breathred just didn't need to add a blue tongue to list of reasons why he was considered weird.
    Breathred jabbed his fingers into his mouth, leaving them there only as long as it took to tap his wiggling tongue. Squinting, he looked at his fingertips. No blue. Then it was confirmed, he wasn't as weird as he thought.
    That left the rest of the whole world to convince, not that he was particularly worried about what they thought. On the whole they tended to think what the way they did, while he thought the way he did. The improbably of the plan seemed to work out for the best, or at least he thought so.
    Pulling himself from the drain, Breathred deemed he was ready to greet the new day. Luckily, his clothes from the previous night were still folded neatly on the dirty clothes hamper, so he wouldn't have to sneak past Luna to get some dry clothes on. He brushed his teeth and hastily dressed, careful to check for any sign of blue on the brush—not to say the mirror was lying, but he had to be sure. There was a lot to get done today and not enough

time to do it all in, especially if he hid in here all day.

Breathred barely opened the door, when Stud crashed through it.

"Out of the way, Human gotta go pee pee," Stud grumbled, as he pushed Breathred from the bathroom.

Well, at least today was starting off normally.

"Hey, Sweetums," Luna shouted from the bed. Breathred noticed his faded Power Station shirt was the only thing she had on besides the flash of white panties he hastened to look away from. "Did you sleep well?"

"Yes. I always wanted a waterbed, now I know what one feels like. Don't think I'll be buying one of those," he mumbled on his way to the kitchenette.

"I don't know, might be fun after we get married," Luna quipped.

Breathred chose that exact moment to go deaf. It was another amazing survival instinct he had developed over the years. Breathred hated to think what would have happened to him, if he had heard her. Thankfully, he hadn't, so all was well in the world. His little corner of it, anyway.

"We don't have a lot of time, so do you want something to eat here or do you want to grab something later?" Breathred yelled from the kitchenette.

"I'm famished. What ya got?" Luna yelled back, as she got dressed.

He grinned, sticking his head into the living room. "Pop Tarts and Fruity Pebbles."

"Not that it doesn't all sound nutritious—"

He couldn't help but note a hint of skepticism in her voice.

"Part of a balanced breakfast."

"Yes, be that as it may. What say we grab something from the Jumper?" Luna offered.

"Sure. Mind if I eat a Pop Tart though?" Breathred was really hungry. Couldn't she see the pangs eating their way across his face? It wasn't like he was made of steel. When you were hungry, you ate. You didn't wait for something better to come along. You ate the first thing you found. Gosh, girls could be stupid sometimes.

"Go ahead. I'm fine. Hey, Breathred, do you mind if we split up for a while? I need to do a few things before we have to meet the Doc."

"I dob tink we neb to dub dat. Wab sob imporbant web canb comb adong?" Breathred asked, through a mouthful of Pop Tart.

"You're welcome to tag along if you want to, but I need to go to the Swang Too Spa. It's time for my bikini wax. You have to book those things weeks in advance. You miss just one, and they won't schedule you again for six months. Say, as long as you're going with me, maybe Lu Lu can fit you in. Then, we can be bikini twinkies."

Breathred choked. It wasn't pretty. A glob of masticated pastry slid from his gaping mouth. Even Stud poked his head in from the bathroom.

"That's where they put, uh, and then they um rip it, you know. And they do it down—" Breathred pointed down, not able to bring himself to say it out loud.

Luna reached for the phone. "So, you know all about it. Do you want me to call Lu Lu and set it up?"

"No, me and Stud have to see a priest about some water, and I'm pretty sure the Pope doesn't approve of bikini waxing. So, it's probably not a good idea to make the Pope mad when you're trying to ask for a favor. What say you go do that, and me and the chimp'll handle everything else?" Breathred rambled on, doing his best not to look her in the eye.

"If you really think that's what we should do, I guess it'll be alright," Luna answered with a smile on her face that made him wonder if he'd been *played*, as Stud liked to put it.

"Of course it's for the best. I wouldn't have said so if it wasn't," Breathred huffed. How dare she think otherwise?

"I know that, Sweetums," Luna said, as she gently patted the side of his face. "I just wanted you to know I agreed with you."

"That's good to know. I guess," Breathred sputtered confused. Did he miss something there?

"Now, you boys'll have to excuse me, but unlike you, it takes time to look this good." Luna strode into the bathroom.

"Boy, your daddy should have named you Guitar Petrifunck," Stud giggled, when Luna shut the bathroom door.

"Why?"

"Because you just got played," Stud chuckled.

Before Breathred could ask another question, Stud waddled off. He saw no sense in trying to get the chimp explain it. Some things you just had to figure out for yourself without rude comments about sex to go along with the explanation.

~ * ~

Dr. Grayson finished signing the last of the documents that would allow her team to leave with the university's permission. A knock at the door, saved her from the pile of term papers she'd have to attend to before leaving. Well, there was no time like later.

"Come in," she announced to her visitor.

The professor was surprised to see Edmund Truehart walk into the room. The Englishman was dressed impeccably, as usual. Grayson wondered how he always managed to look like he just came from a fashion shoot. People in their profession were supposed to be short and dumpy.

His blond hair was combed into a current style. His lean face was handsome, despite his hawkish nose. Even, his bookish glasses could not distract from that fact. His body had an athletic, muscular build—not to say she had spent time imaging it to be so. Well, not all that much time.

"Donna, I do hope I'm not disturbing you? You must be having a devil of a time coordinating this jaunt." Edmund motioned toward a chair beside her desk.

Grayson stifled a yawn. "Sit down. To tell you the truth I just finished the worst of it and I could use a break."

"I wish this was a pleasurable visit," Edmund apologized.

"Oh." He wasn't pulling out, was he? That's all she needed, to lose a key member of her team the day before they left.

"I just wanted to ask you about that bloke you wanted me to meet last night."

She let out a sigh of relief. "I was afraid you were going to say you had decided to withdraw from the expedition."

"Perish the thought. This venture is too important to chuck it." Edmund smiled. "Sorry, didn't mean to give you that idea."

"Then, what did you want to know?" This time her curiosity was piqued.

"This is highly unusual for me to say, but are you sure this Petrifunck character is all that fit to be included in this?"

"For the qualifications I hired him to perform, yes. You have something you want to say about him?" Grayson hazarded a guess this could be trouble.

"You've seen through me, Donna. We've known each other for what, ten years or better? So, I think we know each other well enough to speak our minds. Am I right?" Truehart posed the question in such a way she couldn't deny it, even though for some reason she wanted to.

"I think we can assume so." What was he after, anyway?

"As you know, I am well known in certain circles. These circles span the breadth of Archaeology and this man's name is not unknown to them."

Okay, now this was getting interesting. She had felt Breathred was hiding something. Here could be the proof of it.

"Let me start by saying before last night I never met the man, but through these people I spoke of, I will admit to some knowledge garnered from—gossip—for lack of a better word."

"Look, Edmund. It's not that this isn't all intriguing, but could you get to the point? I do have a lot to clear from my plate," she said with a hint of frustration. Why were all Englishmen so long winded?

"Right to it then. Some ten years ago, Mr. Petrifunck was on a dig, not far from Izmir in Turkey. You know the type, finding old Crusade battlegrounds. Anyway, during the course of the dig, something happened to this Petrifunck. Whatever took place unhinged him, if you will. A couple of my associates who attended Oxford were there. A most unpleasant business, by all accounts. The crux of it is this, the fellow left archaeology altogether, as a result of it. Now, he pops up with you. I find it all a little unnerving."

"Edmund, I appreciate your concern, but Mr. Petrifunck has proved himself to be the right man for this job. I see no reason to exclude him for something that happened over a decade ago. Whatever demons Breathred has, he seems to have worked his way past." What she didn't say was he had found an entire new plethora of demons to plague his mind, but she didn't see any reason to reveal the truth right now.

"I didn't mean to upset you. It's just I felt you should know."

"As I said, I appreciate it, but—" Grayson said.

"But your mind is made up," Edmund finished for her. "I'm sorry to have wasted your time."

"It wasn't a waste. I'm glad you were watching out for me. As archaeologists, we tend to forget there's a world outside the one that's been dead for a thousand years. I promise you if he shows any sign of cracking up, I'll send him back. You have my word." She hated having to defend herself.

"I know you will. Well, I must be off. See you in the morning, luv."

Well, if this wasn't a fine kettle of fish. It seems there was more to Breathred's story than he wanted to tell. If Grayson had time, she'd check him out a little more thoroughly. However, wasting any more time on Mr. Petrifunck was a luxury she didn't have. She would have to play with the cards she had dealt herself. Then again, the dig would present her with time enough to try and find out what this little mystery was all about.

Seventeen

The most important part of any good campaign is planning. If you run in half-cocked you can still end up dead.

It was sometime after eleven before Luna finally managed to find the address her mother had given her for her uncle. She hated lying to Breathred back at his house, but she really needed to do this without him or Stud tagging along. The man she was going to see wasn't her real uncle, but then again, growing up on the reservation Luna had more aunts and uncles than seemed possible. In the truest sense of the word John Prancing Elk was as much an uncle as any blood relation could have ever been. More importantly, he had the gift.

Right now, Luna needed that gift. To her people, the one born with the gift was the most important member of the tribe. When John Prancing Elk left the tribe, everyone was shocked, counting herself among that number. Since coming to Seattle, Luna hadn't found an excuse to go and see him. Truthfully, she was afraid he didn't want to see her. His sudden departure from the reservation left many questions; her mother had kept her own council concerning his leaving. Now, facing the prospect of seeing him after all these years, Luna might finally get the answers to those questions.

Luna saw her visit as killing two birds with one stone, if John could help her. Taking a right onto the street her mother indicated in her directions, Luna thought she must have made a wrong turn. Even when she found the address on the slip of paper, Luna knew she must have been mistaken. The John Prancing Elk she knew wouldn't be caught dead in a place called The Delicious One.

Get real. John was bear of a man, six foot five if he was an inch. All the girls used to swoon over him. The big man always exuded a raw, manly sex appeal that could make a blind woman start to sweat in the middle of a snowstorm. With all those bulging muscles, you'd be hard pressed to mistake him for anything but a man.

Sure, he was quiet and didn't say much. He was just shy. Her mother even used to comment on it. She always said he was the most well behaved man she ever met. Plus, what he knew about interior design would make your head spin.

What would he be doing in a Big and Tall S & M shop? From the looks of the place you'd have to be three sheets to the wind, or a total slut puppy, to even walk through the door. There was no way John Prancing Elk would set one foot inside a place like that.

Luna would have turned around there, but she didn't have any other place to go. She had to get her talisman recharged. Without it she might as well pack up and head home.

Maybe he had lived here and moved after the shop opened. If that was the case, there was a chance someone would know where he'd moved to. You just couldn't forget a man like John. Someone would have to remember him.

The door slid open to the dulcet accompaniment of *Air Supply*. If it hadn't been so blatantly tacky, Luna would have laughed. Instead she suppressed a grimace. The least it could have been playing was some *Culture Club*. She could handle some *Culture Club*, as long as it was the early stuff. Anything after they broke up was just pathetic.

Mirrors lined the store's back wall in a bid to make the tiny space appear larger than it was. All it truly did was tell Luna she could stand to lose the red shirt she had thrown on that morning. Maybe they had something here she could change into. Luna didn't mind wearing something a tad risqué as long as it wasn't downright filthy looking. She did have a wholesome image to uphold after all.

To that end Luna found herself rummaging through the closeout section. The rack had a few things she liked, but nothing Luna would even attempt to wear in public, let alone around Breathred—not that it wouldn't be a lark to see the look on his face, if she did.

"Hey dearie, be right with you," a falsetto voice yelled from out back, breaking her train of thought.

Luna looked up to see a giant of a woman exit a purple-draped dressing-room door. The Amazon was decked out in a skin-tight, pink leather bodysuit. It could have been vinyl, but in the dimly lit store it was hard to tell. A black, studded belt circled the woman's waist. Her cheap blond hair was wrapped up in a beehive that defied gravity.

Luna was stunned to silence. It wasn't from the sight of the woman, herself. Since coming to Seattle she had seen trashier, but never on this scale. Even that wasn't the 'cause for her silence.

"Uncle John?" Luna sputtered.

"Luna Walking Batch, is that you girl?" The woman exclaimed in her best Ru Paul voice. "Let me get a look at you. The last time I saw you, you were running around chasing your momma like a chicken with her head cut off."

"Uncle John," was the only thing her mind and mouth could grasp to say to the man.

"I think we've already established that. I prefer Joan, if you don't mind," Joan stated, throwing her/his hand on his/her hip. *

*Hey, I'm a damn chimpanzee. If you want Shakespeare, read Shakespeare. You bought this drivel, so read it and shut the hell up.

"Uncle Joan," Luna uttered, feeling she had definitely hit a rut. God, what was she going to tell her mother?

~ * ~

"Bless me father, for I have sinned," Breathred whispered. It wasn't that he was ashamed of being in the confessional. Everyone ended up here sooner or later; otherwise they went to the bad place. He was just ashamed of the things that made him go to the confessional in the first place.

"Bless you my son. How long has it been since your last confession?" Father Timothy asked.

"I was just here last week. Don't you remember, Father Tim? I coveted that comic book. Does that help you any?"

"Breathred, is that you?" Father Timothy asked aloud, before mumbling under his breath. "Dear Lord, has it been a week already?"

"Yes, sir." It was best to be polite in such situations. You never knew when God might stop in for a quality evaluation on his priests.

"Are you alone? The chimpanzee isn't with you, by any chance, is he?"

"No, sir. He hasn't been back to St. Catherine's since Sister Ophelia beat him with her rosary," Breathred said, ashamed to admit the chimp's indiscretion. Breathred wondered if he still owed a penance for Stud's transgression.

"Thank heaven for small favors," Father Tim exclaimed, then added, "It isn't that I don't like our little chats, Breathred, but your chimp is the devil's own."

"He has no fondness for the devil, sir," Breathred assured the priest.

"Just Catholic school girls and the occasional novice, if I remember right."

"Excuse me, Father?"

"Nothing my boy. Now, you have something to confess," Father Tim said.

"Well, Father. This past week I got a girlfriend."

"God, be praised! Will miracles never cease?"

"Well, even so. I've found myself thinking thoughts most impure. I know it's wrong to think them, but I can't help myself."

"What manner do these thoughts take?" Father Tim asked, moving his head closer to the screen.

"The worst one is where I think about putting my tongue—"

"Yes, you want to put your tongue where?" the priest gasped excitedly, interrupting Breathred.

"In her mouth. I know you must think me horrible for thinking so," Breathred sobbed.

"That's it? You have a girlfriend for the first time in your entire pathetic life, and the best thing you can come up with is to put you tongue in her mouth? I ought to give you fifty Hail Marys for lack of imagination," Father Tim ranted. "You got anything else? I don't have all day, you know."

"Well, no that's about it. But there's another matter I need to talk to you about."

"What is it?" The priest snapped before lowering his voice. "I need to get transferred to a church with more enlightened parishioners. Someplace full of closet lesbians would be nice."

"Excuse me, Father?"

"Nothing, my son. Please continue."

"My friends and I are going on a mission, a dangerous mission. I fully expect to face all manner of satanic hordes. I was hoping perhaps you could bless my endeavors. I would feel better knowing God watched over me in this," Breathred admitted.

"Be assured, my son, the good Lord will watch over you all your days," Father Tim said with confidence. "Fools and little children—you must fit in there somewhere."

"Uh, thanks. There's one other thing. Would it be possible to get a couple of gallons of holy water?" Breathred hoped he wasn't pushing his luck.

"Check out the gift shop on your way out. Now, if that's all, silently give your Act of Contrition. Do ten Hail Marys and twenty Our Fathers to atone for your impure thoughts." Father Tim sighed.

Bowing his head, Breathred gave his Act of Contrition. "Thank you, Father."

"Then, go with God." Father Tim gave him the sign of the Cross. "And, Breathred—don't come back until you watch some Victoria's Secret commercials."

"Yes, sir." Breathred answered, as he exited the confessional.

Stud was waiting for him when he left the church with two bottles of holy water under each arm. Stud shot him a sneer. Why the boy bothered with this claptrap, he would never understand. At least it gave him a chance to take in the scenery, as the girl's volleyball team sauntered past.

"Don't even think it," Breathred warned, walking up to the chimpanzee.

"Like I could with all these damned penguins haunting the place, especially with Sister O'fillmeup over there leading the pack," Stud groused, catching sight of a flock of nuns giving him a stabbing stare.

"Let's get out of here before they decide a preemptive strike is called for."

"So, what did the old prattle-puss have to say?"

"The usual. Stud, what's a Victoria secret?" Breathred asked.

"Something you wouldn't understand. What's our next move, Chief?" Stud silently hoped it involved food in some form or another.

"As far as I can see, the rest of the day is free. This was the last thing we needed." Breathred indicated the jugs of holy water.

"Let's meet up with Luna and get some chow."

"Luna said she'd be tied up for most of the day. She'll meet back up with us when she's done doing whatever it is she had to do." The faraway look on his face told Stud just how he felt about the girl's absence. "But there's no reason we can't make a guy's day out of it."

"We're one guy shy, but I'm game. Let's get some Mexican," Stud said, cheered by the thought of food.

"No way. There is no way I'm getting on a bus with you for twelve hours after you've eaten a chimichanga—or ten," Breathred stated, firmly.

"Then, what do you wanna eat?" Stud snapped. "And if you mention anything having to do with tofu, I'm slapping my banana in yo' mouth."

"Look, Stud can we get serious? Do you think we're ready for all this? Luna isn't here, so I want your true opinion," Breathred said, as they crossed the street.

"I don't know. We got the skills, but this isn't Resident Evil. We'll be doing this for real. That's enough to make me say, *Hell no*. But, Breathred, you've got something going on here that changes all that. I saw you when you were fighting those vamps at the mall. That was real, you know what I mean?" Stud paused. "If you'd asked me last week, woulda been running for the hills. Today, I think we got a shot at this."

"You mean it?"

"Yeah, but we got to do this as a team. That's the only way we can make this work—the three of us against them," Stud added.

"Then, Mexican it is." Breathred's tears drowned the corners of his eyes.

~ * ~

Luna couldn't believe she had been sitting here for two hours listening to this man pour his soul out to her. In the past two hours Uncle John had said more than she had ever remembered him saying in the entire time she had been around him on the reservation.

Listening intently to his every word, not because she was being polite, but because she truly wanted to hear his story, Luna sat like a statue. This was something he needed to say. John, or Joan, wasn't trying to excuse himself for being what he was. He was just trying to relate the story of his evolution from the man he had been, to the woman he had been born to be. There was no way Luna would have poo-pooed any of it. She had too much respect for her uncle to do that.

John finished and looked at her for some sort of response. Despite the mascara and glitter that adorned his cheeks, his eyes were still those of the John Prancing Elk she remembered. Her initial concerns were gone. He was still the man, or rather the woman, to help her.

"So, momma, knew all along?" she asked, when he finished.

"She was the only one. Your mother was the only true friend I could turn to. I'm sure the others suspected, but she was the only one I dared confide in," he admitted.

"Well, now you have me." She patted the back of his hand. "But what should I call you? John isn't right after what you've told me."

"Thank you for that, Luna." John reached up wiping a tear from the corner of his eye. "And you can call me Uncle Joan, all the *girls* do"

"Alright, Uncle Joan." Luna let the name settle into her mind, finding it fit nicely there. "But how come mom never told me? She gave me your address, but that was it." She wondered what else her mother hid from her.

"That was my fault. She called me right before you moved to Seattle and asked me to watch out for you. I've been to the place you worked once a week to make sure you were doing all right," Joan said, a smug look on her face.

"I never even saw you," Luna said in surprise.

"But I saw you," Joan answered. "And the young man, who you've latched onto."

"That's kinda why I came to see you."

"Explain. I'm always up for a bit of girl-talk."

"The talisman my mother gave me is starting to give me trouble. Last night I felt Coyote's call. The talisman should have blocked it completely, but it didn't," she explained.

Joan eyed her suspiciously. She pulled a feathered pen from her purse. Mumbling under her breath, the big woman passed the pen over Luna's head. After three passes she set it down and took Luna's face in her massive hands. Staring straight through to the soul, Luna knew her uncle had found out what was wrong.

"Your aura is shifting. It is unbalanced. That is what's interfering with the talisman's power." Joan peered into her eyes. "All the signs point to one thing being the cause. What is this young man to you?"

"He's my life mate, though he doesn't know it yet," she said, proudly.

"Then, that's it. The emotions of the bonding are blocking the power of the talisman," Joan said with a flourish.

Luna pulled the talisman from her shirt. "Is there nothing you can do?"

"I must attune it to this new phase of your life. It should be relatively easy to fix. Do you by any chance have something belonging to your potential mate?" Joan took the leather bag from Luna.

"Do I look like someone who would carry something like that

around?" Luna asked, indignantly.

"Honey, you got stalker written all over you. Now, give."

"Okay." Luna pulled a lock of hair from her purse.

"Before I do this…are you sure this man is the one? This is a serious matter, not to be trifled with. If I bind this man to your spirit self, he will always be a part of you, even if he chooses not to be the man you want him to be. After saying this, do you still wish to go forward?" Joan Prancing Elk asked, her eyes peering into Luna's with all seriousness.

"To do less would deny what I know to be true."

"Good, I hoped you'd say that. I do hate people who are wishy-washy when it comes to true love. You're either all in, or not in at all." Joan beamed. "Now tell me, is he worth it?"

"Joan, he's more than worth it."

"Then let's get to it."

Luna sat patiently while Joan delved into the spirit world and tapped its magic. The silent workings fascinated her, just like they had when she was a small girl at her mother's knee. The oneness of it all held her rooted to her seat. Luna knew one day she too, might call this world hers, but that was many years away. Her path was in the modern world. Until that time came to pass, she was content to sit back and watch.

Joan finished the last of the magic and closed the bag. Wiping a bead of sweat from her brow, she handed it back. Luna looked grave and placed it around her neck.

"It's ready to go?" The bag felt different, heavier somehow.

"Would I give it back, if it wasn't?" Joan joked.

"You don't know how much this means to me," Luna said. "This was the only chance I had to get it done before I left for Canada."

"Why the hell would you want to go to Canada? Why would anybody for that matter?"

"Well, Breathred and I have this mission," Luna explained.

"Like De Niro?"

"No, we have to stop some vampires from raising their queen from the dead, so they can take over the world." Luna hoped it didn't sound as crazy to Joan as it did to her.

"Hold it a minute. Did you say Queen?" Joan asked, excitedly.

Luna giggled. "Not that kind, Girlfriend."

"Didn't think so, but it never hurts to dream. This all sounds a tad bit dangerous. Do you think you should be doing this? I mean, your mother would kill me if something happened to you."

"I'll be all right. I'm a big girl now, Uncle. Besides, somebody has to look after my Breathy," Luna said, confidently.

"Okay, but if you need my help, here's my card. It has my cell phone number on it. So, you can reach me anytime, night or day. Understand?"

Luna took it and accepted his question for what it was—an order.

She was happy to know Joan was there if they needed him. It was always good to have an ace in the hole. It wasn't that Luna thought they needed one but you never knew. Get real. They needed all the backup they could get.

Putting the card into her purse, Luna looked at the woman who had been her uncle. Under the makeup and faux weave was the man who had taught her to fish and ride a horse, even if the horse had only been the one in front of the reservation store and took a quarter to get moving. Despite all these changes, Joan Prancing Elk was someone Luna could depend on and was twice the woman she'd ever been as a man. That meant a lot.

"You got it, Uncle Joan," she smiled.

"Now, get out of here, before the straights think I got me a new boyfriend." Joan stood up and straightened her wig, which had slipped to the left while she was working. "It's already getting dark."

"Oh, damn!" Luna exclaimed. Breathred was going to kill her.

Eighteen

If it was easy to slay vampires, would you have bought this book in the first place?

Leopold had decided he wouldn't worry about anything tonight. A good day's sleep had put him in an especially exuberant mood. His hair was doing exactly what he wanted it to do. And if that wasn't good enough, *Vogue* said purple was the new pink. When you added all those things together, it came out heaven in a bottle, and he loved the vintage.

The only thing missing was a double espresso. Oh to be able to indulge in that most human of experiences. It was the only drawback of being a vampire. You could never eat or drink what you wanted. It was sort of like being on Jennie Craig without Kirstie Alley haunting you all the time. How that woman invaded his life at every turn…But one day he would have the last laugh.

Stepping away from his dressing table, Leopold brushed a piece of lint from his collar. He was going to have to get a decorator in here while they were gone. His first plan had been to stay here while the good doctor saw to the unearthing of the Mother. With the addition of Mr. Petmyskunk, those plans had changed.

No, the vampire would need to keep an eye on things. Not a close eye. His agent would take care of that, but Leopold wanted to be near enough to jump in should the need arise. Even Lewis couldn't be trusted to see to his best interests.

The boy was just too young to un-life. The implications of what they were trying to do were beyond his feeble senses. Lewis had potential, but only age would bring that potential to flower. Leopold didn't have that long to wait. He needed experience now. The only place to find it was within himself.

His ego would not admit another vampire of equal age might do the job. Besides, they were all too prissy to get the job done right. He was the only man for it.

That was why Leopold had already reserved a flight, set to leave tomorrow night, as well as a reservation at a lodge not far from the dig site. He would arrive after the team, leaving them none the wiser as to his presence. You didn't get to be as old as he was without thinking ahead. Thanks to *priceline.com,* the entire operation had been a breeze.*

While not an official sponsor of this manuscript, Shatner gives me assurances Nimoy has pull.

Leopold tossed the last of his cravats into his suitcase. They settled like wilted lilies on top of his seersucker suit. He had considered taking something hip and urban, but decided a well-maintained dignity was the best way to go. A vampire of his standing had a certain image to uphold.

Closing the case Leopold went to his door. He could hear Lewis rummaging around in the other room. Lewis knew better than to enter his private suites without knocking first. What the hell had happened to propriety?

"Lewis, you know I don't like you invading my space," Leopold said, as he opened the door. The naughty thing would have to learn.

"Well, if this was Lewis, I'm sure he'd be quaking in his boots," a dark figure answered from the room.

"Marcus, is that you?" Leopold demanded. Anger swelled within him. How dare Marcus invade his sanctum like this! There were rules of etiquette to be followed otherwise they were no better than humans.

"Who else, old friend?" Marcus said, as he walked toward Leopold.

"You think that you can just walk into my home unannounced? I will not brook such umbrage. I expect an explanation," Leopold raged. He felt a good old-fashioned outburst was called for. Not too much, though. He didn't want to look like a crying nilly.

"Oh, Leopold. You never cease to amuse me." Marcus laughed.

"I'm quite serious. Explain yourself, before I get ugly," Leopold warned, throwing his hands on his hips.

"My God, you really have become an old thing haven't you?"

"What makes you say that? What have you heard?" Leopold asked, growing a little nervous. He had overplayed himself. Hadn't he? It was the hip thing. He shouldn't have done the hip thing.

"Oh, please just shut up. Your un-life crisis is no concern of mine. Act the fool if it makes you happy, but don't expect me to follow in your folly." Marcus shook his head.

"No, you shut up. This is my house, not yours. Now, tell me what you want and get the hell out."

"All right, here it is. We want you to stop this madness. The Mother is asleep for a reason. She's too volatile to be loosed on this world. Her world is but dust. Please, Leopold, for whatever friendship we may have once had—let this matter go," Marcus implored.

"It is you, who is playing the fool, Marcus. The Mother will take care of us. She will open this world wide, and we will be her kings to rule it, as she wants."

"She will turn this world into a killing floor. You don't know her. I do. I have seen what the Mother makes of the land when she wakes. I will not see it happen again." Marcus' eyes were cold and hard.

Leopold looked at him. He and Marcus had known each other for centuries. This was the first time his friend had spoken to him in such a manner. Sure, they had had disagreements over the years, but this was different. There was a hardness in the other vampire's voice that hadn't shown itself before. Frankly, it scared Leopold.

But it in no way changed his plans. The Mother would be wakened. Marcus was more than happy to try and stop him, but he would go ahead.

Marcus was no army of one. No, Rambo for damn sure. The vampire was a thinker. His knowledge may be vast, but that was it. Leopold, while born to nobility, had to fight for everything. His youth was one long struggle for survival. His life after becoming a vampire had been no different.

Marcus, on the other hand, had been born to true privilege. He never wanted for anything. He never hungered for anything more than what he had. If he had, it was given to him. He was weak. They both knew it.

The only advantage Marcus had was age. Marcus had been born more than a thousand years ago. That was a lot of time to acquaint yourself with your powers. The vastness of Marcus' power was the only thing to give Leopold pause, but even it didn't give him much worry. Marcus' exaggerated sense of honor would not allow him to fight dirty. Leopold did not have such compulsions.

The silence between them had gone on long enough. Leopold turned to Marcus. The vampire was imploring him with his eyes to forsake this path. Leopold considered lying to him. Falsehoods wouldn't work. They knew each other too well. That left them as enemies at least in this.

"Leopold, do this for me. Do this for our friendship," Marcus pleaded.

"I can't. This is my destiny. Whether it is for good or for bad, this is something I must do."

"Then, know this. We will come to blows over this. Mark my works. You will come to see I was right to your ultimate displeasure," Marcus said, and then was gone.

Leopold saw him fade into nothing. He knew it for what it was—an announcement of war. It was a show that told him Marcus had powers he didn't, as well as the wisdom to use them.

Well, damn him. This was his life, not Marcus'. To impose his demands on him was an insult. Then again, he had always seen himself as everyone's big brother, the sanctimonious prick.

Leopold slammed the lid down on his suitcase. He would not bow to his big brother now, or ever again. Soon, all those high and mighty lords would be bowing to him. That brought a smile to his face. Yes, it would feel good to be worshiped.

~ * ~

Breathred was pumping his foot against the floor when Luna finally made it back to his place. Dusk was long gone, and the night was full against the skyline. Stud finished the packing for the two of them. It had been the only thing keeping the chimp from running off after her.

Breathred, on the other hand, had opted for extreme worry. He paced the floor for the better part of the afternoon. When dusk dropped its coat over the city, he moved on to slamming things. Everything from doors to Nerf basketballs met his fury. Breathred knew Stud sympathized, but refrained from joining him in his misery. He was glad for that. Breathred knew from experience how the little beast acted on his anxiety. To put it bluntly, chimps threw poo to show their anxiety. After all the cheesy burritos Stud consumed over lunch he hoped the chimp was too constipated to manage a fart let alone a full-on poo barrage.

Luna entered the room. "So, guys, how's it hanging

"Is there any reason you couldn't get back here on time, or at the very least call us to let us know where you were?" Breathred demanded.

~ * ~

She reached up and patted his cheek, which earned her a snarl. She had never seen him snarl before. She decided immediately that she didn't like it. She didn't mind him worrying; it was sweet. But the attitude had to go. If this was going to work, it was high time he learned who was in charge.

"Breathred, I think we need to get some things straight. I may be your girlfriend, and I understand you were worried about me, but I can take care of myself. If you keep on thinking you can talk to me like that, you'll find out just how well I can take care of myself," she said in a calm voice. Only her finger slapping the end of his nose let him know just how angry she really was.

"Now, I'm sorry for not calling you, but I couldn't help it. You can either forgive me, or we can keep on like this for the rest of our lives. The choice is yours."

"I'd forgive her, if I was you. That finger looks dangerous," Stud remarked, standing well away from her while he said it.

"Look, Luna. Maybe I overreacted, but that doesn't mean I wasn't worried," Breathred said. "I am really sorry for the way I acted, and the only one who needs to be forgiven around here is me."

"Oh, Silly Puss. How can I stay mad at you?" Luna asked. "You're my big ol' bugger britches." Like putty in my hands.

"Ah, shucks."

"Looks like you're almost all packed. So, what's left to do?" Luna asked, hoping her secret mission was safely out of the way.

"No, thanks to you, missy," Stud grumbled. "Your stuff is still over there. Breathred refused to let me pack it."

"Why not?" She turned to Breathred. It seemed kind of shitty of him to make her pack all the stuff by herself.

"Because he was trying on your, you know, underthingies. And prancing around the room singing *I feel pretty, oh so pretty*," Breathred said, blushing again.

Luna burst out laughing. She didn't know whether to be mad or what. The image of Stud in her thongs was enough to make her forgive the whole matter. Until she was sure which of her things he had put on, the best thing to do was to wash the whole lot of them. She didn't want monkey cooties, after all.

"Stud, how could you? None of my clothes go with your skin color. If you must wear such things, we'll take you to Victoria's Secret and get you some of your own," Luna said, fighting back another wave of laughter at the look on his little chimp face. Who knew you could question a chimpanzee's manhood?

"I think not!" Stud exclaimed. "Can't a guy make a joke without everyone jumping to the wrong conclusions? I think I'm going to see R.J. At least he has a sense of humor."

They watched him storm off. It was only after he slammed the basement door they felt it safe to break down. Their laughter echoed through the room. Breathred fell to the couch in tears. Luna plopped down beside him, her own laughter almost drowning out his.

It took several minutes for it to finally die down. Breathred wiped his wet face. He needed that. It had been a long time, since he had been able to laugh so freely. Breathred owed it all to Luna. She was opening parts of him he never knew existed. How was a woman able to do that? How could Luna make someone whole who didn't even know he wasn't?

He looked over at her. His face hadn't made a quarter turn when it met hers. Breathred was kissing her before he knew what he was doing. Her soft lips pressed into his. He could have stopped it, but he didn't. It was too nice to stop.

Luna was the first to pull away. Breathred felt the emptiness keenly as soon as her lips left his. The feeling was almost too much for him to bear. The loss of her warmth 'caused his eyes to fly open. The look of shock playing across her face stabbed him to his very soul.

"Luna, I didn't mean to." Shame choked his words.

"I'm glad you did," she answered, breathlessly.

"Me too." He lowered his head, blushed and asked. "Is it always supposed to feel like so good?"

"Only when it's with me," she said, stroking his cheek. Even as Luna said it, Breathred hoped it was true. Without her doing the kissing, he just knew it would never be so good.

"I thought so, but I wanted you to tell me, so I could be sure," Breathred said softly.

"Now before you ravish me again, let's get my stuff packed. We have to get up early in the morning," Luna said, as she rose from the couch.

Breathred watched her stand on wobbly legs. He would have joined her, but for some reason his legs refused to move. He doubted kissing could 'cause paralysis but no other explanation seemed plausible. The fact his naughty bits seemed more active than his legs worried him as well. What if it stayed uh… in that condition? Breathred wasn't sure if he could walk with it doing that. There could be a chance of permanent damage if he even tried to move. The best thing to do was sit here and act stupid. It worked for everything else.

~ * ~

Out of sight, Stud closed the door. He had only had it open a crack, but it was enough to let him watch his two lovebirds. If Stud were a hopeless romantic, he would need a tissue after watching that. The whole thing was so Julia Roberts meets Richard Gere in hurt. Thankfully, he was a hardcore he-monkey, so he just used his shirtsleeve.

Nineteen

There are no field trips in this course, but if there were, you'd better believe they'd cost an arm and a leg.

They were traveling in three aging mini vans. That was the first thing Breathred noticed when his father dropped the three of them off. A giddy thrill shot through him. They were going in style. A huge U-haul sat parked off to one side of the parking lot. Several students were packing it with equipment and whatever luggage wouldn't fit in the vans' overhead racks.

Breathred wondered how hard it would be to get to ride in the U-haul. Man, that'd be even cooler than riding in a mini van. It would almost be like being in *Smokey and the Bandit*. He'd let Stud be Fred, and Luna could be Frog. Luna was even cuter than Sally Field in Breathred's book. It would be so cool.

His hopes were dashed when Dr. Grayson motioned for them to join her beside the first van. Life just wasn't fair. He bet old Truehart got to ride in the big rig. Well, let him. Breathred would just call shotgun in the van. Shotgun was better than riding in the stinky old U-haul anyway. That way you got to control the radio.

"Breathred, Luna, over here," Dr. Grayson called.

Luna waved back, and took off across the wet asphalt. Breathred shrugged and followed her. He looked over to find Stud snoring atop their pile of bags and suitcases. The chimpanzee would be all right there for a few minutes. After all, how much trouble could a sleeping chimp get in? Quite a bit, if his name happened to be Stud. He would have to risk it. Besides with Stud out of the way he would have a clear run at the shotgun seat. Stud was a front seat hog.

By the time he caught up to Luna, she and Dr. Grayson were deep in conversation. Breathred hung outside their circle, unwilling to intrude. To tell the truth he was afraid of what he might overhear. Women had peculiar topics of conversation. You never knew what they might be talking about. Some of it was right unfit for male consumption.

"Oh, Breathred, why don't you come here? This affects you as well," Dr. Grayson said, breaking away from Luna.

"I didn't want to interrupt," Breathred said, sheepishly.

"Don't be silly. We don't have time for you to be shy. We have a deadline to keep. You and Luna will be riding in the lead van with me." She pointed behind her.

"What about Stud?" Breathred asked. He didn't like the thought of leaving the chimp alone for a prolonged trip. He shuddered to think of all the mischief that could be done in for the time it'd take to get to the dig. There were international treaties to take into consideration.

Grayson rubbed her temples. "Oh, he'll be riding with us. I wouldn't dream of letting him out of my sight."

"So, is everybody here?" Luna asked.

"Well, there's been a change of plans. A couple of our team members will be flying up later with the rest of our more sensitive equipment. Apparently, my request for a secure carrier was lost in the shuffle." Dr. Grayson frowned. "So, Drs. Truehart and Easily will be accompanying it on a plane chartered by Mr. Chambris Portus."

"Will Mr. Chambris Portus be coming along then?" Breathred asked, not liking the sound of Dr. Grayson's news. It was just a little too convenient.

"Not on the dig itself, but he is flying up with the equipment to make sure everything goes all right. We're lucky to have a man like him funding us."

Breathred's eye twitched. Seems kind of funny how Jessica had been the one to accompany the equipment, not to mention du Chambris Portus. It was another sign she had sided with the vamps. Breathred hated to think she could do such a thing, but what else could he think? Now, that Breathred thought about it, it wasn't too surprising. He once saw her put ketchup on a brownie. Anybody who would do that would be capable of just about anything.

"Ah, here come the last of the stragglers," Dr. Grayson announced as a beat up Cougar pulled into the lot. "That'll be Charles and Chris. They're good students but they'd be late to their own funerals."

Breathred watched the professor check their names on the clipboard she cradled in the crook of her arm. Once finished, she left him and Luna so she could hurry the newcomers along. They were running late as it was. Any further delay would set them way behind schedule.

Not that Breathred cared about it one way or the other. Now with the moment of truth upon him, he was feeling more than a little fearful over the whole thing. Sure, he had the textbook to fall back on, and knew how to handle a vampire. The mall had taught him so.

All right, Breathred hated to admit it but he hated long car trips. Despised them to tell the truth. Enjoying a round or two of a hundred bottles of beer on the wall was always fun, but that was the only thing he liked about them. It would have been even worse, if someone got the idea to force him to drive. Breathred hated driving most of all. The thought of actually getting on the interstate made his butt clinch up so bad it took a month before he could use the bathroom again.

Now as Breathred thought about it, maybe he should let Stud take the front seat. With Stud out of the way, it would give him time to talk to Luna in the back. No, that wouldn't work either. Breathred had heard about what went on in the backs of vans between boys and girls. God, he should have stayed in bed. At least there he could have hid under the covers and pretended none of this was happening.

"Breathred I hate to mention this, but you're drooling," Luna whispered in his ear.

"Huh," he grunted.

"Snap out of it, Big Guy. You're not getting nervous are you?"

"A little. I haven't been this far from home in a long time. It's all a bit daunting."

She smiled up at him. "Hey, I'm going to be with you. I won't let anything happen to you. I promise."

"But that's my job. I'm supposed to protect you, not the other way round." Breathred was a little hurt at her implication he might need protecting.

"Why, because you're the man?" she howled. "Let me tell you one thing, Mr. Petrifunck. I can take care of myself and if you can't see that, I'll be more than happy to find someone who can."

"No, that's not it," he answered, shying away from her.

"Then, what is it?"

"I'm the vampire slayer—not you, not Stud. If I need to be protected, what does that say about my ability to slay? If I thought you couldn't take care of yourself, I wouldn't have let either of you sign up for this job," he said, running his hand through his hair thoughtfully.

"Oh, Breathred. You're such a lunkhead. If I didn't think you could do this, do you think I'd have roped us into this? You're the only man I'd trust to get me out of something like this," she said, giving his jaw a soft tap. "But I'll make a deal with you. You handle all the vamps and other things that go bump in the night, and I'll deal with the frogs."

"Nobody said anything about frogs!" Breathred screamed. "If there are going to be frogs, I need to go home. I'm sure I forgot something on the back of the toilet that won't keep till we get back."

"I said I'd take care of them." Luna slipped her arm around his neck. With a quick snap she locked his head into a sleeper hold. "Now, unless you want me to get ugly, you will get in the van and be a good little boy. Do you understand me?"

"Yes, Ma'am."

"Looks like you're sucking hind tit today, Big Guy," Stud laughed from the front seat when Breathred opened the van's door. "Hit the backseat, Hot Stuff. The big boy's got shotgun."

~ * ~

Leopold stood outside the gate of a private airfield just on the outskirts of Seattle. He was not in a good mood. The drizzling rain did nothing to improve it, either. Fog was rolling in, thick and steady. Hoping the weather would not derail his plans, Leopold sent a mental summons out to Lewis to check on the possibility.

The response came instantly into Leopold's head. The pilot had said no, Lewis thought at him. As much as he hated standing here without his companion, Lewis was better used elsewhere for the time being.

Lewis was seeing to their luggage, as well as helping Dr. Truehart get the university's equipment loaded onboard the plane. Dr. Easily was somewhere in the terminal. Thankfully, out of his hair for the moment. As useful as the woman was to him, she had a tendency to drag on his last nerve. An ill omen, if Leopold had ever heard of one.

Then again tonight had been full of them. It all started with them being late for their departure time, thanks to Lewis' supper. The young were always so hungry. Tonight of all nights, the boy could have waited or taken a bag from the refrigerator. But no, he had to have something fresh. Something that sticks to the bones, Lewis had said. Leopold had something that could stick to his bones, something of the ash or oak variety.

Lewis' tardiness had just been the tip of the iceberg. The limo hadn't shown up, and when it did, the driver was new. To make matters worse, they got lost and had to backtrack. By then it was an hour past the time they were to meet the plane. Lewis had called to tell the pilot they were running late, otherwise the human would have left them sitting on the tarmac.

That thought earned the departing limo a harsh look. Well, the delays didn't matter. They had made it with time to spare. After all, his dime was footing the proverbial bill. Leopold made a mental note to remember the driver's name. It paid to plan your meals ahead. Whoever had said, "revenge was a dish best served cold" must not have been a vampire.

The shifting fog parted, revealing Lewis coming toward him. Good, the plane must be ready. This dreary weather was hell on his complexion. Seattle was like being in London, only without Benny Hill to make it bearable.

In fact Leopold was seriously reconsidering making the city his permanent home. He'd been hearing good things about Green Bay. Well, he'd heard good things about Brett Favre, which amounted to the same thing, if you asked him. Any place that kept so many big brutes on hand for the picking had to be a good place to live in his book. Leopold had always been a pushover for a man in uniform, especially a tight fitting one.

"All packed, boss," Lewis said, as soon as he reached the elder vampire.

"Good. Go get Ms. Easily. I'm ready to get away from this abysmal place," Leopold grumbled.

"Look boss, I appreciate the eye candy as much as the next man, but are you sure about bringing the broad along?"

"I don't need this shite from you, Lewis. I know what I'm doing. They are the perfect decoys. We have nothing to worry about."

"Except for the fact this so-called slayer knows about you and me. I don't call that nothing to worry about. That's a whole pile of shit to worry about," Lewis said.

"Oh, please. Do you think I've never had to deal with these self-styled monster hunters before? They start out like gangbusters, but the first flash of a little fang, they fold up and cry like a baby. This one will be no different."

"I hope you're right."

"Of course I am, now go get that little tart. I'll be waiting in the plane," Leopold said, strolling toward the plane.

Twenty

When dealing with the authorities, the best policy is to act as stupid as you can without getting locked up for it.

Breathred awoke with a start. The van was stopping. When did he fall asleep? Breathred couldn't remember. He had only meant to close his eyes for a second, and ended up sleeping the morning and, from the looks of it, the afternoon away. Night had bloomed some time ago, leaving the van bathed in darkness, except for streetlights that streamed in through the window.

Breathred glanced at his watch. It was a little after eight. Doggone, he must have been tired. He hoped he hadn't snored. Oh God, what if he was drooling? He couldn't stand it if someone saw him drooling. His hand stroked his chin. No, he was all dry. That was one neurosis out of the way.

Through a sleep-filled haze, he glanced over to where Luna sat. She was curled up against the back of the seat, as fast asleep as he must have been. Breathred smiled to himself. Her jacket was pulled tight to her slumping chin. Luna was using his bulky jacket as a pillow tucked neatly behind her head.

Breathred marveled at how childlike she looked. To him Luna never looked more beautiful than she did when she was asleep. He never failed to notice that fact about her. How did women always seem to be able to pull angelic perfection off when they were asleep?

He, on the other hand, was a totally different story. Breathred resembled something akin to a dying moose all sprawled out. Stud had assured him of the fact on more than one occasion, not that the chimp had room to talk. As far as Breathred was concerned, he would rather look like a dying moose than a snoring ape with a habitual pup tent.

The van lurched forward. Breathred shifted slightly in his seat. His arm automatically shot toward Luna, making sure she wasn't thrown forward from the van's unexpected motion. As his hand brushed past her, Luna stirred fitfully from her catnap.

Suddenly, her eyes flipped open. Breathred cringed as she peered wildly at him. He pulled his arm back, away from her. Her lips curled into a wicked snarl. As suddenly as the look appeared, her expression changed to the usual smile Breathred was accustomed to seeing.

"Where are we?" Luna mumbled through a gaping yawn.

"I don't know. Just woke up myself," he answered, wondering if he had morning breath. Breathred had brushed his teeth that morning, but he couldn't be sure if there was a statute of limitations on daily dental hygiene. He hid his mouth behind his hand just to be on the safe side.

"Stud, baby. Do you know where we are?" Luna called to the front seat. Another yawn ended her question.

"He's asleep," Dr. Grayson answered for him. "But we're coming up to the border. We're waiting for our turn to go through. Go ahead and get your passports out."

"Okay," they answered in unison.

"As much as I hate to end the peace and quiet, I'd better wake Stud," Dr. Grayson called back.

"Don't do that!" Breathred yelled, jumping to stop her.

But it was too late. Before he even got the words from his mouth, she shook the chimp awake.

"Estelle, you frosty vixen," Stud moaned, half asleep.

"Oh my God!" Dr. Grayson exclaimed, glancing over to see what the chimp was talking about.

Breathred didn't have to look. He already knew. Shame riddled his face. Why did he have to own the only chimpanzee in the world with a *Golden Girls* fetish? It wouldn't have been so bad if the darned chimpanzee's libido weren't so vocal about his depravity when the little devil first woke up.

The doctor averted her eyes while the monkey stood up and stretched. "That! That! That is the most indecent thing I have ever seen in my entire life. And I watch Cinemax."

Breathred wished he could die. Luna's giggling didn't make it any better, either. He reached over and grabbed his jacket from behind her and tossed it over him. It was too late, but maybe he could minimize the more embarrassing aftereffects.

"I'm going to stop at the Mounty station, and I don't care which one of you changes seats with him, but I refuse to share the front with him for the rest of the trip," Dr. Grayson said through clenched teeth.

"Hey, Toots. Did you take my banana? I'm sure it was between my legs when I went to sleep, Stud grunted as he scratched his ass.

"That's it!" Dr. Grayson yelled, slamming on the brakes.

Stud flew into the windshield. His head left a small crack, before he rebounded into his seat. "Hey! Did you get your license from a gumball machine? You could have killed me with a stunt like that?" Stud snapped.

"You shouldn't have taken your seat belt off, you perverted little beast," Dr. Grayson growled, refusing to look at him.

"I wouldn't have taken my seat belt off if you hadn't stolen my banana."

Dr. Grayson's hand grabbed the chimp by the neck. She slowly dug her fingers into the furry flesh and pulled him toward her until they were nose to nose.

"I'm only going to say this once, so listen close. I have not touched your banana and will never touch your banana for as long as you and I both live." Her voice trembled.

"Why didn't you say so in the first place?" Stud whimpered and she released her hold on him—reluctantly, Breathred couldn't help but notice.

Breathred took in the whole exchange with resigned shame. By now he should be used to Stud and his ways, but every day brought new challenges to his already beleaguered sanity. When Stud's head popped over the seat, Breathred knew he should just jump out of the van before it could get any worse, but knew he wouldn't. Breathred was nothing, if not a glutton for punishment.

"Breathred, see if Luna has any Midol. I think we're looking at a total PMS meltdown up here," the chimp whispered.

"Stud, just shut up and sit down for the love of heaven, before she throws us out and we have to walk all the way back to Seattle," Breathred warned, looking to make sure Dr. Grayson hadn't overheard the chimp.

"Why the hell, should I shut up? She's the one crazed on hormones trying to kill me."

"I don't care. You either sit down, or by God, I'm calling the vet about a vasectomy as soon as we get back."

"Okay, but I'm calling Al Sharpton first. This is another case of the white man, keeping the primate down. He'll organize a million monkey march on your ass," Stud said, before sliding back down in his seat.

Breathred was grateful for the silence that reigned for the thirty minutes it took them to finally reach the checkpoint. For most of that time, Breathred was bopping Stud in the head every time the chimp started to open his mouth. When he missed one, he was glad to note Luna was more than happy to fill in for him. Between the two of them, Stud was nursing a head full of aches when the Mounty came to their window.

Breathred sat up, as Dr. Grayson rolled the window down and handed the officer a stack of papers from over the visor.

The Mounty leafed through the papers. "This all looks to be in order." The officer let them wait while he wrote the information on his clipboard.

"Do you need to see our passports officer?" Dr. Grayson asked.

Breathred could tell she wanted to get as far from there as possible. He did, too. Stud was getting fidgety. All they needed was for him to go on a rampage now. There were international consequences to take into consideration.

"No, ma'am. All the information was in these forms, but you will be asked to show them on your return. So, make sure to keep them with you," the officer replied politely.

"Thanks, Dudley Do Right. Now, can you hurry this up?" Stud said, leaping into Dr. Grayson's lap. "I got to take a wicked poo."

The Mounty fell back, his clipboard dropping to the ground in his shock. He squinted into the car window. Stud stuck his tongue at him, sending the man sprinting toward checkpoint station.

Breathred fell back into his seat, followed by everyone else in the van. He just knew they were going to jail. No, not jail, prison. There was a difference. In jail you could make bail. In prison you did your best not to get Shawshanked in the shower.

"Stud, can't you behave for once in your life?" Luna reached over the seat and smacked him across the back of the head.

"Hell, I got to shit! What do you want me to do, crap on the dash?"

Breathred caught sight of the Mounty returning with another in tow. They were in for it now. He sank down in the seat waiting for the cuffs. Let Luna beat Stud all she wanted. It wouldn't change the fact, he was about to become jail bait for some man named, Skillet.

"Miss, would you all mind stepping out of the vehicle?" The new officer opened the door for Dr. Grayson, while Breathred cringed in the backseat.

None of them said a word as they got out and walked around to where the mounties stood. Even Stud was subdued, which Breathred thanked God for. The chimp's mouth had gotten them into enough trouble without adding any more time onto their sentences.

"Dr. Grayson, we feel it only fair to warn you it is illegal to enter our country with a falsified passport," the first officer said.

"Sir, I assure you every piece of documentation is correct. No one is trying to enter Canada illegally."

"Then how do you explain him?" The Mounty pointed to Stud.

Dr. Grayson threw her hands in the air. "To be honest with you, I can't."

"We thought as much. Normally, we would have to detain you, but seeing as how we're such big fans, we're willing to let the matter drop for a photograph and autograph from Mr. De Vito." The officer smiled.

"Say what?" Breathred said in disbelief. Luna grabbed hold of his arm. He wasn't sure if it was to keep her from laughing or him from falling to the ground in tears.

He pulled a digital camera from his pocket. "We just want our picture taken with the great Danny De Vito. We know he's probably trying to keep a low profile, but we can't help ourselves."

Breathred couldn't believe it. Sure, he was short and hairy but Stud was no Danny De Vito. Heck, he wasn't even Clyde from those silly Clint Eastwood movies. It was a good thing there was a border between Canada and the U.S.A. Otherwise everybody would be on whatever these guys were taking.

"Out of my way. My fans await." Stud pushed his way past Breathred and Luna.

Breathred winced as Luna dug her fingers into his arm and burst out laughing. He wasn't sure but if Luna kept it up she was going to pee herself. To be on the safe side he moved a little to the left.

"Now, be sure to capture my right side. No, my right. This isn't England, boy. Wrong side of the road entirely. Now, Jethro, who should I make this out to?" Stud asked, sounding like an unconvincing Louie De Palma.

"Steve, Mr. Devito. Could you put 'To my best bud, Steve'?" The Mounty asked.

Stud gave Breathred a sly wink. "Sure thing, Jethro."

That was as much as Breathred could stomach. He walked back to the van and leaned against the side. Thankfully, far enough away from Stud and the Mounties he couldn't hear what they were saying. Breathred wasn't sure he could listen to any more without throwing up. There would be no living with Stud after this.

Twenty minutes later they were on their way again. Stud sat smugly in the back next to Luna. Breathred would have sat with him, but the chimp's smug jibes had driven him into the front seat, even before they left the checkpoint.

The van rolled down the road. The other vans and the U-Haul filled with the rest of the team and equipment were close behind. After a while it seemed they were the only four vehicles on the highway. That suited Breathred just fine. He had much to mull over. Least of which was a chimp with an inflated ego.

Luna was drifting off to sleep again. Her sudden sleepiness was beginning to worry him. Ever since they started on this little trip, she had been acting funny. No, that wasn't true either. Luna started acting funny last night after she came back from wherever it was she went for the whole day.

Despite what she said, something was up. As much as Breathred wanted to ask, he wouldn't. She had the right to keep some things secret. Who was he to say she couldn't? Breathred had a whole houseful he was doing his best to keep locked away.

The sudden emergence of his past was the other thing worrying him. Seeing Jessica at the team get-together had been a shock. The woman knew more about him than the friends he trusted with everything—everything but the truth. Stud didn't even have a clue about what had happened to him and why he was the way he was.

His father had an idea, but had never questioned him when he came home from Oxford. R.J. was just glad to have his son home. Glad to have him home safe would have been closer to the truth. His father might be gruff and vocal about his son's shortcomings, but he still loved him.

Breathred had sworn never to look back. For the most part, he kept that promise to himself. Now, he was all but forsaking his promise for a girl. But even that wasn't true. Breathred was forsaking it for THE GIRL. After the past few days Breathred could see she was the one for him, not that he would admit it to her just yet. He still had some male pride. It wasn't much, but it was enough to keep his mouth shut for the time being.

Breathred just didn't know if he could be the man she needed. Face it. He was a geek. Not just a geek, but the king of all geeks. What kind of girl loved a man like that? Sure Luna cared for him, but love? He just couldn't see it.

Luna was beautiful, smart, and funny. The way her eyes twinkled made him feel things he had never felt before. Things Breathred wasn't even sure were legal. He'd seen the way other men looked at her at the Jumper. She had to know how beautiful she was. So, that begged the question—why was she with him?

Blue lights from a passing bus highlighted his face, etching his pain in the window. Maybe, he should just accept the time Luna was willing to spend with him. She made him feel good, better than good. He deserved a little happiness, right? For the first time in his life Breathred felt invincible, and she made him that way.

Breathred knew it probably wouldn't last. Still, he could convince himself it would. He had convinced himself of stranger things, and they came true. If he was really good, maybe this would, too. God, Breathred hoped it did, because the thought of losing her was more than he could stand.

~ * ~

Leopold looked out the plane's window. They had just crossed into Canadian airspace. He felt a momentary twinge. The chosen sacrifice was below them. Well, not directly below. By now the virgin was ten miles behind them, if not more. Damn, planes moved too fast for him.

The vampire missed the days of week-long trips through the peasant-infested villages of Europe, stopping for the night, and getting a quick bite off some buxom lass with her corset cinched up so tight her nipples poked you in the eye when you bent down to feed. God, those were the days.

Those days were behind him, thanks to Lewis and the revelation. Who knew cinema could change a man's outlook so irrevocably? To this day the sight of Tim Curry still made him go weak in the knees. Leopold must remember to send his featured selection in to Columbia House so he could own *Rocky Horror* for his very own and not be troubled with the garish displays prevalent at the midnight showings.

Which brought him back to his original point, now, you didn't know what you were biting. He once bit this marvelous creature only to discover it was a woman. A woman! After that, he avoided flannel with a passion.

Scanning the cabin, Leopold found the dreadful Easily woman asleep in her seat. Her senseless prattle had almost driven him insane, like he cared anything about her trivial concerns. The sooner he had no further use for her, the better.

Lewis and Dr. Truehart were talking in hushed tones. Leopold could have listened in if he wanted to, but lacked sufficient interest to bother. Lewis was still on his shit-list from earlier. He would forgive him eventually, but for now Leopold preferred to let his anger stew. The boy had a lot to learn about the master/vamp-in-training relationship. Leopold was growing tired of the tedium of the whole project.

Truehart, on the other hand, was intriguing. The man was the perfect balance of brains and passion. Given time he could shape up to be the perfect addition to Leopold's little family. But there could only be two—a Master and an apprentice. No, wait a minute, that was Sith Jedi. He always got them confused. Damn George Lucas and his *Star Wars*!

Leopold's eyes shifted back to the blackened window. In less than three hours he would be one step closer to the Mother. Marcus was wrong. Leopold did know what the Mother was capable of. He just didn't care. He wanted this—wanted the power the rebirth of the Mother promised.

For too long Leopold had hidden in the shadows of the night, like a frightened beast. The others might be content to live like mice, but he wasn't. Vampires were born to rule this world, not run from it. Marcus had forgotten that. Leopold wasn't about to make their mistake. That was why he was going to be a king and Marcus would be the footstool he wiped his feet on.

The mental picture brought a smile to his face. Sometimes it was good to be an evil son of a bitch.

Twenty One

Beware the urge to face the unknown alone. There are always enough people who are more than willing to go along for the ride.

"I'm not joking. I really have to poo," Stud whined from the backseat.

The chimp had been complaining for the past fifty miles. Now that Breathred thought about it, he'd been doing it ever since they had left the Mounty checkpoint at the border. Stud had said something about it at the station before the whole Danny De Vito debacle. Maybe, the nasty beast really had to go. Stud did suffer from irritable bowel syndrome from time to time.

"Pipe down, back there. I refuse to stop until we get to the motel," Dr. Grayson grumbled before Breathred could speculate on the matter further.

Stud reached over the seat to give her head a quick tap to illustrate his point. "Look, lady. If I don't see some porcelain soon, I won't be responsible for what happens. You know what I mean."

Breathred looked over at the chimp. Stud wasn't fooling. His face had a scrunched up look to it and he was doing the one legged jig he reserved only for special occasions and the odd Bar Mitzvah. Stud's bowel situation wasn't the problem though. The real problem would be convincing the good doctor of the fact. Before he could open his mouth Old Stankful blew.

"Oh, my God. Roll down the windows," Luna gasped, as an explosion reverberated from the back of the van.

Before the words finished leaving her mouth, the cloud of methane hit Breathred like a steam engine going full tilt. His nose hairs curled at the foul stench permeating the entire interior of the mini-van. Sucking in what little clean oxygen he could, Breathred rushed to roll down his window on the off chance Stud happened to let loose a second booty barrage.

Once the first wave of nausea passed, Breathred looked over to see Dr. Grayson was doing her best Fido impression, her head slung from the driver's side window, as she too gasped for clean air. The wind whipped her hair so wildly, he wondered how the woman could possibly see, let alone drive. The truth be told, his eyes were burning so badly he could barely see her himself.

"Stud, what did I tell you about eating convenience store egg salad sandwiches!" Luna exclaimed, as she fanned the air back toward him.

"It was either them or the pimento cheese, and I hate how they smell on my breath," Stud grabbed the pine tree hanging from the rear view mirror and waved it toward the back of the van.

"Well, I don't like how the other smells on your ass."

"Luna! Language, please!" Breathred shouted, his voice shrill with his shock and displeasure. Sometimes the things that came out of that girl's mouth would make the Devil himself blush. Didn't women know how to act like ladies anymore?

"Oh, just give me a break. Can't the three of you act like normal human beings for five minutes?" Dr. Grayson asked, rounding out the dissension.

Breathred sulked up against the window, not even daring to look in her direction. He could tell after three hours of *I've got to poo*, she was bordering on a nervous breakdown—if she wasn't already having one. Stud could be a handful, but in the chimp's defense he did have to see to his bodily functions. Breathred wasn't sure how much longer the chimp could hold out. He just hoped Dr. Grayson's mood improved and the professor stopped at the next gas station she saw. He didn't even want to think of the damage monkey poop could do to the rented upholstery.

When the van pulled off the highway fifteen minutes later, Breathred let out a sigh of relief.

~ * ~

Luna stood under the harsh lights flooding the convenience store parking lot. While the others rushed toward the store, she had elected to remain outside and watch the vehicles. Breathred had suggested staying with her, but she told him to go. Luna smiled at the relief that flooded his face. She knew him well enough to know that somewhere in the store; a Twinkie was calling his name.

Walking around the yellow and black gas pumps, Lunarealized just how glad she was to be free of the van. She hadn't been on a trip this lengthy since coming to Seattle over a year ago. Luna hated it then, and this jaunt was no different. If anything, it was worse. At least then she had the excitement of college to drive the demons from her mind.

Luna had hoped after Uncle Joan had readjusted her medicine bag things would be different, but they weren't. The closed-in confines of the van were just too restricting. Her heritage rebelled against being enclosed in such a small space. Her spirit self needed the freedom of the outside world and made her body suffer along with its imprisonment.

Her thoughts drifted back to those early days of being in Seattle. They had been both a blessing and a curse. The gray streets and buildings loomed over her every day, driving the sky away with their built-in gloom.

The first few weeks in the big city had been the most frightening of her life. Nothing at all was like the home she had always known. It had been like crash landing on an alien planet.

Then, Luna found her salvation. If it hadn't been for the parks and forests that bordered her adopted city, Luna wouldn't have been able to stand the thought of staying in Seattle. At least once a day she had to taste the freedom of the grass licking at her bare feet, the feel of the wind as it brushed through the trees touching her face. Only then, did she feel at one with herself.

The van voided all those feelings. Breathred's presence wasn't even enough to make the claustrophobia endurable. Her every instinct told her to run into the wild northern woods that surrounded the gas station. Her soul burned to run among them. Luna looked forlornly at the thick forest just beyond her grasp. Luna could feel the closeness of home in the world around her. The smell of the pines and firs filled her with a homesick feeling she hadn't felt in a long time. Luna nearly wept as it overwhelmed her.

All too soon she would have to get back in the van and they would be off again. Breathred had been watching her, worrying. Luna had seen him casting glances at her ever since the border checkpoint. His concern had poured off him. She loved him for his concern, but there was nothing he could do. This was one battle she had to fight on her own. Thankfully, the darkness had hid much of her pain from his notice. She would snap out of it, but for the time being she wanted to sulk for lack of a better word to describe how she felt.

She looked around, as she heard them exit the store. They were grouped together, her group and the ones from the other vans, in a huddled bunch. It was hard to see Breathred in the crowd, but he was there. She could sense him.

The bond between them because of the new talisman was growing stronger. Uncle Joan warned her it would. She just hadn't realized how much it would affect her. Luna wondered if Breathred could sense it as well. Could he tell how she felt? What did she feel? Luna had to dampen his worry down a notch before he went all puppy dog on her.

As the crowd parted, she put on her happy face. Luna didn't know who she was trying to fool more—Breathred or herself. Either way, it was necessary.

"Hey, Luna. Look, they had caribou jerky," Stud said, running up to her. He flashed the most inedible thing she had ever seen in her face, like it was the most important find since the Rosetta Stone.

"That's nice, dear." She hoped he wouldn't ask her to try it. The thought of taking even a small bite of the foul concoction made her tummy do a belly flop.

"Luna, I got you a Slurpie," Breathred said, tentatively. The others were already in the vans, but Luna could tell he didn't want to leave her sitting out here all alone.

"Thanks, sweetie." She took the cup. Her lips took a hard tug on the straw. Watermelon, her favorite. Breathred always remembered her favorite.

"Something wrong?"

"I'm just tired, Breathy. That's all." Luna sighed.

"If you're sure," he said.

"We'd better get in the van. Stud's sucking the window," Luna said, taking his hand and giving it a quick squeeze.

Breathred swooned slightly at her touch. It was like a jolt of electricity ran through him, as her fingers brushed against his. That had never happened before. For one brief second, he almost thought he could hear what Luna was thinking, but the concept was ridiculous.

Breathred allowed her to lead him back to the van. Against her better judgment, Dr. Grayson must have let Stud return to the front seat. That was okay with Breathred. He wanted to be close to Luna. Didn't know why, but he did. Somehow Breathred felt she needed him, instead of it being the other way round, as it usually was.

Protectively, he wrapped his arm around her. Luna nestled herself into the crook of his arm, laying her head against the side of his head. It felt good to have her there. More than that, it felt right—like she belonged there.

For the first time in a long time, Breathred was content. His being was at one with the cosmos. She was the reason for this new awareness. His brow knotted. Despite what he thought earlier, he wouldn't ever give her up. Breathred could see that now. If he did, Breathred knew he would surely die from the lack of her. He swore then he would protect her with everything he had—with his very life if need be.

Breathred laid his head atop hers. As Luna snuggled up into the protection of his body, the sound of a low satisfied growl escaped her pursed lips. Smiling, he tightened his hold on her, not wanting this moment to ever end.

~ * ~

Leopold stepped from the plane in a foul mood. Between the turbulence and the company he had been forced to keep, the vampire wished old man Stoker had been right. Leopold would have given anything to be able to turn into a bat, a wisp of smoke—anything was preferable to the agony of forced enclosure with cretins. Lewis was just as bad as the humans. The younger vampire acted almost like them when he was around them. It was irritating.

Leopold was finally free of them. Well, not exactly free, but he didn't have to smell them all over him. That was the important thing. Two cars awaited them at the front entrance of the hangar on the desolate airstrip. He would happily place Lewis and the two professors in one car, while he blissfully rode in the last car all by himself. It would be sure ecstasy.

Twinklings of snow filtered through the ebony night. Damn it! No one said anything about snow falling in Canada. The one thing the vamp despised more than polyester was snow. Here he was surrounded by it. Someone in his research department was going to hear about this as soon as he got back home.

Leopold always liked to be well informed before traveling to new locales. That way, if he didn't like the weather, he could be prepared for it. When confronted with such things, he tended to change his plans all together. Thinking back, he never once saw the word snow mentioned in any of his briefs. Leopold couldn't even remember seeing the phrase wintery precipitation. Now, he was forced to accept it without an Armani jacket to make it bearable. This sucked serious ass, as the obnoxious Hilton child liked to say.

Lewis came up behind Leopold. "Boss, the trucks are loaded."

"Lewis, did you know it snowed in Canada?"

"Sure. Everybody knows that." Lewis scratched his head. "Why, what's wrong with snow?"

"And you didn't feel the need to share such pertinent information with me?"

"Look. Chill, man. It's gonna be okay. We'll get you some winter togs and you'll be fine. Leopold, you seriously need to take it down a notch."

"It's snowing you imbecile. How much chillier do you want me to get?" Leopold tapped the younger vampire on the forehead.

"All I meant was calm down. We can work through this, as long as you don't wig out on me."

"I am calm. Now, since I can't change the weather I will deal with it. That is what nobility does," Leopold said strolling toward the car.

How dare Lewis intimate he was anything less than calm? He was the epitome of calm. He was Belgian, for the love of heaven. Unlike the French, Belgians knew how to be composed under pressure.

Leopold jumped in his limo and slammed the door before Lewis or the others could follow. As the car pulled away, Leopold flipped him the bird. He knew it was vulgar, but after all he had been through, a little vulgarity was called for.

The freedom to express one's ire with colorful non-verbal expressions was one of the few things of the modern world that truly thrilled him. In his day who knew the middle finger could invoke such derogatory feelings in your fellow man? It was empowering in its simplicity. Just raise your finger and insight a riot. Leopold found himself doing it sometimes just to shock old women driving slowly in the fast lane.

His need to be vulgar was neither here nor there. More important things needed to be contemplated at the moment, finding a good clothing store, being at the top of his list. Then, he could worry about Dr. Grayson and her team. Leopold checked his watch. 11:27. Damn, he doubted anything would be open at this time of night, except for a chain store. He would not shop at a chain department store. Heaven forbid he should ever stoop to something as mundane as retail shopping with yokels.

He'd call his solicitor and have the man get him something shipped up. Something from New York would do nicely. But, until then Lewis was so sleeping in the doghouse.

The ringing of his cell phone jarred him from his thoughts. Leopold fumbled for it in his bag on the seat. He flicked it open, fully expecting Lewis to be on the other end.

"Leopold, there is still time to end this foolishness," came Marcus' grating voice.

"Marcus, have you nothing better to do than stalk me through the auspices of T Mobile?" Leopold laughed to hide his discomfort. How had the old fool found him? The vampire wasn't in his top five.

"This is deadly serious, my old friend. The Lords are prepared to move against you if you don't stop this frivolity."

"Let them. Soon, not even they will be able to move against me," Leopold said, growing angry.

"I pity you your senility. To think my old friend has succumbed to such a human frailty."

"The only frailty I hear comes from your feeble mouth. Don't darken my phone again with your dire warnings of doom. The best thing for you to do is to stay out of it. When I come to power, I will spare you from the purging to come," Leopold advised, before hanging up on the elder vampire.

Well, wasn't this great? Not only did he have to worry about Lewis' stupidity, now the geriatric squad of the damned was breathing down his neck. This night couldn't get any worse.

The car pulled up to a red light. Leopold looked out the tinted window. A reindeer was standing at the crosswalk. He stood corrected. It couldn't get any worse, but it definitely was getting weirder. All he wanted was one night where the universe wasn't against him. Was that too much to ask? And, would it be too much to fucking ask for it to please quit snowing?

Twenty Two

Beware of long drives. The tendency to obsess over the inane is highest at this time. Keep your mind focused on the important thing—not looking stupid when you die.

(*Authors Note: Due to the tedium of automobile travel, I regret to inform the reader the remainder of the trip is not located within this volume. Besides the self-deprecation was more than I could stand. So, to speed things along we will begin this chapter as we enter the campgrounds leading to the dig site. If any of you have a problem with that, tough shit.)

Breathred woke to find sometime after he fell asleep, his head had become wedged between the seat and the van's window. He'd still be asleep if it hadn't been for the fevered dreams that had fueled his rest.

Breathred wasn't used to such things. Sure, the occasional rampaging nun might pop up from time to time, but nothing like what he just experienced. For one thing he couldn't ever remember wanting to be a dog. Yet there he was in the middle of the forest chasing the moon through the high trees. His fur bristled, as the wind washed over him. It felt good. More than good in fact, it felt right.

The strange thing was Breathred knew even while it could only be a dream he wasn't the wolf. The wolf in his dream had been female. Of the wolf's sex, Breathred was certain. He knew it to be true because his nipples hurt from the cold, all eight of them. From there things got worse, or weirder depending on your point of view.

Breathred could smell a male in the woods, his/her mate. The scent drove all other thoughts from his mind. He had to find his/her mate. Everything depended on it.

The knotty pines and redwoods flew past him as he ran. The world was a blur around him. Still, he ran. The scent was too strong to ignore. The blooding moon sang and he had to answer it. The time of mating had come, and nature would not be denied.

The forest thinned, Breathred saw the mate standing in a clearing and his anger flared. This hairless scarecrow couldn't be his mate. Where was the majesty of the wolf? Where were the claws and teeth that marked his protector? This MAN was none of those things. The very thought of the aberration in the hallowed role filled his lupine heart with anger.

In a single bound, his wolfen form cleared the forest. As stealthy as any cat, he crept across the matted pine straw and struggling saplings. The sound of his paws crunching the dry carpet of the forest floor brought the man's head up. The man turned and faced him.

Breathred the wolf drew up. His hackles rose at the impossibility of the sight that greeted him. It was him. Not the mate he had been chasing, but him, Breathred the man stood facing him. The horror of it drove him from his sleep.

A sudden pain jerked his head up. His neck was crooked in an impossible position and Breathred couldn't be sure, but he thought his face might be frozen to the window. Tugging his head slightly, Breathred's lip peeled away from his teeth, but that was as far as it went. Yep, he was frozen in place. A thin line of spittle ran from his mouth to his puckered chin. The drool must have freeze-dried his face to the window while he slept. Nothing short of a lip-ectomy would get him loose, now. Man, where was everybody? This was starting to hurt.

Breathred fumbled around with his left hand, hoping maybe Luna was still asleep beside him. A few seconds of useless grabbing told him she wasn't. He couldn't even hear Stud's nasally snores.

This was just great. He was all alone with his face glued to the window in the middle of the Canadian nowhere. All he needed now was for little green men to pop up at the window, and Breathred could be reliving his ninth grade Civics class.

He reached down to open the door. The handle clicked up but gave no sign of opening. Stud must have hit the child locks before he left. The stupid chimp always did that. Breathred felt like a Chihuahua trapped in a mid-sized sedan at a Wal-Mart parking lot. Since he was obviously stuck for the time being, he had better come up with something more constructive than sitting here like a goob.

Breathred strained to hear any sign that he hadn't been totally deserted. From the looks of things it wasn't a bad bet to take. It took him a couple of minutes, but he was able to hear voices off to the right. Breathred pricked an eye open—luckily the one that hadn't succumbed to the same fate as his lower jaw. Through the squinted lid, he could make out a crowd of people grouped around a bank of cabins.

So, they had made it to the Eh Ya Campgrounds. That was a relief. After the way Dr. Grayson had been driving, Breathred was beginning to think this was hell and he was paying for looking at Sally Mc Alistair's panties in kindergarten. He couldn't help himself. Sally threw her dress over his head in the sandbox. It was either look or plant his face in a freshly laid pile of cat poop. Thinking back, he should have taken the poop. To this day he still wasn't sure what he'd seen, or why the nuns had been so upset over it. He thought the Care Bears were cute.

Whoever was out there, Breathred had to get their attention. The last thing he needed was for some wandering bear with a working opposable thumb to come along and have Breathred under glass for morning brunch. The problem was how to get their attention without looking like a total dweeb. Somehow, he didn't think it was normal for a vampire slayer to be found frozen to his car window. It just didn't seem proper for someone in his profession.

Surely, one of his friends would have to come back and check on him. Luna wouldn't leave him out here. At least Breathred hoped she wouldn't. His grasp on the finer points of the female psychology were still rudimentary at best. For all Breathred knew this could be all a dream and he really was a female wolf sleeping in the woods. His life was strange enough he couldn't completely rule out the possibility.

Breathred jumped as he heard a roar come from the crowd. What was going on now? The sound of trampling feet swept past the van. Good, they were breaking up. Somebody was bound to find him now. He just hoped it wasn't Stud.

~ * ~

Luna stretched. She didn't remember nodding off, yet here she was dead on her feet. She must be more tired than she thought. Luna moved away from the rustic fence she'd been using as a makeshift bed. Snot-wallop, she couldn't even recall just when she fell asleep. She'd probably still be asleep if it wasn't for her weird dream. Luna couldn't remember all too much of it. All she could really see was a lot of sand and a freaking Care Bear. If that wasn't weird, she didn't know what was. She had been a Strawberry Shortcake girl.

Luna idly fingered the medicine bag hanging around her neck. The smooth leather felt warm to the touch, despite the chill air. She wondered if the dream could be a result of the spell Uncle Joan had worked upon the bag.

She was beginning to feel Breathred's emotions. Being inside his dreams wouldn't be too much of a stretch of the imagination. That couldn't be it, Luna decided. What would he be doing dreaming about a Care Bear? That wasn't true either. He was weird enough to be dreaming about the Care Bears. The only question that bothered her was why would he be dreaming about them?

Luna shook her head. All this was getting her nowhere, except confused as hell. Her feelings for Breathred shouldn't be making her so crazy. He was just a man. Oh yeah, just a man, right? Breathred was THE man. The man who completed her was nearer to the point.

Uncle Joan's spell had made the connection between them stronger than it otherwise might have been. Luna had known there would be side affects. She just hadn't figured she and Breathred would be sharing a brain because of it.

Well, Uncle Joan had warned her not to go into this lightly. Luna hadn't, either. Breathred was the One. Even he was beginning to realize it more and more each day. Maybe in hindsight, she had rushed into it a little bit, but it was for a good 'cause. Otherwise she would have had to stay behind.

Even worse, she would have had to return home. The thought filled her with dread. Returning home meant Luna might never see Breathred again. Knowing that, she would have done anything. Anything! Even telling him the truth was preferable to never seeing him again.

Luna stepped away from her thoughts. They were getting her nowhere but lost inside herself—a place she had no intention of lingering. Besides, Breathred must be awake by now. She couldn't think of what was keeping him bottled up in that stinky van.

Taking one last look at the forest, she turned and almost fell over at the sight of Breathred's face squished against the window of the van. Was his lip glued to the window or what? Luna squinted a second time to make sure she wasn't seeing things. Yep, he was actually glued to the window.

Luna immediately looked around for Stud. This smacked of his devious mind. She was going to kill that primate. No, he was over talking to one of the Graduate Assistants. If this were one of his schemes, he'd be here to exploit it. For once, this one was all Breathred's faux pas.

Look at him. Wasn't that the cutest thing? He looked like a goldfish with his face all puckered like that. Luna fought the urge to make kissy faces at him. He wouldn't like it. She had better get over there and get him loose before Stud had a chance to see what was going on.

Luna meandered to the van nonchalantly. She poked her head over the top of the van. Having made sure the chimp was none the wiser, she bent down to talk to Breathred.

"Honey, are you okay?" Luna whispered into the glass.

"Meb lup dis froob," he muttered in reply. His eyebrows rose dangerously on his forehead, making him look, like a frog through the frost-distorted glass.

"Give me a minute and I'll have you free," Luna said, giving the glass a kiss where his lip was glued.

Luna rubbed the glass with her warm fingers until the frost was gone from the outside. Then, she cupped her hands over his lips and blew onto the glass. Within seconds it warmed enough for Breathred's lip to loosen from the window. It took relatively no time to slip free.

"Tank du," he said. His lip was still numb and dry from the experience. He pointed toward the door handle. "Dud, tit de tilddoks."

"Sure thing, sugar," Luna said, deciphering his new language. She popped the front door open and hit the button on the panel, opening his door for him.

"Me lib turts," Breathred pouted, stretching his cramped limbs upon exiting the van. His fingers touched them tenderly to show where they hurt.

Luna couldn't help herself. She stood on tiptoe and kissed them, surprised to feel him return the lip embrace. She was more surprised to hear a low growl come from him. It was a low guttural sound, enough like a wolf's to send a shockwave down her spine.

Her eyes snapped open to find his staring into hers. They were his eyes but something else was behind them. They were wild, almost bestial. His sudden change frightened her, more so because it mirrored her own hidden thoughts than anything else. She seriously had to talk to her uncle when she got back to Seattle.

Luna was the first to back away. The gravel parking lot separated them by a few inches but it felt like miles, years—the time that existed between the kiss and the forever it promised. Luna sidled away, unsure of what had just happened. The sound of Stud yelling their names further pushed the distance between them. For the first time since they'd met, Luna was scared—scared of him, scared of the way she felt. Not saying a word, she turned and ran toward the yelling chimp.

Watching her go, a wave of shame washed over Breathred. Suddenly, he felt dirty all over. Breathred had never felt like that before, but he liked it. Liked the touch of her on him. The smell of her filling his nostrils was like the nectar from the gods, or the smell of freshly minted comic books. Breathred wasn't entirely sure, but he thought he might have just felt his testicles dropping.

Twenty Three

Beware of locals; they can be even weirder than the usual crowd of creatures of the night.

As the day wore on, Stud grew tired of watching the pair of lovesick fools. Breathred kept to himself for the remainder of the day. He avoided even the most basic of eye contact with Luna. She did her best to do the same. Stud had noticed their comedic attempts at melodrama but kept his opinions to himself. It was no skin off his nose how humans preformed their mating rituals. If they wanted to ignore each other for a while, that was alright with him. All that kissy-kissy stuff was quite frankly making him sick to his stomach.

Not to say, Stud wasn't worried about the whole thing. Being lifted from his real family at an early age had traumatized him so that no amount of therapy could hope to correct it. After so much misery, the chimp found himself loath to lose the new family he was in the process of raising.

Stud's past wasn't even the real reason for his worry. To tell the God's honest truth, he put a lot of effort into training Breathred up and would hate to see the big goob blow it. Hell, he knew whatever the problem was it sure as hell wasn't Luna's fault. The girl wasn't the type to screw things up. Breathred, on the other hand, excelled in such things. If things weren't set right soon, he'd just have to see to matters himself. It wouldn't be all that hard. He'd got them this far, hadn't he? Right now, Stud had important things to do. Well not important, but anything was better than being a party to their adolescent mooning.

Stud skirted the brooding pair on his way to the team meeting. The guide from the Canadian Archeological Cultural Agency had just arrived to brief them on the do's and don'ts of their excursion. As if he was in the mood for another lecture.

As an advanced form of primate, and not some lowly human, Stud couldn't see the sense in sitting down for a prolonged speech guaranteed to bore him into a coma. Besides, apes didn't settle things in committee. They threw shit and screamed at each other until it was all over but the crying. Anything not settled by then, you ran off, like a scared hyena. It was a sight more civilized than anything the so-called human race had come up with in three thousand years.

Seeing as how he had given his word to behave as long as they were trapped in this Canadian wilderness, Stud would be a good little boy. All bets were off if he had to listen to the word 'eh' more times than was necessary in the course of a normal conversation. It wasn't that he was a cultural bigot. Unnecessary pauses during a conversation led to the eventual breakdown of the esoteric balance of harmony in the universe. Aside from that, it made his ass itch.

Stud glanced back. The morose twosome fell in behind him. Good, if he couldn't irritate on a grand scale, he could at the very least agitate them enough to hopefully make them forget this funk they were drowning in. If that was what love did to people, Stud was damn glad he hadn't found someone to pick the fleas off his back.

The cabin was cramped with all sixteen team members bunched together. He wormed his diminutive body through the mass of bodies and took a seat in the back row. Stud wasn't enthused to find eight more people crowded around the side wall. They smelled of bear funk, which made his sinuses do belly flops. From the looks of them, he guessed they must be the yokels Dr. Grayson said would be joining them as laborers. Man, and he thought Breathred's relatives looked inbred.

"Everyone, find a seat. Mr. Brogan will be here in a moment to brief us on the regulations set down by the Canadian government, so get ready to listen." Dr. Grayson's eye automatically aimed toward Stud. "And no goofing off in back."

On the general principle of the matter Stud stuck his tongue out. Let her stick that in her snap, crackle, and pop. He may have to behave but wasn't dead.

Stud chuckled when he noticed Dr. Grayson was ignoring him. True, he was just trying to get her goat, but he had given his word to behave. Stud would too, as long as he could manage it before gagging on the boredom. By his watch that gave him about five minutes and thirty-seven seconds before blowing his internal Tourette's fuse to hell and back. Which for him would be a personal record. Almost.

The room grew quiet. Stud raised up in his seat trying to see what was causing it. Apparently, so was everyone else, because all he could see was the back of some lard-butt's head. Stud toyed with the idea of a Vulcan nerve pinch, but let it go. The last time he tried it Breathred voided his bladder, but didn't go to sleep. Damn, Leonard Nimoy's lying ass.

It wasn't long before the room again broke out in a wave of hushed mumbles. Stud still had no idea what the hell was going on. Saying to hell with it the chimp pushed his way through the seated throng. He made his way to the front, paused briefly to shoot lard-butt a one-fingered hello. Hey, how good was he expected to be? A chimpanzee had his limits after all. He made it to the front, just as the Canadian official began to speak.

All right, for you purists out there I'm about to step outside the usual voice of this story. Sure some of you might say bad form or some such drivel. But, seeing as how I'm the monkey at the keyboard driving this thing, I figure I can pretty much do what I want. If stepping from a third person narrative to a first person one is my idea of telling the story, that's my prerogative, the Bobby Brown one, not the Brittany Skanks one.

But really, you would have had to see this guy in the flesh to understand why I'm doing this. I'm a good three foot nine in my bare feet and this freak of nature wasn't much taller than me. He was maybe five foot zero, even with his boots on. If that wasn't enough to make you think Darwin was on the right track, he looked more like an ape than I do.

And he was wearing flannel with thermals sticking out from the arms. My God, flannel. Could you ask for a more clichéd look? The hair. The guy's hair was sticking up like wings on either side of his head with the biggest pair of chops cropping his face I'd ever seen. The whole thing looked like somebody had, *Something about Mary*-ed his entire follicle system.

So basically, what we have here is a sawed off runt with bad hair and a flannel fetish. Did I forget to mention the cigar? Well, if I did, I'm sorry. He was chomping, not smoking, the biggest damn cigar I've ever seen. It was big enough to make White House interns run in fear.

Okay, I've said my piece so you all can return to the story and stop looking for my editor to hang for letting me get away with this. Oh, and get a life. If the worse thing you got to bitch about is the voice of a fricking book, consider yourself lucky. I'm due for my monthly flea dip, tomorrow. Top that, you silly bastards.

"The name is Brogan, bub. Not Mr. Brogan. Just, Brogan," the little man began, drawing more than a few chuckles from the crowd. He snarled but went on. "It's my job to keep you alive and in one piece. Canada is more than hockey pucks and maple leaves. Half of what you'll find in the wilderness will kill you; the other half will make your pants go all squishy, if you know what I mean."

"Well, yes. Uh, Mm—" Dr. Grayson started to say. The man gave her a blood-curdling glare that stopped her in mid-mister. "I mean Brogan. I'm sure we all would love to hear more of your colorful anecdotes, but could you get straight to the regulations from CACA? The time is growing quite late, and I'm sure we'd all like to get settled in. It's been an extremely long trip."

"Sure thing, Toots. Here's the low-down. If I say it's all right, it's all right. If I tell you, no can do, you better stop before I rip your arms off. Is that clear enough for you?" Brogan grinned. "If not, I can draw some insightful diagrams to enlighten you."

Stud rocked back in his seat, grinning from ear to ear. Now this was a man after his own heart. The same family tree, from the looks of it, too.

"So if that's all wrapped up, what say me and you go grab a brew and think about some horizontal Macarena, good looking?" Brogan patted Dr. Grayson on the bottom.

"Mr. Brogan!" Dr. Grayson exclaimed in a high-pitched shriek. "That will be quite enough of your suggestions. Thank you very much."

"No offense intended, Sweet Cheeks. But I feel it only fair to tell you nine out of ten dental hygienists say I'm the best at what I do." Brogan smirked.

"What about the tenth one?" Stud yelled out. He couldn't help himself. It was just too damn easy.

"His name was Bob," Brogan snarled. He clearly wasn't in need of a straight man, nor did he want one, but what did Stud care?

"Bob what?" Stud yelled back. God, this was better than a triple banana frappe with a mocha twist. Just the look on ol' Doc Grayson's face was enough to see him through many a cold night.

"Bob up and kiss my ass. Now, shut the hell up," Brogan answered. He then turned to Dr. Grayson and snapped, "Could somebody tell that hairy-ass little kid to shut the hell up before I smack his momma blind for having relations with her brother?"

That was it. Sure a joke was a joke, but the freak has just gone too far. International relations be damned, that sawed-off shit-eater had pushed the limits of good taste. Anyway, his father was a third cousin at the very least. Okay, there was an off chance it was really his Uncle Herb, but the tests came back inconclusive.

"Look here, you maple-wrapped pygmy," Stud growled, as he rushed the stage.

"Who, the hell, are you calling me a pigmy, monkey-butt?" Brogan growled back.

"Unless you got a mouse in your pocket, I guess we can narrow it down to you."

"Okay kid, I'm about five seconds from pulling down your Osh Goshes and teaching you some manners." Brogan bent down to shove his cigar firmly under Stud's nose.

"That's it. Ain't no way in hell some Canuck shit-wad's gonna teach me manners. Hell, this country hasn't even learned what bacon looks like. Let's take this outside before the women folk see you get your ass handed to you," Stud said, slapping the cigar straight up the Canadian's nose.

~ * ~

Breathred was used to Stud's tantrums, so at first was not really all too concerned. Most people usually laughed at the chimp's rantings and left him to his own devices. From the looks of this hunk of meat, that wasn't going to be the case. Breathred made a beeline for the bristling pair. He cleared the circle of spectators to find Luna had beaten him there.

"Break it up, you two," Luna ordered, pushing them apart.

"You the kid's momma?" Brogan asked, giving her more attention than Breathred thought decent, especially the roundy bits he, himself, did his best to ignore.

"No, I'm not. I'm his friend," Luna said proudly.

"That's a relief 'cause, if you were, I'd have to double up on my little soldier before we played sink the puck."

Before Breathred knew what was happening, he decked the man. Even decking didn't cover it. It was more correct to say he slammed his fist so hard into the man the guy rebounded off the back wall. It was a toss-up on who was more surprised—Breathred, Stud, Luna, or Brogan. The fact Breathred was drooling and couldn't stop looking at his balled up fist, made him the safe bet.

Twenty Four

Sometimes you have to show the locals who's boss. Otherwise they'll walk all over you.

"You got knocked the fuck out!" Stud howled over the unconscious face of Brogan. "See I told you these Canucks were all talk, no action."

The chimp gasped, as the man's hand shot up and closed around his hairy throat. Through bulging eyes, he looked down to see the man wide awake with a grimace hard enough to crack marble. The man's fingers felt like corded steel, growing tighter with each passing second.

"Okay, Bub. The geek might have got in a cheap shot, but there ain't no chance in hell you're getting away," Brogan promised, spitting a wad of cigar past the chimp's ear.

Stud saw only two ways out of this. Die with the dignity all primates were instinctively born with. The second way was much harder. Put up a fight to end all fights and leave this world like a man. Naturally Stud went with option one.

Brogan dangled the chimp above him, all set to give the beast a good and lasting throttle, when he felt a warm flood drench his chest and neck. Brogan scrambled to his feet, holding Stud well away from him. His faded flannel shirt was now a rich red it hadn't been in a long number of years. The acidic stench of chimpanzee pee permeated the air about them.

"You tinkled on me," was all the burly man said.

Stud swung his body toward the man's face. "You know primates have two functional bladders."

Brogan dropped the chimp post-haste. Stud gave him a wink, backing the official up three steps to avoid the chances of another deluge. The ape may be small, but even toddlers shot for distance. Stud could tell the man wasn't sure if the chimp could back up his threat, and didn't look to be one to taking unnecessary chances.

"They do not. Stud, you behave or I'll stomp a mud-hole in you," Luna warned the monkey.

"It was an accident. He scared me. He's just lucky I got rid of that breakfast burrito before we got here," Stud whined.

"Mr. Brogan, I hope you'll accept my apologies. They assured me he was housebroken." Dr. Grayson stepped in.

"Lady, a pissing monkey is one thing, but that S.O.B sucker-punched me." Brogan's gnarled finger swept the room until it settled on the still-gibbering Breathred. "And this dog ain't taking that."

He took a step toward Breathred, who was still lost in his post-traumatic episode. Brogan got two feet before Luna stepped in his path. The man raised his hand to push her slightly to the left of center. Her eyes locked with his stopping him cold in his tracks. Something in the way she looked at him, made his blood run cold.

"I don't think you want to be doing that," Luna said.

It wasn't anything Brogan could pinpoint, but he believed her. Taking a deep breath, the scent of the girl filled his sinuses. A faint hint of something rode the wave of air. It was a smell he knew from old. A smell he respected enough to give the girl space. There would be time to see to the boy, when the bit of fluff wasn't around to play bodyguard.

~ * ~

Luna held herself in place waiting for the little man to make his move. She saw the debate raging in his mind. She'd hate to back up that threat, but was willing to do it if he pushed her. After all, Breathred defended her. The least Luna could do was do the same for him.

A collective gasp filled the room when the man turned around and walked out the side door. Luna fell back. Dad-gum-it, that was close. She felt Stud's hand on hers, looked down and gave him a smile. Squeezing her hand, the chimp sat down. Luna dropped beside him. Neither noticed the rest of the room empty once it was clear there would be no fight.

"Uh, Luna. Thanks for, well…you know," Stud stammered.

"Forget it. That's what friends are for. Just don't let it happen again. The little guy's trouble in more ways than one," Luna said, wondering just how much trouble he really was.

Stud bent his head toward Breathred, who was still dribbling puddles on his chin. "Sure thing. What are we going to do about Dufus?"

"Why don't you head on out and let me deal with him? I heard Dr. Grayson say they were heading over to get something to eat." Luna smiled.

"If you think you'll be alright," Stud said. From the look on his face he clearly hoped she would be. Luna knew his looks by now to know the chimp was famished or at least thought he was.

"Go on. Just be good. I won't be there to save your bacon this time."

"You got it," he said, running for the door.

Luna watched him go in a detached sort of way. She suddenly felt the need to be alone with Breathred. A lot was happening and none of it was his fault, yet she was blaming him. The girl just wished she knew how to make it right again.

She rose from her seat and walked over to Breathred. He was in the same position he had been in since decking Brogan. Breathred had surprised her by doing it. Except for the mall with those vampires, she had never seen him so much as swat a fly. Luna wished she could attribute his actions to his undying love, but was realistic. Breathred was not a man ruled by his emotions, unless it came to comic books. No, he was just defending his friends against harm.

Sure, he'd agreed to be her boyfriend, but love was different. She loved him. Luna made no bones about admitting her emotional attachment. Breathred, while he felt something for her, was not ready to admit undying love. Luna knew it, but a girl could dream.

And daydreaming was all she was doing. One day the dream would come true, but not today. She had better get Breathred unwound. The goob was going to run out drool, if she didn't.

"Breathy, baby. Snap out of it." Luna popped her fingers in front of his face.

~ * ~

Breathred heard her, but was unable to respond. He had hit another human being. Not in the 'Hey there's a Volzwagon, slug bug' way but had lashed out in pure, unadulterated anger. He had never done something so evil before. Breathred might have wanted to, but never had. But, when the man said that dirty, dirty thing to Luna, he'd flipped out.

Breathred couldn't stand the thought of anyone talking to her that way. You could almost see the man's filthy little parts tingling as he spoke to her. Still, it was no reason to punch the man. You were supposed to act civilized, not resort to brute force to inflict your will.

But, it had felt so good. Breathred could still feel the crunch of the man's cheek against his knuckles. There was even the crunch from bone breaking when the fist connected. No, he had to stop thinking like that. It wasn't good. It was bad. Bad Breathred! Sister Marie Angelle said bad Breathreds went to h-e-l-l. He sure didn't want to go there. His skin burned so easily.

"Breathred, look at me. You have to come out of it. All you did was punch a creep, that's all," Luna cried in his ear.

Her tears broke the spell. Breathred slowly turned to her and found tears of his own running down his face. "I didn't mean to do it. He just made me so mad, when he said those things to you."

"It's okay, Sweetie. I know you didn't mean to hit him, but thank you for doing it."

"You're not mad at me for being a brute?"

"Of course not. I thought it was quite nice to see you defending my honor." She stroked his cheek.

Breathred smiled, wiping his nose with the back of a hand. "You did?"

"You're my boyfriend, now. It's your job to do things like that."

"It is? I thought women didn't want you to do that nowadays."

Luna reached up and wiped a stray tear from his cheek. "Those girls are crazy. I'm more the romance novel heroine type. I can take care of myself, but it's nice to know I have somebody looking out for me."

Breathred beamed. "I can do that."

"I know you can, that's why I love you," Luna whispered, kissing him lightly on his quivering lips.

"Luna, I uh, well you know."

"Yes, Breathred," she said, her voice a husky whisper in his ear.

"I, uh, think we better go find Dr. Grayson. She's probably sore at me for hitting poor Mr. Brogan."

Why had Luna had her nose scrunched up that way? She looked almost frustrated. Breathred hoped it wasn't something he said. For a minute there he'd been so close to making a fool of himself by saying something totally inappropriate. Breathred wasn't sure what but was sure he shouldn't say it quite yet. For some reason Breathred knew Luna wanted him to say whatever it was. Before this little adventure was over, who knew what could happen? Breathred might even figure it out before Luna told him what he was supposed to say.

~ * ~

Leopold stood at the opulent bay window and watched as the last of the evening's snow drizzled to a stop. The vampire was glad to see the end of it. All this white goodness was frankly getting on his nerves. Leopold guessed he didn't have much to complain about. It hadn't accumulated or anything.

It was still the principle of the matter. In a few short days he was to become one of the princes of the new world—the only prince, if Leopold had anything to say about it. How dare the weather not co-operate with his grand scheme!

Leopold thought about killing a weatherman or two to settle his frazzled nerves. He would have, but they tended to be pudgy and dressed in polyester blends. That would have clashed with what his current color scheme, so dismissed the idea as being too horrible to contemplate. Besides, bad taste in clothes might be contagious. It was best not to chance it.

It was half past eight. The sun had been down for a little over two hours. By this time, Lewis should be rendezvousing with Easily and Truehart at the dig site. He could have probably left the two scientists to their own devices, but thought it better to have his companion check up on them.

His plans were coming together and Leopold was hesitant to risk their failure to the human factor. He might have to depend on his human agent to get things done while he slept, but it didn't mean he had to trust the mortal completely. It was too much to ask.

Lewis would have to be his go between. Not that he trusted the youngster all that much, either. The youngster was still too human himself to be totally dependable. In a century or two that might not be the case. It took a couple of lifetimes before a vampire realized his place in the world. Lewis was still at the potty-training stage.

So, the great Leopold du Chambris Portus sat and waited while the game was played out beyond his control. For now the vampire contented to be the chess master. As long as his pieces did as ordered, that would be the case until the time of his rise finally came.

Leopold sat by the roaring fireplace, fumbling with the flowing cuffs of his shirt. He could have been thinking many majestic thoughts at a time like this, but wasn't. The only thought that dominated his mind was the unanswered desire for a cup of hot cocoa with those colored marshmallows floating on top.

Twenty Five

After a good night's sleep, everything looks better, especially if you're alive to wake up and enjoy it.

Breathred woke fully refreshed. It was like the preceding day had never happened. He rolled over and saw Stud was still asleep. That gave him about an hour of uninterrupted peace and quiet. Breathred looked up at his alarm clock. It read 7:32 in the blessed a.m. On second thought, Stud would be asleep for another two hours. The chimp hated to get up before ten, eleven thirty if he could manage it. Today, like the day before, would be an exception. According to Dr. Grayson's schedule, they would be heading to the dig around noon. By his figuring, he could wake Stud by eleven and still have time to whip the monkey into shape for the short hike to the site.

Breathred threw his lanky legs over the side of the bed. A half-hearted yawn followed him to the bathroom. He tried not to scratch his itchy parts, but couldn't help himself. He looked around to make sure Stud was really asleep, and the blinds were closed. Once sure he wouldn't be caught, Breathred reached down and hyper-scratched, keeping one eye on the window. Even though he knew it was a necessary function, doing it still made him feel dirty for touching himself in such an unladylike manner. He just knew there was a nun with a ruler hiding behind the bathroom door, ready to pound him. It was irrational, but a solid Catholic education was a hard thing to shake.

The urge to yell *Naked Nun, Naked Nun* and run around the room almost paralyzed him to the spot. Breathred sucked the impulse down into his brain, as far as he could knowing if he didn't he would go blind. You didn't mess with nuns. They had ways to make St. Peter look at you funny when you went to see him.

Finishing his business, Breathred crept to the bathroom door. He pushed it open with his socked toe. The light was still on from his last trip to bathroom at about three a.m. He checked the floor for any nun-like shadows. None revealed themselves so it must be safe. Dog-gone it, the shower curtain was closed. He would just have to risk it. Breathred drew the paranoia line at nuns hiding in showers. That would lead to other more disturbing questions, like what did nuns wear in the shower? That single impure thought would send him to hell alone.

Breathred shambled over to sink and stared at his reflection. It shocked him. When did he get so old? Tiny lines wormed their way from the corners of his eyes. If wrinkles weren't bad enough, he was beginning to grow his father's wattle. When did that happen? By the time forty rolled around he'd be a turkey from the neck up. The thought was so depressing Breathred didn't even floss after brushing his teeth. He was just thankful male pattern baldness wasn't an issue. If it ever become one, they could just put him in the ground and call him Petunia.

The mirror must be lying. It was shoddy workmanship somewhere. No, it had to be the fact that it was a Canadian mirror. They just weren't up to the high standards the American government required of those made in the good ol' U.S.A.

Feeling better about it, Breathred went over and hastily finished his morning ablutions. He did such things with both eyes closed. Again, fear of nuns prevented him from looking at those parts of his anatomy that could possibly lead to blindness, hairy palms or eternal damnation. It never hurt to be cautious with such things.

Leaving the bathroom, Breathred hastily dressed. After spending the whole day in the cramped mini-van he felt the need to be out in the open, yearning to smell fresh, unpolluted air. He grabbed his heavy jacket from the chair beside the door and left Stud snoring blissfully in the darkened room.

For some reason he wasn't surprised to see Luna leaning over the handrail outside the cabin. She always was an early riser. After his episode the day before, Breathred didn't know how to approach her. She was still the same girl, but he felt different. Somehow, he wasn't the same man who had left Seattle less than two days ago.

Sure, he was still the same on the outside, but inside he felt not the same. It was hard to explain. Luna had changed him. Breathred knew for a fact, he wasn't about to change on his own. The would-be slayer liked who he was, or at least he had. Now Breathred wasn't as confident of that statement.

Breathred wanted to be a hero, like one of those guys on the covers of Kinley MacGregor novels. All right, his dark secret was out. He read romance novels. Breathred never went to Target to get them, not even at the run down used-book store, where he bought his old Sci-fi books. Breathred had the good sense to buy them online and used Stud's credit card to pay for them.

But, there it was. He yearned to be a roguish, dashing man. Breathred wanted to be the type of man who swept women off their feet. No, he wanted to sweep one woman in particular off her feet. Breathred was surprised to hear such a revealing thought rolling around inside his head, but knew it was true. Luna made him feel like one of those men. Just by looking at him, she made him feel like a Malory or a MacAllister, instead of the klutz who was afraid to look at himself naked, let alone allow a woman see him in such a condition.

Breathred coughed softly so Luna would know he was here. She turned and gave him a warming smile. He walked over to her and leaned down beside her. She took his hand into hers. For once he didn't pull away. Her hand was cold. He brushed his other hand on top of it, cradling it until it warmed under his touch.

"You better stop that or people might begin to think you're sweet on me." She smirked.

Breathred jerked his hand back and looked around for innocent bystanders.

"You mean you're not sweet on me?" she asked with a sullen pout.

"Well, you know I am. No, I didn't mean that."

"Then, I had better find me another vampire slayer," she said, throwing her hand across her brow.

"You better not."

"Then, you are sweet on me?" She prodded.

"If it stops you from throwing yourself at some total stranger, then I am sweet on you."

"As long as you realize you were the first one to say it."

Breathred wasn't sure, but he thought she was hiding a smirk behind her hand. Breathred stopped dead in his tracks. Wait a minute! She was. Not only that, she had tricked him. He wouldn't have said that, if she hadn't. He might think it, even feel it, but it was highly unfair for her to make him say it. The tactic must be against the Geneva Convention or something. What else she could make him admit to? It was the most sobering thought he had ever had.

"So what you doing out here so early?" Luna asked.

"Guess I was excited about getting started," he said, guardedly. "Couldn't stay asleep, so I decided to come outside for a little fresh air."

"Me, too, Breathred." She paused. "Do you think we'll really find this vampire mother?"

"Yes. Vampires had to come from somewhere. Boffrend doesn't even explain why they're here. Something about this seems like it's the real thing. Call it intuition, but I think the Mother is out there in these woods. Ever since we got here, I've had this tingling at the back of my head telling me she's out there."

"How do you know it's not just wishful thinking?" Luna asked in all seriousness.

"After we fought those vampires at the mall, it's like my mind became attuned to them. A part of me can feel them moving in the world around us. Just like at the meeting the other night. I could feel the wrongness in that Leopold guy. It screamed to me, saying this guy ain't right. I wanted to go after him and tell him he didn't belong here," he explained, as he looked at the thick tree line that bordered the campground.

Luna took his words in. For the first time she realized this wasn't a game. She could get hurt. More importantly Breathred could get hurt. Or worse. There was always a worse. Why hadn't she thought this through?

She looked back to Breathred. He was still lost in his own thoughts. He looked different. The naiveté was gone from his face. A hardness had replaced it.

How much of that came from the bond between them? Was her meddling with her own spirit affecting him? No, he'd had the same look in the shoe store, when they were attacked by those vamps. It could only mean this was something to do with his vampire slayer thingie. But that shouldn't have anything to do with the way he was acting.

If you became a doctor, you didn't stop being goofy. You were just a goofy doctor. Right? When this thing was over, she would get to the bottom of this. The only thing that should be able to change her Breathy was her.

"Say, you want to go over to the dining room and see if they have any cherry pop tarts?" He asked in his normal goofy voice.

Luna smiled. There were some things you just couldn't change. "Sure, they might even have some Fruity Pebbles."

"Ya think!" Breathred exclaimed.

Luna could see a thing line of drool forming in the corners of his mouth.

"If they don't, we'll just have to go find some. There's no way I'm going into the Canadian wilderness without some good old fashion junk food to start the day," Luna assured him.

"We could get some powered milk, too. I like powered milk." He grabbed her hand and dragged her toward the dining room.

"I know you do, but let's not go crazy."

Okay, Breathred might not be perfect, but he was as close as she wanted to get.

Twenty Six

Getting there is only half the battle, but the easiest part of the whole damn thing.

After breakfast, Breathred didn't have much time to think much about Luna, sparking, or the fact he might be sweet on anybody. Dr. Grayson had announced her decision to leave early to avoid any more unpleasantness due to Stud and his altercation with Brogan of the day before during his second bowl of cereal. Breathred got the idea the professor was more worried the Canadian representative would have them all deported for bringing an unlicensed chimpanzee into the country. Whatever the case. At promptly 10:47 they headed out.

Breathred was no stranger to walking. Except for the occasional bus ride, he walked all over Seattle, from one end to the other. But this hiking was totally different. For one thing the forest wasn't paved. Not that he had given it much thought, but at the very least, they could have put down some heavily packed gravel to match the rustic surroundings. There was none of that. If the uneven path wasn't harsh enough, there were tiny acorns hidden among the slippery pine straw littering the path. Even through his thick hiking boots, the tiny nuisances were making mincemeat of his feet. Why couldn't they have some of those ATV's or at the very least a few pack mules? Leopold might be an undead bloodsucking fiend, but he could have forked out a few more dollars for a little more convenience. Breathred wasn't one to grouse over a hardship or two, but sore feet were an exception to any rule.

They had been trampling through this gnat-infested jungle for three hours. How could it be cold and there still be gnats flying around? That had to go against the laws of nature. But who did you report that sort of thing to? Mother Nature didn't exactly have an e-mail address. If she did, Breathred hadn't been able to find it. Over the years, he had been having some serious doubts about what Michael Jackson was doing to himself and wanted some answers. For all his time and effort, all he'd been able to find was a site called mothersnaughtynature.com. In all honesty, he couldn't find anything remotely connected to mothers or nature. The place was full of women wearing barely anything. In some cases nothing at all. It was all so disturbing he forgot the whole thing. If Mother Nature wanted to talk to him, she could find him.

Wait a minute! Breathred's thinking process jumped-started into overdrive. His mind wandered over to some fact he wanted to make sure of. Yes, he knew what insects in winter meant. Skirting out of the procession, the slayer plopped down beside the first tree he came to.

~ * ~

Luna noticed him squatting on the ground and angled back to see what was going on. When she caught up to him, Breathred was digging in his backpack. He had scattered its contents all over the ground in his search. She thought about asking him what he was doing, but knew how her boyfriend was when he got his mind wrapped around something. She just eased herself down beside him. The last of the group crested the rise and disappeared down the sloping hill. Well, she'd waited long enough.

"Breathred, what are you doing?" she whispered. Once when they had first met, she had tried yelling to get his attention, but that had just frightened him so badly he forgot what he was thinking. It had taken him fifteen minutes to remember his own name, so after a period of trial and error she found whispering in his ear achieved the desired effect.

"I'm looking for something."

"I can see that, but what are you looking for?" Why did everything have to be pulling teeth with him, when he got into his moods?

"Have you noticed there are a lot of insects flying around?"

From the sound of his voice Luna felt she should know what he was talking about. Well, she didn't. "Yeah, but it's the woods. Bugs live in the woods." Along with birds, rodents and snakes, but Luna didn't feel the need to say any of those things. It would only distract him from telling her what he was up to.

"But it's below thirty degrees. At that temperature they should be in hibernation, or dead," Breathred explained, absently while still digging in his backpack.

"You're right, but it still doesn't explain why you're sitting down when we should be following the rest of the group."

"Because of this," Breathred beamed, holding up his Boffrend handbook.

Damn, he was sitting on the ground—wet ground she might add—looking for a makeshift fly swatter. She should have known it would be something silly. With him could it be anything but?

Luna waited patiently while he thumbed through the book until Breathred found what he wanted, then pushed the book into her face. "According to Boffrend, insects swarm around the lairs of the undead."

"So, you think the insects are here because of the Mother's tomb!" Well, she'd learn not to doubt him. He might be goofy, but had his moments.

"Stands to reason. If the Mother's as powerful as the tablet says, she would be a magnet for them and any other loathsome beast that lives off the carrion of evil."

"What is it supposed to mean?" Luna asked in a worried voice. Okay, vampires she could handle, but if there were any type of insect that may or may not be pre-deposed to crawl about her person, she was all for going home.

"That there may be things worse than vampires loose in these woods, feeding off the power the Mother projects. We would be well-advised to be watchful."

"Hello there, stragglers!"

Both of them jumped from where they sat. Luna looked up to see Edmund Truehart waving at them from the top of the hill. Breathred motioned for Luna to keep their talk to herself. She nodded and they strode to the waiting man.

"I thought you were already at the dig with the equipment?" Breathred asked, when they reached the archeologist.

"The camp is on the other side of that rise." The Englishman pointed over his shoulder. "Dr. Grayson sent me back while she got everyone settled in. She was kind of worried you might have gotten lost."

There was a smugness to the man's voice that grated on Breathred's nerves. Ever since the meeting back at the hotel in Seattle, Breathred had wondered why the man looked so familiar. No matter how hard he tried, Breathred just couldn't figure out where he knew the archeologist from. It was like the annoying feeling you had, when you knew the name of one of those old actors in a movie, but the only name that came to mind was Walter Brennan. No matter how hard you tried to force the name on the person's face, you just knew it wasn't right.

Luna threw her arm around Breathred. "No, we just stopped for a quick snuggle."

"Well, yes... erm..." Truehart stammered.

"Erm, indeed," Luna snarked, popping her eyebrow nearly to her hairline.

"Dr. Truehart, as you can see we're quite all right," Breathred broke in, knowing when she started doing Spock, there was trouble brewing. Best to nip it in the bud before anybody got hurt: namely Dr. Truehart. "But we would appreciate you escorting us the rest of the way."

"Be happy to," Truehart answered. Breathred could tell the man was glad to be free of Luna's freezing glare. "You know the site is quite exciting, even in its raw state."

"How so?" Breathred couldn't help but ask. He loved a good mystery.

"Well, Dr. Easily and I have been here since yesterday morning and just our preliminary scan of the area has unearthed some outstanding discoveries. We found several pottery shards predating anything unearthed in this region before. If I'm correct, they may even predate the Incan and Aztec ruins in Central and South America!"

"But, it is a well-known fact the Native Americans indigenous to North American were here at the same time as those peoples. To find artifacts that predate those other cultures isn't too spectacular. The common theory is the entire shooting match came over on a land bridge in the Bering Sea." Breathred's comment drew a puzzled stare from Luna.

"Yes, but these artifacts prove this northern culture had a written language before either of their southern relatives did," Truehart answered back.

"That's impossible. The northern peoples used no written language. Their histories were passed down verbally. If you're right, this would totally change history as we know it. At least where this is concerned."

"That's what I've been trying to tell you," Truehart said.

Breathred mumbled under his breath and walked past Luna and Truehart, who had stopped to watch him. After less than twenty paces he stopped too, and turned around.

"My God, what if this site is proof the theorized link between the Egyptians and Incans was true?"

"I believe that was one of your less idiotic theories. Wasn't it, Petrifunck?" Truehart asked in a haughty voice.

"Excuse me, but do we know each other?" Breathred asked, totally ignoring the jab. He had finally given up trying to figure it out on his own. It was hurting his brain. Besides, Truehart knew the answer, so why not let him give it, since the man wanted to, anyway?

"Not personally, but you were a classmate of my brother Reginald,"

"That's it. I've been trying to sort it out for four days. Thank you ever so much. You just don't know what a load that is off my mind," Breathred said, wiping an imaginary bead of sweat from his brow. "Where is Reginald now?"

"He's dead. He died at the Shrine of the Seven Veils to be exact." Truehart's voice was cold and hard.

"Yes, that's right. Must have forgotten it."

"I think you can find your way from here. It's just past that tree line. I need to check the outer perimeter. If you have any trouble, just yell. Someone from camp should be able to hear you."

With that the archeologist strode into the forest and disappeared. Luna watched him go. She didn't know what had just passed between the two men, but it was enough to shake them both. For the first time Luna realized just how much she didn't know about Breathred. She had just always assumed he'd lived his entire life in his father's basement. Now, it appeared she was wrong. He had gone to school with Truehart's brother, which meant he had gone to school in England, or somewhere other than Seattle. She seriously doubted a Truehart would go to a college anywhere in the U.S., let alone near Seattle. And, let's not forget about Slutty MacSlutty, Jessica Easily.

What did this all mean? What else was Breathred keeping from her? No, that wasn't fair. She had never asked him about his past. So, he wasn't hiding anything. But he wasn't forthcoming with any information either. Now that she thought about it, Breathred never talked about himself. The closest he came was rambling on about whatever had caught his childlike fancy. The more she thought about it, Luna doubted even Stud knew much about Breathred's past.

Silly twit, just ask him.

She couldn't do that. What if he didn't want to tell her anything? She wasn't prepared for a brush-off, or a big fight. Breathred was just now beginning to come to grips with being her boyfriend. She really hadn't scheduled a fight for at least a few more months. It was always best to let men think they were in charge of things before hitting them with the hard truth of the matter. Her mother had been quite adamant about that fact, which was a good lesson to learn and helped explain why her father was hiding out in parts unknown to this day. Apparently, Mother was a little late learning the lesson herself.

Luna knew what to do. She would arrange a quiet word with Stud. Nothing that would reveal she was searching for anything specific mind you, just a few general questions. The last thing she wanted was to let Stud know anything was up. All she needed was a suspicious Stud running around. The chimp had a big mouth and would run straight to Breathred, asking all the right questions at the wrong time. Luna would have to be subtle with them both. How hard would it be to fool a monkey and a man? She was a woman after all.

Twenty Seven

Looks can be deceiving—you never know where the bodies are buried and when they'll get mad at who's walking on their heads

The site was nothing like Luna expected. It all seemed rather ordinary, like a recently buried trash heap, only with fewer beer cans sticking out of the muck. She expected something, you know—grand. Luna wasn't thinking pyramids or anything, but something more than nearly-flat ground with a few pine trees peeking through. She couldn't see any evidence anything had ever been here at all except for two stone pillars sticking up from the earth at odd angles across. Even they looked like nothing more than two plain rocks.

Breathred, on the other hand, saw it for what it was: un-panned gold. Beneath centuries of earth, a whole civilization awaited them. He could see the possibilities for knowledge lying at their very feet. After what all he'd heard from Dr. Grayson, the thought scared him.

He was afraid even to touch the ground. Breathred had no idea, what kind of evil the Mother of all vampires might have pumped into the earth over the years, but it couldn't be good. He knew from the Boffrend handbook evil had a way of infecting everything around it. A three thousand year old vampire's corpse was a large amount of evil with a lot of time on its hands. For all Breathred knew, this whole place could be a giant sponge for the darkest power the earth had ever seen.

Or, he could be overly paranoid. The thought had occurred to him. From practical experience Breathred found there was no such thing as being overly paranoid. Overly crazy, yes. Overly paranoid, no. As one of his many therapists told him after a grueling session—crazy you could cure, or at least control, with the proper balance of chemicals. Paranoid was with you for life, or until better chemicals came along. For the amount of money R.J. had been paying for that sage advice, Breathred tended to believe the man's statement.

His gaze wandered back over to the clearing the team had inhabited for the time being. It was alive with activity. The site had been sectioned off into three areas. A row of tents was being set up for living quarters to one side. Stud was helping a pair of undergraduates set them up. Slightly to the right stood the main tent the team would be using for the documentation of any artifacts they found. It would also act as a radio base for contact with the authorities in case of trouble.

Finally, encompassing the remainder of the area was the main dig. Drs. Truehart and Easily had already set up a grid over the space. It was from there the team would split into individual groups to cover as much area as they could before they were forced to leave.

The setup was pretty much standard operating procedure for these things. The main hope was they would find what they were looking for in those grids already laid out without having to redraw another grid in a different area. They had only five weeks to uncover the tomb before they would run out of funding.

Dr. Grayson's last dig found the antechamber, but sediment and storms had erased the evidence of the discovery in the time since she had left. Even the homing beacon she planted during her earlier excavation was gone. So, basically, they had to start from scratch.

It was like the land didn't want the tomb to be found. Maybe Breathred was reading too much into it. Vampire slayers tended to do that. Living in the supernatural world, you saw ghosts behind every tree and vampires under the bed. That's why his box spring sat securely on the floor and there was a padlock on his closet door.

Luna grabbed his jacket sleeve and pointed toward Dr. Grayson, who was making her way toward them.

"Good to see you two. Guess Truehart found you, okay. Where is he by the way?" she asked breathlessly.

"He went to check the perimeter," Luna answered. Breathred could tell from the sound of her voice she, like him, hoped the man wasn't in any hurry to return to camp.

"Good. There have been several animal attacks, according to the locals who have been watching over the site for us. He spent the day setting up early warning sensors," Dr. Grayson explained.

Breathred shot Luna a knowing look, then changed the subject, "It looks like the camp's already in shape." He saw no reason to let Dr. Grayson in on his suspicions until he had more proof.

"Yes, it is. Doctor Easily has worked wonders. Hasn't she? With Doctor Truehart handling the security measures, I was afraid we'd be behind schedule."

"When do we start excavating?" Luna asked. Breathred was happy to see her getting excited at the prospect.

"Tomorrow, first light," Grayson said with a huge grin.

Breathred watched the activity going on below them. "Do we just pick out a grid and get started?"

"I've already got them assigned, but that's just for those already marked out. Drs. Easily and Truehart will head the teams, while the three of us and Stud will concentrate on the area around the stone pillars," Grayson explained, pointing to the twin daggers of stone. "I can't be sure but I think they may be all that remain of the temple discovered during our last excavation. The storms over the past years have been strong enough to destroy everything but those pillars which I believe to be the columns that held the roof aloft."

"What about the statues and wooden box?" Breathred scratched his head.

"There is evidence of fires around the pillars, so I can only assume a lightning strike reduced everything made of wood to little more than ash. It isn't uncommon for fires to go unchecked in this isolated an area. I'm just surprised it didn't spread any further."

Breathred wondered if it was a natural 'cause or something more sinister covering traces of the Mother after Dr. Grayson's last visit. "How can you be so sure it's the right spot? I thought you told us earlier the marker was gone."

"I can't be. Those pillars are the only things I'm basing my assumptions on. They weren't here when we left the site three years ago. As a totally new development, I'm all the more convinced this is the right spot. Call me crazy, but I can't help but feel like the site itself is showing me where to look," she said.

Breathred had his own thoughts and none of them were good. This whole line of thinking was disturbing, because in his heart Breathred knew Grayson's assumption was true. For whatever reason the area went to such lengths to hide itself before, the site seemed to want them to find the tomb now. Or more importantly, The Mother wanted to be found and she was more than willing to show them the way. At the heart of this fact were the twin monoliths under whose shadow they'd be working.

Breathred couldn't break his eyes away from them. He felt as though their shadows were licking at his soul. Pure and simple, the two stone columns gave him the willies. The sun moved from behind a bank of clouds, framing them in darkness against the dark green line of trees. Breathred shuddered, as he suddenly thought of what they reminded him of: fangs rising from the bowels of hell.

Breathred was happy to see he wasn't the only one captured by their spell. Both Dr. Grayson and Luna were staring at them, intently. He had better break this up before they formed a religion and drank tainted fruit punch.

"What say we get a closer look at things?" he asked, giving the two women a slap on their backs.

"Y-yes, w-why don't we do that?" Dr. Grayson stammered. She appeared visibly shaken by his touch.

Breathred and Luna shouldered their packs and followed the professor down the path to the camp. Very little vegetation grew past the overlooking ledge that bordered the southern entrance to the clearing. On further examination, the entire space was nearly devoid of life. With the exception of a few stunted pines, nothing occupied the area till a hundred yards from the center of the clearing. Past that, the forest was alive with trees and assorted shrubbery.

Another indication his theory about the vampire queen sapping the life from the area might be true. How long would it take before this entire region looked just like where they were standing? It was enough to make him want to plant some flowers to hide the fact from himself.

Breathred watched Stud detach himself from tent-raising to lumber toward them. From the worn out expression on the chimpanzee's face it wasn't going to be a dull evening.

"Hey, Buds. Decided to miss out on all the work, I see," he all but yelled. He bent toward Breathred and spoke just low enough for Breathred to hear. "Stopped off to kiss and make up, huh? Hoped you used some protection, 'cuz this chimpanzee *don't know nothing about birthing no babies*."

Breathred turned five shades of red before stuttering out, "I would never."

"Don't I just know it? At this rate I'll never get any grandchildren." Stud laughed.

"You know I haven't exactly seen you swinging from any chandeliers yourself, Monkey Boy," Luna said.

Stud poked a finger in Breathred's chest. "Hey, that's not my fault. In that Clint Eastwood flick they at least drugged the orangutan's date to the prom."

"I told you I wasn't slipping ecstasy to that chimpanzee at the Seattle zoo," Breathred said, shamefaced at the very idea.

"No, Mr. Goody Goody, if you'll remember correctly I said just hand it to me and I'd do it. You still owe me for that wasted Viagra. A four-hour pup tent for nothing," Stud griped to no one in particular.

"And where, may I ask, did you get Viagra?" Luna demanded, tapping her toe.

"Same place I got the ecstasy—the Internet."

"Can we please just forget about illicit drugs and fornicating monkeys?" Breathred asked.

"Sure, but she brought it up." Stud pointed at Luna.

"No, I didn't!" Luna shouted.

"Yes you did. I was discussing Breathred's lack of a sex life, and you dragged me into it. Seems to me you're the one with the problem. Not me."

"What problem would that be?" Luna demanded.

"You're frustrated," Stud said.

"I am not!"

"Look, honey. You're a healthy young woman with a boyfriend with the sex drive of a petrified turnip. If that isn't the definition of frustrated, I don't know what is," Stud stated, as cool as you please.

Luna howled before storming off with Dr. Grayson close behind her.

Stud turned to Breathred. "See? Frustration. Most clear-cut case I've ever seen."

Breathred gave the chimp a puzzled look but didn't say anything. That was because he wasn't exactly sure what frustrated meant. From the look on Luna's face the slayer wasn't sure he wanted to know, but sure hoped she found a cure for it—whatever it was. If Stud was right and Luna had it, it looked painful.

Twenty Eight

To get the job done, you have to be prepared to get your hands dirty—or at the very least, slightly dusty.

Breathred watched Brogan sitting beside the dwindling fire. Its orange halo cast dark shadows that all but obliterated the man's face. It was late—too late for anybody to be up. After all the hard work to get here and then setting up the camp, Breathred hoped he'd be the only one fool enough to be up this late. The Fates decided to give him company, and who did they pick? The only guy he'd ever struck in anger, well struck at all. He hoped the man was the forgiving sort, but seriously doubted it. Still, that was no reason to stand here like a goob.

"Er, excuse me, sir. Uh, Brogan, do you mind if I join you?"

"Clamp a log between your ass cheeks."

Breathred sat quietly beside the fire. He bristled under Brogan's scrutiny. Something in the man's eye told him the Canadian was sizing him up. Breathred kept his eyes facing down afraid to antagonize the man any more than he already had. Finally, the silence got to him. Any minute now he would have *say* something or it would kill him.

"I'm sorry about, you know—hitting you yesterday." Breathred nearly jumped at the sound of his own voice. Then what he'd said hit him. Oh great, remind the homicidal Canadian who wants to kill you, that you hit him. Was it too late to run back to his tent for a witness or two?

Brogan looked up and gave Breathred a smile that would have made a shark take to land. "Seeing as how I'm in a good mood, I'll let it slide. You were just protecting your woman, after all. Can't blame a man for looking after a prime piece of real estate like that."

Breathred stiffened but wasn't stupid enough to try his luck a second time. The look on the man's face did make him want to give it a good hard think. Brogan was just trying to get his goat. Well, fool him. He didn't have a goat.

Brogan reached over and punched him in the shoulder. "You know if you don't loosen up, you're gonna blow an artery."

Breathred looked down. His fists were clinched so tight his knuckles were white. He let his hands go slack. The tension eased from his shoulders, but a knot had settled in the back of his neck. It might be the start of a tumor, but he'd have to wait until they returned to Seattle for verification.

Breathred finally spoke up. "I'll take your advice under advisement." It seemed the only polite thing to say, even if it was said through gritted teeth.

"You do that. You can breathe now, if you want." Brogan chuckled.

Breathred let out a gasp of air. "Do you mind if I ask you ask a question?"

"If it'll help you sleep at night, shoot," Brogan poked the fire with a stick.

"Are you just mean, or do you enjoy making people nervous?" Breathred asked.

"Both."

"Well, that's not very nice."

"Never claimed to be nice. Look, I get the job done. That's it. I don't make friends. Making people happy isn't my purpose in life. The Canadian government wants you here and wants you safe. It's my job to see both of those things happen. It's been my experience tourists can't seem to manage either on their own. You, my friend, are proof of that." Brogan jabbed the ember-tipped stick in Breathred's face.

Breathred couldn't dispute his words. Most of the team had never been in the wilderness before. The true archeologists weren't much better. The minute their hands touched earth, they'd forget their own names let alone remember the dangers that surrounded them. Brogan was right. They were babes in the woods, and he was their only protection from the environment and themselves.

Instead of drawing the man into further conversation, Breathred sat in silence. His mind was a maze of doubts. He couldn't back down from this. After failing at so many things, this was his last chance at being something other than a geek who lived in his old man's basement.

As the night gave way to the first streaks of dawn, Breathred gently slipped into sleep with a log for his pillow.

~ * ~

Breathred awoke to the smell of burning bacon. Opening one eye expecting his mother to be fighting smoke at the old family stove, he was relieved to see a boy of about nineteen manning the fire with a flat pan full of smoldering meat. Breathred sat up and rubbed the sleep from his eyes.

"What time is it?" Breathred mumbled, trying his best to disguise his chronic morning breath.

"Half past nine, Doctor Petrifunck," the boy answered.

"I'm not a doctor." Breathred grumbled, wondering what all Dr. Grayson had been saying about him. "Call me Breathred. Where are the others?"

"They're already at the dig site. Mr. Brogan said to let you sleep.

Doctor Grayson took the rest of the team over to the grid to get an early start." The boy grinned, oblivious to the fire shooting up from his frying pan.

"Better watch that pan," Breathred advised, rising from the ground and heading toward the sound of digging.

He stopped by his tent and quickly brushed his teeth before running a comb through his hair. Like the rest of the team, Breathred would have to wait for a good bath until they went back to civilization. He could handle everything but the Porta-johns. His twenty-five can stockpile of disinfectant and hand sanitizer took care of most of his reservations. The rest he filed under *memories to be repressed and to agonize over later.*

It was a short walk to the main grid. On the way Breathred sidestepped the boy who had awakened him. The boy's arm was on fire, and he was streaking toward the small stream that ran through the western edge of the clearing.

Told him to watch that pan. Breathred brushed a stray ember from the arm of his jacket. He stopped long enough to hear the hissing sound of the boy's arm sinking into the stream, then wandered to the site.

Even after all these years, he heard his first professor's voice in his head. "The first thing to get out of your head is the Indiana Jones mentality about archeology."

Dirt wasn't flying from heaping shovels. There was no chanting in rhythm to get the work done. As Breathred looked across the clearing, all he saw were a bunch of bowed heads and knotted backs. The movies painted a picture that was romantic and exciting. Unfortunately, the movie version was as far from the truth as you could get, short of reading a comic book.

The meat of real Archeology was delicate and boring repetition. Shovels rarely came into play. Most of the work was done with computers, thanks to modern technology and military research that had filtered down to the scientific community. After that, the majority of the hard labor was done with brushes and trowels. When shovels did come into play, they were used judiciously and sparingly, so as not to damage any of the finds to be unearthed. Over the years amazing discoveries had been lost due to sloppy handling of the tools of the trade. Dr. Grayson wasn't about to let that happen here, Breathred was happy to note.

He moved through the grid workers, careful not to disturb their work. Most of them paid him no attention. They were so enthralled in the job that he simply didn't exist in their pocket-universes. For the majority, a comet could come crashing to earth on top of them and they wouldn't know it. Breathred gave them a clinched smile and kept on going.

He had seen the most docile of archeologists turn to rabid Chihuahuas, when they were broken from the spell of the dig. Nothing was more pathetic than having to watch a middle-aged balding man foam at the mouth. Breathred had witnessed it firsthand, and it wasn't pretty.

Breathred skirted the rest of the dig-zombies and made a beeline for

Dr. Grayson. The top of her head peeked over a bank of monitors sitting in front of the two pillars. He waited to hear Stud's voice, but it never came, thank his lucky stars. Even the extra sleep wasn't enough of a balm to sooth over the sound of raw chimp voice, the way he was feeling this morning.

Rounding a freshly turned mound of earth, Breathred found himself in something more like NASA ground control than an archeological dig. Three monitors sat on a card table facing away from the pillars. Two keyboards rested in front of them with a third monitor controlled by a device that looked like a cross between a metal detector and a bazooka.

He wasn't surprised to see the huge *gun* in Luna's petite hands. She ran the machine over the top of a freshly tilled patch of ground in the center of the stone monoliths. The device sent a grainy image to the third monitor, where Dr. Grayson was busy tabulating data in a worn-out notebook.

The most amazing thing of all was Stud, manning the other keyboard feeding in Luna's data, as fast as she wrote it down. Breathred had never seen the chimp so serious. All the time Stud spent on the Internet ogling girls and posting love stories under the pseudonym Mistress Spank My Monkie must finally be paying off.

Breathred stepped over a bunch of taped-up wires that ran to the solar-powered generator. He snagged his toe and knocked the edge of the computer table before he stopped his downward slide. His misstep earned him a stern look from Stud, of all people. Dr. Grayson just kept on scribbling in her tablet, not even noticing the flickering screen his clumsiness 'caused. Again he was amazed by academic zombification at work.

"Sorry." Breathred stepped carefully over another bank of wires.

"Oh, Breathred, you're up," Dr. Grayson said, hearing his voice. Before he could respond, she continued, "You won't believe what we've already found. According to the radio telemetry, we're sitting atop a huge void in the bedrock structure."

"Should we move to the other side of the camp, or something?" Breathred asked, stepping deftly to her left.

"No, it means we're over the tomb, Numb Nuts," Stud answered for her.

Breathred scratched his head. "Well, that's different."

"Stud, be nice. Can't you see Breathy's still half asleep?" Luna put the radar gun down and walked over to join them.

"I'll be nice when I get to sleep till noon," Stud snapped.

Luna smacked him on the head. "It isn't noon. It's only nine o'clock. Now shush."

"Look you guys. The telemetry is telling us is there's an open space underneath us. It may not be the tomb. This area's riddled with caves. The void could be nothing more than one of them. Until we can locate the entrance, it's all speculation," Doctor Grayson warned them.

"What did the last sweep tell us?" Luna asked.

Dr. Grayson handed the tablet over to the chimp. "If Stud will feed the last of my figures into the computer, we can see."

Stud hunkered over the keyboard and fed the row of numbers into the computer. He rechecked the data and ran the program. All four heads bent over the monitor waiting for the results. It didn't take long.

In the span of seconds a map flashed on the screen. It was scratchy and blurred along the edges, but clear enough to show a workable schematic of a series of tunnels and rooms that could only be the tomb.

"There she blows. Looks like we have a tomb. Anybody got some popcorn while we wait for the mummy to come get us?" Stud joked.

Breathred was slightly peeved. You sleep late once in thirty-five years and look what happens. You miss all the fun stuff and end up being around for the hard part—the shoveling.

Twenty Nine

Okay you've found the grave. What are you going to do now?

Excitement ran through the camp, like Jell-o through a nursing home inmate. Everybody caught the fever except for one notable person—Brogan. Dr. Grayson was surprised to find he saw the discovery as a headache. Before any digging could commence, he had to radio the Canadian Archeological Cultural Agency, which explained the headache. It seems CACA was the one who had to make the last decision on whether or not the team could actually excavate, now that they had found something.

Dr. Grayson, herself, was distraught over this fact. Like most scientists, she had forgotten to read the small print in the contract. After breaking out a handheld magnifying glass and a miniature electron microscope, they were able to read the negative five-point type at the bottom of the contract. It read simply— "Hey Bub, it's our country. If you don't like doing what we say, haul your ass back to America."

Needless to say, it threw the entire camp into a tailspin. Without CACA's go ahead they were royally screwed. Most of the team retired to the tents, while Dr. Grayson and her handpicked crew waited with Brogan for word.

"So, does anybody want to play Yahtzee, while we wait?" Brogan smirked through a haze of cigar smoke.

"Tournament rules or regular?" Stud chimed in from where he sat on the ground.

"Stud, shut up. Mr. Brogan, is this really necessary? All my documentation was in order before we even came here. If it wasn't, why let us come here to begin with? There is absolutely no need for you to continue with this farce," Dr. Grayson harped. It was enough to make her want to scream. The very idea she wasn't fully authorized to conduct an archeological expedition.

"According to my boss—namely me—you do," Brogan countered.

"What is the reasoning behind this course of action? This is an accredited archeological dig. Surely you can't think we're fortune hunters," Luna interjected.

"Honey, that I believe." Brogan laughed. "Let me be honest with you. I've been on a lot of these little excursions, and I know when something doesn't smell right." He held his hand up before anybody could speak. "It isn't you. It's this place. Something about this mud-hole makes my nose hair itch. Before I let even one shovel touch ground, I want confirmation this place is kosher."

"If you trust us, why hold us up?" Breathred asked. "This is all very confusing."

"Despite our rocky start, I like you all, even the dirty-mouth monkey. I'd hate to see something happen to you. I've learned to trust my instincts, and they tell me to haul ass."

"You don't mean to say you're allowing superstition to impede our work. I thought we were past the age of bogeymen hiding in tombs and ancient curses. Science has come so far since Carter and Tutankhamen's tomb, and I flatly refuse to think that such outdated reasoning is truly the case," Dr. Grayson exclaimed.

"Darlin', believe what you want, but my nose is never wrong." Brogan tapped the side of his nose with his thick finger.

Before Dr. Grayson could reply, the radio chimed to life. The tension was so thick, they all jumped at the static-filled burst. Brogan grabbed the receiver, while they piled in closer to listen.

"Wombat, this is Blackbird, over," the radio crackled.

"Wombat, here, over," Brogan answered back.

"Checked over your inquiry. No sign of extracurricular activity. Proceed with all caution, over."

"Repeat, no sign of extracurricular activity?"

"Checked with CAPP SAT. Area shows no sign of activity. Advise daily reports. Any sign of activity call in task force to contain. Copy Wombat? Over."

"Copy. Over and out." Brogan slapped the receiver down hard on the table.

"What the hell was that all about? The last time I looked we didn't have cheerleaders along, so what was all that extracurricular activity bullshit?" Stud demanded.

"When I called in my reservations, my bosses called CAPP SAT to check things out. If they confirmed my suspicions, I would have packed you up and headed home," he told them.

"Brogan, what exactly is a CAPP SAT?" Breathred asked.

"CAPP SAT's an agency that works closely with CACA. It stands for Canadian Agency for Paranormal Protectorate," Brogan answered.

"What does SAT stand for, Mulder?" Stud snorted.

"Nothing. Some dumb-ass in the publicity department said a government agency needed to end with SAT to look official, so they put it in at the end so it'd look on the up and up. Let me tell you, I'm still trying not to laugh at the millions of political dollars that went into that decision."

"Who the hell would believe something as stupid as that?"

"A politician, who else? I'm just glad the Prime Minister didn't go with the idiot's first choice of names. Thankfully, the *X-Men* was already taken, even the government can't get around copyright infringement."

Brogan leaned back in his chair watching the team debate issues they couldn't change if they wanted to. Damn, the government was finally getting its shit straight, and these Americans were coming in and screwing that up. We'd got Dan Akroyd and Mike Myers firmly entrenched on American soil. Pamela Anderson was none too quietly sleeping her way through the Headbangers Ball, effectively putting Canadian hockey stats on the rise again. Maple syrup sales were on the upswing again after the low calorie craze of the past few years. What more could a Canadian ask for?

Now, all that was in jeopardy. Brogan saw it as a direct result of NAFTA, the proliferation of the importation of American television programs, especially *X-Files*, which was the very reason CAPP SAT was put into power in the first place. Worst of all, if he was right, these Yanks were about to open a can of worms that could make even the Pam Anderson thing seem unsavory.

But, who was he to criticize how they did things? His own government gave them free rein to loose the hounds of hell. He never should have come in from his self-imposed exile in the first place. If he hadn't run out of Double Stuf Oreos, he'd still be in his little cabin, happily ignorant of cellular communications and Internet spam.

But that was not to be. He would learn to mind his own business one day. Sure, right, and donkeys would fly out his ass and bring him a handful of Cuban cigars. Brogan leaned back in his chair and listened to the professor and the other loonies decide when to get started. It was so sad it made him want a beer. Then again, when didn't he want a beer?

"Uh, Brogan. Is it all right, if we plan to get an early start? Most of the day is already gone and there's really no reason to try to start anything this late," Dr. Grayson said.

"Lady, as far as I'm concerned, you can slap a two-by-four up the monkey's ass and play sit and spin," Brogan grumbled, not believing the agency had disregarded his fears.

No, he believed it all right. That's what happened when you let a politician run the show. What happened to the good old days, when a blood thirsty General was head honcho? They knew how to get shit done. Now, you had touchy-feely intellectuals telling you to get in contact with some feminine side you had no idea you even had. It was more than a man could stand.

"Mr. Brogan, are you supposed to eat that cigar?" Breathred asked.

"Shut up. I'm going for a beer. If I ain't back by morning, dig till your ass falls off." Brogan pushed his way out of the tent.

"Well, that sounds like an okay to me," Stud said, picking a matted piece of pine straw from between his toes.

"He didn't sound too happy, did he?"

"It doesn't matter. You heard the guy on the radio. He said we could do whatever we wanted," Luna said.

"No, he didn't," Dr. Grayson said. "He said to proceed, but he also said Brogan has the power to call in a task force. Whatever that means."

"I think it means if old Mighty Mite thinks the bogeyman is coming, he can blow our butts to the moon," Stud said, his voice as serious as death, and as sure as sin.

Breathred felt a quiver turn his noodly bits to Jell-O. He knew with all certainty Stud was right. Brogan wasn't one to jump the gun, but something had the man spooked. Breathred wondered just how spooked they'd all be, if Dr. Grayson was right and there really was a three thousand year old vampire lying under their feet. With cold certainty he knew in the next couple of days the truth would be something they'd find out one way or another, whether they wanted to or not.

~ * ~

Lewis checked his e-mail, while Leopold pranced in front of his full-length mirror. The young vampire did his best to ignore the older one, but it was hard. How could you not notice a white guy dressed in a purple lamé jumpsuit with a feather sticking out of the lapel. The boss man was getting worse. Before long it would look like the Rocky Horror Picture show around here.

A ting from his messenger told him their contact had come through. He surfed through the pop-ups and assorted spam until he navigated the web to his inbox. He could have gone straight to the e-mail, but he didn't. Without knowing it, Lewis had become addicted to getting mail.

Lewis sneaked a look at Leopold. The head vampire was preening over a magenta scarf as he tried to decide whether it clashed with his ensemble, or if he should go with the midnight-blue one. Leo's preoccupation with couture should give him plenty of time to read a few e-mails before he got to the agent's message.

Forty-seven minutes, and twenty-six IMs later, he finally clicked open the message. Lewis ran through the message twice to make sure he read it right. Seeing no sense in rushing into one of Leopold's flights of fancy, he took a minute to gather his thoughts. Once properly steeled for the elder vamp's response, he turned toward his master. "Leo, got a message from our plant."

"Lewis, I told you to never mention that again. My glaucoma has been acting up, and I brought it to settle my nerves." Leopold dropped the magenta scarf in favor of the blue one.

"Dip-shit," Lewis whispered. "No, your inside man has sent word they've located the Mother's tomb."

"Well, that's entirely different! Good. Now we'll see some results.

Have they opened it yet?" Leopold asked, joining Lewis at the computer.

"Not yet. According to the e-mail, it's still buried. It should take about three or four days to dig down to it. We'll get another e-mail when they have it completely dug out," Lewis said, minimizing the screen before Leopold could look at his other windows.

The last thing Lewis needed was for the old fop to read the latest installment of the adventures of Mistress Spank My Monkie. Damn, that broad could write some smut. One day he had to hook up with her. If she looked half as good as she wrote and did half of the things she wrote about, he'd turn her just to see what it'd be like to spend all eternity finding out if you could kill a vampire with hot monkey-love.

Thirty

Neck deep in vampire shit and don't know how to get out? Buy the Boffrend Handbook Volume Three on sale soon.

The next three days were a blur of activity with little time for anything resembling true human interaction. For most of that time the friends found time to do little more than grunt at each other in passing. The rest of the time they did their utmost to snore, as coherently as possible at each other.

At 2:57 p.m. on the third day after locating the tomb, rounded metal struck carved stone and the world went silent. Well, not the entire world, but the general area surrounding the team did go mighty quiet. Totally quiet would have been achieved except for the clicking of a lone cricket, who had not received the memo concerning the approaching winter.

"Send in the expendable bearers," Stud shouted, as the last of the dirt was cleared away. "That has to be a couple of grad students nobody would miss."

"Be quiet, you," Dr. Grayson snapped. "I guessed it was too much to hope your mouth would be too tired to move."

"He may have a point. No telling what gases have been building up, since it's been sealed," Breathred cautioned.

"See," Stud said. "What about those two guys in the back swapping buggers? They look like they'd to do it for a coupla Scoobie snacks."

"Stud, we are not using anyone as human guinea pigs, and that is final. We have a tool which will enable us to vent the opening without any harm to us." The professor rubbed her temples.

"Then, vent that sucker. I'm growing old sitting here."

"It's not that easy, my friend," Truehart said. "It will take us a few hours to set up the machine. Then, we'll have to put on Haz-Mat suits to insure there is no damage from contamination, should there be poisonous gas built up."

"Stud, just be quiet. They know what they're doing, and they don't need you butting in," Luna ordered, tweaking the monkey's ear.

"Ow," Stud cried. The sight of her making pinching motions was enough to silence him.

"Look, I can begin setting up the machine. Why don't the rest of you get some food and rest? We could all use both after the past few days," Dr. Truehart offered.

"I could stay and help, Edmund," Easily piped up. "I'm familiar with its setup."

"No, need, Jessica. You'll get your chance to help tomorrow. Believe me," he assured her with a wave of his hand.

"Thank you, Edmund," Dr. Grayson said before Jessica could voice an objection. "We all appreciate it."

"Just doing my part."

"Okay, people, you heard the Limey. Let's go grub." Stud dashed from the hole.

Breathred waited while everyone filed after the chimpanzee. Something told him to stick around and offer to help Truehart, despite the man's reluctance to take Jessica's offer. Somehow, Breathred doubted he would accept his, especially after what he said the other day on the trail. Still, it was the polite thing to do.

Breathred turned as he felt Luna's hand on his shoulder. She looked as exhausted as he felt. Perhaps Truehart was right. They all needed a good meal and a good night's sleep. If Truehart wanted to be pig-headed and do it himself, why should he try and stop him? The man obviously didn't like him, so why bother? From the look on Luna's face she felt the same way. He shrugged and let her lead him to the tents.

Breathred shoved the last bite of his roasted hot dog into his mouth, realizing he felt a bit lonely despite the crowd of people around him. He found the loneliness unsettling. Luna and Stud had gone off in search of wild berries a little while ago. Dr. Grayson was asleep in her tent. He should be asleep too, but couldn't seem to relax. So instead, Breathred sat and listened half-heartedly to the whispers that flitted through the night air.

As tired as everyone felt, he couldn't help but notice they appeared as loath to sleep as he was. Most of them sat around in huddled conversations about the expectations of the coming day. Except for Breathred and the three professors, none had ever experienced a dig before. They didn't see the dangers of an unopened tomb. All they saw was the treasure the tomb held. Whether it was real or imagined, it was on everyone's mind, Breathred's included. He looked over to the secluded spot where Brogan had taken up watch. Breathred wondered what the man thought about all this. Ever since the radio message, the Canadian hadn't said a word. Breathred knew how he felt.

The closer they got to actually opening the tomb, the more the dread closed in on him. It was like a black cloud descending on them. The funny thing was, he and Brogan seemed to be the only ones who felt it. He wasn't even sure Luna or Stud knew what was going on.

That scared him. He needed them both to be on their toes. They were treating this like a summer camp adventure. If the Mother of Vampire's really was down in that tomb, the entire team was in trouble. They had forgotten all about Jessica leaving the meeting with Leopold. It was bad enough having a vampire lurking around at night without worrying about a human coming after you during the day.

And where was Leopold at? He wasn't back in Seattle. No, he would be close by, just in case they found something, but there was no sign of him since they had crossed the border. Which made it more likely Jessica was working for the vampire, feeding him information. Breathred had tried to keep an eye on her; she didn't act suspiciously. Truthfully, he had been too busy to do a good job of it. Any time during the past three days, she could have used the radio to call Leopold. She might even have a radio of her own.

"Breathred. Mind if I join you?" Jessica Easily asked, jarring him off the log he was sitting on. She reached down and helped him back up. "I didn't mean to scare you."

"I wasn't scared. I guess I dozed off." Breathred brushed dirt from his pants.

"Whatever," she laughed. "So, do you mind if I sit down?"

He moved down the log to give her room. "No, go right ahead."

"We haven't had time to get reacquainted. I'm beginning to think you're avoiding me. Or are you under orders from your girlfriend to avoid me?"

"Luna isn't like that," Breathred said, defensively, because she was like that.

"You could have fooled me. I don't mean to offend you but it looks to me like she keeps you on a short leash."

Breathred didn't say a word. Several choice ones sprang to mind. He ran them over a few times in his head to hear how they would sound, but didn't say them. It wouldn't be polite. He had always been told if you didn't have anything nice to say, don't say anything at all. This was one of those times to do just that, but saying them in his head was alright. God would forgive him, but Jessica probably wouldn't, if she heard what he was thinking.

"Oh, I have offended you," she said in the most mocking voice Breathred ever heard. "I didn't come over here to fight. I just wanted to ask you something."

"Go ahead, ask. You know how I get." See, I found something nice to say.

"What happened to you? I mean it's been over ten years and not a word from you. I'm not fooling myself into thinking we were anything but friends, but even friends write each other."

This time Breathred heard no condescension in her voice.

"Things went bad," Breathred mumbled.

"And that's why I haven't heard from you? I don't accept it as an answer. I heard what happened. Sure it was bad, but not bad enough to make your friends desert you."

"Maybe, I needed to desert them."

"Why? Just tell me why," she demanded.

"Because I didn't want you to get caught up in my misery. I didn't want you becoming a pariah because you were my friend," he tried to explain, but it all came out sounding like hooey.

"You silly bastard! I would have stood beside you. What happened wasn't your fault. Nobody blamed you, except for you."

"Easy to say now. Then, it didn't seem like that." Breathred looked away.

Jessica eased close and put her arm around him. "Breathred, I was your friend. Whether you believe me or not, I was. I still am, if you'll have me."

Breathred looked up and saw she meant it.

"Thank you, Jessica. That means a lot to me. It really does. There's one thing though."

"Shoot."

"Don't tell anybody about what happened. My friends don't know and neither does Dr. Grayson. I know it's silly, but I'd rather keep it that way." The truth was he didn't remember a whole lot about what happened. He was afraid if he did know, it might scare him more than not knowing.

"You got it. Now, give me a hug." She threw her arms around him.

The action shocked him so much Breathred didn't notice Luna and Stud entering camp at that exact moment. Needless to say, if he had, the past would have held no fear for him. The look on Luna's face was more than enough to scare the devil himself into relocating were he nearby.

~ * ~

Lewis woke up just as the computer chimed that he had a new message. He hoped it was from the contact. Leopold had driven him bug-shit for the past few days. "Have they got there?"

"What's taking them so long?" It was enough to make him want to drive a stake into his own heart.

Easing from his darkened bed and stumbled over to his computer, he slapped the pink fuzzy cozy from his mouse. Damn Leopold and Martha Stewart. You couldn't go to sleep without Leo putting the damn things on everything. One night he would wake up and be wrapped in one.

He grumbled and called up the mail. No, Mistress Spank My Monkie tonight, he was sorry to see. It was like she dropped off the face of the earth. Well, Leopold wasn't letting him enjoy it, anyway. He scrolled down until he saw the mole's addy. He opened it and leaned in to read.

Tomb uncovered. Will delay entrance until you can get here. No one will enter tomb, until you have secured the Mother. Hurry. I don't know how long I can hold them off.

Mis Staked

Well, well. Looked like Leopold was going to crap his silk panties. Leo would be all for rushing up there tonight, but this homeboy wasn't going until they had a place to sleep. Lewis wouldn't get caught out in the open if they couldn't make it back in time.

Hell, they didn't even know how to get into the place anyway. Leopold had a few hints from an old scroll he stole from Marcus, but nothing that told them exactly how to get in. He wasn't about to trust brute force would be enough to get the job done.

Lewis rose from his chair and walked toward the other room. Might as well get it over with and tell Leopold the good news. Otherwise he would just come in here and nag him to death. He could always go out for a bite then come back to tell Leopold. No, Canadians tasted too much like maple syrup and herring for him to eat out. That settled it. He was on the bag stuff until they got back home.

It could be worse. They could be in Wisconsin. Everybody there tasted like cheese.

Thirty One

Okay take a deep breath. Turn around slowly. Boogiedy, boogiedy. That gets them every time.

"Alright, Bitch! You have five seconds to let go of my man before I shove this monkey up in your ass," Luna howled.

"Hey!" Stud exclaimed.

Luna watched as her inhuman screech sent Breathred falling off his log, carrying Jessica with him. They landed in a crumpled heap with her provocatively positioned on top of him. She didn't blame Breathred of course. He was innocent—maybe not totally, but she'd see to him later. The fact he was trying to untangle himself from the skank was a move in the right direction, but did he have to touch her squishy parts to do it? She didn't think so!

Jessica must have caught sight of her because the skank was squirming like hell, trying to get to her feet. Luna was sure this wasn't the first time the woman found herself in this compromising position. She bet Easily had to know what was coming next. The woman managed to get to her knees when Luna jerked off her feet with the help of two handfuls of bleached blond hair, and sent her flying. Luna had the good manners to wait until she slammed into the ground before making her next move.

"Hussy, I'm going to explain this in terms even a skank like you can understand. See that?" Luna pointed toward Breathred. "That's mine. If I see your hands on him again, I'll pull every bit of Miss Clairol-soaked hair from your head."

"Luna, we weren't doing anything. We were just talking," Breathred spoke up.

Luna turned to him. One eye twitched uncontrollably, while the other one spit fire. Her lips were turned up to a horrifying snarl. If good old-fashioned common sense wasn't enough to put the fear of God into him, in the pale light of the moon it looked like she was growing a beard.

"You need to shut up. I'll talk to you, when I get through with this bitch," Luna growled.

Breathred opened his mouth to reason with her. A hairy hand caught him before he could get a syllable out. Breathred started to pull Stud's hand away and stopped.

Jessica regained her composure. "Sweetie, you've had your say, now it's my turn. I've known Breathred a helluva lot longer than you. If I want to talk to him, no scrawny pissant girl is going to stop me."

"Oh, really," Luna hissed.

"Yes, and another thing. You may be all-that where you come from, but where I come from you couldn't get a date to a dogcatcher's picnic. So, stop copping an attitude with me." Easily flicked her hair over her shoulder.

"I guess a bitch like you'd know about things like that. Woof, woof."

Easily leapt at Luna with her hands outstretched into twisted bird-like claws. Luna accepted the woman's challenge with a leap of her own. They met in midair like two enraged harpies.

Over the centuries epic battles have long been recorded, David vs. Goliath, Custer vs. the Sioux, and the North vs. the South. They all had one thing in common. They were fought with honor and dignity. This was nothing like that.

Basically, it was a full tilt boogie of estrogen-induced lunacy. Those who watched were subjected to eye gouging, hair pulling, below the belt hitting, and once a truly devastating double Texas titty twister, that would have made soap opera vixens blush with shame. Several people considered jumping in and breaking up the ill-fated battle, but seeing the emotions involved, thought better of it. Life is too precious to waste on a fruitless enterprise. At one point Dr. Grayson poked her head from her tent. Upon seeing the 'cause of the commotion, she promptly closed the flap behind her and went back to bed. She always found it best to let these things work themselves out—besides Blue Cross doesn't cover stupidity.

Ten minutes into the catfight, they exhibited signs of male pattern baldness, bitch-slap tattoos and rabies, but that was only to be expected. What wasn't was the sight of a petite brunette riding a blond around the camp using a two foot long piece of braided blond hair with dark roots as a bridle. For those of you into such things the video can be found on YouTube. After thirty minutes, the combatants showed the first signs of exhaustion.

In all likelihood it would still be going on, if it hadn't been for the sound of helicopter blades filling the campsite. Luna looked up, a tuft of hair protruding from the corners of her mouth. Jessica joined her, spitting a ragged piece of bloody cloth from between her own lips. A whirlwind of dust and pine straw shot through the camp, knocking the two women to the ground, effectively ending the battle.

Dust continued to swirl after the sound of the helicopter died down. The entire team stood entranced as two figures strode out from the dust storm.

"Look, Lewis. We missed the floor show." Leopold grinned, walking past the dazed women. "Remind me to bring the hot oil next time we visit.

These events must to held according to established protocol, or they lose their rustic charm."

Jessica finger-combed what remained of her hair back into place. "Mr. Chambris Portus. I can explain."

Leopold patted her on the head. "I'm sure you can, Honey, but I prefer to let my imagination run wild. So, what say you don't. Now, where is that delightful Doctor Grayson?"

"What now?" Dr. Grayson growled, stumbling from her tent. "I'm trying to get some damn sleep."

"Oh, my. The things you see when you don't have any concealer," Leopold said, both shocked and dismayed. "Lewis you must remind me to drop-ship these people some Revlon before they revert to cannibalism." He leaned in close to Lewis and whispered, "Better make that Avon. No sense throwing good money at bad complexions."

Dr. Grayson pulled her robe tight around her. "Mr. Chambris Portus, it is a pleasure to see you, but this is quite a surprise. I thought you wouldn't be available to come to the site."

"I had a business meeting in Calgary and decided to stop by on my way back to Seattle. Is there any chance I could get a tour of the dig before I depart?"

"Sure. If you'll let me change, I'll take you over now," Dr. Grayson said. "It shouldn't take me more than a minute, if you care to wait?"

"Doctor Easily can take me over while you get dressed. I am most excited to see it. If that is acceptable to you?" Leopold motioned for Lewis to help Dr. Easily to her feet. "Unless she has to get ready for round two, of course."

"Jessica, would you mind? I promise I won't be long," Dr. Grayson said.

"No problem." Jessica wiped a droplet of blood from her cheek.

Breathred shot Stud a look. The chimp nodded. Something was fishy. It was mighty strange the head vamp showed up just when they had finally reached the tomb. The whole thing smelled like a tip-off.

As much as Breathred would have liked to tag along, he didn't dare. Luna was irked enough without adding fuel to the fire. He'd have to stay here and let Stud keep an eye on things. Breathred motioned for Stud to follow the vamps and Jessica. The chimp nodded and took off after them.

Well, that was one problem out of the way. Now, to tackle the big one—namely Luna. She was still sitting on the ground, her chest bellowing in and out, looking more dead than alive. Her hair stuck out at odd angles. Unlike Jessica none of it was missing. Blood seeped from numerous cuts, and her clothes hung like rags.

The team followed Leopold over to the site. For the first time in three days, Breathred and Luna were alone. He didn't know if the idea was a good thing, or not. Breathred sat down beside her. Luna gave him a dirty look, but made no move to vent her frustration in a physical way. Even if she had, he was too tired to run.

"Luna?"

"Breathred, don't say anything," she said, coldly. "You were hugging that cow. Don't deny it. I saw you."

"I can't deny it, but me and Jessica are just friends. That's all."

"I thought I knew you, but suddenly I find out I don't. You're like a different person now. How come you never told me you went to college?"

"Because, I don't like to think about it. Bad things happened. Things I don't want to remember."

"But you could talk to her about it, that's what hurts," Luna all but sobbed.

"No, I couldn't. I never want to talk about it. She knows part of what happened, but not all of it. I'm not even sure if I know what truly happened, and I was there."

"Then, why couldn't you trust me enough to tell me about your past?"

"Because it wasn't important. You liked me, not my past. Not who I was or what I have done. This is who I am." Breathred slapped himself in the chest. "I am the same person I was back then. I've never asked you about your past. Why so suddenly is it important for you to know about mine?"

"I don't know. I just hate to think she could have been a part of it," Luna cried. "And the thought that she might try to be a part of it again makes me mad as hell."

"Don't make me laugh. Jessica is, quite frankly, a tart. I could never be with her. I promise you there isn't anybody else but you."

"What are you trying to say then, Mr. Petrifunck?"

There was a weird twinkle in her eye that made him more than a little nervous.

"That I—Well…you know."

"Pretend I don't. If you feel it, say it."

"Okay…I love you," Breathred mumbled.

Luna slid closer into him. "Do you really?"

"Yes, but please don't ask me to say it again."

"What if I asked you to kiss me instead?" Luna cooed in his ear.

"I might could manage a kiss, if you promised to keep your tongue to yourself." Breathred blushed, but meant every word he said.

"Okay, cross my heart," Luna smiled, as she bent in to kiss him.

Breathred was happy to note she lied about the tongue.

Thirty Two

Always be sure to sharpen your stakes away from you. It isn't exactly rocket science, but it is good practical advice.

Leopold was not amused being surrounded by the horde of people crowding around him. They all smelled of body funk and pine needles. He found himself wishing for little air fresheners to be dangling from their ears. In the absence of your basic good hygiene, he pulled a Calvin Klein magazine sample from his pocket and flashed it under his nose. He just thanked heaven the new GQ arrived before they left for this God forsaken wilderness.

The vampire wished for the good old days, where you could drive these mewling insects away with the tiniest of effort and without the fear of reprisal. Oh to once again be able to terrorize the peasants without fear of crazed scientists performing anal probes to see what made you tick. The very idea made him want to seek solace in a pair of vintage Versace slacks.

If the press of unwashed bodies wasn't bad enough, thanks to that damn, Anne Rice everyone wanted to be a vampire. Try a good hiss and blah on anyone nowadays, and they'd laugh in your face. You have to dress like Prince and look like Brad Pitt to get any kind of respect nowadays. Even then, all you get is a sneer. Goth had done nothing but kill the heart of the vampire's soul. It made Leopold want to hit the malls and bitch slap everyone dressed in black.

The rush of so many bodies choked him. He did his best to turn around. An arm full of flannel stopped him cold. Where the hell was Lewis? The sorry excuse for a vampire was supposed to be running interference, so he wouldn't have to be touched by flannel, or anything closely resembling low-grade cotton blends. Here he was neck deep in the damnable stuff with no possibility of escape short of wholesale slaughter. Which, as far as Leopold was concerned, wasn't a bad idea—just impractical.

Leopold elbowed past a particularly inbred example of manhood to get back to Dr. Easily's side. He spotted Lewis standing on the rise of a massive pile of earth directly ahead. The young vamp slid a finger along his nose, letting Leopold know everything was clear. Good, now all he had to do was get rid of these people so he could have an undisturbed look around.

"Okay, people. Mr. Chambris Portus didn't come all this way to be overrun. He came here to make sure he got his money's worth." Jessica laughed, taking care of the problem for him. "So, you can all just go on back and let him look around."

A collective groan issued from the crowd. They made no move to leave, but all it took was one evil eyed glare from the disheveled-looking Dr. Easily to send them packing. As the group filed away, a diminutive shadow, unnoticed even by Leopold—who thought himself all-seeing—eased to the side out of view unnoticed even by Leopold.

"Well, that's that. They should leave you alone," Jessica snorted. "For about five minutes, if you're lucky."

"We will make the best of it then." Leopold smiled, satisfied with the shiver he saw go through her at the sight of his bared teeth.

"Let me call Doctor Truehart for you, and let him know you're coming down," she offered.

Lewis swiftly slipped up beside her. "That won't be necessary. Why don't you head on back with the others? I'm sure the good doctor won't mind giving us a tour."

"Okay, if you think it's best."

"We do," Lewis said in her ear, using his best graveyard voice.

"Now, Lewis, don't frighten the poor girl." Leopold turned to Dr. Easily. "My dear, Doctor Truehart will be more than adequate to perform the task." Leopold placed his cold hand on her shoulder.

"If you're sure?" Jessica's gaze darted to the path.

"Put it out of your mind. We'll be fine. Now head on back." Leopold gently pushed her back toward the camp.

"Do you think it was a good idea to throw the mojo on her?" Lewis asked, when she was too far to overhear him.

"I had no choice, Dimwit. After the crap you pulled it was either that or drain her." Leopold snorted in disgust. Like he would have done anything so pedestrian in this climate; besides she had neck boogers. There was no way he would touch that neck without a whole truckload of wet wipes on hand.

"What if she blows our cover?" Lewis asked.

"She won't. You have my word on it."

"As long as you're sure."

"I am. Now let's get this over with. This damp, cold air is making my hair go all frizzy." Without a second glance he pulled Lewis into the sloping tunnel of earth.

~ * ~

Stud slid from his hiding place as the two vampires descended into the stygian gloom. These guys were nuts. *Nobody home* didn't even begin to cover it. Jeez, you'd think vampires had some sort of test to screen these guys before they got all dark and toothy.

This was just too bizarre. He could deal with scary vampires, even the odd silly vampires thrown in here and there. Shit, Breathred had made him sit through *Love at First Bite* a hundred times, so *silly* the chimp could understand. Not like, but comprehend in a sadistic sort of way. Neurotic vampires were a totally different matter. It was like following a satanic Woody Allen, dressed in full Bela Lugosi regalia.

The sound of their muffled voices died away. Stud thought it safe to tiptoe to the edge of the embankment and peek down. This 007 shit was hard on his nerves. He placed his hand on the rim and a trickle of dirt cascaded down the slope. The unmistakable sound of the two vampires coming to a halt paralyzed him with fear. Stud waited breathlessly for them to come rushing back to see what had 'caused the waterfall of dirt.

Seconds droned by as Stud clutched dirt to himself, knowing at any minute he would be vampire chow. Well, let the fuckers bite him. He'd shit on them, not that he would be able to help himself. Defecation was a chimpanzee's natural defense mechanism against danger. Just ask Tarzan, if you don't believe it. The goob was known as Shithead of the Apes until he was old enough to realize rain wasn't brown and lumpy.

The crunch of footsteps sent him scampering back into the darkness that hugged the night. The chimp had just made it to safety when Lewis poked his head above the rim of the hole. The vampire's eyes pivoted around, drinking in every inch of the dig site. Stud slithered further between a mound of dirt and a warped piece of plywood that had been thrown against it haphazardly. It wasn't much, but it was better than nothing.

Stud's heart sank as the vampire breached the top and stood motionless. Lewis' eyes flashed yellow in the pale darkness, stopping close to the spot where Stud was hidden. Well, wasn't this a fine kettle of fish? He was trapped like a mole-man by Huggy Bear's idiot nephew.

Stud's breath caught in his throat when a sound came from the direction of camp; the vamp whipped around. Stud lifted his head for a closer look. Dr. Grayson stumbled along in the dark with a flickering flashlight gripped tightly in her trembling hand. He peeked back. The vampire had composed himself and had a smile in place as the professor reached him.

"Doctor Grayson, so good to see you," Lewis said.

Stud shifted around expecting him to vamp out at any moment.

"Hope, I didn't scare you. I must have looked like a zombie or something."

"Not at all. Leopold is already below. He asked me to wait for you. He was afraid you might stumble. The area is very treacherous going in the darkness." Stud had to admit the vamp lied quite convincingly.

"Oh, you shouldn't have. I'm sure you're just as anxious as Mr. Chambris Portus to get a look."

"Not in the least. This is Leopold's passion. As far as I'm concerned the past is dead. The future…now, that's something worth worrying about."

"I see," Doctor Grayson said, not hiding the disdain in her voice.

"I hope I haven't offended you." Stud could tell the vamp didn't really care if he did.

"It's strange to find a man with your obvious enlightenment being so cavalier about something as important as this."

"Look. I'm not knocking what you do, but Leopold has pretty much killed my historical bent. This is important to him, so I get dragged along, whether I want to be or not, which explains why I'm up here in the cold instead of down there in the cold."

"Lewis, how many times have I told you not to show your ignorance to strangers?" Leopold said, as he returned from the excavation. "You must excuse him, Dr. Grayson. He's from a purely pedestrian background with no sense of the importance of this endeavor."

Stud couldn't help but notice, 1) the sneer that plastered Lewis' face at the remark or 2) the fact Leopold chose to ignore it. Trouble in paradise was something they could use. He couldn't wait to tell Breathred and Luna when they hooked back up. From the look on the other vampire's face, he almost thought they might come to blows over it. The Leopold guy noticed too. Instead of defusing the situation, he swept past Lewis, grabbed Dr. Grayson by the arm and headed back to camp.

"Did Edmund show you around?" Dr. Grayson asked.

"No, he wasn't there. I took the liberty of making myself at home, so to speak. It was quite exciting. All the machinery, and the door itself set my heart to fluttering with expectation." Leopold grinned and waved his hand behind his back, signaling Lewis to follow them.

Stud counted to five, then followed at a safe distance, keeping to the shadows, but well within earshot.

"So, you'll be staying to see the grand opening," Dr. Grayson asked.

"Unfortunately, that is not possible. Lewis and I have to be in New York by tomorrow night. In fact, if we want to catch our flight, we really should be leaving," Leopold said, absently looking at his watch.

"Is there no way you could postpone your visit? We hope to break through by late afternoon tomorrow."

"Would that I could, but the business world waits for no man," Leopold said with a flourish. "You will keep me updated, I hope?"

"Of course. I believe I have your e-mail address in my files. If we find anything, you'll be the first to know."

"That is most reassuring. Now, I must bid you good night. We have already kept you up too late. Good night, doctor." Leopold gave her hand a hard shake. He turned to Lewis. "Come, Lewis. Our pilot is probably threatening to leave without us, as we speak."

Stud followed after a few minutes. He waited behind a boulder near where the copter had landed, until the two men climbed inside. He had hoped they might say something to give him an idea of what they were planning.

But not a peep. What did he expect—for them to reveal everything like a bad episode of Scooby Doo? Stud shrugged and decided to hit the sheets. If he was lucky, Breathred would still be awake. Nothing was worse than trying to sleep with the goofus' snoring filling the tent.

    His shoulders drooping, Stud walked toward the bank of tents. As he did, a shadow detached itself from the darkness and tailed him all the way back.

Thirty Three

If you find yourself hopelessly lost, look to the handbook as a guide. If that doesn't work, bend over...Hell, you know the rest.

Lewis watched the landscape slip past under them. Leopold was still not talking, and it was driving him crazy. It was so unlike the old vamp Lewis began to suspect Leopold was losing it. He had begun to suspect it some time ago, but was still waiting for confirmation before saying anything.

Sitting here like a dumb-ass wasn't getting him anywhere. Lewis didn't want to admit he actually wanted to know, but dammit, the younger vampire did. He might not be as interested as old needle britches, but he was curious. Lewis knew if he asked, Leopold wouldn't let him forget who brought the subject up. Sometimes, being one of the undead was like being in kindergarten, only without the finger paints.

Luckily, Leopold cleared his throat, which meant he was ready to talk. Lewis suppressed a smile. He knew Leopold would break sooner or later. It just took longer than expected.

"Yes, Leopold?" Lewis asked. Hell, no sense in drawing it out. A little prompting never hurt anybody.

"Knew you wouldn't be able to contain yourself," Leopold said, jabbing him in the ribs with his elbow.

Asshole, Lewis thought. Then he said aloud. "So, did you get in or what?"

"Unfortunately, not. Whoever placed the Mother in the tomb was afraid one day her children might find a way to release her. Beneath the dirt and grime, a series of runes prevents our kind from entering," Leopold grumbled.

"So, we're screwed."

"No, my colorful sidekick, just derailed. Instead of seeing to the Mother ourselves, we'll have to let Grayson and her team liberate her."

"But, what if they wake the Mother?" Lewis asked, not really convinced the older vampire had thought things all the way through.

"They can't. If I'm correct, they can enter her chamber but will be unable to open the sarcophagus. According to the scrolls, it takes the blood of a Vampiric Lord to open it."

"We can't be sure of that. If the Mother is exposed to daylight, there is still a chance our entire race could be destroyed—if your scrolls are to be believed," Lewis mused aloud.

"Dear Lewis, we have nothing to worry about. The validity of the scrolls is unquestionable. The very fact you quote proves it. They will not be able to open the coffin." Leopold rubbed his chin thoughtfully. "But we must not take any chances. Let our agent know under no circumstances should they attempt to open her coffin. The agent is smart enough to find a way to accomplish so simple a task."

"So, what are we supposed to do in the mean time?"

Leopold motioned for Lewis to write things down. "We make plans. The first thing you do is locate a truck to transport the coffin. Something big, maybe a U-haul. You should be able to do that easily enough. We can place it at the campsite at the ready. From there we can have a plane ready to fly us and the Mother to Seattle."

"Won't the professor try to stop us?" Lewis smiled, seeing a flaw in the big guy's plan.

"No, I will explain the truck is in her best interest. Security concerns should be enough to convince her of the validity of the lie."

"You got it all figured out," Lewis hated to say.

"That's why I'm the boss. Now, have the pilot swing past a donut shop. I'm in the mood for a sugar high." Leopold folded his arms and settled back in his chair.

Lewis just grunted and went to the forward cabin that separated them from the pilot. As much as he hated to admit it, Leo was on the ball. That was no guarantee it would work. With Leopold at the helm it was a good bet it wouldn't.

Despite that, Lewis couldn't just walk away. He owed Leopold too much. If it hadn't been for the vampire, he'd more than likely be just another dead pusher. Instead, he was one of the glorious undead. Which wasn't a bad trade-off in Lewis' opinion. So, he'd stick it out and see what happened. After all the old man might actually pull this shit off.

~ * ~

"What do you mean it won't cut through?" Dr. Grayson screamed over the sound of the grinding drill.

It was already past mid-day. Dr. Truehart had been up since dawn trying to calibrate the delicate mechanics of the drill. He had attempted no less than ten times to break the stone door's surface—to no avail. In fact, on the fifth try the diamond-tipped bit had actually shattered. Luckily, they had brought a second for just such an occasion...but it wasn't doing much better.

Truehart looked up to find Dr. Grayson's glaring face breathing down his neck. *Well, take a breath mint and calm down.* He squeezed away from her and went to the door. Nothing. All the last attempt did was knock about an inch of dirt off the slick surface.

Wait a minute. What the hell was this? The Englishman peered at the clean area, detecting a thin pattern of lines in the stone. Why didn't he see those before? "Doctor Grayson, come look at this."

Grayson pushed him to the side and peered at the door. "Any idea what it means, Edmund?"

"Languages were never my forte. They look like a form of pictograms," Dr. Truehart surmised.

"They bear a remarkable resemblance to those on the tablet, but I won't know if they're the same until we uncover the entire structure." She poked a fingernail at the flaking dirt that covered the door. "How could we have missed this?"

Edmund traced one of the figures through the grime. "We were in too much of a hurry. We made the most basic of mistakes. We were over-eager."

"Too, true. Do we have any language specialists with us? I can't remember," Grayson said, absently.

"Sharbano and Roberts have some skill in that area, but they're both too inexperienced to be trusted to give an accurate translation. Dammit, we should have brought someone more qualified, instead of depending on graduate assistants."

"We didn't, so we're stuck with what we have. Before we do anything more to gain entry, the door's surface must be cleaned and a tracing made. We'll try a digital scan, as well, but I'm leery of depending on modern technology. I've seen too much lost due to poorly handled equipment, so we'll make an effort to back up everything. If we have to damage the door, we'll still have a record." Dr. Grayson rose from the door.

"I should be able to translate it." The sound of Petrifunck's voice brought Truehart's head whipping around from the door.

"Really, Petrifunck? Are you qualified for this sort of thing?"

"My degree is in ancient languages. From what I see it's a variation of ancient Babylonian with a few minor deviations," Breathred answered.

"Preposterous!" Truehart exclaimed. This was truly too much. Grayson had lost her mind for allowing this bumpkin to tag along. "Babylonians in Canada? Forgive me if I say *bullshit*."

"Say whatever you want."

"Edmund, he's right. Look here…" Grayson pointed to one of the runes. "This symbol, here, is clearly one of the most widely used pictographs in the Babylonian language. I recognize this one also. It's the symbol of life."

Breathred drew a brush from his back pocket and swept at the mud until the row of symbols was completely uncovered. The symbols were as clear as the day they had been etched into the stone door. Breathred clicked them off in his head until they formed a sentence. When he finished, his mind was a blob of cold fear.

"Well, what does it say, man?" Truehart demanded.

"In the darkness born, life grows in death and hungers," Breathred chanted in a voice, as cold as hell itself.

Everyone who heard him stopped in their tracks. Eighteen heads pivoted toward the door. A hushed fear ran through the crowd. Breathred knew no one would admit it, but they all felt it. When the moment passed, they would attribute it as foolishness, but it would still fester inside them. Maybe not openly, but it would sit in the backs of their minds until the door was open and its treasure revealed.

"Poppycock," Truehart finally said

"Edmund, please," Dr. Grayson snapped. "Breathred, are you sure that's what it says?"

"One hundred percent sure."

"Next thing you know, we'll be running around actually believing this madness," Truehart continued.

"You know as well as I, these ancient cultures used these curses to ward off those who would defile their holy places. This is nothing more than a warning to evildoers. We are archeologists, Edmund, not actors in some cheap movie. Give us more credit than that." Dr. Grayson said it loud enough for everyone to hear. "Breathred, I'm leaving you in charge of finishing the translation. Luna and Stud can help you with the tracing and digital record. Make sure to back up to disc as soon as you're finished."

"We will," Luna answered for him.

"Thank you, Luna. I'll send Roberts back with the camera and discs. Breathred, is there anything else you need?"

"Can you have someone bring a couple buckets of fresh water to help break up the outer covering of dirt? I'd rather try that first. I'm afraid to chip away at the mud in case it mars the inscription."

"Roberts can do that, as well. In fact he'll act as your assistant for as long as you need him. Understand, Roberts? You'll be working directly under Doctor Petrifunck for the time being." She turned toward a youth with a mass of unruly hair and a none-too-trimmed beard.

The boy gave an exaggerated thumb's up. "Gotcha, Doc."

"Anything else you need, just send him and I'll okay it," Grayson told them.

"Donna, you can't be serious," Truehart said.

"I am. Remember, I am the one in charge of this dig, not you."

"I'll try to remember. But if this goes to hell, it'll fall on your shoulders not mine." The Englishman turned on his heel and strode away from the excavation.

"Okay, everybody, the show's over. Get a life, we have work to do," Stud shouted, grabbing Robert's by the arm. "Kid, bring me back a low-carb banana latte, and don't skimp on the foam. Don't stand there looking stupid. Chop! Chop!"

"Stud, he isn't your slave." Breathred snatched the chimp by the scruff of the neck. "Chris, don't mind him. Just bring the water."

"Sure thing, Doc," Roberts said. Breathred couldn't help but notice the boy stuck his tongue out at the chimp before leaving.

"Now, let's get to work," Breathred said, once they were alone.

"What do you think the rest of the inscription will say?" Luna asked, nervously.

"Nothing we really want to know."

The next five hours were the most tedious of their life. Breathred began by gently brushing loose dirt from the door. The initial cleaning took the better part of the first hour. After the last stroke of his brush they applied coats of water to the door, washing away yet another layer of the deposited earth. Gradually, the door became an open book set in stone.

What amazed Breathred the most was the door showed no sign of deterioration. Even after centuries under the earth, the door showed none of the pockmarks one associated with nature's effect on man-made artifacts. It was almost as if the door had just been set into place.

Another thing about the door was it was smooth—too smooth to be made with the tools available at the time it was made. Egyptian structures made from that era showed the marks of the tools used to construct them. If Breathred didn't know better, he would have sworn the door had been machine tooled.

Even the inscription was too precise to have been made with the nearly prehistoric tools of that time. His fingers traced the writing and never once snagged on irregular chips or cracks. It was too much to be believed.

"So, smarty pants. What does it say?" Stud asked. "Watching you fondle this door is getting old."

"Hush, let him finish," Luna hissed.

"That's okay. I've got it all. I just can't believe what it says," Breathred uttered.

"Well, what does it say?" Stud snapped.

"I won't bother you with the actual translation. But roughly it says a goddess descended from the heavens in the dead of night. In her glory she claimed the villagers as her children and ruled them wisely for untold generations. Then, in the thousandth year of her reign a consort came on the wings of darkness. The people grew afraid because her prince began to see her chosen people as cattle to feed his growing hunger. In time the people became bold and beseeched their goddess to rid them of the demon who preyed upon them.

"It goes on to say she confronted her consort and took his power into herself to free her people from his evil. How she did that, it doesn't say, but I imagine she drained him. In time the people became afraid their goddess had become tainted by the consort's blood. The goddess herself saw the change coming over her.

"So she had the villagers construct the tomb, making the door herself, and infused it with a part of her own powers, so none of her children could open it. She hoped this would stop them from awakening the evil consuming her," Breathred related.

"But how do we open the frigging door?" Stud asked in frustration.

"That's the funny part. It says only a warrior who is pure in soul and willing to pour his blood out in righteousness' sake can breach the bonds of the dead, but to beware. For in darkness, life grows in death and hungers," Breathred finished.

"Which explains the part you translated earlier," Luna said.

"But what does the last bit mean?" Stud wondered aloud.

"You got me, but it begs the question. Now that we know the vampires can't get in, should we even try to do it ourselves?" Breathred pondered.

Thirty Four

Go back and read the damn thing again. There will be a pop quiz in your future.

Luna watched Breathred sleeping. The sweetie hadn't even made it to the tent. He had curled up waiting for supper, and was out before she knew it. Breathie was kind of cute all relaxed and snoring, almost like he wasn't hiding things from her.

The thought made her wince. Luna had been over this before. He wasn't hiding anything. She was just too afraid to ask, which as far as she was concern amounted to the same thing. The past three days made her realize she knew almost nothing about Breathred. Like today, who knew he could read dead languages? She sure as hell didn't. From the look on Stud's face the chimp was just as clueless. If Breathred didn't trust him, how could he trust her? That was what hurt. They were going together. Some amount of trust was implied with that statement.

All of a sudden the little voice in her head spoke up. *Luna Walking Batch, aren't you the hypocrite? He's not the only one who's holding back dirty little secrets. What about yours? Did you ever think how he'd feel if he knew yours? But you aren't about to jump up and tell him, now are you? So ask yourself who's the bad guy here—you or him?*

"He is!" she answered back, hurt that her little voice would turn on her.

Really now. He might be hiding his past, but you're hiding so much more. So the truth now, missy.

"Okay, it might be me, but there's a good reason why I haven't told him mine."

You don't think he might have a good reason, too? Look at the big goof. He loves you. He said so, didn't he? You know how hard it was for him to admit. You have to give him time. Love is hard, but trust is harder by far.

"For an imaginary little voice, you're pretty smart."

That's because I'm you, dummy. So, listen to me. He'll tell you when he's ready or when you get the guts to ask. Now, I'm going to watch some

Food Network. *Try to keep it together. I can't keep bailing you out like this. By the way the chimp is back and he's giving you the padded room look.*

Luna looked up just in time to see the look the voice had been talking about. It was a cross between worry and where's my net. "He must think I'm nuts."

Told you, the voice said just to get in the last word.

"Hey, Stud. How's it going?" Luna asked, hoping if she sounded happy enough he might forget the whole *Is she talking to herself?* thing. It didn't work.

"Pretty good. How about you? Heard any good voices lately?" Stud asked.

"I was just thinking."

"What were you thinking about?"

"Stud, can I ask you a serious question?" Luna asked, looking him in the eye.

"Of course. As long as we aren't talking about a feminine hygiene moment or anything."

"How much do you know about—?" Luna asked, pointing toward the sleeping Breathred.

"Let's take a walk." Stud gave her a look that said he wasn't about to say anything while they were still near Breathred.

Luna reluctantly got to her feet and followed the chimpanzee away from camp. Okay, this wasn't exactly instilling a trust-filled relationship, but dammit she wasn't about to ask him about himself without doing a little recon first.

Luna followed Stud into a secluded clearing, about a hundred yards from camp. He jumped up on a half-buried boulder. Luna shrugged and sat down beside him. She waited for him to start speaking but the chimpanzee simply cradled his head in the fold of his crossed arms for what seemed like forever.

The moon rose gently over the fractured tree line, and when he began to speak it shocked Luna into sliding from the boulder. "This is about today, huh?"

"Kinda, but it's more than that. Is it just me or is Breathred a little bit more than he seems?"

Luna waited for an answer, but none seemed to be coming. Stud stared at her but his mouth refused to work, a first for him. Then he suddenly opened his mouth to speak only to shut it before he could say anything. It was so totally unlike him Luna saw for the first time where the chimp's true loyalty stood.

"Stud, I would never hurt him or talk behind his back. This is different. I just don't know what to think anymore."

Stud jabbed his finger at her menacingly. "Okay, but this is between us. Got that?"

"Cross my heart."

"Back when I first learned to talk, I had a heart-to-heart with ol' R.J. one night. The big guy was more than a little inebriated, which is a rare occasion in itself, but Breathred had just set fire to the toilet so he had a good reason for tickling the bottom of the bottle. Anyway, since he thought I was a figment of his imagination, R.J. opened up. He said Breathred had once been in college—graduated even. Anyway, the guy's a genius, if you can believe that. His I.Q. is so high the goofball makes Einstein look like a dummy. I think it explains how he could make the spell work that made me talk. When R.J. opened up, I just figured Breathred was eccentric. You know, like mad-scientist crazy," Stud paused. "But it wasn't the whole story, not by far."

"So, what are you saying? That Breathred is just so smart he makes his own rules and living in his father's basement is part of those rules?"

"No, something happened when Breathred was away. Something bad," Stud said, glumly. "R.J. said when Breathred came back home, he was different. Still goofy, but something had changed. He wasn't all there, if you know what I mean."

"So, what happened?"

"R.J. didn't know and Breathred wouldn't talk about it. I tried to find out about it, like you want to, but I couldn't find anything. I even asked Breathred, but he just clammed up. So, I wouldn't suggest bringing it up. Whatever happened to him was bad enough he tries not to think about it. I don't even think he can. It's like he's blocked it from his mind. This is as close as he's got, and it's scaring him. I see it in his eyes. He's afraid it's going to happen again and this time he won't come back from it." Stud stopped talking and put his head between his legs.

Luna sat for a moment letting Stud's words sink in. This explained so much. She had seen the pained look in Breathred's eyes, but had dismissed it as nothing. She had even felt the fear in him through the talisman, but just explained it away. Now, Luna couldn't ignore the signs. If she couldn't ask him about it, what was to do?

Another thing bothering her was that Truehart was involved in this somehow. The other day out on the trail, the Englishman had said as much. At the mention of his brother, Breathred had gone all weird. Did the connection between the two have something to do with what happened to Breathred? Well one thing was for sure, she wasn't about to ask Truehart about it. The guy gave her the creeps. Which meant she was right back where she started.

A light snow began to fall. She turned her face up into the swirling glitter. The flakes felt good on her face. The bits of ice turned to tiny rivers on her warm flesh, but washed away none of the worry that filled her.

"Stud, I'm afraid for him. Something else is going on here and it has nothing to do with vampires or archeology. Truehart's mixed up in it somehow. I don't think it's a coincidence he and that woman are here. Two people who know Breathred from his past don't just pop up out of nowhere. What if someone's trying to get him to crack, or worse—what if they want him dead?" She could barely get the words out through the tears that swelled in her throat.

"We stop them," Stud said, defiantly.

"Damn, straight we do."

She accepted his hand as he helped her down from the boulder. Luna was grateful for the silence as they walked back to camp. The conversation had frightened her, and could tell it had Stud, too. Luna found herself seeing conspiracies behind every bush and tree. One thing was certain, she wasn't alone in this. They both were resolved in their need to protect Breathred.

Luna let out a sigh of relief on seeing him safe and sound, sitting by the fire with Dr. Grayson, pouring over the translation from the door. She was just glad to see the Easily tramp had the good sense to sit in front of her tent instead of near Breathred. The woman didn't have enough hair left to lose if she made that mistake again.

Entering the camp, Breathred looked up and saw them. He waved them over with a goofy grin on his face. Stud put his hand on hers before they reached him to remind her to keep quiet about their conversation. She nodded, but didn't like being reprimanded. The fruit should know by now she could keep a secret. She hadn't told anybody about his failed bikini wax, had she?

They sat down. "Where've you guys been?" Breathred asked.

"We went for a walk. The camp was starting to close in on us."

"Well, while you guys were out fooling around, we solved the riddle of the translation."

"We still aren't sure, but it does look like a promising hypothesis," Dr. Grayson added.

"Well, spill it. I ain't sitting in the snow to play thirty questions," Stud grumbled, as the snow quickened.

"If we base our question on Babylonian customs, it follows that the answer must fall to their way of thinking. So, we believe, to open the door you must be a virgin who is pure in spirit, but the warrior bit is throwing us. We still don't know how that fits into it," Breathred explained.

"What if it's like the Knights Templar? You know how they were supposed to be God's chosen warriors. It could be something similar," Luna offered, failing to notice the grimace that covered Breathred's face at her mention of the Knights.

"She could be right. Many ancient cultures had warrior priests, who were dedicated to the gods and served as their holy arms of retribution," Dr. Grayson said. Luna could see the woman was excited by the new input.

"But, where in the hell are we supposed to find a virgin warrior who fights for the powers of good?" Stud countered.

As soon as it was out of his mouth, every eye turned toward

Breathred.

Thirty Five

Be assured of one very important fact, they're out for blood and you're on the menu.

"Wait a minute!" Breathred jumped to his feet. "Why am I automatically picked to be the guinea pig here?"

"Because you fit the bill, Buddy-ro," Stud smirked.

The chimp had him there.

"But it doesn't mean I know what to do," Breathred said in his defense. Let them try to tell him different.

"I think I know how," Dr. Grayson piped up.

Darn it. How did he know she was going to say that?

"See this part of the translation." She laid the paper out in front of them. "It talks of being pure in spirit and blood. I think it means the door is a test. I know it's crazy, but I think it means you have to put your blood on the door."

"Lady, you're nuts. You're telling us the door is a vampire too," Stud snorted.

"No, she could be right. We've already established this isn't your normal dig. It wouldn't be a stretch of the imagination to say the door is an ancient sensor that can detect goodness and evil. We're dealing with vampires. If we can accept the fact vampires exist, anything's possible," Luna said, giving Stud a shut-up-or-else look.

"Breathred, are you willing to test this theory out?" Dr. Grayson asked. Her tone said please in a very big way.

"If you think it'll work, okay," he answered after a few minutes of thought. Breathred wasn't all too convinced, but he wasn't about to let them down just because he was a little squeamish.

"Breathy, you don't have to do this, if you don't want to," Luna told him. "I've got a bad feeling about this. Something in my gut says this isn't a good idea."

"It'll be all right. It's just a little blood. What could happen?" Breathred reassured her, not really believing it himself.

"Then it's settled. First thing tomorrow, we give it a try," Dr. Grayson said, clasping her hands together. "Now let's get a good night's sleep and pray for success."

~ * ~

Breathred tossed and turned in his sleep. Even in his exhausted state of mind he knew the dreams were back. It had been a long time, yet recognized the smoky vision. A part of him even welcomed it—thirsted for it. It was more than a dream. He knew subconsciously for what it was, a memory of shades and shadows bathed in light.

The darkness swelled over him, as the door in his dream closed like a setting sun. Someone was in the darkness with him. The sound of whimpering came from the shadows to let him know the dream hadn't changed. He tried to ignore the sobs, but he couldn't. The sound filled the darkness. In the void it was the only sensory input left to him.

The blackness was total. The presence of his own hand in front of him was no longer a given. His hands fumbled over his body to reassure himself he was indeed still real, and not a figment of the dream. It wasn't enough.

He needed to breathe. Breathred choked as he dragged in his first mouthful. The air was stale and lifeless. He panicked, scrambling to cleanse his lungs of the graveyard taste that filled them. Tears ran down his face as he strained to keep himself from going over the edge. In the back of his mind he saw the dead air as something cloistering him, as sure as the darkness itself was doing.

Breathred knew it was a dream, yet struggled to force himself to move, but couldn't. The dream wouldn't let him go. Fear rooted him in place. To escape he had to allow it to flow until it ended. Knowing this truth from old, he waited. The darkness would soon lift. It always did, because the never-more thing wouldn't come until the void was ripe for its rebirth.

Then it came. Light exploded around him. Breathred felt the light burning his skin, but refused to open his eyes. If he kept them closed, he wouldn't see it. Behind him the whimpering faded to nothing, only to be replaced by a maddening scream that shook his resolve. He almost broke and let his eyes flicker open. The screaming ended. The silence stopped him. It was his turn to suffer. There was no way he wanted to see the things to come

His skin tingled in expectation. The shadow thing was coming. Cold breath sang across the back of his neck, harkening its arrival. Breathred felt his own breath catch in his throat. It wasn't from fear. It was something more.

The frigid air that came from the thing's mouth rolled over his ears and came to a stop on his face. Then his eyes did open. When they did, Breathred did scream.

"I choose you. You will be my avatar, my redemption," a voice whispered in his mind.

A hundred lifetimes later, in the middle of the night, Breathred came awake, sweat covering his chilled flesh. His sleeping bag slithered down his bare chest and pooled around his paunchy waist. He groped aimlessly in the pale moonlight that filtered through the translucent tent for the comfort of anything real. Touching the quilted bag, Breathred at last knew he was awake. He caressed the silky fabric, afraid it would turn to smoke and vanish from around him.

Breathred unzipped the sleeping bag the rest of the way. Goose bumps ran up his legs in spite of the thermal undies he wore. He rummaged at the foot of his cot for his pants and shirt. His jacket was curled up under his pillow to keep it warm and toasty. Breathred silently wished he'd done the same with the rest of his clothes. Making sure Stud was still asleep, Breathred threw on his clothes.

After the dream, the tent was just too confining. He needed the fresh air. Doing his best not to make a peep Breathred tiptoed past the snoring chimpanzee. He slipped from the tent without so much as causing Stud to turn in his sleep, grateful for the small favor. His head still ached from the nightmare. The last thing he needed was for Stud to turn it into a full-fledged migraine. There would be enough of that tomorrow.

As clear as the dream had been, his waking had diminished it to nothing more than flashing images. It was always like that. Breathred was missing something. It lurked in the edges of his consciousness, beyond his grasp. As much as Breathred wanted to know what it was, he was afraid—afraid to know the truth. Over the past ten years he had done a pretty good job of avoiding the truth and was quite proud of the fact.

Now, it wasn't so simple. The past few days had made him realize he wasn't in total control of himself. If he ever had been. The thing at the mall had cemented the idea in his gut. At the time Breathred could have sworn there was a voice in his head telling him what to do. Thinking back, he saw the lunacy in thinking along those lines, but then it had been so real.

The thing that troubled him the most was he knew what was going on. He just couldn't dredge the reason from his brain. It was like something was blocking him from opening the page in his mind. Breathred could trace the feeling all the way back to the tomb at the Shrine of the Seven Veils. It was right after that he first noticed the change in himself. The doctors told him it was a normal reaction to what had happened. But, what had happened? The whole thing was a blank spot. The doctors also said memory loss was to be expected. The trauma would eventually pass and the memories would return. The last doctor visit was ten years ago and still nothing.

"We can't seem to stop meeting like this. Can we Petrifunck?"

Breathred snapped around to see Brogan leaning against a tree, smoking a cigar. Just great. Didn't this guy ever sleep?

"Brogan, I thought everybody was asleep," Breathred grunted, not really feeling sociable and hoping the man would take the hint.

"Wrong, Bub. So, the doc says you guys got the door all figured out." The man blew a huge wheel of smoke toward him.

"We haven't seen you around for the past day or two. Where have you been hiding?" Breathred countered. He really didn't want to talk about tomorrow either. Couldn't a guy just mope around in the dark in peace?

"I've been around, just didn't want to get in the way." Brogan dropped the cigar and stepped on the still-burning ember. "But you didn't answer my question."

"You didn't answer mine. I think it makes us even, don't you?"

"Looks like you grew a set, Petrifunck. Don't think I like it, but it was bound to happen sooner or later," Brogan said, as he stooped to poke the dying fire into a weak, but growing blaze.

"Is there a reason for this conversation, or do you just like to pester me?" Breathred asked, growing more than a little irritated.

"Both, but you knew that."

"You don't like us."

"That's the funny thing—I do. I just think you're a bit on the naive side." He tossed a log on the fire. A haze of flames and smoke flew into the air between them.

"What do you mean by that?" Breathred snapped.

"You come up here with the best intentions. I know a whole road paved with those and my friend, you are slap dab in the middle of it. Your doctor has no idea what she's playing at, but I think you, your girlfriend and the monkey do." Brogan shot him an accusatory wink.

"Are you trying to scare me?"

"Nope, just making an observation."

"Okay, let's say you're right, what next? Do you plan to call in the troops?" Breathred sputtered, as the wind changed direction and blew a gust of smoke into his face.

"Depends on what happens tomorrow."

"When we open the door, you mean?" Breathred waved his hand to clear the smoke.

"You got it, Bub. Appears to me it could go two ways. I could be wrong and you get a dried up corpse or two hunkered down there, or the shit hits the fan. Before you get any delusions of grandeur, understand this one thing—I am never wrong," Brogan stated in a voice that said it was a stone-cold fact.

"What if I said I thought you were right?"

"Then we're in more trouble than I thought, if a dweeb like you agrees with me," Brogan said. He lit another cigar and did not say another word.

Thirty Six

Okay roll up your sleeves, it's time to get this ball rolling.

Vampire hunters do not faint. Vampire hunters do not faint. The mantra rolled over and over in Breathred's mind like a wave of nausea on a roller coaster. The slayer hoped if he kept repeating it over and over it would have to work. He stared at the cold, stone door of the tomb, mocking him with its silence.

He slammed his eyes shut to ward off the voice, but it kept pestering him. Breathred knew the voice was his own, but that didn't seem to matter. In fact it made it worse. Breathred tried not to think about his friends staring, waiting for him to open the door. He wished they would just go away. It was like trying to pee in a public restroom. You knew what to do, but the guy next to you wouldn't stop grinning. It kind of blocked the process.

Standing here wasn't going to open the door. If it would, the door would have opened an hour ago. His hand tightened on the slender scalpel Dr. Grayson had handed him. Breathred almost dropped it, as the fear of it welled up inside him yet again. He was abnormally afraid of paper cuts and was about to slash his own whatever. Did that make sense? It, sure as heck didn't to him.

This was the kind of thing that kept him up at night. Breathred couldn't count the number of times he'd awakened from a sound sleep with rampant fears doing cartwheels in his brain. True, this wasn't ever one of those fears, but given time Breathred was sure it would have made it to the convention. Now faced with it, he was glad it hadn't. This was definitely something he only wanted to experience once.

He gulped down a lung full of air and brought the blade up to his hand. Without looking let the scalpel fall. The knife bit softly into the tender flesh of his palm. Breathred had played with the notion of simply pricking his finger, but he wasn't sure how much blood it would take to open the door. If he drew too little, he might have to do it all over again. Breathred wasn't sure he could manage a second cut.

Blood swelled in his cupped palm. He was spellbound by it. For one thing the shock of actually doing it was still pretty strong. Second, he was always under the insane belief his blood might possibly be green. Silly he knew, but the call of Vulcan was a thing Breathred had long since stopped trying to deny.

Letting the warmness fill his hand, his eyes searched the door for the spot he'd noticed on the tracing. In the left-hand corner, Breathred saw the slight indentation that marked the outline of a hand pressed into the stone. He squinted to make sure it wasn't bird poo or something. No, it was a handprint all right. The door sure looked cold. Maybe he should wait until it warmed up a bit. He wouldn't want to get freezer–burn, or anything.

"Stop the dilly dallying and touch the damn door!" Stud yelled, nearly sending Breathred falling into the rising mound of snow. "I'm freezing my nuts off over here."

"Leave him alone, Stud. He's just a little nervous," Luna scolded the chimp, before turning to Breathred. "You take your time, sweetie. We'll wait until you're good and ready." She gave Stud a dirty look to shut him up before he could say another word, which from the look on his face he was about to do.

Breathred gave them an apologetic look only to catch sight of Brogan frowning at him from behind the chimp. Breathred tried to ignore the look, but he couldn't. Their talk last night had cemented a bond between them. Whatever happened in the next few minutes, Breathred knew the man would be ready to face anything that came out the door.

A little more relaxed knowing they were there, he lifted his blood-soaked hand to the door. Breathred hesitated a second, then slapped his palm against the stone. The chill from the door ran up his hand and moved quickly to his arm and shoulder. He didn't have time to acknowledge the sensation before it was replaced by another—pain.

Raw electricity shot through his body. It was visible, as a halo that surrounded him. Breathred blinked through the pain and saw his blood racing across the surface of the door. It filled the cracks and lines making up the pictograms. They burned with an unholy radiance that consumed the dull, gray stone, blocking out everything but their ancient promise.

In the midst of the agony erupting around him Breathred heard a soft voice question the dark interiors of his very soul. He fought to drive the voice out, but couldn't. It wanted him. He staggered to the snow-covered ground. He couldn't get the voice to quit.

Come to me, little warrior. I thirst, the voice beckoned.

"No!" Breathred howled.

I need you. You have breached my resting place. I can taste the richness of the purity coursing through your veins. Give it to me.

"I said no!" Breathred screamed through a wave of agony, drawing concerned stares from his friends who weren't sure what was going on.

Then why do you seek to open my tomb, if not to submit to my touch? the voice demanded.

"Because, others seek to use you for their own evil gains. I won't allow them to succeed," Breathred stated through clinched teeth as the pain intensified.

It is not your place to allow, but mine. I am the Mother of Damnation. In me rest the seeds of forever for those who come to me. Will you accept my charms, little warrior? the voice asked, seductively.

"Never!" Breathred exclaimed.

Then, enter freely and of your own accord, the voice announced sadly before fading into nothingness.

A burst of power rocketed through Breathred, sending him flying from the door. He landed in a mound of melting snow. It took him a minute to realize he was the reason it was melting. Steam billowed from him, as the last of the energy evaporated away. Groggily Breathred raised his aching head, but waited a minute before deciding vampire hunters did indeed faint, and did so, as fast as he could.

~ * ~

"Hey, wake up," Stud said, his voice a mass of unspoken emotion. It took everything the chimp had not to smack the big goob upside the head, figuring it would be the only thing to wake the goofus up.

"Oh God, what if he's dead?" Luna sobbed hysterically beside him, as they hunched over the unconscious Breathred.

"He's not dead. See, his chest is moving. You can't be dead and still be breathing," Stud said, relieved.

Dr. Grayson poked her head between the two friends. "I think Breathred just passed out. He took quite a jolt. It must have been a shock to his system."

"He could be brain-dead. I heard electrical shocks could do that," Luna said, continuing to sob.

"How could you tell, even if he was?" Stud knew the remark was gonna get him in trouble the minute it left his mouth, but didn't care. Being a smart ass was his defense mechanism. Breathred may be her boyfriend, but the goob was—what the hell did it matter what Breathred was? Breathred was his, and nothing else mattered.

"Stud!" Luna gasped.

"Luna, it's all right. The shock wasn't electrical. I believe it was more mystical in nature. He should be fine. We need to give him time to recover, though. Breathred could be out for some time," Dr. Grayson assured the sobbing girl.

"Not with everyone shouting, I won't." Breathred moaned.

Stud let a totally uncharacteristic prayer of thanks escape his lips, but internally dared anyone to call him on it.

"Oh, Breathy! You're okay!" Luna exclaimed, throwing her arms around him. She didn't stop crying, but the timbre of her voice was definitely of better quality than before, Stud was happy to note.

"Come on, Toots. Let him catch his breath," Stud said, pulling her back, afraid she was going to suffocate the goob.

"How long have I been out?" Breathred asked, lifting himself up to a semi-sitting position.

"Here let me help you up, Big Guy." Stud slipped his arms around Breathred and pulled him up to a sitting position.

"How long was I out for?" Breathred asked again.

"Not long, twenty minutes at the most," Dr. Grayson said.

"Seemed like longer," Breathred mumbled, then he tried to jump to his feet, but Stud put his hand on his shoulder slamming him back to the wet ground. "The tomb! Has anyone gone into the tomb?"

"No. After what happened to you, I thought it best to proceed cautiously. Until we're sure the tomb is safe, no one gets in," Dr. Grayson stated. Stud thought a better idea was to blow the damn thing shut again, but nobody asked him.

"You got that right, lady," Brogan said, pushing his way through the crowd of people. "I've been in contact with my superiors. They've raised the threat level to five. While a lev five won't get CAPP SAT involved, it has CACA on standby should we need them."

"Really, Brogan, was it necessary to do call in your superiors?" Dr. Grayson asked.

"You bet your ass it was. When I see a man shot through the air by a door, my ass hair starts twitching. Let me tell you—it's doing the Mambo, as we speak," Brogan shot back.

"Sounds to me like you need to leave the canned beans alone." Stud couldn't resist the cheap shot. The man was such a maroon.

"So what do you suggest? We get our guns and shoot the place up until nothing comes out to get us in our sleep?" Dr. Grayson snapped.

"Sounds good to me," Brogan said.

"It would," Grayson huffed.

"Look, we can post guards," Breathred offered. "Brogan, you can't guard it around the clock. Don't deny that wasn't your plan. We can put two men to watch over the opening. That way nobody is left alone."

"Good thinking, but I'll have a radio set up at the base camp. Each guard will carry a walkie-talkie. I want somebody at camp in case something goes down," Brogan countered.

"I can live with the suggestion, if you can," Dr. Grayson said. "But I want to be notified next time, before you call your superiors."

"Can't make any promises, but I'll see what I can do." He grinned.

"See you do," Dr. Grayson warned.

"So what do we do now?" Stud was tired of all this back and forth. Humans tended to talk things to death, when all they needed was to let a chimp take charge. "I vote for going back to the tent and crawling into my sleeping bag, if anybody hasn't got a better idea."

"Sounds like a plan to me," Breathred piped up. "I'm kinda wet and my tender parts're all numb from the snow."

"I agree," Grayson smiled. She turned to Dr. Truehart, who was standing beside the open doorway leading to the tomb. "Edmund, do you mind helping Brogan set up the radio equipment? I'll assign guards once I've had a chance to warm up."

"I'll be glad to, Donna. If you wouldn't mind, could you have somebody bring back some coffee? I'm half past frozen, myself," he chuckled.

"As soon as we get back, I promise." She smiled. "And some sandwiches. You look like you could use a bite to eat."

"I wouldn't turn it down," he answered.

"Good. Whoever you send can stay with the limey while I get the equipment set up at camp and bring the walkie-talkies for the guards," Brogan said, lighting a cigar.

Stud almost offered to stay behind just to give Truehart grief, but Breathred needed him. Something weird had gone on at that door, besides the static shock from hell. He could tell from the look on Breathred's face, some bad shit was about to go down and wondered if all Brogan's precautions would be enough to stop it once started.

Breathred took all this in absently. His gaze was riveted to the hollow void of the tomb's entrance. He tried to peer into the darkness, but except for fleeting shadows playing off the waning sun, nothing could be seen. Despite this, he felt the malevolence leaching from the opening. No matter how seductive the voice had been in his head, he knew without a doubt like Pandora, he had loosed an old evil upon the world. He just hoped he would fare better than she had.

~ * ~

"Thank you, Doctor. That is exciting news. I do wish I could be there to enjoy this moment with you, but unfortunately, duty calls." Leopold grimaced.

Lewis knew the look on the elder vampire's all too well. Leopold was not getting what he wanted. That always put him in a bad mood. He had seen it coming, as soon as he saw the doctor's name on the caller ID. From the expression on the old vampire's face they must have gotten the tomb open.

"Get in touch with me as soon as you can. Perhaps Lewis and I can make time in our schedule to get back up to site. Thank you again," Leopold said before slamming the phone down on the table.

"Things not going well?" Lewis said, trying not to crack a smile.

"No, that foolish woman opened the tomb. I thought our agent was going to stop her until we could figure out a way for us to be present," Leopold ranted.

"I don't know. You handled that side of things." This time Lewis couldn't help himself—a huge smile split his ebony face. He quickly put his hand over his face to cover it up. No sense in making Leopold any madder than he already was.

"Just shut up. Well, since you don't know shit about it, let's talk about something you do know. Did you get the truck like I told you to?" Leopold demanded.

"Yeah, it's on standby."

"I want you to have it here by sunset tomorrow. I feel a road trip coming on."

"Hey, Leo. Look on the bright side. If they got the door open, it means your virgin is still intact," Lewis said, hoping it would calm the vamp down some.

Leopold poked his long finger in the younger vampire's face. "It does, doesn't it? You had better just hope he stays that way."

"Why do I have to worry about your virgin?" Lewis asked indignantly. This didn't sound good at all.

"Because, if this blows up in my face, somebody has to pay and you can't very well expect me to pay for your mistake," Leopold snapped.

Before Lewis could respond, Leopold swept from the room. Lewis was torn between being grateful the old poof was gone, and hating the fact he had let Leopold get in the last word. In any case this wouldn't do. It was just like the man to make being dead a pain in the ass.

Thirty Seven

There are things your Mother never told you, and things you wish she'd kept to herself.

Christopher Roberts was not happy. Drawing guard duty was bad enough, but to have to sit out here in the fricking cold with that goof off Sharbano was more than he could stand. Looking over his shoulder, he saw his fellow guard propped up against a pile of snow-covered dirt, snoring. Hell, the dumbass was already asleep. Just great. They had three more hours until they got relief and Sharbano was already acting like he was off duty. Two o'clock couldn't get here fast enough. A warm bed was calling his name.

Chris walked over to the sleeping man and kicked his feet out from under him. Sharbano fell crashing to the ground. Roberts let out a satisfied chuckle. Served the bastard right. Good thing Brogan hadn't caught him. The Canadian had been checking up on them since they came on duty. If the sawed-off runt was going to keep coming out here, why wasn't he on duty? This was a pain in the old vertical upright.

"What the hell'd you do that for?" Sharbano groused, rubbing his sore backside.

"Thought I saw Brogan coming," Roberts lied.

"Man, that guy's a freak," Sharbano whispered, just in case Brogan was within hearing distance.

"I got to hit the head, Chuck. Think you can handle it for a few minutes until I get back?"

"Sure, go ahead. You better call it in, though. Whoever's manning the radio'll have a fit, if we both don't check in."

"Okay, can you do it for me? I can't squeeze it shut for much longer. If you need me, give a yell." Roberts duck-walked back toward camp.

"Got it. Hey, Chris, better watch out for critters. They might take a liking to that backside," Sharbano shouted after him.

"If they can stand the smell, let 'em try," Roberts yelled back.

Sharbano lifted the radio to his ear and called in. It took about two minutes to explain the situation. It would have taken less time, but felt he owed it to Roberts to make sure everyone knew about his leaky bowels.

Releasing the button, Sharbano was left with the realization he was the only one who was stirring this far from camp. It frankly gave him the willies. Who knew what was hiding out there? There could be anything from rabbits to a frigging Big-Foot. His gaze shifted uneasily over the night-drenched landscape. Uncertainty filled him at the thought of being alone guarding a grave. The whole thing was too much like a bad horror movie, or a good one for that matter.

This was not what he had had signed up for. Chuck was only in this class because of a girl anyway, and the chick hadn't even made the cut to come along. Chuck wasn't even sure how he'd made it, to tell the truth. He kicked at a lump of snow, only to have his toe crash into a hidden rock. After hopping around for a more than suitable time, he collapsed onto a bare patch of ground that had not been touched by the early snow.

Chuck let his head fall to his chest. Man, when would he learn not to let women get him into things like this? He was a Liberal Arts major for Pete's sake. Last time he looked, liberal arts majors didn't squat in the snow in the middle of nowhere. They, on the whole, preferred squatting in smoky bars. If it wasn't for the extra credit, he wouldn't be here at all.

A shadow passed over the moon, making him glance skyward. The biggest owl he'd ever seen was flying toward the tree line. The bird let out an eerie hoot that sent him flying to his feet. This was just too spooky. Where the hell was Chris? How long did it take to drop a stinky load, anyway?

He settled down facing the open tomb door, trying not to think about it. The black hole glared back at him, taunting him. Chuck found himself sliding back from the opening. He didn't like it one bit. This whole damn thing was freaky. He was beginning to think the extra credit wasn't worth it.

Wait a minute! Was he crazy or did something just move in there?

Brogan had told them under no circumstances were they to enter the tomb. If anything strange happened, they were to call it in and let him handle it. He picked up his radio to call base camp, almost had it to his mouth when something made him stop. What if it was nothing? Then he really would look like a scared puppy. But, what if it was something? He sure as hell wasn't getting enough extra credit to die out here.

Fuck it! He was calling Brogan. After all, the Canadian was the one who got paid for doing this shit. As he raised the walkie-talkie to his mouth, a feather light touch danced at the base of his neck. He was instantly frozen in place.

Chuck my love. You do not need their help. Come to me and I'll give you all the help you'll need, a voice whispered in his ear.

The soft, sultry voice sent a shiver down his spine. Chuck, who was no stranger to erotic dreams, recognized the voice as being of that nature. Against his own volition, he felt himself drop the walkie-talkie to the ground.

You don't need those fools. Enter the darkness and know the pleasure that awaits you, the likes of which you have never dreamed possible, the voice cooed.

"Chris is that you? If it is, this isn't funny," Chuck howled into the darkness.

Does this look like Chris to you?

Chuck's entire body was cold with sweat and fear. His brain quaked with the fact something was here with him—something other than human. The part of the human mind that couldn't help but look into the unknown took over. All of Chuck's survival instincts went into quiet remission. In a move that defied all semblance of logic itself, the frightened boy turned to the shrouded tomb.

Light shimmered within the darkness. Gradually the light condensed and took form. Chuck stared breathlessly at a vision that would have quickened even a priest's libido. A woman—no, a goddess—stood framed by the blackness of the night. She was every bit of six feet and every inch of it was woman. Bountiful curves strained against the tight-fitting gossamer barely concealing the pleasures they held in check. He licked his lips, which had suddenly gone dry. His eyes roamed the vision, lingering shamelessly on certain areas longer than seemed necessary, before finally settling onto her perfectly formed face.

Large almond eyes the color of the forest under the fullness of the midday sun beckoned to him from a cage of sweeping lashes. He wanted to look away, but his gaze was imprisoned by her stare. Her lips were plump ribbons under her Romanesque nose. His mind replayed the fantasy of holding those lips in his, until his body burned with the want of them.

He shook his head trying to clear her from his eyes. The vision's flowing auburn hair and perfect face just wouldn't allow it. Chuck closed his eyes and counted slowly to ten. He went ahead and added eleven and twelve, just to be on the safe side. Finally, feeling he had let enough time go by to clear whatever mirages had decided to populate his waking mind, Sharbano forced his eyes open.

The woman was still there. So, maybe this wasn't a dream. He liked the idea. It was probably a Canadian honey who just happened to be wandering around in the forest looking for a little fun. He had already decided this would be a perfect spot for a nudist colony. What if there already was one, and she was the welcoming committee? He liked that even better. It made him forget all about the voice in his head.

"You know you're not supposed to be around here. We kinda got a situation going on," Chuck said, deciding to wow her with his authority.

You don't say. What kind of situation could bring a man of your obvious strength into the night, good sir? the woman whispered in his mind.

"Well. It seems we've unlocked a gateway straight to hell." He gave her a sly wink. "And they sent ol' Sharbano out here to keep things from getting out of hand."

So brave you are. It makes a woman feel safe to know a man like you is here to protect us. She all but swooned into his arms, as she spoke.

"Don't worry, little lady. I'm not about to let a fine piece of womanhood such as yourself get hurt. No sir, this good ol' boy knows how to take care of things," he boasted. Then added silently to himself, "Man, she's eating this up."

Oh, I feel ever so much better.

"You should, baby," he smirked.

Don't think me forward, but I think you deserve a reward for being such a selfless warrior, to brave this blistering cold to protect little ol' me. Her fingers tweaked the top of her shift, letting it drift slowly to the ground. *Come, my love, let me show you how appreciative I truly am.*

Chuck sputtered at the sight and followed the twinkling figure, as it receded into the stygian tomb. As the darkness swept over him, he suddenly came to his senses. By then it was too late. His muffled screams fell on dead air.

~ * ~

Breathred's head flew from his pillow. His hand fell to the crucifix. In the near dark of the tent, the cross throbbed a deep crimson beneath his sleep-shirt. He instantly drew back his blistered fingers. It was only then he noticed the burning sensation running across his chest where the crucifix sat. In spite of the pain, he left the icon where it lay. Something told him removing it wasn't a good idea.

Swinging his legs from the bed, he felt the wrongness in the air. His thoughts went out to the tomb. It was emanating from there. Breathred was sure of it. The Mother must have come awake. It was the only explanation that made any sense. Breathred hastily shoved his boots over his thermal underwear, not even bothering to pull on his pants. Grabbing his jacket from the edge of the cot, he rushed out of the closed tent-flap.

Exiting the tent he saw Stud stirring on his cot. Breathred guessed his footsteps pounding through the tent flap must have shaken Stud from his sleep. As sorry as he felt for waking his friend, he welcomed the company of not being the only one awake. Something bad was going on and he needed all the help he could get.

Breathred looked back to see Luna joining Stud in his mad dash to catch up with him. Apparently whatever was going on, was affecting more than just him. He crested the rise that dropped into the dig, searching for some sign his gut was lying to him. Only darkness greeted him and he knew what they said about what hid in the dark. Breathred waited long enough for Stud and Luna to catch up before taking off again. He wasn't afraid of the dark or anything, but they might be, so he was just being courteous of their feelings and not a scaredy cat.

~ * ~

Leopold smiled in the darkness. He, too, felt the stirrings in the air, as the Mother moved once again in the world. It was only her astral self, but she was awake. The Mother was weak and not fully aware, but could feel her moving about the world. Her true awaking would not come until the ceremony took place. This was but a flexing of her powers, a way to attain sustenance after her long slumber. He was close enough to draw strength from her, but far enough away that her presence was but a mere tickle in the back of his mind.

He was glad Lewis wasn't here to share this moment. The experience was something to be savored in solitude. All too soon, he would be forced to share her with the world. Leopold would take this time to relish the glow of success. Lewis would return with the truck, and the moment would pass. Tomorrow they would make the journey to meet their maker. Until then, he would enjoy the gentle touch of the oblivion to come.

Thirty Eight

Boffrend's in no way endorses the use of second-rate materials in the performance of vampire slaying. To that end a catalogue at the back of this handbook offers a full line of slaying essentials at low, low prices.

Breathred met Brogan as he reached the tomb. No one was there other than the two of them. He'd lost his friends after topping the rise overlooking the tomb. The two guards were gone, and the tomb sat empty. Brogan pointed to the snow, to a line of footprints that led into the tomb. Breathred took a step toward the tomb, only to have Brogan throw his arm in front of him.

"No way, Kid. Until we find out what's going on, nobody sets foot near that damn hole."

"What if the guards are in there? We have to help them."

"Then, they'll damn well stay there until morning. Even if they need help, they're beyond any help we can give them," the man answered flatly.

"We can't just leave them in there!"

"That's exactly what we're going to do," Brogan snapped. "I won't risk another member of this team because those two can't follow orders."

They were about to go at it again when Stud and Luna sprinted up. They were closely followed by Roberts, hiking up his pants. Their arrival broke up Breathred's and Brogan's argument. The sight of Roberts gave them both a new focal point for their anger.

"Where in the hell, have you been?" Brogan demanded, jumping in the boy's face.

"I had to take a dump. Chuck was supposed to call it in," Chris said. "Why what's going on? Where's Chuck? He'll tell you."

"That's what we want to know," Brogan snapped.

"Roberts, how long were you gone?" Breathred asked, hoping to divert some of Brogan's anger.

"I don't know," Chris said, scratching his head. "Maybe, twenty, twenty-five minutes. The cold kind of froze up the plumbing, if you know what I mean. Took a few minutes to flush the system out."

"Well...er...that's more info than I needed," Breathred stammered.

"More than any of us needed," Stud snarked. "Now, would

somebody mind telling us what the snot is going on?"

"It looks like Sharbano took a look-see in the tomb while Roberts here was playing Commander Turdsaway," Brogan snarled.

"Hey, it's not like you can bottle that stuff up," Roberts yelped.

"Whatever the case, Sharbano is missing," Breathred said.

"No he's not. Look!" Luna exclaimed, pointing toward the open tomb.

The twenty-two year old student was staggering out of the darkness. His face was drawn and haggard. His hair hadn't turned white, but it was sticking out at odd angles. What remained of his clothes hung in a tattered mess. Chuck's mouth worked feverishly to make words but all that came out was a muffled gasp. His blank gaze poured over the huddled crowd, haunting them with the deadness it contained.

Luna was the first to run over to him. Her hand on his shoulder sent shrill screams from his gaping mouth. He pushed away. His hands clawed at the air between them, as if warding off an unseen attack. Brogan and Roberts rushed over to restrain the man. Luna staggered back to Breathred's arms in shock.

Breathred wrapped his arms around her. "What's wrong with him?" she asked.

"I don't know, but if I had to guess I'd say something in the tomb got to him," Breathred whispered in her ear, hoping Brogan couldn't hear him.

"You think the vampire mother is awake?"

"All I know is I felt something just before we got here and whatever it was woke me from a dead sleep."

"Me too," she said, fearfully. "Breathred, I'm scared. This isn't a game is it?"

"No." Was all Breathred could say.

Sharbano's screams became muffled sobs, as they looked on. They were so entranced by the tableaux neither noticed a shadow had detached itself from the darkened tomb and slipped across the ground to become lost in the blending black of the night.

~ * ~

Luna let the steam from her coffee flow across her face before taking a sip from the cup. She looked up to see she wasn't the only one. Even Stud was nursing a cup, and he usually didn't touch coffee unless it had a donut attached to it. No one was talking about what had happened. They were all waiting for Dr. Grayson to join them. As soon as they got Sharbano settled in his tent, Brogan had sent Roberts to wake her.

They still weren't sure what to do about him. Physically, the boy was fine. Mentally, he was out there. Hopefully, Dr. Grayson would have some ideas. Luna looked over to the brooding Brogan. She could tell by the set of his jaw he had definite ideas of what to do and knew just what those ideas involved—tanking the whole dig and calling in the Marines, or whatever the

Canadian equivalent happened to be. Luna just hoped Dr. Grayson could talk him out of it. As if on cue, the professor walked through the tent flap.

"So, is there a good reason for me being torn from a perfectly delightful dream?" she grumbled, taking the empty chair beside Brogan.

"We have a situation," Brogan said.

"I figured that much out. Is anyone going to tell me what it is or do I have to guess?"

"Sharbano was attacked by something while he was on watch. We think whatever attacked him, may have come from inside the tomb," Breathred explained.

"How sure are you of this?" the professor gasped.

"We could ask Sharbano—if he could still talk," Brogan offered.

Grayson turned to Breathred. "He's dead?"

"No, but he isn't exactly in his right mind, either. He appears to be suffering from shock," Luna answered before the professor had a heart attack.

"Dear God!" Dr. Grayson exclaimed.

"Look, Doc. This little meeting is just a formality. I told you I'd let you know before I called my bosses, and this is it. As of now, this is in the hands of the Canadian government," Brogan informed them.

"You can't do that!" Luna shouted.

"Watch me," Brogan stated.

"Luna, he's right. If something is in the tomb, Brogan has every right to do what he sees fit to keep the team safe. I won't be party to any more of this team being hurt." Dr. Grayson's voice was coated with remorse. "He was a bit scatterbrained and on the lazy side, but he didn't deserve to be hurt."

"But that's what you hired Breathred for. Give him a chance to handle it before Grumpy over there, calls in the cavalry," Luna suggested. Somebody had to stand up for her sweetie. This was his shot to prove himself. They couldn't take the chance away from him.

"Excuse me," Brogan snapped. "Perhaps somebody would care to explain what she meant by that."

"Needle britches is a vampire slayer. The doc hired him to take the Mother out if she woke up," Stud butted in.

Brogan jumped to his feet. "You don't expect me to believe this pile of monkey crap, do you? No offense to the chimp, but this is just plain crazy. I can buy into vampires. I can even buy into geek boy knowing a thing or two about this paranormal bullshit, but there is no way in hell he's a vampire slayer and there's an all powerful vamp queen under our feet. What we have here is a random ghosting at the best."

"I am what she says, and this is the tomb of the Mother of all vamps," Breathred said. "Doctor Grayson found evidence of it on her last dig. She thought it a good idea to have an expert along in case the tablet was authentic."

Brogan slapped his fist down on the table in front of them. "Just great. I've looked over your papers and not once was this mentioned in any of them."

"I thought it would sound crazy, so I left out that teensy little piece of information. We weren't even sure the tablet was speaking of vampires," Dr. Grayson said. "If I said I was looking for evidence of vampires in ancient history, your superiors would have thought me a loon at best."

"Got me there, Toots. So, do you really think a vampire got the kid?" Brogan asked no one in particular.

"For all we know, he might've just gone stir crazy. It's been known to happen," Breathred said. "But, for what it's worth, I think it was a vampire."

"Then, I have no choice but to get CAPP SAT involved. This is their ballpark now," Brogan answered, just loving how this would sound when he called it in. "Now, if you'll excuse me, I have a phone call to make."

Luna rose to stop him, but before she had the chance the tent flap billowed in, bringing a tornado of snow into the tent. She stepped back as the ice-clad figure of Roberts followed in its wake. Instinctively she pushed past the freezing man and looked through the flap. The campground was covered in piles of snow that seemed to be growing by the minute. Any second now she fully expected the entire landscape to turn into one giant white blob.

"We got trouble," Roberts chattered excitedly behind her.

"What now?" Brogan snapped.

Luna held back the flap for him to see the whirling landscape. "I think you should come look at this."

"One thing at a time, Sweetheart." She gave him a dirty look as he turned back to the freezing boy. "Roberts, you first."

"The radio's down. The snow and wind just blew the whole tent away. The radio shorted out before we could get it out of the weather," Roberts reported, his teeth clanking the whole time.

"What about the cell phones, or the computers?" Brogan demanded.

"The antennas and all the computer equipment were in the same tent as the radio. It was the freakiest thing you ever saw. It was like it wanted to destroy that one tent. Nothing else was damaged."

Luna let the flap fall back into place as the companions went dead silent. No one wanted to say what was on their minds. Luna's mouth hung open like the rest of them. It was too frightening for them to speak aloud. All the what-ifs had come crashing down on them. There were things that went bump in the night and the Queen Bee of all those things was waking up, and man, was she hungry.

Brogan, naturally, was the first to make a move toward the tent's opening. Luna fell back as he brushed the flap back with an urgency they all felt. Even though she knew what awaited them outside, she couldn't bring herself to join him. Instead she went to the others huddling for warmth that wouldn't come. In the darkness of night, the stark white was a curse upon their hearts even a blazing fire couldn't heat.

~ * ~

Breathred followed the Canadian as he walked out into the swirling, icy mist. In the span of an hour, the landscape had been retooled by something other than nature. Snow was piled a good two feet deep in some places.

Breathred could smell the mystical energies flowing around him. The storm was a product of the awakening. He sensed the Mother's power in every snowflake that swept past him and could tell Brogan sensed it too. Maybe not on the level he, himself, did, but something close to it. Fear traced every inch of the man's face.

The storm wasn't the worse part. What frightened him the most was she was not fully awake. For all intents and purposes the Mother was nothing more than a dried up corpse lying on a slab. If she could affect the world in the state she was in now, what kind of chaos would be enacted should she become fully awake? Breathred shuddered. As much as he would like to, couldn't blame the cold for it.

~ * ~

The shadow watched the two men. The substance from the other had given her enough strength to break the bonds of her self-imposed prison. True, her physical form was trapped, but her soul was free to walk the shadows that fell between. Soon, such weakness would not be the case. She would be able to walk—flesh and blood among the human world again.

In her slumber, she had heard the people above her. It took a while to remember who she was. She had begun slowly leaching the energy of small animals that burrowed in the earth of her tomb. Time passed slowly, then remembered she had a name. In the old days she had been known as D'brea Asksafomoore in the language of the people of the icy wastes, as her people called themselves. Her name meant *She Who Thirsts For Men In Bad Places And Does Things To Them That Would Make A Walrus Blush.* She thought the name fit, especially the walrus part.

Thinking back, maybe she had been too rough with her first meal in eons. How was she to know these modern men were so fragile? He passed out in the first five minutes, and D'brea hadn't even got to the part where she threw her leg over. Well, it didn't matter, because she didn't get to do it. Most disappointing. Now, the little hairy one looked like he had stamina. She liked stamina in a man. It wasn't her favorite thing, but it came in a close second.

As good as he looked, the one next to him smelled like pure heaven. He wasn't much to look at, but man did he have blood to make a girl sweat for. She toyed with the idea of taking a sample. Not too much, just enough to settle her nerves. Well, what would it hurt? It wasn't like anyone could see her in this form. She'd just nip on down there, slip in, get a quick bite, and come on back up. It would be good for her. After that, maybe she could get the dreamy hunk of a man with him to follow her back to the tomb for a quick tumble.

D'brea let herself flow into shadow. The earth echoed against her touch. Almost to her target, she caught wind of something foul on the air. She stopped and clung to the shadows that called the forest's edge their home. A slip of a girl was walking toward the two men. If D'brea had been in her physical form, she would have hissed. Not very ladylike, but it was in her to do so.

The girl was a Dushato. So, their race still roamed the earth. D'brea wondered if the same could be said of her own race. Perhaps the Dushato had purged the land of them. The war between their races was as old as time, itself. D'brea, herself, had started the war, so knew how deep the hatreds ran. Seduce one Dushato prince and they take offense for all eternity. Talk about big babies.

Well, from the looks of it, the Dushato was the tall one's bodyguard. No, the way she looked at him said they were undedicated mates. Ah, a challenge. She loved a challenge. For a taste of that one, it was a challenge she was more than willing to accept.

D'brea eased back into forest. She was tired. She had expended too much energy. The man would have to wait. Already the night waned toward day. She would rest. There would be time enough for her new quest. After all she had forever to look forward to.

Thirty Nine

Stake first, and ask questions when the dust settles.

Luna couldn't shake the feeling from the night before. It itched at her brain like an old scab. It had started as soon as she walked out to join Breathred and Brogan. She had only felt it once or twice before. Both of them had coincided with the times they had been around the vamps. This was like that only a hundred times itchier. The fact the feeling still sat with her almost seven hours later was a testament to the intensity of the sensation.

She stared into the snowblown camp. The storm had yet to let up. In places snow had already obliterated once easily-recognizable landmarks. Against Brogan's orders, Dr. Grayson had the students keeping the entrance of the tomb clear of snow. They worked in teams of four and none of them stayed for more than an hour at a time, the only way Brogan would allow them out of the tents. So far, they had no repeats of what had happened to Sharbano.

As much as Luna hated the thought of going inside, she turned back to the main tent. The sound of arguing could easily be heard coming from inside. She grimaced. They were still at it. Four hours and still they couldn't decide what to do. It was enough to make her scream. In spite of her frustration, she pushed her way into the tent.

"Come on, we're trapped here. We might as well go ahead and see what's in there," Stud shouted in Brogan's face while jumping up and down on the table in front of him.

"That's all the more reason, not to mess with it," Brogan yelled back.

Breathred shoved the chimp off the table and appealed to Brogan. "We're not asking for everyone to go in, just Doctor Grayson and the three of us," he pointed to Luna, Stud and himself. "You can keep everyone else out of the way. If anything happens, you can get them as far away as you can."

"Watch it, Petrifunck. Last time I looked I was more qualified than you to enter," Truehart stated.

"Me, as well," Jessica added, glaring at Truehart.

"People, can we focus on the important thing—getting someone inside?" Dr. Grayson broke in.

"She's right," Breathred agreed. "Brogan, give us a chance to find what we came for. You have my word we won't disturb anything."

Brogan rocked back in his chair. This was getting them nowhere and giving him a headache. They were right. They needed to find out what was going on inside the tomb. He'd checked out all the routes at dawn. Every one of them was packed with snow. They weren't getting out of here anytime soon. He was a soldier and knew facing an enemy without knowing what you faced was suicide. He would give in, but he wouldn't make it easy for them. "Okay, you win, but I pick who goes in. Agreed?"

"If that's the only way to get in, I guess we'll have to agree," Dr. Grayson answered.

"So who's it going to be secret agent man?" Stud asked, getting back in the man's face.

"It, sure as hell won't be you," Brogan snapped.

"But who will it be?" Jessica spoke up.

"I want to keep it to a small group. Dr. Grayson goes of course. The rest of the team will consist of Breathred and Truehart," Brogan stated.

"That's not fair. I know as much as Truehart," Jessica shouted.

"That's why you'll be here at the short-range radio with me. I need somebody to interpret what these eggheads are spouting. Before you say another word, it's ended. The rest of you will stay in camp. I don't want anybody near the tomb. In case you're wondering, I mean you and the monkey, Luna."

"But—"

Brogan cut Luna off, "No buts, or we can all sit here and wonder what's in that damn hole,"

"Then, we want to be on radio duty, too."

"Fine with me. One more thing. We only have four hours of daylight, so we do this tomorrow. I don't want anybody near that place after dark. Are we clear?" Brogan asked, his steely gaze sweeping the crowd.

"After what happened last night, I don't think you'll have a problem keeping people away from the tomb," Dr. Grayson said, her voice showing the tension they all felt.

~ * ~

Luna stood in the opening of the tent she now shared with Breathred and Stud. As night fell across the treetops she sensed a pack of wolves heading north not far from the camp. A part of her wished she could join them, but that path was denied to her. Her place was with Breathred now. He and Stud tossed uneasily on their cots. It had been too early to turn in, but after the restless night before, they had decided to try. Tomorrow would come all too soon.

Rest was something she desperately needed, but still couldn't bring herself to go to sleep. Her body was all keyed up. It was more than just the groundswell of events. Her instincts told her she had a job to do. Luna

Walking Batch wracked her brain, trying to figure out what her instincts were trying to tell her. She dredged up the memories of her childhood. Every lesson learned at her mother's knee flooded her. Somewhere in there was a snippet to explain it all to her. She just had to sort through them to find it.

The crunch of feet on snow broke her from her thoughts. She glanced into the gloom expecting to see Brogan making another round of the camp. To her surprise Sharbano stumbled across the camp, heading toward the tomb. Dammit, where was Roberts? He was supposed to be watching the man.

She turned to wake Breathred, but stopped herself. He needed his rest. Besides, she could handle this. A tug on her arm stopped her from running after the man. Luna looked down to see Stud rubbing sleep from his eyes.

"What's going on?" he asked between yawns.

"Shhh," Luna hissed.

"Don't tell me to shhh."

"Be quiet. I just saw Sharbano heading for the tomb," Luna told him in a hushed whisper.

"Why are you whispering? That zombie can't hear you. Let's go get his ass, so I can get back to bed." Stud took a step toward the staggering Sharbano.

"No, Stud. I want to see what's going on. Let's follow him and see what he does."

Stud crossed his arms. "Look here, Velma. I ain't Scooby-doo and Shaggy's ass is asleep. So, unless you got a hippo in your pocket, we're getting the dead weight back in bed and that's that."

"Just help me. There's two Scooby snacks in it for you, if you do," Luna laughed.

"Make it a triple banana latte, and you got a deal." Stud winked.

"You got it. Now let's get going. He's almost out of sight," Luna said, as Sharbano slipped into the sparse tree line.

Not waiting for Stud, Luna took off after the fleeing man. She danced over the snow. Her feet made deep ridges in the loosely-packed whiteness. She was pleased to hear the soft crunch of Stud closely behind her. Despite her earlier bravado, she was glad to have some help. While Sharbano might not present much trouble by himself, she was not sure what might be waiting for them out there in the darkness.

She brushed past the first few stunted pines and kept going. It took her several seconds to realize they were heading away from camp instead of toward the tomb. Luna slowed down and scanned the forest. Luna saw no sign of Sharbano, but she was just as sure they hadn't passed him, either. He had been in full sight up until that last turn. The boy had to be close by.

Luna signaled for Stud to draw up beside her. Maybe between the two of them, they could figure this out. Before she could begin her search, a wall of flesh dropped from the sky and slammed her to the ground.

Expecting another attack, Luna rolled out of the way, as soon as she hit the ground. The press of her attacker's weight pressed down on her feet. She kicked out and scrambled further from his reach. Over the blood pounding in her ears, Luna heard Stud shouting at her. She didn't have time to listen. Her only thoughts were of getting away.

"You can't stop me!" a hysterical yell rang out.

Luna flipped onto her knees and looked in the direction of her attacker. Sharbano was hunched over, foaming at the mouth. His face contorted into a mask of hate. The sight of him made her hair stand on end. He barely looked human anymore. She felt herself being pulled apart at the seams; the urge to give in to what she had been holding in for so long, tore at her. Deep inside her, heritage demanded release.

"Sharbano, we just want to help you. Nobody's trying to hurt you. Just let us take you back to camp," Luna said, sounding a lot calmer than she felt. Something about him set off a whole orchestra full of bells and whistles. It was getting harder to hold it all in.

"You lie! You want to keep me from her. She told me you would try to keep us apart. Well, I won't let you!" His teeth gnashed his lower lip, drawing twin waterfalls of blood down his chin where his canines were.

"Look, Chuck. Calm down. This is getting us nowhere," Luna all but growled, as she inched closer to him. Looking to the left, she saw Stud doing the same.

Without warning, Sharbano leapt. He clawed the air, striking Luna as he came down. She was thrown back on the unfamiliar ground. Chuck didn't give her a chance to recover. He bowled into her, driving her to the ground. She struggled to free herself from his grasp but blow after blow kept her pinned to the ground. She just couldn't get her arms free to stage an offensive. It was all she could do to defend herself.

"You can't beat me, girl. She's given me her strength, her power," Sharbano screamed into her face. His breath was fetid and hot against her bruised face.

That was the last straw. A beating she could take. Luna could even take a good tongue lashing, if she deserved it, but there was no way she was going to take chronic halitosis on top of everything else.

"Asshole, you don't want to get me angry," Luna warned him, but it was already too late. She was pissed and sure as hell not going to take it anymore.

The urge to fight her nature was gone. Like slipping into a second skin, the beast took over. The change was subtle at first. Only she could even tell it was taking place. Distantly, she could hear Stud crying out her name, but the fact was beyond her caring. There was only one thing that mattered— the acceptance of her true nature, the birthright of Coyote.

Her body burned. The moon kissing her fevered face, Luna smiled at her heavenly mother's touch. The smile was frightening to behold. Her teeth had grown long and pointed to match the elongation of her nose and mouth into a single unit. In that last minute she gave herself to it totally and without reservation. The child of Coyote had come.

Luna howled at Sharbano, who looked at her oblivious to her change. She smiled as the rustle of fur beneath him brought his attack came to an abrupt halt. The look on his face pleased the beast for it was one it knew well. It was called fear. Before he could regain his composure, Luna threw him across the small clearing.

~ * ~

Stud had been all but blind. He saw Luna go down, but that was it. The last clear sight of her he had was when she rolled under the rabid Sharbano. Stud looked for an opening he could exploit, but found none. He was kept rooted in place by the uncertainty of the situation. For the first time in his life, Stud didn't know what to do. If he rushed in, he could do nothing more than get hurt himself. The chimp was no fighter. Stud hated to admit it, but he was too small to be of any help, hated himself for thinking it, but knew it was true.

Then, the situation changed. Sharbano flew through the air, right toward him. Stud ducked out of the way, as the boy skidded into the snow. Sharbano landed hard, throwing a blanket of snow into the air with his impact. The man flinched twice and didn't move again. Stud didn't know what kind of kung fu she had used, but good for her.

Jumping to his feet, Stud looked for Luna. His eyes went to the spot he last remembered seeing her and Sharbano. Instead of his friend, a hulking shadow moved from the darkness toward him. The moon moved from a bank of clouds lighting the land. Stud let out a strangled gasp. Okay, now was definitely the right time to wet himself.

A wolf the size of a small horse drifted across the ground. It was huge. Stud was no fool, he watched Animal Planet. These things were killers. Oh my God! It was covered in blood. The big-ass dog had eaten Luna and was coming at him, like he was dessert. He'd seen the Temple of Doom. He knew what they did to chimps. He was just a little chimpanzee. He was too young to be served chilled.

Fumbling for his last shred of bravery, Stud ran. His little legs pumped for all they were worth, but it wasn't enough. He felt the wolf sink its teeth in the loose folds of his jacket. Closing his eyes, decided to face death with all the strength he could muster and promptly passed out to avoid the whole thing, all together.

Forty

Okay, vampires can have bad days, but don't expect it to be today.

The tire was flat and there was nothing Lewis could do to change the fact. Leopold thought differently and was quite vocal about it. As a result, Lewis had tuned him out thirty minutes ago. It was the only thing that had stopped him from finding a stake and driving it through Leopold's old ass. Before his death Lewis had been a pimp and a player. Players did not change flats. They had 'hos to do that shit. Just because he was a vampire did not mean he had magically changed into the type of man who changed tires.

He reached over and hit the clock button on the radio. It flashed 9:42. They had been sitting in the truck for over an hour. Leopold slapped his hand away from the dash, continuing his tirade, blissfully unaware Lewis had stopped listening. Okay, maybe he could change a flat. Anything was better than listening to Leopold bitch all night.

Without a word Lewis opened the door and jumped to the ground. His legs sank up to the knees in snow. Shit. These pants were dry-clean only. Well, Mr. High and Mighty was going to buy him a new pair. Grumbling under his breath, he walked around the truck looking for the flat. The vamp made two circuits before giving up. He had heard the pop and felt the truck drag to the right. The tire had to be flat. Checking the tires again, nope, they were all aired up. What the hell was going on?

"Having car trouble?" a voice asked, sending Lewis tumbling into the truck. The bundled up owner of the voice bent over and gave his hand to the floundering man. "Here, let me help you up, young feller."

Lewis got back to his feet. "Where the hell did you come from?"

"South Dakota originally, but I've been about everyplace."

In the light from the open truck door, Lewis gave the man a good once-over. What little he could see of him, he appeared to be an Indian—an old one at that. The rest of him was covered in the biggest parka Lewis had ever seen. Except for his face, there wasn't an inch of the man was left bare to the weather. But, it was the old man's eye that haunted him. They were black as coal. As dark as they were, the twin orbs contained a twinkle that made Lewis nervous. The eyes belonged to a man who was liable to do anything.

Mis Staked

Lewis found the voice to ask, "No, I mean, what are you doing out here in the middle of nowhere?"

"Oh, you'll have to speak plainer than that. My granddaughter ran off with some white boy from the States and I came up here to make sure he didn't try anything funny. I don't have to tell you what them pale-skins will try to get away with. Do I?" The old man gave Lewis a jab in his ribs with his elbow. "But you don't want to listen to an old man jabbering away in the middle of a blizzard, do you?"

"No, I really don't," Lewis sneered.

"See there. I told you so." The old man laughed. "Now, what seems to be the trouble with your truck?"

"I thought we had a flat, but it looks like we just bogged down in the snow," Lewis said, hoping the man would just walk on down the road.

"Well, old Coy knows a thing or two about these tricky suckers. Why don't you just hop back on up in the cab, and I'll see what I can do to get you back on your way." Coy pushed Lewis back toward the front of the truck.

Lewis grumbled the entire way to the cab. The old man was crazy as a loon, but anything was better than standing out in the cold.

"Now, I'm going to try and wedge something under your back wheels. When I give the word, you gas it and pull it forward," Coy said, walking away. His voice was almost lost on the rising wind.

Lewis shook his head and jumped back into the cab. He ignored Leopold, who was ranting to his own reflection. Lewis didn't know what was worse—a crazy vampire in the truck, or a crazy Indian outside. He turned the key. The engine sputtered, but he pumped the gas until it finally caught. Sticking his head out the open window, Lewis waited for the man's call. He didn't have to wait long. The cab was just beginning to warm up when he heard the Indian call out. Throwing the truck into gear Lewis slammed on the gas.

The truck rolled back. Lewis rocked back and forth in his seat to help it get going. After several attempts the truck rolled free. He let it coast forward for about twenty yards before putting it into neutral and letting the truck idle.

"About damn time," Leopold told his reflection.

Lewis ignored him. He threw the truck door open and hopped down. He looked back expecting the old man to come ambling up. Lewis saw no one. Thinking maybe the old guy slipped when the truck broke free, he walked back to where the truck had been sitting.

Even though the snow had yet to let up, Lewis could see his own footprints in the snow, for the life of him he couldn't find any for the old man. He saw the hole where the back tire had been stuck. There was even a broken slab of wood with streaks of rubber where the back tire had run up it, but nowhere was there a single sign the Indian had been anywhere near the

231

truck.

Standing in the blowing snow, Lewis rubbed his head. He was losing it. Being cooped up with Leopold had finally driven him mad. It was bound to happen. He'd just thought it would have taken him longer than thirty years to do it. The wind picked up, deluging him in a shower of fresh snow from the treetops. Not about to stand in the dark nursing his paranoia, Lewis ran back to the truck and hopped in. Lewis wasn't even in his seat when he threw the truck into gear and took off.

The belching of the truck vanished into the night. When the sound was nothing more than distant thunder, the old Indian walked out of the woods. He smiled a shifty grin. It might not have been his best trick, but it had been enough to get the job done. Then again, Coyote had been known to be subtle when the need called for it.

In spite of his efforts, he wasn't sure it would be enough. Luna and her man had a wall of trouble heading for them, and there was little more he could do to stop it. This wasn't his game to play out. He might be able to wiggle his finger here and there, but that was about it. As much as his children meant to him, there was little he could do when he wasn't running the show. True, he had his own scheme in play. So he could dabble a bit to keep it going. Ultimately, the main event was out of his hands.

Soberly, he walked back the way the truck had come from. The old man hoped the white boy could handle this. A lot of people seemed to think he could. For Luna's sake, Coyote prayed they were right.

~ * ~

Stud was in the middle of praying, a sport he rarely played. He had already worked his way through the Egyptian, Greek and Roman Pantheons and was about to start on the Hindus, when he felt himself being slowly lowered to the ground. Here it comes, the last chomp before that last trip to the great banana tree in the sky.

"Stud, I can't believe you wet yourself," a gruff voice laughed.

Stud's ears perked up. Luna! It sounded like Luna, but it didn't. What if it was Luna talking from inside the wolf's belly? He didn't remember hearing a wolf could swallow somebody whole, but anything was possible.

Against his better judgment, he cracked a single eyelid. Then, promptly slammed it shut again. The wolf was right over him. It was a talking wolf. How dare a wolf talk, and with Luna's voice to boot! Everyone knew animals couldn't talk. It was ridiculous. Wait till he got home. He was going to start an Internet campaign to put an end to this talking animal shit, if it was the last thing he did.

"Come on. Open your eyes, Silly Butt," the Luna-wolf ordered.

"I am not. Now, take your wolf-talking ass somewhere else."

"You're one to talk. You're a monkey and you talk."

Stud crept one eyelid open. "That's different. Besides I didn't just eat a perfectly good girl and then start talking like her."

"Stud, it's me, Luna," the wolf said.

"What chou talkin' 'bout. Willis?"

Luna sat back on her haunches beside the flinching chimp. This would be harder than she thought. If it hadn't been for Sharbano, her secret would have been safe. Now, it was out in the open, and she was scared—scared of what she would say to Stud. Most of all she was scared of what Breathred would say when he found out. Sighing, Luna guessed the best thing to do was tell the whole truth. It wasn't like she could lie her way out of this.

"I was born like this," she said, turning her head to look at Stud's reaction.

"You were born a dog!" Stud exclaimed.

"No, a werewolf. See, in my tribe, in every generation a daughter of Coyote is born. My family has had the honor of being the heirs of Coyote since the dawn of time."

"And you've been hiding this from us?" Stud asked, sounding a little hurt.

"I didn't want to, but look at it from my side. By the time I knew I could trust you, I was afraid you wouldn't like me, if you knew the truth."

"Then, why tell me? I mean you could've run off or changed back before I saw you."

"I can't change back until morning, and I couldn't just leave you out here with Sharbano," Luna said, tears rolling down her furry face. "Please don't hate me. I'll understand if you do, but please don't tell Breathred. Let me do it."

"I don't hate you. You're my best friend," Stud said, tearing up himself.

"I am?"

"Yep." He threw his arms around her neck. All right, he was a big softy.

"What about Breathred? Are you going to tell him?" she asked, worried by what he was going to say.

Stud released her. "I won't tell him, but you're going to have to. He loves you, and he has a right to know."

"I know, but I don't want to tell him right now. With everything else I don't think he could handle it. Do you?" Luna asked.

"No, the boy ain't exactly flexible, when it comes to change," Stud agreed. "But you can't keep something like this a secret from him forever."

"I'll tell him, when he's ready."

"So can I ask you something?" Stud asked with a devilish grin.

"Yes…"

"Does this mean I can call you a bitch without getting my head chewed off?"

"No," she growled, giving him a good look at her teeth.

"Just checking. So what are we going to do with Sharbano?"

"Take him back to camp," Luna said, looking over at the unconscious man.

"You mean he's not dead?" Stud asked.

"No, I just knocked him out. He should wake up soon, though, so we better get going," Luna said, butting him to his feet with her muzzle.

"How do you expect to get back into camp like that? Hey, you aren't going to be able to. Are you?"

"No, I won't. You'll have to take him into camp. I'll help you get him there. You'll have to do the rest."

"Okay, but what am I going to tell Breathred, if he asks where you're at?" Stud asked.

"We just better hope he's still asleep. Otherwise, 'Lucy we got a lot of 'splaining to do!'" She laughed in spite of herself.

~ * ~

Luckily, the clearing was deserted when Stud dragged Sharbano's limp body the last few feet into camp after Luna had drifted back into the shadows. Seeing no one moving about, he assumed everyone must be asleep. He looked back to see Luna's golden eyes flashing in the darkness and waved to let her know it was all clear. He heard the rustle of leaves, as she slipped back into the forest. Stud hoped she would be okay. She might be a wolf-girl, but it didn't mean she was Wonder Woman. There were worse things than wolves out there. You just had to look at the lights by the tomb to know that for a fact.

He'd made it about half way across the camp when Stud heard the unmistakable sound of Brogan lighting a cigar. Just great! Did that bastard ever sleep?

"Wondered where he got to," Brogan said, through a haze of smoke.

"If you wondered, why the hell didn't you go after him?" Stud snapped.

"Saw you and the girl take off after him. Figured if you needed help, you would have called."

"Thanks." Stud dropped Sharbano's head to the ground. "So, where was Roberts?"

"He fell asleep. Said he didn't think Sharbano was going anywhere."

"Guess, he was wrong."

"Looks that way. So, where's the girl?"

"She went on into the tent," Stud lied, hoping Brogan hadn't been watching him come into camp, but doubting it.

"Must have missed her while I was taking a whiz," Brogan answered.

Stud could tell the man clearly didn't believe him, but was unwilling to push it. That was good, because he was in no mood for bullshit at the moment. "Do you ever sleep?" Stud blurted out. He couldn't help himself.

Brogan puffed on his cigar. "Not if I can help it. Look, you better get some rest. I'll put sleeping beauty to bed."

"Thanks, but aren't you going to ask me what he was doing running away from camp?" Stud asked.

"He was going to whatever's in the tomb. Am I right?"

"Basically, yes. Is anybody guarding it by the way?"

"Nope, I rigged some alarms across the opening. If anything tries to come out, I'll know before it does," Brogan said.

"Before I go to bed, let me ask you one more thing. What if whatever is in the tomb doesn't trip your precious alarms?" Stud asked, smugly.

"Then, none of us has to worry about waking up with morning breath tomorrow."

~ * ~

D'brea tried to stir, but was too weak. She had expended too much energy last night and would have to wait for one of the humans to come to her. The sound of them moving about kept her awake all day, but none ventured close to her tomb. Even the one from last night had not answered her call. Despite her best efforts, she was powerless.

She had acted too quickly with the first one. D'brea knew through experience you must sample slowly, so as not to draw suspicion, but she had been too hungry and let need override good judgment. That was a mistake she would not make again.

A forgotten sensation broke into her thoughts. Two faint echoes pinged in the back of her mind. Two of her children were close by. The storm was hampering them, but they were close enough for her to feel. For the first time in eons she knew her kind still existed. By tomorrow night they would reach her. D'brea saw into their minds they were coming for her. She didn't know if she liked that. From what little the Mother gleaned from their minds, her race had not changed since her entombment. How sad.

There was little she could do to stop them. So, she would wait for their arrival. Whatever their purpose, they were in for a rude awakening. D'brea was no man's slave. Her will was her own, and it was a lesson she was willing to teach this new generation. She hoped they were smarter than the old one. If not, it was a lesson they would not survive.

Forty One

Don't try to wake a vampire up, unless you know what you're doing. They don't like that.

Yawning, Luna walked back into camp, just as everyone was heading out to the tomb. A night on the cold ground had done little to improve her temperament after the fight with Sharbano. She had prowled through the forest for most of the night. Sometime during the middle of the night she had ventured close to camp.

Luna would have come on in and hid in her tent till morning, but damn if Brogan wasn't on guard duty all night, making it next too impossible to get anywhere near it. She contented herself with bedding down within earshot of the collection of tents. All in all, she was totally disgusted by the whole turn of events.

Waking up naked in a snowdrift hadn't helped her mood, either. She had at least remembered to tell Stud to leave her a set of clothes outside of camp before he had left. Otherwise, she would have had to walk starkers back into camp. That would have shocked everyone's modesty to the core, especially Breathred's. Not that she worried about that; her own modesty was enough she wasn't about to flaunt her goodies for everyone. She was saving all her flauntiness for Breathred—well, when the time was right, of course.

Across the clearing, Breathred caught sight of her walking in and waved. She smiled back and took off across the camp at a brisk trot. Breathred broke away from the small group heading to the tomb to meet her halfway. It was a rare thing for him to openly show affection like this. She almost broke into tears. He was finally opening up.

"I was worried when you weren't in the tent this morning," Breathred told her, slightly out of breath. "I thought something might have happened to you."

"I was okay."

Breathred shook his finger at her. "Stud told me what happened. You shouldn't have left so early without telling me."

"Aren't you cute," she said, reaching up to tweak his ear. This earned her a puckered snarl Breathred usually reserved for aunts and the occasional visit from his mother. Luna just laughed it off and went on. "I do know how to take care of myself, Mr. Petrifunck."

"I know." He dug his toe into the ground. "But why did you have to leave so early? Stud said you lost something when you and Sharbano were fighting, but you could have waited for me to go with you."

Luna thanked heavens Stud had come up with something, because she was clueless as to what to say, if the subject came up. "You needed to get your rest before you went into the tomb. Besides, I wasn't gone all that long."

"So, did you find it?"

"Find what?" She shot him a confused look, then caught herself. "Oh, yeah. It was right where I thought it was." She pulled out the only thing she could think of, the talisman—not that it did her any good, when she really needed it to—and showed it to him.

"Breathred, we're burning daylight. Get the drag out," Brogan shouted.

"Well, I guess I gotta go. They're waiting for me," Breathred said. She could tell he wanted to say something more about last night, but was holding back.

"Yeah, you better," Luna answered back. "If you need me, I'll be in the radio tent."

"I know." The expression on his face was enough to make her want to cry. He really was a puppy dog.

"Kiss her, for the love of hockey," Brogan yelled. The statement was followed by a round of less-than-subtle snickers.

Suddenly, Breathred realized he did want to kiss her. That was strange. Maybe this was what boyfriends were supposed to feel. Before he could think himself out of it, he leaned in and gave her a quick peck on the check.

*Author's note:
What did you expect, a long blistering smooch that'd make a hooker blush? Get real. This is Breathred we're dealing with here.

"I'll see ya later," he mumbled.

"You better," Luna yelled, as he started back to the others. Not able to help herself, she yelled after him. "And I'll have the rest of that kiss waiting for you when you get back."

Breathred gagged, but kept going. Hopefully, no one noticed her remark. She was across the camp. Even if they did, they were all grownups. Surely they had better things to do than eavesdrop on a private conversation.

"So, what do the think she meant by *the rest of the kiss* thing?" Brogan grinned, when Breathred reached them. "You don't think she plans to curl your toenails, do you?"

"Hush, Brogan. That is none of your business. You should be ashamed for even saying such a thing," Dr. Grayson snapped. "Can't you see from the look on Breathred's face, this is a matter he'd rather not discuss publicly?"

Brogan threw up his hands. "Hey, I'm just glad he has something to look forward to." He bent over and whispered in Breathred's ear. "If you decide to back out on the rest of that kiss, let me know. My toes haven't been curled in a long time. Might be fun to see if they still know how."

Breathred blanched at the very idea, but couldn't help wondering what toenail curling had to do with kissing.

"Can we please stop all this foolishness? It's bad enough to be ensconced in this hive of imbeciles without having to be constantly harangued by it," Truehart griped.

"Looks like we're not the only ones who need a good toe-curling, Petrifunck," Brogan howled.

"Bloody yanks!" Truehart exclaimed, as he stomped away.

"Hey, ya dumb Limey! I'm a Canuck," Brogan shouted after him.

"What you are is a distraction I can frankly do without at the moment. All your foolishness is cutting into my time. You promised me this one day to venture into the tomb, and so far all you've done is hamper the opportunity," Dr. Grayson informed the man.

"Okay, Doc. Lead the way, and never let it be said I left a woman unsatisfied."

As quickly as he moved, Brogan was unable to dodge the hastily constructed snowball that slammed into the back of his head.

"Shall we go, Breathred?" Grayson asked, wiping the snow from her hand. Grabbing him by the arm, she pulled him after Brogan, who was bobbing down the path. Breathred was more than a little unsettled by the way she uncharacteristically giggled the whole way, but the sight of Brogan wiggling, as he fought to keep the snowball from sliding down the inside lining of his jacket, was more than enough to make her forget her usual stoic demeanor he supposed. Breathred was having the devil of a time trying to keep from laughing, but he knew better than to give in to the urge. The sound of Brogan grumbling was enough to let him know to keep his mouth zipped. A hundred yards from the tomb, still mumbling, the man called them to halt a few minutes later.

"Before we jump our asses into this crap I think I need to reiterate the seriousness of what you're about to do. I'd be lying to ya' if I didn't tell ya' I'm having second thoughts about letting you yahoos go in there. I hate to admit it, but the only thing stopping me is I'd like to know what the hell's in there, too."

"Then stop holding us up, and let us get to it," Truehart grumbled.

"Let him finish talking first. I'd like to find out what's in there as much as you, but going in half-cocked is just plain stupid," Breathred cut the

Englishman off, glad for the reprieve Brogan's speech was giving them. Being this close to the tomb was giving him the heebie jeebies.

"Thanks, Breathred," Brogan gave him a nod before continuing. "I was able to salvage enough equipment from the wreckage of the radio tent for you to take a limited video hook-up in with you. Putting you three in the lion's den scares the crap out of me, but at least this way I can keep an eye on you in case things go south. As much as I'd like to say to hell with it, I can't. CAPP SAT wants answers and, my friends, this is my only chance to get those answers."

"You make us sound like bloody cannon fodder," Truehart snapped.

"Bub, you wanted to go in, not me. Don't bitch because you might get your ass handed to you. Feel free to back out anytime you want. Easily can fill your shoes and you can ride the chair beside me." Breathred saw the look on Brogan's face and knew the man was calling the Englishman's bluff.

"Kiss my arse, Canuck."

"Thought you'd see it my way." Breathred caught Brogan's sly wink, but kept his face blank.

"Brogan, is there anything else we should know before we go in?" Dr. Grayson asked.

He shook his head. "You all know what you have to do, but I want to make sure everybody knows this isn't a game. The first sign of trouble I want you to haul your asses out of there. This isn't the place for fools."

Truehart sneered. "And that does little to explain the inclusion of Petrifunck in this group. Perhaps we should have invited the monkey. At least then we'd have an excuse for this circus you have assembled."

"Well, he'd be the perfect match for the talking horse's ass we got now," Brogan snapped. "Now, shut your pie-hole so I can finish."

"Edmund, please show a little decorum. We are all colleagues in this," Dr. Grayson stated.

"It may be true of you and I, but Petrifunck is a farce, and you damn well know it. For the life of me, I can't see what madness consumed you to include him on this team," Truehart remarked, snidely.

"That is quite enough. Breathred is on this team because he has skills that are needed, much as yourself. If you can't accept the fact, maybe Doctor Easily should join us as Brogan suggested. I'm sure she would be more than happy to."

"You are quite right, Donna. My behavior was atrocious. Forgive me. I will endeavor to comport myself with more dignity in the future. Petrifunck, I apologize." Truehart begrudgingly extended his hand.

As Breathred shook the man's hand, he could tell by the look in the man's eyes this was a token gesture, at best. As long as it kept the peace, he would accept it in the spirit it should have been meant. He just hoped whatever animosity Truehart felt toward him would subside. This had to do with Truehart's brother, but he couldn't change the past. Heck, he couldn't even remember it.

"Good. Now that we've all made up and gone all Dr. Phil with each other, do you want to do this or not? "Brogan asked.

"I think you know the answer," Dr. Grayson stated.

"Good, while you three were bonding, I disabled the alarms and traps. I'm giving you four hours to look around. That's four hours by my watch, not yours." He tapped his wrist to illustrate his point. "I'll call you fifteen minutes before time to haul ass out, so you can wrap it up."

"That is scarcely enough time to do an adequate study of the tomb, let alone the detailed one we need to do!" Truehart exclaimed.

"Tough. You're under the misconception this is still your mission. The minute Sharbano went all psycho, this fell under the sole providence of the Canadian government. So, you can shove all your haughty speeches up your English wahzoos," Brogan explained in no certain terms.

"Edmund, if that is all the time Brogan is allowing us, we will have to make it work. Don't worry, we will still have a video record to work from, once we're back in Seattle," Dr. Grayson assured him.

"If the bloody barbarian doesn't confiscate it," Truehart warned.

"Don't give me any ideas, Bub," Brogan snarled.

"Stop all this. We have a job to do and all this bickering isn't helping. Brogan, if you have anything productive to say, say it. Edmund, you can be quiet and let him say it," Breathred ordered, frustrated by the whole thing.

"I only got one thing to say. Turn on your equipment and get going. I'll be in the radio tent waiting for your transmission," Brogan said. Breathred could tell he was making it a point to ignore Truehart.

"Now, was that so hard?" Breathred asked.

No one said a word. Dr. Grayson and Truehart shouldered their packs and walked down the slope to the tomb. Breathred held back, and moved closer to Brogan.

"I'd appreciate it if you kept an eye on Stud and Luna for me. You know, if anything should go wrong," Breathred said in a hushed whisper.

Brogan gave Breathred a look of concern. "Are you expecting trouble?"

"I've got a bad feeling about this. It's nothing I can put a finger on, but I'd feel better knowing you're watching out for them."

"Don't worry, Kid. I got the same feeling. If it gets hairy, I'll get 'em clear. You have my word on it."

"That's all I needed to hear." Breathred smiled, in spite of his doubts.

Brogan slapped him on the back. "You know, for an addle-brained dweeb you're okay. Now, get on down there."

Breathred didn't know whether to take it as a compliment or an insult, but Brogan was right. Daylight was slowly slipping away. With the overcast sky, it was almost non-existent. Shrugging, Breathred made for the two doctors, who were waiting for him just inside the doorway. Seeing him coming, they switched on their halogen flashlights and ducked into the darkness. Taking a last look over his shoulder at Brogan, he joined them.

Brogan held his breath. He'd been dreading this moment. Once they were inside, they were on their own. All his warnings were for nothing. He had been around scientists enough to know they were absent-minded at best, and hardheaded by nature. Left to their own devices, they'd be in their till the end of time.

With nothing left to do but worry, the man headed back to camp. Brogan hadn't walked twenty feet, when he heard the unmistakable sound of stone grinding on stone. His head whipped around in time to see the door sliding back into place, locking Breathred and the others inside the dusty tomb.

Damn it all to hell! He should have seen this coming and left someone on the outside to make sure the door stayed open. Second-guessing himself wasn't the answer. What was done was done. The sentiment didn't change the truth. He had failed them. It was his job to keep them safe. Instead of protecting them, he'd just given them to whatever was in that hole served up on a silver platter.

Forty Two

Okay, you've made it into the fiend's den. What you going to do now?

Luna lost all semblance of self-control when Brogan finished telling them about the tomb. It was all Stud could do to keep her from running from the tent. Not for the first time, Stud found himself being a rock when all he wanted to do was fall apart. Being a highly evolved chimpanzee was tough work. Keeping his emotions in check, he held the sobbing girl while Brogan went on to give the rest of the team orders.

"I want all non-essential personnel packed and ready to move out in an hour's time," Brogan finished, as Luna regained a little hold on her composure.

"You can't be serious!" she shouted, amid a storm of sobs. "I'm not leaving here without Breathred."

"Damn straight," Stud added.

"That's why you're essential personal," Brogan told them. "If I thought either of you would leave, it would be different. Since you won't, I'm leaving you in charge while I get the rest started back down to the base camp. I promised Breathred I'd get you two out of here, but dammit I need somebody I can trust to watch things until he got back. Unfortunately, you two bozos are it."

"So, we can stay?" Luna sobbed.

"Yes. Along with Doctor Easily, if she'll stay, I want the two of you to keep track of the tomb. I checked. The video feed seems to be working, but the audio isn't."

"The snow's let up. The rest of the team can find their way down on their own. Why do you have to go?" Stud asked. "It's not that I hate the thought of being left on our own, but let's face it you're the only chance Breathred has of getting out of that tomb alive."

"Dontcha think I know that? But unless I got a rocket launcher stashed up my ass, I can't open the flipping door. Since I don't, we need something more than picks and shovels." Brogan grinned, wickedly. "I've got some C-4 in my truck. If a bad case of high explosives won't open the door, nothing will."

"How long do you think you'll be?" Luna asked.

"I should be back sometime tomorrow morning at the latest."

"Tomorrow won't help them, if something happens between now and then," Dr. Easily interjected.

"No, it doesn't. But I can't think of anything that will, if we don't get the tomb door open." Brogan said, throwing his pack over his shoulder.

"And if we don't get it open?" Stud asked.

"Then, we're screwed."

~ * ~

Breathred watched as Dr. Grayson played her flashlight over the picture-filled wall. Behind him, Truehart continued to bang on the stone door, like he'd been doing ever since the thing had slammed shut. It was growing quite annoying, but Breathred didn't say anything. If it made Truehart happy, he could live with the noise, but the Englishman's profanity was really getting raunchy. Half of it Breathred couldn't understand, and what he did was not fit for human hearing.

Breathred let his head fall to his chest as he flicked the camcorder's power switch between on and off. He finally decided to leave it on. There was always a chance the feed might help the others find a way to get them out.

They had been trapped in here for about a half an hour. It may have been longer, but he didn't know for sure. Breathred couldn't really judge time. His watch didn't work all too well. They tended to do that, when you got them from a Burger King promotion.

Despite the fact the door had been open for a day or so, the air was starting to taste a bit on the stale side. He guessed it was Truehart's exertions depleting the air. If the man didn't stop soon, they'd be out of breathable air in no time. He was too tired to fight with the man over it, though. Edmund would run out of steam soon enough. Breathred would just let him tire himself out. If it didn't happen soon, he could always try a sleeper hold on him. It always worked for Captain Blamo.

Sitting there was getting him nowhere. Breathred looked up and took in the tomb for the first time. Flashing the camcorder across the room, made him realize he had been mistaken. This wasn't the tomb. It must be an antechamber, or corridor, that led down to the tomb. The similarities to Egyptian tomb construction were not lost on him. He pulled out his own flashlight, letting the extra light play across the walls.

The corridor, as he decided to call it, was about six feet by what looked to be forty feet in length. The walls on either side of the stairs were painted with rows of pictographs. Breathred walked slowly down the flight of steps. The pictographs were a hodge-podge of different cultures. Some looked like stylized Egyptian hieroglyphics while others looked to be from Babylonia. Stranger still, he detected some that resembled Japanese and Greek symbols. If he didn't know this place had been sealed for thousands of years, Breathred would have thought the paintings fakes.

He glanced up when Truehart's banging stopped. Seconds later, agitated footsteps came toward him. Breathred fell back as Truehart rudely pushed past him. The animosity was boiling off the man in waves that could have killed, if they had been able. Breathred held his place against the wall and let Dr. Grayson handle the man. Anything he said would have just set Truehart off, anyway.

"Are you through?" Dr. Grayson asked, not even bothering to look up from the door at the bottom of the steps.

"Yes," Truehart snapped.

"Good, all of your ranting and banging around was driving me mad."

"If the two of you had bothered to assist me, perhaps we would be out of this hole."

Dr. Grayson ran her hand over the second door. "It would not have helped any. If I'm right, the only way out lies behind this door, in the tomb itself."

"How can you be so sure?" Truehart mocked.

"I can't, but it stands to reason the door closed for a definite purpose."

"Yes, to trap us inside."

"Partly, but I believe also in the past the natives entered the tomb and left sacrifices and alms to the Mother," she said looking up.

She then pointed down. More than a dozen plates littered the floor. Bones of small animals, and in some cases, pieces of larger bones lay upon the plates. Truehart looked up from them to see a smug look on Grayson's face.

"See, they must have had a way to exit, if the door closed on them as it did on us."

He kicked the plates into the door. "These may be left over from the time of the original entombment."

"No, they appear to be from different periods. If you look, the level of development in the pieces seems to deteriorate in a strange manner. The plates on top look crude compared to those at the bottom of the pile. I'm sure with carbon dating we'd see the newer pieces aren't as refined as the older ones," she stated.

"That doesn't make sense. If your hypothesis is true, we're looking at a total reversal of established doctrine."

"Then, that's what we're looking at. This is evidence illustrating this culture was in a decline. As to it not making sense, it would if you factored in the fact the level diminished because the Mother was not around to lead the later generations," Breathred said, as he joined the conversation.

"Poppycock! This is all speculation. Without getting that door open a fanciful guess is all it'll ever be."

"I thought you were more concerned with the other door, Truehart,"

Breathred couldn't resist saying.

"Let's just say that proving the two of you wrong is of more importance at the moment."

"Then, you'll help us?" Dr. Grayson asked.

"Of course. Never let it be said a Truehart wasn't a man of action."

"Breathred, can you decipher the symbols and see if they're of any help?" She indicated the row of pictographs on the door with her flashlight.

Breathred didn't say a word. He simply brought his own light to bear on the door, adding the camcorder so a visual record would flash back to the other team members. Like the door outside, the symbols were of Babylonian origin. The dim light did little to help him, but after a while, he was able to make a passable translation. Doubt stopped him from blurting out what he read. Breathred had been a goofball for so long it was hard to remember he could be something more. The past few days might have erased a lot of his fears, but that fear of failure still refused to budge.

Giving the door a soft pat, he rose to his feet. He had the translation. No one else in this room could have done it. That had to count for something. Maybe, it counted for everything. "I've got it."

"Well, are you going to tell us?" Truehart huffed.

For a second Breathred felt the power of the words he was about to say course through him. It passed as suddenly as it came up. He coughed softy into his hand before he began to speak. "The Mother of the Dark slumbers in the void, awaiting the coming of the righteous one. He will wake her with a touch. A kiss in the darkness to once again bring the glorious light of her being into the world."

"Is that all, Breathred?" Dr. Grayson asked, feeling he was holding something back.

"No ma'am. It goes on to say, 'Beware her children. In them are born the seeds of destruction. They will seek out the Mother, and through her bring about the end of all things. Seek the warrior pure. Only he may defeat them.'"

"Breathred, what does that mean?" Dr. Grayson asked.

"It means if we get out of this tomb, we may very well unleash a plague upon the Earth so destructive it would have given Pandora pause," Breathred said, his voice cold and distant.

"Excuse me, but *bullshit*. You can't be seriously considering this is anything more than a myth." Truehart sneered at them.

"The proof is inside that door, Truehart. Whether you choose to believe it or not, something beyond your feeble grip on reality exists. Your brother had the same problem, and look at what it did to him," Breathred bellowed, tired of the man's tirades.

"How dare you mention my brother!" Truehart screamed. "You aren't fit to breathe air while he lies dead. I don't care what you or the authorities say. You had something to do with his death, and it's high time I found out the truth."

"I don't know the truth anymore. Can't you see that? Whatever happened in the Shrine is gone, if it was ever there in the first place. Don't you think I want to know what happened? I wake up with the tips of memories burning in my mind. I want it all to end. Even if it drives me insane, it would be better than this emptiness," Breathred cried, slapping the sides of his head.

"You're fecking lying!"

Before Breathred could move, Truehart slammed his fist into his face. Breathred staggered back into the door. Blood poured from Breathred's ruptured nose and mouth. He lifted his head only to have another blow strike the side of his head. His head rang with the sound of crushed muscle and bone. He let his body slide down the rough surface of the door. Breathred didn't have to open his eyes to know Truehart was waiting for him to get back up.

He couldn't. It wasn't because he was coward. The simple truth was, he couldn't fight back. Getting up meant he would have to confront the man on a physical level. Edmund was just letting his bottled up emotions over his brother's death take over. Breathred couldn't blame him. So, he lay there.

Dr. Grayson jerked him back. "Edmund that is enough. I don't know what's going on with you two, but this is the end of it. You can settle this when we get out of here, but until then we will work as a team. It isn't a suggestion. It isn't even an order. What it is, is a stone-cold fact."

Breathred eased his bloody face up, so he could see the confrontation. When he did, his lips caressed the cold stone. The touch surprised him. He looked over to see a pair of painted-on eyes staring back at him. As his own eyes focused a little more, he saw a whole face was painted on the wall. Amid the arguing, an idea came to him.

He hopped around until he faced the door. The face on the door was in the exact spot someone would be if they were kneeling. Breathred brushed some of the loose dirt away with his hand. His quick cleaning revealed the face of a beautiful woman. A pair of lips was pursed, as if awaiting a lover's kiss. The door's inscription had mentioned a kiss.

What if it wasn't a metaphorical one, but a real kiss? Thousands of years ago, this village's people had come to this door to offer the Mother her worship. It wasn't strange to think they would genuflect and kiss the object of that worship.

If that was the case, then as crazy as it sounded, all he had to do was pucker up and kiss a stone wall to open the door. He was just a tad bit weirded out by the idea. Breathred had never admitted it, but over the years he had practiced his kissing skills on mirrors and assorted posters. He wasn't proud of the fact or proud of the fact he had gotten quite good at it. Peeking over his shoulder, he saw Dr. Grayson and Truehart were still in the middle of their argument. Good. Just because he was going to kiss a rock, didn't mean he wanted to advertise the fact.

Holding his breath, he leaned in and planted his lips on the door. He fought the urge to jerk back. For a brief second it felt like the door was kissing him back. He didn't have time to think about the absurdity of it, because the panel slowly inched open. He fell back, as a whoosh of air rushed over him.

Foul air filled his nose. Against his own volition, Breathred found himself blacking out. He struggled to keep hold on his lucidity, but it was a losing battle. As the last spark of consciousness left him, he looked over and saw the flashing light on the camcorder. It had been transmitting the whole time. Man, if Stud saw him kissing the door...

Then, every thing went black.

Forty Four

It's time to talk about post-traumatic stress disorder.

"Don't worry about your companions. They're safe for the moment," D'brea said, startling Breathred.

She let out a giggle. The sound of her voice drove the poor man flying toward the open door. That wouldn't do. With a twist of her mind D'brea slammed the door shut. Breathred skidded to a stop. The look on his fright-filled face sent another wave of giggles ushering from her non-existent mouth. It had been a long time since she'd been able to do that, and without a physical form no less. It felt so good she didn't want to stop, bu had to.

There were things to be done. D'brea had patiently watched the trio of interlopers ever since they had entered her tomb. Unlike the pitiful example of manhood from the other night, she had gleaned much from their minds. There was still more she must know to prepare her for this new world she had awakened into.

D'brea knew she was in the twenty-first century. From the woman, the scientific advances of this modern world filtered into her mind. Cars, airplanes, DNA, an endless list of the things humans had discovered while she slumbered. Some she knew of from old, but the names were different. Most of it had been magic to those she once ruled over. To her it had been nothing more than simply the nature of things. Now, these truths were so commonplace most humans took them for granted.

Their attitude disturbed her. To take nature for granted was an unspeakable crime. The gift of life and its bounty was no small thing. Seeing these modern men disregard its importance shocked her. Her long slumber had dulled her to the stupidity of humans.

The one called Truehart was easy to manipulate. The knowledge dredged from his mind was mundane, yet interesting. The thing called Internet was most intriguing. To be able to communicate with the entire world from the safety of one's home was exciting in itself. You could even see tiny images of people you would never see in the flesh. And television— the idea was so impossible she almost couldn't believe it to be true. Whole segments of society did nothing except watch continuing drivel for hours upon end. As far as she could see, this television was no different from the

Internet. It tore humans from the natural order of things. D'brea would relish the experience of seeing both of them first hand, but could not see the attraction of losing oneself in the want of it.

Time would tell. She was a fickle creature. D'brea knew this about herself. Though she could not remember ever being human, the woman knew she was as prone to the same distractions as they were. Perhaps for a time she would indulge in some harmless experimentation. That would be for later. Now, a more pressing engagement presented itself.

The one called Breathred was a stone wall. Except for his purity, D'brea had been unable to delve into his mind as she had the others. Only glimpses of surface thoughts floated in the forefront of his mind. The remainder was locked away behind a screen of loosely assembled safeguards. Instead of being infuriated, D'brea was content to pry what she could from him.

Oh, wasn't that cute. He was trying to look brave. At least he wasn't running around screaming. She couldn't stand loud noises coming from a man. It upset her cosmic balance.

"Release my friends from your fiendish embrace, creature of the night," Breathred shouted. She wondered if he realized melodrama would get him nowhere.

"Freeing them would not be prudent at this time. I wish to converse with you alone first," D'brea cooed.

"What are you doing to them?" Breathred asked.

"Nothing at the moment."

"Then, why aren't they moving?"

"Because I have suspended time around them, so we could talk. Weren't you listening? I'm sure I told you before," D'brea said confused.

"Well, you didn't. How do I know you're not sucking their blood?"

"Because, I'm not. My body is still resting, there in the coffin. This is just my astral body." D'brea was starting to get a headache from dealing with this fool. What did she have to do? Give this guy diagrams and a full lecture on being an undead spirit? "Now look, this is getting us nowhere. I see men have gotten no smarter since I went to sleep. I knew I should have tried talking to the woman first."

"So, you're not sucking their blood?"

"No," she answered curtly. She was leeching a fraction of their life force to reinforce her dwindling power, but saw no sense in telling him. It would just set him off again. "What say I slip into something a little bit more form fitting, and we can talk?"

"You can do that?"

"Not really, but I can do a fair imitation of a ghost." *As long as I suck enough energy from your friends.*

"Say, how come you can speak English?" he asked, as she shimmered into being across from him.

"Is that what this language is called? How quaint. I simply pulled it from your minds. An easy thing for one with my powers." D'brea sidled up beside him. He hastily shuffled away. "Still afraid of me, I see."

"I tend to be leery of vampires, especially ones who have been asleep for three thousand years. So, why don't you just tell me what you want?"

"Dear boy, my list of wants could take up most of the night. Unfortunately, we don't have that much time."

"Why not?"

"Because my children are coming for me," D'brea said, turning toward the closed door.

~ * ~

Lewis staggered toward the truck. He had been wrong. Being a vampire did nothing to stop it from hurting. The vampire felt like he had been shoved through a meat grinder instead of a busted windshield. With all the cuts on his body, he was lucky vampire blood clotted quickly, or he would be a bloodless corpse waiting for a fat squirrel to come along.

From the looks of it, the truck had fared better than him. The impact had only dented the front bumper and busted out the windshield. Lewis could see cracks in the side windows and a ripple in the left side fender, but nothing more to indicate major damage. Hell, he might even be able to drive this sucker back home, as long as the frame wasn't bent or the drive shaft wasn't warped. Even if they were, Lewis could still make the truck limp back to the road, if he didn't try any fancy driving.

Now, his only problem was finding Leopold. Reaching the truck, he peered through the cracked window. Leopold wasn't in the cab. There was no sign of blood either. The seat belt wasn't torn, so Leopold must have walked away after the crash. Knowing Leopold, the old vampire hadn't gone far. It was just a matter of finding him. Or not finding, whichever turned out to be easiest. Lewis rounded the corner of the vehicle and slammed right into Leopold.

"Lewis, are you trying to kill me?"

"Not that I know of, but I'll let you know when I start."

"See that you do. I hope you know your ineffectual driving has cost me my new frock coat." He lifted a torn sleeve to illustrate his point.

"Sorry, boss," Lewis said, not caring if Leopold believed him or not. None of this would have happened if they had just left the truck back at the campgrounds like he wanted to do.

"So how far from the dig site do you think, we are?"

"Not far." Lewis looked for a landmark. He saw a stone outcropping he recognized from their last flight to the camp. "I think the dig is right over that rise. We should be there inside an hour."

"Good, it's a little past eight o'clock. That will give us nine hours to get the Mother and to get back under cover before the sun rises. I just hope this truck will run after all the damage you've done to it."

"It'll run," Lewis assured him.

"I'm glad you think so. Now, get your gear together. I will deal with your inadequacies when we get back home."

Lewis snorted a less than favorable flurry of words under his breath, as Leopold took off. He wasn't vindictive by nature, but Leopold tended to bring out those tendencies in him. For now he was content with the knowledge those new suede pumps Leopold just bought weren't going to make it to the next season. Leo's ire over his ruined couture in itself was worth the discomfort of wet socks and soggy toes.

~ * ~

Luna felt her heart stop yet again. The feed from the tomb was gone. One minute Breathred was talking to thin air, then nothing but static. For one brief second Luna could have sworn she had seen a woman standing in front of him. Luna could have dismissed it as a figment of her imagination, but she wasn't one to imagine drop dead gorgeous women talking to her man.

It could only mean one thing—the Mother was awake. More than that, she was awake and putting the moves on Breathred. One second was all it took for Luna to recognize a skank when she saw one. The fact the skank in question was the three thousand year old Mother of the entire vampire race made no difference. This was about propriety and Breathred was her property, which marked him as off limits to everything from Catholic school girls to decrepit, dried up vampire skanks.

"Easily, get the feed back up," Luna hissed.

"I'm trying to, but it was cut from the sender. All I'm getting is dead air." Jessica slapped the keyboard in frustration. "If you think you can do better, be my guest."

"I can…" Luna began then closed her mouth. Easily was right. If the feed was cut off from the camera itself, there was nothing any of them could do. Feeling bad about her outburst, she turned to Easily. "I'm sorry, Jessica. It's just I can't stand the thought of Breathred alone in there."

"It's okay. I know how you feel. I would give anything to go rushing in there and help them," Jessica smiled weakly and patted the girl on the hand.

"Thank you," Luna smiled back.

"For what?"

"For understanding."

"Well, buy me a hanky. Look, you two may be fine with sitting here and mopping up each other's tears, but I'm not. My buddy's trapped with some undead cow from hell and I'm going to do something about it," Stud said, his face a mask of pain and defiance. "So, excuse me while I go save his ass."

"And how do you plan on doing that? Turn into King Kong and bash the door down?" Easily snapped, giving him a mock monkey face and beating her chest with her balled up fists.

"Kiss my ass, bitch." Stud jumped from his seat. "You've been nothing but trouble since I first saw you. So, you can keep your smart remarks to yourself."

"I'll tell you something, you dirty little shit thrower. I have had enough of you." Jessica slowly rose to her feet.

"Bring it on, you blonde-haired hoochie."

"Stop it, both of you. This fighting isn't going to save Breathred or the others," Luna turned to Jessica. "Look, he's right. We have to do something. There's another walkie-talkie on the table. You stay here and monitor the radio, while Stud and I see if there isn't some way we can get the door to the tomb back open."

"Ms. Walking Batch I don't think you should do that," a voice called from the doorway.

Luna whipped her head around to see Leopold and Lewis standing in the tent's open flap. She reached down and put her hand on Stud's head to hold him in place. He tried to pull away, but she held him firmly. This was no time for the chimp to go off half-cocked.

Leopold swirled into the tent with a flourish. Even soaked to the bone by snow and wearing torn and muddy clothes, the vamp acted like he owned the world. Luna wished she could say she was surprised to see him. In fact she'd been wondering why he hadn't showed up before now. The thought didn't make the sinking feeling in her gut any better. It was obvious this wasn't a pleasure visit. From the looks of him, all the cards were fixing to be put on the table.

"Mr. Chambris du Portus, what a pleasant surprise." Luna gave him her best fake smile.

"You can cut the horse manure, Ms. Walking Batch. I think we're past the silly games and pretenses. You know what I'm here for, so let's just get down to it. Shall we?" Leopold gave a smile in answer to her own, but his voice was cold and hard.

"Look here Froggy, you can shove..." Stud got out, before Luna clapped her hand over his mouth.

"I think what he was trying to say was, we don't know what you mean," Luna said, trying to keep the struggling Stud in hand.

"Please, don't insult either one of our intelligences. This little game is over, and I do so hate to have these scenes drag on. Now, shut up and do what I say." Leopold motioned for Lewis to come forward. "Lewis, would you be so kind as to see the nice lady and her monkey back to their chairs? I would hate for them to come to any harm."

"What makes you think you can tell us what to do?" Stud asked.

"Because as you very well know by now, I'm a vampire and if you don't, I'll snap your neck and suck you dry until you are nothing more than a sock monkey dangling from my hand."

"As long as we're clear on your plans, I'll do it. But don't expect me to like it."

"You, as well, my dear," Leopold said to Luna.

Luna growled low in the back of her throat, but did as the vampire demanded. He had them at a disadvantage at the moment, but it wouldn't be the case for long, if she had anything to say about it.

"Good, now that we're all comfy. I think it's time to find out what's been going on. You know all the juicy gossip. Who's sleeping with whom? Who is feeling springtime fresh? I want it all. Especially the part where you tell me how to get to the Mother," Leopold said, taking an empty chair next to Dr. Easily.

"We ain't telling you shit, fang boy." Stud gave the vampire a smug sneer before Lewis slapped the side of his head. Stud jerked his head up and gave the vamp a nose thumb. "Hey, itty bitty pimpin'. You touch me again, and I'm going to shove your hand so far up your ass your sphincter will think its going steady with your tonsils."

"Such a nasty brute you are, Mr. Chimp. Lewis, leave the poor thing alone before it gives you rabies or some other monkey illness. You know how unsanitary they are, and me without my wet wipes," Leopold warned.

"I still ain't telling you shit," Stud said, making chomping noises at Lewis, who had backed out of biting distance.

"I never thought you would, but I was never one to walk blindly into the lion's den, so to speak." Leopold demonstrated a condescending flip of the hand. With a knowing smirk he faced Jessica. "Then again, I wasn't speaking to you. Was I, Doctor Easily?"

Luna shot from her chair, narrowly missing Stud as he eased his head around to join her to glare at the woman behind the monitor. The smug look on the bitch's face was the last straw. She'd known that skank was trouble from day one and now had proof. She should have thrown her ass in the fire when she had the chance. Well, that was one bitch slap she wouldn't let slip through her hands a second time. Miss Thang and the vamp squad would screw up sooner or later and when they did, she was going to be there. And God help them when it happened.

Forty Five

If your check hasn't cleared, don't expect to find out what happens next.

Let me see if I got this straight. Chambris du Portus is on his way, if he isn't here already. Luna and Stud are all that's left out there to face him and there isn't much I can do to help them cooped up in here, Breathred thought. *Was there anything I missed? Nope, I think I got it all.*

"You seem to have covered everything. I see I've upset you," D'brea said, a little worried for his grip on what passed for sanity. "I can see this Chambris Portus worries you, as does the fate of your friends."

"No, but how can you be sure they're coming? Wait a minute. You read my mind!"

"Reading your thoughts is a simple matter, but you were mumbling them out loud to yourself while you were thinking." Yep, his sanity was going bye bye.

"Well, for your information that was a private conversation, so stop eavesdropping. Before you even try reading my mind, it isn't polite to go traipsing around in someone's mind."

"Why, you got dirty thoughts you're trying to hide?" D'brea peered into his eyes just to be sure. It'd been awhile since she'd seen a really good dirty thought, and a virgin's at that.

"No! Can we get back to the other vampires and how you know they're coming?"

"Even in this distant generation, I can sense my offspring. I had hoped my great grandchildren would be smarter than the firstborn, but from the looks of these two I might as well have been pissing in the wind for all the good that did," she chuckled. "You can't pick your family, that's for damn sure."

"But aren't vampires—you know—made, not born?"

"Don't try to get all philosophical with me. It's a real buzz kill," D'brea snapped. "I really like this new language. I'm gleaning such delightful things from your mind."

The language was so flowing and descriptive. D'brea had been picking up loose thoughts for the past century and also been receiving something called radio transmissions, especially old television ones. Until these three had entered her tomb, she hadn't been sure what they were. D'brea now knew the basis of her speech had come from a program called *Designing Women* and another, newer one, called *Reba*. She had no idea this form of speech was not the norm for the entire world, but liked it nonetheless. One day she hoped to meet this Suzanne Sugarbaker. D'brea was sure they were sisters from another mother.

What else had changed while she slept? She had picked up a vague picture from the female of men dancing with no clothes on. Now, that was something worth looking into, because in her time men didn't have muscles like those. She wasn't sure what six-pack abs were, but damn if it wouldn't be fun finding out.

"Did you know you're drooling?" Breathred asked.

"Sorry, Hon. Forgot you were there. Now, what was I saying?"

"Your children are coming and they're not too smart."

"Yes, that's it. So, if it's all the same to you, I'd rather not be here when they come," she said, twisting a ghostly strand of hair.

"But why? I'd think you'd want to be freed," Breathred said in surprise.

"I do. It's just I'd rather not be freed by them. They're the reason I locked myself up in here in the first place. Always hounding me. Always so needy. It's all my fault, you see. Back then all I made were male vampires. I had these grand ideas of harems full of men at my disposal whenever I felt the urge to do the hanky-panky. A big frigging mistake let me tell you." D'brea laughed.

"It was?" Breathred asked in between fits of blushing.

"Sure as hell was. Men might be good eye candy, but quite frankly the lot of them are dumb as bricks. No offense."

"None taken. I'm not sure if I should be offended or not, but since you're probably reading my thoughts anyway would you please spare me an in-depth explanation?"

"Sure thing, Hon. Anyway, that's where all this talk of calling me the Mother came from. They wanted somebody to nurse them, baby them, tell them when to pick up their loincloths and lust after in their pathetic little dreams. So, finally I decided to say to hell with it and go to sleep. After wiping their asses for a hundred years I was ready for a nap." D'brea sighed.

"I imagine so."

"But you know what the worst part was?"

"No," he said meekly. "Not eating?"

"No. I needed to lose a couple of pounds anyway. It was that I've been locked up for so long without a man. They may be annoying as hell, but dammit when you want one, you damn well want one. My juices are so bottled up I could drown a whole village, if you know what I mean." She gave him a spectral nudge to the ribs. "Hell, I might even qualify for virginity again."

"Well, I'm sure that is, what I mean is...N-no, I don't know what you mean," Breathred stammered. D'brea waited for it, knowing he couldn't hold it in. "So, you can become a virgin again? I didn't know women could do that."

"Boy, you kill me." D'brea guffawed and slapped him across the back, which didn't work all too well because her ghostlike hand slipped right through him.

"You really need to meet my chimp," Breathred mumbled under his breath.

"Ohhh." D'brea walked over to him and said with a perverted leer. "That's the kind of talk that's going to get you walking bowlegged."

"Ewwww!" Breathred whined his face scrunched up in horror and disgust.

D'brea leaned in and licked his quivering ear. She purposely let her ectoplasmic touch send a jolt of pleasure through his naughty bits. Biting her lip as he tried to fight off the sensation, she increased the sensation until the tingling felt so good the boy nearly forgot what he was trying to do. Reaching into his mind, she felt it took his entire concentration to push the naughty sensation from his mind.

"Sugar, don't knock the ride until you buy the ticket, strap in and ride the rapids," D'brea whispered in his ear.

"Madam, would you kindly refrain from doing that?" Breathred hissed, swatting his ear, as he backed away from her. "I'll have you know I'm saving myself for marriage."

He stopped her cold. With a look of confusion D'brea looked him over from head to toe. Taking a ghostly sniff, she decided he was indeed telling the truth. Which begged the question. "How old are you?"

"Thirty-six."

"Honey, you ain't saving yourself. You're letting that shit wither on the vine." She didn't bother to hide the amusement from her voice.

"Be that as it may, I would like to keep this relationship platonic, if you please."

"If that's the way you want it. You're not my type anyway."

"So, if you don't want the vampires to help you, what do you want me to do? I don't want to hurt your feelings, but I'm not comfortable with the idea of being your love-slave and I know Luna—that's my girlfriend—will have a few things to say on the subject, if that's your intention."

"Your tough luck, Hon. You don't know what you're missing." D'brea was clearly not in the mood to forgive him for rebutting her advances. "If you're not up for a bit of the in and out, I want you to get me out of here, and if you don't, your two friends over there are going to be my first meal in eons."

~ * ~

After calming down, Luna let Leopold's statement sink in. The initial shock had worn off and denial was setting in. She didn't want to believe Jessica could be a traitor. Sure, she might have had her differences with Easily, but after the other night Luna had marked the woman off her list of suspects. She should have known better. Never trust a woman who tries to steal your man. That's Girlfriend 101 and she had forgotten it. Damn bitch probably double-dipped her chips to boot. She looked the type to do just about anything, including selling them out to an undead freak like Leopold.

"Don't look so surprised, Luna," Jessica said.

"Why?" was the only thing Luna could find to say.

"How can you ask? You stole my man. This was supposed to be my chance to get him back after all these years, but no—you had to drag your little butt into it. When I saw the two of you together at Grayson's party, I knew I had to do something. I couldn't just let you get away with horning in on my party. Do you know how long I waited for him?"

"I can imagine," Luna said, trying not to smirk. Breathred was nothing if not a bit sluggish when it came to women.

"Breathred would have been mine all those years ago, if it hadn't been for the accident. Then, he just disappeared. I spent years trying to find him, but he just vanished. Then finally, I when I thought I could live my life again, Doctor Grayson called and asked me to join this expedition. I was fine with throwing myself into a little work, but then she said *he* would be part of this dig. After all these years I found him again, but you…" Jessica said, all but foaming at the mouth. "Came along and ruined it. Well, I decided then and there you weren't going to get away with it."

"Girly, you need a serious dose of Prozac," Stud snorted.

"No, what I need is for you to shut up, you vile little shit," Jessica screamed into his face.

"Now, Doctor Easily there is no need for vulgarities," Leopold interjected.

"You just stay out of this. This is between me and the girl."

Leopold raised his hands and backed up. "By all means. Who am I to stand in the way of a woman scorned?"

"So, what did he promise you? Were you to become a vampire? Is that it? That he'd let you have Breathred for all eternity to yourself? Well, let me tell you something, Breathred would rather die than become one of those things." Luna wiggled her finger at Leopold and Lewis.

"Oh no, nothing so pedestrian. Seeing the two of you together, it was clear Breathred was no longer fit to be with me. He had to pay for his stupidity. Breathred could have had me, but chose you," Easily said with an up-turned nose. "When Leopold told me about the sacrifice he needed to wake the Mother, I was only too happy to help him."

"What sacrifice?" Stud butted in.

"Breathred, you silly primate! They're going to sacrifice Breathred

257

in some ceremony to wake the Mother. They need a virgin and there you go. Who else fits the bill? I even offered to do the deed," Jessica said, a faint giggle hiding beneath her words.

"You're insane," Luna said.

"Think what you like, but it doesn't change the fact your boyfriend's about to become vampire chow." Jessica unleashed a barrage of laughter that made Luna's blood run cold.

"Lewis, I think it's time for Doctor Easily to take a little break," Leopold whispered to the other vampire.

"I heard you," Easily shouted. "I was promised immortality you twit. I want it, now."

"I think you need to calm down, Doctor. We had a deal and you will get it in all good time, but for now we need to get into the tomb. In your present state of mind I don't think you can aid us with much of anything," Leopold said in a calming tone.

"The hell I can't. You're just trying to get me out of the way. Well, think again. I know how to open the door. Unless you can open it yourself, you had better just think about giving me what I want."

"How do propose to do that? It was my understanding Mr. Petrifunck was the only one able to open it," Leopold stated, motioning for Lewis to slip around the woman.

"No, you give me your word and then I'll tell you."

He held his hand up for Lewis to stop. "Okay, you have my word."

"That's better. You don't need Breathred. You need his blood. When he first opened the door, I made sure I kept the gauze he used to dress the wound. Keeping it in a moist environment, I was able to keep the blood fresh in case the tomb closed, which it did."

"Very astute, doctor. I congratulate you." Leopold stood, clapping his hands. "And I'll make good on our deal, once the Mother is in my hands."

"But, you said..." Easily started to say.

"I said I would honor our agreement and I shall, but not without the Mother safely in my hands. If my word isn't good enough for you, I will nullify our deal now." Leopold's features shifted slightly, revealing a totally inhuman countenance that brought her protests to an abrupt end.

Luna had watched the exchange with growing horror. She knew her and Stud's time was reaching an end. Once Leopold no longer had a use for them, they were as good as dead. The only hope they had was the vampires would wait to kill them until after they opened the tomb. At least then she might have time to come up with a plan.

"Lewis, change of plans. Tie up Ms. Walking Batch and the chimp. I'll escort Doctor Easily to the tomb. Join us as soon as you're done," Leopold ordered.

Lewis licked his lips. "Sure you don't want me to just kill 'em now?"

"No, we might need them to keep Mr. Petrifunck in line."

Luna let out a silent sigh of relief. Things were finally looking up. Now, all she had to was hope for either a plan or a miracle. At this point she was willing to take whichever one she could get.

Forty Six

If you can't hold a stake without shaking, how do you plan to kill a vampire?

Brogan watched the sky with growing concern. Clouds were gathering on the horizon, big fluffy ones that could only mean trouble. He knew snow clouds when he saw them and these weren't them, but somehow he doubted they were anything but. The clouds looked heavy and dark, more like storm heads than snow. Brogan'd been in Kansas once during a tornado. That was what those clouds made him think of. The whole damn mess was turning to crap. Opening the tomb was coming back to bite him in the ass, and he had a feeling it wasn't going to leave him much of one before this night was done.

Having enough of daydreaming, Borgan let his body slide down an embankment. The snow easily gave way beneath his short, heavy legs. The earlier snow had obliterated his tracks. Luckily, he had kept track of landmarks on the first trip. If the approaching storm hit before he made it back to the dig site, landmarks weren't going to be worth diddlysquat. By his reckoning, he was almost there. A mile or so, and the camp should be within sight.

But, he was going to scope things out before rushing into the belly of the beast. His gut told him things were about to get rough. The last thing he needed to do was stumble into any surprises.

Brogan stopped suddenly. His hand reached up to catch a broken branch. It wasn't the first. The trail had been littered with them. Now, he regretted his laziness. The dangling bit of tree sat high enough Brogan doubted an animal had been the 'cause of the damage. His fingers caressed the broken branch. Letting the branch snap back to its place, Brogan brought his fingers up to his nose. They smelled faintly metallic.

His curiosity piqued, Brogan let his eyes roamed the nearby landscape a little more closely. Above eye level, more branches hung at odd angles. As he mulled over the evidence, his gaze fell to the ground itself. Barely noticeable after the snowfall, Brogan made out faded but discernable tire tracks. Who would be crazy enough to drive a truck through a forest at night?

A short detour was worth the delay back to camp. Somehow, Brogan thought this mystery might be tied into whatever was happening back in the camp. He set off at a slow but steady pace. Once or twice, he lost track of the trail, because of snow falling from the heavy-laden trees, but was able to pick up the trail with little effort. From the damage, whoever was driving the truck hadn't been too worried about being followed.

Fifteen minutes later, Brogan caught sight of the truck half-buried against a tree some hundred yards from the main trail. From the looks of it, the driver had lost control and slammed it into the tree. It was a big four-wheel drive U-haul. What had Roberts had told him?

One of the team had seen a U-haul back at the Eh Ya Campgrounds. He'd dismissed it back then. Suddenly, it made sense. There was only one reason to bring a truck like this into these woods. Somebody wanted to get something big from the site. It had to be whatever was buried in the tomb. Suddenly Breathred's talk of this vampire mother suddenly seemed all too real.

If the kid was right, then that meant a truckload of vampires was probably waiting back at camp. Normally, this might worry him, but the way Brogan saw it, he had the advantage. This was his home turf, not theirs. The last time he checked he was the baddest mutha this side of the border. A vamp might make the Americans shiver their short and curlies straight, but he was Canadian. Canadians were the toughest S.O.B.s in the world. At least this one was.

~ * ~

Lewis grinned as he tightened the makeshift rope around Stud's arms and chest. The chimp let out a pained gasp. Lewis cinched the knotted up sheets a little tighter before tying them off behind Stud's back. After thinking about gagging the foul-mouthed beast, one flash of its abnormally large incisors gave him second thoughts. It wasn't like the beast could reach down and gnaw through the ropes.

The girl had been easy. Lewis made the monkey do it. Glancing over to make sure she was still strapped in place, the vampire wasn't all too sure the chimp had tied her up, but wanted to wait until the chimp was secure before checking her bonds. All left to do was tie down the little sucker's legs then he could see for himself.

Luna watched the vampire bend down to tie Stud's legs. Stud shot her a questioning look over the vamp's shoulder. Luna wished she knew what to tell him, but she didn't. That was a lie. Luna knew what she had to do, just didn't want to do it, especially in front of this Lewis person. Luna wasn't ashamed of her true self but didn't want to advertise it to the whole world yet. If she wolfed out and the vampire got away…

Luna didn't even want to think about the consequences. Hearing the news from a vampire wasn't the way she wanted Breathred to discover her secret. He deserved to hear it from her, not some freak.

Luna turned her head away from Stud's accusing stare. When the vampire was gone, she'd tell him her plan. With Lewis out of the way, she could change and get them free without Breathred finding out. It was the coward's way, but it worked for her. Luna just hoped it wouldn't be too late. She glanced up to see Lewis finish with Stud's bonds.

He was coming over to make sure Stud had tied her up right. Luna was glad she told the chimp to do it the way Lewis wanted. Otherwise, the vamp would have had to do it again. Every minute they had to stay here was a minute wasted. Luna was sure Leopold and that slut, Easily, weren't wasting any time.

"Okay folks. That's it. We'll be back with your boyfriend in a minute, so don't even think about trying any funny stuff," Lewis warned, as he gave Luna's bonds a final tug.

"Or what, you'll kill him? You're already going to do that, so don't try to scare us with lies," Stud snarled, straining at his ropes.

"No? How do you think he'll feel, watching me suck his girlfriend dry as a bone?" Lewis took a quick swipe across Luna's neck o drive his point across.

"When I get out of this, I'm going to drive a stake straight through your sorry butt," Stud promised the gloating vampire.

"Feel free to try, but I don't think you'll get the chance." Lewis said, slipping from the tent.

"Why didn't you wolf out and kill that piece of crap?" Stud asked.

"Because, he might have gotten away."

"He might have shit himself is more like it. Whatever you're going to do, do it. I don't like the idea of Breathred trapped with those two bloodsuckers breathing down his neck."

Luna knew Stud was concerned about Breathred and forgave his abruptness.

"Give me a few minutes and then we'll go after him."

Luna tuned out Stud's reply, so she could focus her thoughts. Her mind swam to her secret place. This wouldn't be like the other night. The change then had been pure reflex in answer to Sharbano's attack. She still couldn't explain why it happened like that. As hard as she concentrated, the tug of power that marked the start of the change wouldn't come.

She was trying too hard. Luna let her mind flow free, letting her spirit flow toward the living well of Coyote's will. Something was blocking her from reaching it. Luna grunted in frustration. This wasn't going to work. They were trapped like rats and there wasn't one damn thing she could do about it.

~ * ~

"That's harsh, don't you think?" Breathred said.

It had taken several minutes for him to even say that. Her words had struck him as a last resort on her part. Seduction hadn't worked. So, this was it. Breathred had to admit it was working. Dr. Grayson had taken a chance on him, and didn't want to see her die because he wasn't up to the job she hired him for.

"Not as far as I can see. If you don't help me, you're going to die anyway," D'brea said.

"How do you figure that?"

"It's simple. My body has been sleeping for too long. It's going to take a lot to kick-start it back into shape. Regular blood won't work. It's going to take something special to do it."

Breathred didn't even have to listen to know what she planned to say next.

"It's going to take the blood of a ripe virgin. Well, an over-ripe one in your case. And knowing my offspring, they're going to make a big thing out of it."

"A ceremony you mean?" Breathred said absently.

"That's the way they did it back in my day. Goofy looking headdress and a big ol' knife. You might even get a fancy slab to lie on while they funnel your blood into my body," she stated, her words doing little to improve his mood.

"How much time do we have?"

"Not much. I can hear them right outside the door."

"Well, don't worry. They can't get in without me. You're safe."

"Don't get too confident. The blonde girl you're with is helping them," D'brea stated.

"Jessica's the mole?" Breathred said, shocked. He was sure it had been Truehart.

"Yep, and she has some of your blood. Looks like we've got about ten minutes til they come busting through the outer door. If you've got a plan, now would be the time to get going."

Breathred looked worriedly to the door. "Can't you do anything to help out here?"

"Not really. No body, remember?" She ran her hand down her ectoplasmic body. It shimmered as her fingers danced through the edges.

"Is there a back door to this place we might be able to scurry out?" Breathred knew he was grasping at straws, but darn it—there had to be another way out.

"Nope. I didn't see the need for one. I was hoping they'd forget about me to tell you the truth."

"Well, they didn't," Breathred snapped.

"Don't get all mad at me. I didn't ask them to come," she snapped back. "I was content to sleep until the end of time in my hidey-hole. If anybody's to blame, blame her." D'brea shook her finger at Dr. Grayson.

Dejectedly, Breathred slumped down until the cold stone of the tomb floor pressed against the entire length of his body. He dejectedly jammed his thumb between his puckered lips and promptly decided to give up. What else should he do? He was out of time, out of ideas and out of his mind to think he could do this.

Who was he trying to kid? Breathred had been a failure his entire life. Why should this case be any different? Sure, the downside was he was most probably going to die. On the bright side—if he was dead, he wouldn't have to spend the rest of his life living in his father's basement with Stud. See, when you looked at things with your Sunshine glasses on, even death didn't seem so bad.

But, what about Luna? If Leopold was outside, she must be in danger. What kind of boyfriend would Breathred be if he died with her in mortal peril? He couldn't leave her to the whims of an undead fiend. Breathred unseated his thumb with a puckered pop. His depression slipping away in the face of true love, he flipped up into a seated position. He might not have a plan, but he sure as heck wasn't about to give up just yet.

Breathred looked over at D'brea. Her expression shifted from pouting to frustrated anger. Her being distracted by his distraction was better than finding her sucking the life from Doctors Grayson and Truehart. Good thing she was still a ghost or he might have found her chomping down on his two companions.

That's it! Since D'brea didn't have a body, there was a slim chance she could leave the tomb. After all, the ghosts in the movies could pass through walls. Breathred saw no reason why she couldn't do it, too. If D'brea could just get to Luna, maybe she had an idea about how to get out of this. All they really needed was something to hold Leopold up long enough for them to get away. How hard could that be?

"D'brea," Breathred shouted, earning him a dirty look from the specter.

"Yeah. I've been listening to Leopold and the woman. From the sound of it, it won't take long for them to get past the outer door."

"Can you leave the tomb in your ghosty form?"

"I can't leave my body for long, but I should be able to make a short hop. Why?"

"My friends on the outside might be able to help us. I was hoping you could go out and tell them what's going on," Breathred explained.

"You're talking about the girl and the monkey, right?"

"Yes."

"Well, that might be a problem. The vampires tied them up." She paused with a faraway look on her face. "The short one is returning."

"Short one?"

"You know the stumpy one who took the others away." She rolled her eyes as if to say that he should have known who she meant.

"Brogan!" Breathred exclaimed. This might work after all.

"He's the one." He tried not to read too much into the dreamy look in her eye at the man's name. "Just go tell them. Brogan will get them loose."

"Okay, but you should know there's a chance I might lose myself, if I'm gone from my body too long." D'brea didn't seem pleased with the idea either.

"What do you mean?"

"Basically, what you're looking at is my soul. If it's away from my body for a prolonged period of time, it may not be able to find its way back. That happens, and it's not me anymore. What you'd end up with is one great looking corpse, and one highly pissed-off ghost. I don't know about you, but being discombobulated isn't my idea of how I plan to spend the rest of eternity."

"So you're saying if your soul wasn't near your body, they could still bring it back to life?" Breathred asked, wondering if he might have found a way to get them out of this.

"Hon, you wouldn't want that to happen. Without my soul guiding my body, you'll end up with a fabulous-looking killing machine. Which would be a very bad thing."

"Then scratch that plan. Just get to Luna and see what you can come up with." The outer door slide open. "And hurry!"

D'brea gave him a wink and vanished. Breathred turned away from the shimmering air left by her disappearance. Even through the thick stone walls, he could hear footsteps coming from the stairs leading to the tomb. Slow dread crept over him. Left alone with his thoughts, Breathred prayed Luna had something up her sleeve, 'cause he'd just used up his last good idea and it wasn't all that good to begin with.

Forty Seven

What do you mean, garlic only works in the movies?

Luna kicked feebly at her bonds. Not for the first time in the past hour, she wished she hadn't told Stud to be so thorough with his tying. This whole night had been a disaster. Leopold showing up had been the topping on the cake. If she could just get the damn medicine bag off, she could change and set them free. Might as well wish for something sensible, like a Sherman tank.

Her only consolation was Stud was quiet for once. From his brooding silence, Luna knew he was in full-on pout mode. She had never seen him so depressed. He was blaming himself for this. It was as if all the smart-ass had just drained from him.

Outside the tent, D'brea heard the pitiful thoughts drifting from the two mortals. She had never heard such sentiments in her life. These people cared for each other in ways the people of her time never had. Breathred was more concerned for these two than he was for himself. Strangely, the girl and the monkey were more concerned for him than they were for their own dire situation. In the days of her reign, there was a sense of community among her people, but nothing like this.

If these three souls, who were not even of the same species, were any indication, she still had much to learn about this new world. No one focused on the community as a whole anymore. Now the concerns of the individual were what mattered. This individuality intrigued her. It gave her a spark of hope she hadn't felt in a long time. Perhaps, there was no longer a need to be a goddess to her people. D'brea could be the sexpot she always yearned to be.

When time permitted, she would have to ponder this further. Unfortunately, she had a mission to accomplish first. Already, her two children had nearly breached the inner door to her resting place. Amid this, she sensed the fear coming from the one called Breathred. D'brea felt a darker thing lurking behind his fear. Whatever it was, this thing almost seemed to overwhelm his fear.

This bore investigating. After all, she was entrusting her future to this person. Sure it might be an invasion of his privacy, but what did she care? Who was the vampire mother around here, him or her? Flinging a piece of herself back to him, D'brea attempted to touch this darkness and gently probed past the outer-most barriers of Breathred's mind. Her ectoplasmic body shuddered as she felt her touch wither against the formless reaches of the man's mind. D'brea suddenly remembered the reality of pain.

The woman drew back in confusion. Now she was the one who was afraid. This human was not as he first appeared. The power of a spirit that rivaled her own was the only thing which could rebuke her with such ease. The boy was indeed a holy warrior, if he was able to do this to her. His naiveté had lulled her into a false sense of security. She would do well not to overestimate him. To that end, D'brea would do as he asked, so long as it served her purposes to do so.

D'brea floated unseen above the bound pair, still hesitant to reveal herself. There was still much she did not understand, but time was growing short. Even with his untapped strength, Breathred could not hold off her two offspring for long. Taking a deep metaphysical breath, D'brea willed herself into being.

The look on the monkey's face was worth the expenditure of her flagging strength. The girl had not yet seen her. From the drool cascading down the chimpanzee's chin, the situation wouldn't be the case for much longer.

"Lu-lu-luba-luba," Stud stammered, his eyes wide and crazed.

"What's wrong? You sound like you got an Umpa Lumpa trapped in your throat." Luna strained against the ties that held her.

"Big honking ghost!" Stud shouted, his confined body bouncing up and down in his chair.

"Say what?"

"Excitable little fellow, isn't he," D'brea laughed in her ear. "Do you think he needs a banana?"

Luna jumped at the sound of the voice. D'brea could see it took everything the girl had not to join the chimp in his bid for hysterical flight.

"Calm down girly, one nutty-bunny is enough, thank you very much," D'brea said.

"What do you want?" Luna calmed down enough to ask.

"Your boyfriend sent me to give you a rundown on what's happening."

"He's alright?"

"He was when I left him, but won't be for long, if you don't help us."

"What can I do? I don't know if you noticed it or not but I'm kind of tied up at the moment," Luna snapped.

"That's what I told him, but he was convinced you'd know what to do. I don't know if you know this, but the guy's not all too bright. His one redeeming quality was he had the good sense to turn to a woman for brain power." D'brea cackled.

"Yeah, he is smarter than the average male." Luna joined in her laughter.

"So, any ideas? Because time's kind of running out?" D'brea turned a worried look in the direction of the tomb.

"If I was untied, I have a lot of ideas, most of them unpleasant and involving a big ass honking rectally-inserted wooden stake. Unless you can do something about getting me loose, I'd say we're pretty much screwed."

"That tasty Brogan is on his way back to camp, so you may get your wish." D'brea lifted her head and listened to the man's loud approach.

"Then go get him, and bring his ass here," Luna ordered.

"Can't do it, Hon. I'm at my breaking point. If I tried to reach him, I'd dissipate into nothing."

"Shit!" Luna snarled.

"Don't worry. He should be here in about five minutes. He's moving slowly, but heading this way."

"Stud, did you hear her? Brogan's coming!"

"Honking big booby ghost," Stud murmured spraying the air with a fountain of fresh spittle.

"Even scared out of his gourd, he can't stop being a perv." Luna sighed.

The ghost suddenly let out an inhuman howl. D'brea's face twisted into a mask of pure anguish. Her voice cracking with the heavy sounds of her sobs, she cried. "It's too late. They're breaking into the tomb."

~ * ~

Leopold found himself staring at yet another door. This would not do. Easily had informed him there was only one door. Now, there were two. Surely, a college education had included a seminar on basic mathematics. Even in the seventeenth century they knew the difference between one and two. He sincerely hoped this was not indicative of modern education.

"Doctor Easily, would you mind explaining where this door came from?" Leopold demanded.

"From its construction I'd have to say from a nearby stone quarry," she answered, absently.

"You know very well what I mean. You never mentioned a second door in your computerized missives," Leopold exploded. He hoped the vein in his forehead wasn't popping out. It didn't match his outfit.

"Breathred and the others only just entered the tomb. How was I to know what was in it?"

"Don't take that tone with me. I will not be shouted at by a college professor who can't count to two."

"You sanctimonious bastard! I told you everything I knew. If you're too stupid to realize it, you can kiss my rosy pink ass," Easily announced to the vampire's dismay.

"Then, obviously you knew too little. You have five minutes to get the door open before I decide our deal is null and void," Leopold said, his voice tight with unrestrained anger.

"You try to back out on me, and I'll shove a stake through your heart, you froggy fop."

"Don't try to scare me, doctor. Your threats mean nothing to me. You cannot scare a man who has been schooled in fear by the masters of fear itself, Carmelite nuns," he sneered in her face. "Now, open that door!"

Easily grumbled under her breath, but kept her thoughts to herself. She would not lower herself to a war of words with this fool. Besides, she was too close to her revenge to jeopardize it now. She could put up with this for a little while longer. To do that, all she had to do was get this flipping door open.

In the video feed Breathred had bent over and kissed the door. If this door worked like the other one, she wouldn't be able to open it. They all might work on the same trigger, which seemed to be purity of spirit and body, neither of which afflicted her. Now, twenty or so years earlier she might have had a shot. Unfortunately, Bobby Bigalloe had taken care of the little deed.

The scuffle of approaching steps made her look up. The other vampire, Lewis, was joining them. He must have finished dealing with Breathred's girlfriend and pet. Easily wished Leopold had just killed them and gotten it over with. The fact they still lived was an affront to her, personally. Her feelings aside, Jessica knew the girl was more dangerous than she appeared. The monkey might look like a dimwit, but he was just as dangerous as the girl. Leopold hadn't bothered to consult her before making his decision, so wasn't about to offer her two cents worth. Let him find out for himself.

"So, are they secured? I don't want to look up and see them coming merrily up behind us." Jessica did her best to tune out Leopold's grumbling, but found she couldn't stop listening in spite of herself.

"They're tied up like a pair of new shoes. Stop worrying." Lewis grinned.

"It's my job to worry," Leopold said.

"Then, you're doing a good job."

"I'm glad you think so. Now, why don't you do yours and convince this woman she needs to get this door open?" Leopold snapped.

"What's the hold up?" Lewis asked, sidestepping a wicked glare from Leopold.

"For one thing there are two doors instead of the one I was told about." Leopold gave Easily a snide look.

"Get over it, already," Easily snapped.

"You hush," Leopold ordered. "Unless you know how to open the second door, I don't want to hear another word from you."

"Well, then cover your ears."

"What was that?" Leopold asked. "Lewis did you hear her? Am I mistaken or did she just talk back to me?"

"Sounds like it, Boss." Jessica didn't have to look up to know the younger vamp was grinning.

"Clearly, I need to rethink this whole human sidekick thing. Whatever happened to the sniveling Renfields of old? I ask you. Maybe, I should try putting an ad in the personals. You know something like, 'Dominant male seeking subservient companion, commitment a must, light housework optional. Smokers need not apply.'"

"Sounds crazy to me, but you're the boss."

This time Jessica knew he was smiling. Well, let them laugh. She'd be the one who had the last laugh.

"Before you look start looking into placing that ad, I can open your damn door," she snarled.

"Then shut up and do it. You can go pre-menstrual on your own time." Leopold threw a dismissive wave of the hand.

The bastard was asking for it. If she had been pre-menstrual, he'd be picking his teeth out of his colon, and his balls out of the dirt. She was a highly respected scientist, not some lackey. So, she didn't know about the second door, so what? She'd gotten him this far. What did he expect? To waltz in here and throw the damn Mother over his shoulder and walk right back out? If du Chambris Portus thought it would be so easy, he was a bigger fool than what he looked like in that cheap ass Armani knock-off.

The sooner she got this over with, the sooner she could get what she wanted. That was the important thing. Breathred and his floozy had to pay. Putting up with this half-wit was a small price to pay to see the girl got her comeupense, and more importantly to see Breathred get what he deserved.

Easily turned back to the door. In the pale light from the weak flashlight, she saw a faint hint of faded paint in the dust. Brushing the dirt from the door, the outlines of a face appeared. That must be where Breathred had kissed it. Thinking along the same lines, she bent over and placed her lips over the spot where he had an hour before.

Her lips cramped, as Easily waited for something—anything—to happen. How long did you have to kiss a door? This was crazy. She was kissing a door. How low could you get? She'd gone from being a respected archeologist to flagrant door molester, and all because of a man. What next? A contestant on a reality show. She'd almost decided to stop the whole charade, when a slight tremor came from door. It was opening! The mechanism that operated it must be sluggish after sitting dormant for so many years.

All that mattered was the thing was opening. Nothing was going to spoil this moment for her. In a few more minutes, she would get everything she wanted, and Mr. Breathred E. Petrifunck was getting what he had coming to him. It couldn't get any better than this.

Forty Eight

Forget it. If you've gotten this far and can't get out of a tough situation, you might as well apply to your local technical college.

"Would you just shut the hell up!" Luna shouted at the gibbering Stud. "It's just a ghost."

"Bu-bu-bu-Boogedy, Boobedy ghost," Stud slobbered.

"She's trying to help us you dumb shit!"

"Look, sweetie. I've seen this type of thing happen before. There's only one way to get them to calm down." D'brea laughed. "Sure, I've only seen it in men of the human variety, but there's a first time for everything."

Before Luna knew what was happening the ghost walked over to Stud. Stopping in front of the whimpering chimp, D'brea turned and gave Luna a sly wink. With a jiggly shake D'brea let her top dissolve in a puff of smoke. Stud's reaction was instantaneous. His eyes got as big as saucers and his tongue fell to his hairy chest. Luna didn't like it, but couldn't argue with the results. Stud stopped his hysterical gibbering. His pupils properly dilated, and he even managed to stop drooling. Well, almost.

"See, works every time." D'brea turned around. Luna was relieved to see her top was back in place.

"Stud, are you okay?" Luna asked.

The chimp's head rocked back and a smile the size of a Winnebago graced his serene face. He said in a dreamy faraway voice. "She showed me her boobies, and I like them too."

"Pervy little fucker ain't he?" Luna could tell D'brea was trying to look shocked, but couldn't quite pull it off. "Who am I kidding? If he was a little taller, and a little less hairy, I'd be all over him like dentures on a neck bone."

"Ew, so not an image I want to have to carry with me. Thank you, very not." Luna did her best not to gag.

"Any chance of an encore, Toots?" Stud asked, wistfully.

"No!" They answered in unison.

"Just checking."

"Stud!"

"Hey, she showed them once. I would have been remiss if I hadn't asked for a second showing. If it got out I'd be drummed out of the perv-of-the-month club."

"Then check somewhere else, Turd Knocker," D'brea snapped. "Now, where is that hunka-hunka-burning Brogan? He should be here by now."

Luna was about to tell her to be patient when Brogan shredded his way through the back of the tent. In a fury of flailing arms he emerged from the shadows. He catapulted past them, his momentum carrying him straight out the tent flap and back into the night.

"Was it just me or did he look like he was auditioning for Edward Scissorhands Two?" Stud asked.

"I think those ropes are cutting off the blood flow to your brain," Luna said. "Try not to be an ass when he gets back in here."

"Don't panic. It's just me," Brogan said, as he rushed back into the tent.

Luna looked up to see in expectation of his return, D'brea had let her form-fitting top dip ever so slightly, so the swell of her breasts nearly cascaded over the top of it. If her exploding cleavage wasn't enough to make a man salute the Canadian flag, her loincloth had gone obscenely transparent. Luna was shocked to see it revealed everything, including what she had tucked away under the kitchen sink.

"What was that about panicking, short, broad and manly?" D'brea whispered in a husky velveteen voice.

"D'brea stop it! Poor Brogan can't even breathe," Luna ordered the ghost.

"Ooh, I like a man who knows how to hold his breath."

"Ma'am, would you mind putting some clothes on? I don't think my jeans fit anymore," Brogan gasped out in short ragged breaths.

"See, he's gone all stupid. Men can't function, when you cut off the blood flow to the brain like that," Luna warned.

"I'm sorry. It's just been so long I forgot myself," D'brea said. Luna caught the ghost shoot Brogan a sly wink when the vamp thought she wasn't looking.

"When this is over, you can do whatever you want to him. Until then, don't let it happen again," Luna chided her.

"She didn't say anything about me, though," Stud remarked, his tongue rolling from the side of his mouth.

"Stud!" Luna shouted, and then turned to D'brea. "Clothes, now!"

"Did you see how she talked to me?" D'brea whispered in Stud's ear, as her clothing became more opaque. "Let me tell you, if I still had my body, she wouldn't dare talk to me like that."

"If I had your body," Stud leered.

"Stop it right there before I forget I'm a lady."

"I can hear you both. So, stop it!" Luna didn't have time for this.

Breathred was in danger. The Skank and Chimp Show could wait until he was safe and sound.

They both gave her apologetic looks, but Luna wasn't buying it. She ignored them for the time being. Brogan was her more immediate concern. The man looked positively confused, not that she could blame him. From the look on his face, he could see D'brea, which wouldn't make explanations any easier. If she wasn't mistaken, he was mumbling to himself, which was never a good sign.

"Okay, when I left, the only thing I had to worry about was frostbite and crazy people who thought they were going to wake up a billion-year-old vampire. Now, not only do I have REAL vampires running around, but now I've a ghost to worry about. True, that's the sexiest damn ghost I've ever seen, but still a ghost." Luna watched him narrow his eyes and give D'brea an once-over. "Oh, yeah, baby. You'd definitely make a corpse sweat."

Luna couldn't stop herself from laughing.

"Look at what you did." Stud pointed at Brogan. "You broke the Canuck."

"I did not. See, he's back to normal." D'brea pointed a finger in Brogan's direction, which made Luna only laugh harder.

"Ah, could somebody explain what's going on?" Brogan stammered.

Luna turned to see the vampire was now dressed like a nun, albeit a sexy nun—but a nun nonetheless. Exactly, how she managed the feat, Luna would die to know. Luna held up her hand. She had to put an end to this or they'd never get around to saving Breathy. "Brogan, if you'll untie us, I'll try to bring you up to date."

"Only if you promise to make the skirt stop making me sweat until you finish."

"D'brea, put some clothes on and leave him alone." Luna cocked her head toward the vamp.

"Spoilsport," D'brea pouted, but Luna was glad to see she complied.

Things finally calmed down, as Brogan bent down to untie her and Stud. Rubbing her blood-starved arms and legs, she told Brogan what had happened after he and the others left. Grateful D'brea refrained from any more lewd comments Luna took all of about ten minutes to bring the Canadian up to date.

"Okay, the vamps have Breathred and her body," Brogan summarized, giving a hasty nod toward D'brea.

"That's about it. So, whatya gonna do about it?" Stud demanded.

Brogan sat back in his chair. "Damn good question. Right now the only thing comes to mind is to run like hell till we all hit Mexico. Somehow, I don't think that's what you want to hear, but it's all I got."

~ * ~

"Mr. Petrifunck, so good to see you again," Leopold said, as Breathred watched him push the kneeling Dr. Easily out of the way to enter the tomb.

"Du Chambris Portus," Breathred growled

"No need to repress your anger, Breathred. I may call you Breathred? Of course I can," Leopold shushed him with a wave of his hand. "Now, I really must thank you for all your invaluable assistance. Without you we would be all standing out in the cold."

"I know what you are," Breathred said, as the knot in his stomach tightened.

"Of course you do." Leopold smiled.

Leopold swept past him, making for the stone coffin in the center of the room. He paused briefly at the paralyzed Grayson and Truehart. Breathred heard a faint laugh escape the vampire, as he pushed the unresponsive Truehart to the side.

Breathred took a step toward the vampire. A hand on his shoulder halted him. Lewis' smiling face asked him wordlessly to stop. The sight of Jessica stepping into the tomb behind them did little to improve his mood.

"The Mother's work?" Leopold asked, gesturing to Grayson and Truehart.

"Answer the man," Lewis commanded with a harsh shove.

"Yes," Breathred spat between gritted teeth.

"So powerful. Even in her slumber, she can move mountains," Leopold mused wistfully.

Breathred shook off Lewis' hand. "Don't even think about it. She won't help you."

"Dear, boy. I am her child. What mother wouldn't help one of her children ascend to the power that is rightfully his?"

"You obviously haven't met my mother," Breathred mumbled.

"This is the finest hour of the Vampiric race. I will not let your churlish words diminish its importance. Lewis, restrain Mr. Petrifunck."

Breathred felt his body go rigid when the vampire reached around to take hold of him. It was like fire was channeling its way through every cell in his body. His ring burned into the flesh of his finger. His hand shot out involuntarily and slammed the vampire back into the wall. "Don't touch me."

"Lewis, it appears the virgin has a backbone after all. It must be all that pent up energy." Leopold chuckled.

"Then, you come over here and restrain his ass." Lewis rubbed his tender back.

"Neither one of you will do anything," Breathred stated, his voice a cold lump in the stale air.

"Believe what you will, but I think if you want your two friends to remain among the living, you will do what we say." Leopold pulled Truehart over to him and raked his teeth along the man's neck. "I am growing quite peckish. If you want to try my patience, feel free." The point of his fang pricked the meat of Truehart's neck enough to draw a single drop of blood.

"Okay, leave them alone!" Breathred shouted.

"Glad to see that bravado of yours has its limits. As tasty as Doctor Truehart appears, he isn't my type." Leopold pushed Truehart into the comatose Dr. Grayson.

"Leopold cut this bullshit. Let's get the Mother and get out of here," Jessica snapped, elbowing past Lewis and Breathred to face Leopold.

"You must excuse, Dr. Easily. She confided in us earlier she is premenstrual at the moment and quite touchy about it," Leopold whispered to Breathred. "So, it would be best not to antagonize her, if you know what I mean."

"I am not!" Easily exclaimed.

"Well, uh, yes. Perhaps it would be best if we got down to business. Mr. Petrifunck, if you and Lewis would kindly remove the lid. I hear Mother calling."

~ * ~

"You better get the drag out, hunky man," D'brea said. "I'm listening in on Leopold and Breathred at the tomb, and it isn't sounding too good."

Brogan shot the ghost a dirty look. She might be a knockout, but that didn't mean he had to take her crap. Brogan knew what he had to do, and didn't need a pushy, undead broad telling him that. The hound-dog looks from Luna and Stud were bad enough. He could deal with D'brea. What kind of name was that anyway? But those two sad sacks were breaking his heart.

He let out a sigh. "Okay here goes. They're already in the tomb, so there's no way we get to them in there without taking the chance the vamps will take Breathred and the doctors out."

"Well, I ain't sitting here with my thumb up my butt," Stud announced to nobody's surprise.

"I don't expect you to. I'm just asking you to be realistic. If we rush into the tomb, they're dead, we're dead, and if we're lucky we don't come back in three days to a steady diet of blood," Brogan said, looking to D'brea for agreement.

"He's right, you know. Things at the tomb are about to get worse, so if you got a plan let's hear it."

"Then, what are we gonna do, Brogan?" Luna asked, trying not to let her emotions get the best of her.

Brogan slammed his hands together. "We wait until they come out of the tomb. They'll have their hands full with the ghost-chick's body and Breathred. Counting Easily, there's only three of them. We can hide, and when they come out, we take 'em down."

"I love it, when you're all forceful," D'brea cooed.

"Lady, you need a cold shower."

"Are you offering to scrub my back, if I take one?" the ghost asked, seductively showing a bit more of her ample chest than Brogan was happy seeing up close. It wasn't that the view didn't tickle his cigar straight, but he just liked his woman more solid and a lot less dead.

"D'brea, you promised," Luna corrected the naughty spirit.

"I know, but he's just so…" D'brea ended her statement with a squeal of delight.

"Can we get back to the reason for this little meeting?" Brogan demanded.

"I'm sorry. Is there anything I can do to help?" D'brea asked,.

"Yeah, if you can rein in them hormones, I need to know a few things before we go jumping into the thick of it."

"Go ahead. Ghost's honor, I'll be good." D'brea crossed her heart.

Brogan couldn't help but notice the crossing ended with a nipple tweak. "First thing—can we kill those two vamps without getting the others killed?"

"I wouldn't advise it. The young one will be no problem. The blood hasn't had time to take a good hold, yet. It's the other one who'll give you trouble. He's old enough that a stake won't kill him right away."

"Then, how do we kill him?" Stud snapped.

"You don't. You just need to get my body away from him."

"That won't work. He'll just keep coming after you," Stud shot back.

"Not, if you can revive me before they get the chance," D'brea said.

"You'd still have to kill Breathred to bring you back. Sorry, not going to happen," Luna was quick to say.

"I only need a drop of his blood to bring my body back. What the others are planning is overkill and wasteful to boot."

"When your body reaches full power, how do we know you won't come after us?" Brogan asked, the whole thing sounding fishy to him.

"I've done the Queen of the Damned shit. It's a drag. Give me a man or twelve to call my own, and I'm happy. As far as I'm concerned, my children can take care of themselves."

"Good enough for me," Luna said and turned to Brogan. "And it should be good enough for you."

Brogan laughed. "Luna, if she's got you convinced, that's good enough for me."

"Then, let's get this show on the road," Stud said.

Forty Nine

Now would be a good time to look into cut-rate burial plots.

The coffin lid shifted in Breathred's shaky hands. He had to drop his knee to the floor to keep it from falling. Looking up, he saw the strain on Lewis' face, as all the weight shifted to him. Feeling bad for his misstep, Breathred gave a half-hearted smile. From the look on the vampire's face apparently, Lewis felt the same way. The veins in the vampire's arms and neck looked like corded snakes, as he strained to keep his own end from tipping.

"Don't break it, you incompetent buffoons!" Leopold ordered. "I trust you'll forgive me if I move back a step or two. I'm not about to risk damage to my person because of your tomfoolery."

"Maybe, if you came over here and lent a hand, we could do this to your satisfaction," Lewis snarled.

"Wouldn't think of interfering. Someone has to see that the job is done properly. Doctor Easily, give them a hand." Leopold waved his hand at the woman.

"Bite me," Jessica growled.

"All in due time."

With a loud thump Breathred and Lewis let the coffin lid fall to the tomb floor. Letting out a huge sigh, Breathred slipped to the floor beside it, surprised to see Lewis settling down beside him.

"Times like this I miss a good beer," Lewis confided, under his breath. "Don't let Leopold know I said that. Beer is on his list of bourgeois articles not to be brought up in his presence. So's the Westminster Dog Show, but for entirely different reasons—something about a cocker spaniel and sock drawers."

"Excuse me, but I have to ask you. Why are you with that nut job? You seem normal. Well, normal for a vampire," Breathred whispered.

"Leo's all right. He's just a little confused at the moment," Lewis replied.

Breathred gave Leopold a quick glance to make sure he wasn't listening. "Come on. This goes beyond confused and straight into rubber room dairies."

Lewis shrugged. "You got me there, but he's my maker. I'm not trying to justify it or anything, but it's the way things are with vampires. You just gotta go with it."

"My Dad made me, but you don't see me kidnapping people and trying to take over the world so the sales at his convenience store'll go up," Breathred replied.

"Lewis, do stop fraternizing with the help. We have work to do," Leopold said.

Leopold leaned over the edge of the sarcophagus. He gently brushed aside the eons of cobwebs and dust that covered the lifeless body of the Mother of vampires. He had imagined this moment differently when he first embarked to bring about the mother's return. Now, faced with the reality of it, the vampire found the moment not as he pictured it at all. For one thing, there were no male strippers.

No, it wasn't how he pictured it at all. He expected her to look a bit more lifelike. You would think the Mother of them all would look more well-preserved. She certainly had let herself go. You would never catch him looking so... He didn't even want to think of the words it'd take to describe her. She wasn't even wearing make-up. What kind of woman would allow herself to be found without even a smidgen of concealer to hide the imperfections?

"She looks a bit gristly to me," Lewis said, popping his head over Leopold's shoulder.

"Philistine, show more respect," Leopold snapped, the force of his voice driving Lewis from the coffin. Leopold couldn't help but agree with him, but it didn't mean he would let him get away with saying it.

"There's still time to walk away," Breathred said.

"Shut up. I have had quite enough of your tongue for this evening," Leopold grumbled. Why did everyone think he was open to discussion?

"Just letting you know you don't have to do this. Your Mother isn't what you think she is."

"Oh, and how would you know? This is beyond your feeble little world, Petrifunck."

"I know she won't serve you or give you what you want," Breathred said.

"I guess she told you this, did she?"

"Well, yeah. She did," Breathred admitted.

"You lying little shit! She would not talk to a lowly human." Leopold grabbed Breathred by his collar, lifting him into the air. "Now, you take it back before I scuff my new Pradas kicking you in the butt."

"Kick away, because I'm telling the truth," Breathred said, as he dangled in the vampire's grasp.

"Hey, boss. I think he's telling the truth," Lewis leaned in and offered.

"Just kill him and bring her back, here and now," Easily interjected.

"No, I had Laurence Llewelyn-Bowen, himself, design the sacrificial room. I will not have it take place in a drafty tomb, when a perfectly delightful room is waiting for us back in Seattle," Leopold said, flatly.

"You're shitting me! We could get this over with right now, and you're waiting because you don't like the ambience?" Easily cried in disbelief.

"One must consider decorum in such matters. I wouldn't want the Mother to think I'm not of sufficient station to be the one to wake her. I will not have her thinking I am lowbrow. I am unanimous in that," Leopold said, to end the conversation whether Dr. Easily wanted it ended or not. "Lewis, please gag Mr. Petrifunck. I can't even bring myself to call him Breathred after all the lies he's been telling."

Breathred didn't even struggle when Leopold handed him off to Lewis. There was no need to fight it. He had to trust D'brea had reached Luna and had something planned to help. He hadn't seen her in almost an hour, so could only assume she was with them. If not, he was on his own and didn't like the thought. Didn't like it at all.

Lewis made short work of tying him up. Once he was deposited on the floor, they set to work on removing D'brea's body from the sarcophagus. Despite his reluctance to their tampering, Breathred was glad to see Jessica was overseeing the project. Somehow he doubted D'brea would appreciate a broken body when she made it back.

"Damn right, I won't," D'brea whispered in his ear.

Breathred mumbled something understandably incoherent through the gag.

"Shut up. It's not like I can hear you through that piece of rag," she ordered.

He continued to mumble. "Blubby whubber rrr doo?"

"Bit daft, aren't you? They can't see me. I'm invisible. I had to come back and reconnect with my body. I was beginning to feel lost."

"Whubber rrrr du udders?"

"They're outside waiting for you to come out. Brogan has a plan. Don't worry, we'll have you free in a jiffy. Now, be quiet. The young one's looking over here. I have to go."

Breathred turned his head to see Lewis was giving him a strange look. The vampire's reaction didn't surprise him. If he were looking at himself, he'd be giving himself a strange look, too.

They had removed the body from the sarcophagus while he had been talking to D'brea. Jessica was already wrapping the body for transport. Doing a good job of it, too. He'd forgotten she'd spent two years studying ancient burial techniques. When Easily was finished, D'brea's body could survive just about anything. Breathred smiled when he saw her do a secondary wrap with waterproof cloth to end the job. Jessica might be a low down dirty traitor, but she knew how to treat antiquities.

Jessica wiped a sheen of sweat from her brow. "All finished, Leopold. The body is ready for transport."

"Good. Then let's head 'em up and move 'em out. I always wanted to say that." Leopold beamed.

"Leopold, what about them?" Lewis pointed to Dr. Grayson and Truehart.

"Leave them, as they are. No sense carrying around anymore dead weight than we need to."

"What about Petrifunck?" Jessica asked.

Leopold dismissed her question with a wave of his hand. Instead, he walked over to Breathred. Bending down, he pulled Breathred's head up by his chin.

"You will be a good boy. Won't you? I have to untie your legs so you can walk. Just understand, it doesn't give you license to run away or play the hero. I'm going to pull this dreadful gag out of your mouth, so you can answer."

"You won't get away with this," Breathred said.

"I feel it redundant to say I already have, but I have. So there," Leopold mocked, adding an uncharacteristic raspberry to his statement. "Your friends are tied up. There is no one else to stop me."

"D'brea will stop you."

"And who is this new figment of your imagination?"

"If you don't know, I pity you, because you're more ignorant than I thought you were." Breathred looked for some sign D'brea was still around but the woman was nowhere to be found.

"Ew! Lewis, tie his hands behind his back and put the gag back in. I will not be called ignorant by a virgin," Leopold ordered, drawing a giggle from Jessica. "You stow it before I have Lewis gag you, as well. Virgin smack is bad enough without having to take it from the vindictive slut contingent."

"Bastard!" Jessica shouted.

"Bitch!"

"Oh, I am sorry to have offended you with my name calling," Jessica said in a sickeningly sweet voice. "Sometimes I forget what kind of man you are."

"That's more like it."

"What I meant to have said was DRIED UP OLD BITCH!" she shot back with a furious howl.

Leopold dabbed his nose with a purple handkerchief. "We do know the scent of our own kind, don't we?"

"Kiss my ass."

"It's not like I couldn't find it in the dark." Leopold laughed.

"Are you saying I have a big butt?" Jessica fumed.

Leopold did a passable rendition of the Cabbage Batch. "And I cannot lie."

"People, aren't we forgetting a little something, like getting out of here?" Lewis intervened. "And stop doing that, Leo, my man. You're making me regret giving you a copy of *Monster Booty* for your birthday."

Leopold turned on Lewis with his fangs bared. Breathred took a nervous step back, glad he was standing behind the younger vampire. He kept waiting for the other shoe to drop, hoping the two vamps would take each other out, saving his friends from having to rescue him.

"Lewis, you are quite correct," Leopold said, retracting his fangs.

"Glad, you noticed." Lewis smiled.

"Don't get all smug. You're still lugging the Mother out of here. Easily, if you would take please keep Breathred in hand, I think we can depart."

Breathred couldn't help but notice the evil smile play over the woman's face. He still couldn't understand why she would betray them to Leopold. Breathred knew she could be domineering at times, but this went way beyond being cranky or bossy. A rough shove ended his confusing thoughts. They were off.

Breathred hoped he would have time to talk to her. Maybe, he would have an opportunity to speak with her before they got around to killing him. Breathred did so hate to have people mad at him. If he actually was going to die, he hated to think he would die without giving her a chance to get what was bothering her off her chest. He was stupid like that.

Fifty

Boffrend's accepts no responsibility for any wrongful death suits your career as a vampire hunter may bring about.

Exiting the tomb, Leopold flinched, as the first snowflake hit him. He turned around to make some comment on the event to Lewis. Remembering his fellow vampire was burdened with the Mother, Leo grumpily clamped his mouth shut. Why was everyone busy when he felt the need to rant? He could have told Ms. Easily about the matter, but the thought of putting up with another of the woman's verbal barrages was more than he could stand.

Instead, he would store the comment for later discussion. It was a long trip back to Seattle and would need something to talk about to break the monotony of his brooding. Over the course of his life, Leopold had discovered being broody on long trips was the best way to avoid unwanted conversation. If he managed it right, he could get what he wanted to say out, then make some stray remark from Lewis appear more dire than it was and bypass any of Lewis' bland reminiscing of the good old days when pimps were pimps and women could bring in enough to afford the finer things in life, like gold lame and crystal pumps.

Leopold pointedly ignored the grunts that announced Lewis exiting the tomb. If he couldn't talk about those things he wished to, the vampire saw no need to speak to the man at all. He wasn't being petty. He was just being practical. Besides, conversation might distract Lewis from the job at hand. All they needed was for the clumsy oaf to drop the Mother in a pile of snow because the younger vampire couldn't listen and walk at the same time.

Perhaps he should have had Petrifunck assist dear Lewis. No, it would be too risky. Petrifunck was obviously unbalanced. It was the only explanation for the man's outrageous claims about talking to the Mother. The very idea the Mother would converse with a lowly human was ludicrous. Leopold was certain someone as powerful as the Mother would only talk to well-dressed people of discernable breeding who shopped at only the finer upscale establishments. Neiman Marcus sprang to mind, but he wasn't one to drop names willy-nilly.

Leopold topped the mound of the dig that had, until recently, covered the tomb. The flurries were flying even harder above the tomb. He flipped up the collar on his jacket, hoping it would ward off the majority of the icy flakes. Leopold moved away from the edge before he was enlisted by Lewis to aid him in his extraction from the gaping hole. Propriety dictated he remain aloof from such menial endeavors. To that end, the vampire stared blissfully at the sky until he heard his party stagger to rest beside him.

As Leopold opened his mouth say something particularly snide, Brogan launched his attack. The first snowball struck Leopold full in the chest. The second one caught him in the face. The stinging projectiles sent him sailing back into the other three. He screeched, as three more snowballs slashed into him on his downward descent.

"I have been violated by Frosty the Snowman," he howled, frantically wiping snow from his face and chest.

"That's right Buster! If you don't want to meet his throbbing icicle, hand over Breathred," Stud shouted from the darkness.

"Don't forget about me," D'brea whispered in Stud's ear.

"Yeah, and the moldy corpse, too."

"You really are an unpleasant little creature. Do you realize that?"

"I call 'em like I see 'em, Sugar Dumpling."

"You two, shut the hell up," Brogan hissed from across the cluttered area.

"If you humans are through, I feel it incumbent to inform you the virgin is mine." Leopold grabbed Breathred by the neck and dragged him in front of himself. "I also feel it relevant to tell you if another snowball so much as grazes my person, I will rip his head clean from his shoulders."

"You're bluffing." Stud jumped from his hiding place with a snowball in hand.

"Ah, the monkey." Leopold jerked Breathred's head back sharply, revealing his pulsating jugular. "Try me."

"Stud!" Luna screamed from where she sat beside Brogan.

"Look, Vampy. All we want is Breathred," Brogan said, before things got any worse.

"Well, you can't have him. He's my virgin and I'm keeping him," Leopold ranted.

Luna jumped from cover. "He's my boyfriend and I want him back, now!"

"If he wanted you, we wouldn't be having this conversation. Now, would we?" Leopold asked. "Perhaps he wouldn't be a virgin, if you actually had something he wanted."

Leopold inched further behind Breathred as Luna took a step toward them. Not that he was afraid, but the girl did look quite upset, so no need to take chances. The Canadian reached for her, but she swept away his arm, the force of the blow staggering him back. Leopold wasn't sure but thought girls her size weren't supposed to toss men around like that, unless Canadians weren't as tough as their reputations reputed.

He was about to point the observation out when he noticed the girl didn't look quite right. She didn't even look human, to be perfectly honest. Leopold was ready to think an outbreak of the premenstrual syndrome affected the women in the area when it dawned on him perhaps the girl wasn't human to begin with. Hair growing everywhere suddenly was a dead giveaway. After a few minutes she looked nothing close to human. The girl was something different. If anything, she looked like a giant Schnauzer.

At least he wasn't the only one shocked. Breathred ceased struggling to get away. Leopold guessed the virgin was in shock after seeing his girlfriend turning into a Great Dane. The boy shouldn't be all too surprised. Leopold hadn't known her all that long and had already figured out she was a bitch. Now the outside just matched the inside.

Leopold was old enough to know what he was seeing. He had never seen one before, but this creature could only be a Dushato. While vampires were children of the spirit world, the Dushato were creatures of the earth. That being the case, the two races had been sworn enemies since time began, or for as long as he knew. The vampire had long thought the creatures were nothing more than a myth the elders used to frighten newly-dead vampires. Seeing this one, he knew his assumptions were not the case.

The Dushato's existence was not as shocking as who the Dushato was. The girl had hidden her origin well. Leopold had never suspected. As the girl approached, he tried to remember the Dushato's weaknesses. He couldn't think of any off hand, at least none that didn't mirror his own. They really were opposite sides of the same coin. If it might kill her, he knew it would surely kill him. It was the main reason why the two peoples tended to avoid each other. Avoided each other so well Leopold hadn't even seen one in his three hundred some-odd years of existence. Well, he was making up for the slight now, wasn't he?

So, what should he do about it? He wasn't about to hand Petrifunck over to her. Virgins were hard to come by, and you didn't go throwing them away once you got one. It was like throwing out the chamberpot before the indoor plumbing was hooked up.

"Vampire, let my man go," Luna growled.

Leopold could only watch as she made her way toward him with slow and measured steps, every muscle tensed and ready.

Leopold, like Breathred, was slow to realize he no longer had a hand on the man in question. The vampire hastily reached out and grabbed Breathred, before the man could run off.

"Why is the big doggie talking with Luna's voice?" Breathred asked, but Leopold chose to ignore him. He had bigger problems to deal with at the moment than a confused virgin.

"I don't think so, Dushato," Leopold said, regaining some of the confidence he had lost upon seeing her transformation.

"Give him to me before I rip you apart." Luna snarled. "Blood Drinker, you're holding my mate. Do you have any idea who you're dealing with? I'm a child of Coyote, not some pampered Pomeranian. Give me what I want or by God you will die."

"Nothing has changed. If you try to take him, I will kill him," Leopold stated, his voice telling her he wasn't lying.

Leopold watched the Dushato stop in mid-step, turning her nose into the air. He could tell she was sniffing for some sign of deceit on his part. Well she'd find none. He'd kill the virgin here and now, his finely decorated room be damned. She wouldn't risk the life of her mate with a foolish bid at saving him, especially if the attack meant his death. The scent of her frustration filled the air between them. Leopold smiled as her head snapped up and she let loose a howl that shook the entire clearing. When its last echoes faded into the night, she sank to the ground.

"Hey, I think that doggie is Luna!" Breathred exclaimed.

"Ya think?" Lewis said, right next to him. "Leopold, I didn't sign up to fight no werewolf. You de bad-ass. I'll be the chicken-shit in back. You can be the goofy white guy in front. Acting as the shield, dig?"

Brogan ran up to the girl, a look of surprise on his face. "Look, Darlin'. This werewolf thing you got going is impressive, but the vamps ain't buying."

"Yes, Girlie. We ain't buying, so peddle your doggie Avon somewhere else," Leopold yelled.

"We can't just let them take Breathred," Luna growled.

"Babe, you ain't in no shape to take them on and if we try they're holding all the cards. Do you want to see Breathred get killed?"

"No!"

"Then we got to let them walk. They'll slip up, I promise and we'll be there to kick their ass."

Leopold listened intently while the two finished the rest of the conversation in hushed whispers, growing irritated he could not make out a damn thing they were saying. The virgin was getting twitchy, which made it all the more harder to concentrate. Finally, the vampire just gave up. The Canadian was right. He was holding all the cards. The only thing they could do was let them go. All Leopold had to do was wait for them to come to their senses and realize it.

"Okay, Snaggletooth. Walk," Brogan shouted.

"Finally, a voice of reason in this motley crew." Leopold applauded.

"It doesn't mean I like it, Bub," Brogan snarled.

"I'm sure you don't but there isn't a lot you can do about it. Kindly, put a leash on your little dog, so we can get about our business."

~ * ~

Luna growled, but her heart wasn't in it. She lifted her head toward Breathred. A soft whine issued from her trembling snout. Breathred pulled

Leopold to a stop just short of her. With the vampire's hand gripping his arm, Breathred fell to his knees and reached out and gently stroked her tousled head.

Luna looked up into his smiling face. "Don't look at me, Breathred. I didn't want you to see me like this."

"You're a doggie."

"I know what you must think. You hate me, don't you?" She broke down into a sobbing wreck.

"I like doggies," Breathred swore. "But I love you."

"You do?" she asked, not believing her ears. She lifted her head until their eyes met. All she could see was love staring back at her. "But I should have told you."

Breathred stroked her tear-soaked cheek. "Yeah, but if you can put up with me, my weirdness—and let's not forget Stud—who am I to get all crazy just because you're a dog?"

"Werewolf."

"You're a werewolf? I thought you were a dog."

"Does what I am change anything?"

"Do I have to sniff your butt?" Breathred asked, a look of horror on his face.

"Not, if you don't want to."

"Then, I'm okay."

Before she could say anything else Breathred reached over and kissed her on the end of her muzzle, letting out a giggle. "The prickly hair tickles my lips. It's sorta like kissing my Aunt Sue, only you're not my Aunt Sue." He grinned.

Leopold jerked him away, ending the moment. "Stop that! I will not have my virgin consorting with animals in my presence. What will the neighbors say?"

"Breathred!" Luna howled, as Leopold dragged him away.

"Down Fido," Jessica laughed, stopping just outside of her reach.

"Bitch!"

"Well, if that ain't the pot calling the kettle black."

Luna lunged at her but the woman dodged easily out of her way. Before she could make another try, Easily took off sprinting after Leopold and the rest of her party. Luna fell back to the ground. Her paws pounded the ground in frustration, sending up a spray of snow and chunks of frozen earth.

"Don't worry, Luna. We'll get him back," Brogan said.

She appreciated the fact he was trying to console her but it wasn't helping. "How can you be so positive? They've won. They have Breathred and D'brea's body."

"They might have won the battle, but the war ain't over with yet," Brogan assured her.

"Yeah, yeah, but we got another little problem," D'brea said.

Brogan and Luna turned around to see Stud standing alone in the center of the clearing. They looked around for the ghost but couldn't find her. They had almost given up, when Stud began to speak.

"Looks, like I've reached the edge of how far I can stay away from my body. Lucky for me, the chimp was nearby," Stud said calmly, using D'brea's voice.

Fifty One

After doing this for a while, you'll realize there are just some things you don't want to know, or have to see.

"What's the matter? Never seen a woman in drag before?" D'brea/Stud said, as she hiked up her leg to scratch his butt.

"Stud?" Luna asked, the words sounding more human. The wolf side of her nature was giving way to the human. She didn't know if the shift in the status quo was a good thing, but was grateful for it. She couldn't prove it, but swore she was catching fleas from being close to Stud.

"He's in here somewhere, but damned if I know where," D'brea answered, flippantly.

"Don't listen to the crazy-ass bitch! She's got me chained up in here," Stud's voice shouted from the other side of his mouth.

"Shut up, you monkey! It was either this or I went back in my body," D'brea told the chimp, which was weird because the two voices started fighting.

Two voices shouting at each other from the same mouth was a little more than Luna could take. "Both of you shut up."

The chimp's body snapped to attention.

"Now, D'brea. What have you done to Stud?" Luna demanded. "And Stud be quiet. I want to hear this from her, not you."

"Don't get all snippy. Do you think I'd do this, if I didn't have to? I felt my spirit slipping away. For a second I got scared. Then, something you or Breathred said, I can't remember which, got me to thinking. Maybe I could jump into another body," D'brea explained.

"Why not just go back to your own?" Brogan asked.

"You saw those goof-balls. Would you want to go with them? Besides, I thought if I was in somebody else, they might not be able to bring my body back."

"But, why me?" Stud interrupted her.

"You were closest. I didn't have much time to think about it. I just did it. It wasn't like you weren't thinking about getting in my pants. I just went one better."

Luna's thoughts kept going out to Breathred. Every minute they stayed here, the vampires were carrying him further away. Who knew what they were doing to him? "So, what do we do now?"

"We follow them," Brogan said.

"In this storm that won't be easy."

"Well, I can do something about the storm," D'brea replied.

"What do you mean?" Brogan snapped.

"I did start it after all. Even in this body, all I have to do is snap my fingers and poof no more storm," Stud's face smiled. "See?"

True to her words, she snapped Stud's fingers and the snow stopped.

"Can you do anything about the radio interference?" Brogan prompted.

"Sure thing," she said with another snap of Stud's fingers.

Brogan didn't even wait for her reply. He ran straight to the radio tent with the rest of them following close behind. He dashed over to the radio and clicked on the handset. It buzzed to life in his hand. Finally, Luna was happy to see something was going right.

"Agent Brogan, report. Again, report. Over," a voice crackled over the long-dead line.

He winked at Luna. "HQ this is Brogan. Over."

"Good. Thought we'd lost you there. Received unconfirmed report from Eh Ya Campgrounds about vampire invasion. Can you confirm?" the voice demanded.

"Report, affirmative. We have vampire contact." Brogan waved the others away from the radio, as they huddled around him.

"Do you have coordinates of hostiles? Repeat, send coordinates for immediate wet work," the voice crackled.

"Negative, hostiles have bugged out. Over."

The voice on the other end paused. Luna felt like grabbing the handset from Brogan and banging the receiver against the table. She noticed he wasn't too happy with his bosses either. His fingers were digging grooves into the thin plastic. She hoped he remembered the radio was their only way out of this.

"Affirmative on hostile location. Anything else? Over," the voice finally said.

Brogan gave her a thumb's up. "Need ETA on extraction."

Luna wasn't stupid. She knew as well as he did CAPP SAT probably didn't have anything close to them. Unless Elvis came waltzing in here on a UFO in the next twenty minutes, they would lose any chance they had of gaining on the vamps and Breathred.

"We're looking at a thirty minute window," the voice stated.

"If that's the best you can do, we'll be waiting. Over." Brogan slammed the receiver on the table.

"We'll never catch them," Luna moaned.

"Sure we will, Darlin'. You heard Leopold. They won't do anything until they get back to Seattle. We'll get him back. I promise."

"That's right, sugar," D'brea/Stud said, wrapping his arm around her neck. "Those goobers didn't look like they could blow their noses, let alone bring me back. They probably can't even prick his finger without an owner's manual to tell them how."

"Hell yeah, Luna! We're going to kick their blood-sucking butts," the Stud half chimed in, drowning out D'brea.

"You really, think so?" Luna wanted to believe, but the odds were against them. She wasn't a fool. If they didn't catch the vamps, Breathred stood a good chance of dying. She just had to have faith.

"You have my word on it," Brogan assured her.

She looked up and gave him a tearful, silent thank you.

"Hey I just thought of something!" D'brea exclaimed.

"Don't tell me, you've figured out a way to get to them before the extraction team gets here," Brogan said, hopefully.

"No, I got a weenie. I always wondered what it'd be like to have one of those." D'brea pulled out on the elastic of Stud's pants to peek below. After a confused minute, she looked up with a strange look on Stud's face.

"What is it?" Luna giggled at the face she was making.

"Somehow, I hoped it would be bigger than this."

"Bet you aren't the only one," Brogan laughed, evoking a round of laughter that erased their fears for a moment or two.

~ * ~

The dented U-Haul pulled out onto the highway and headed south. It was a little after two in the morning. Lewis eased the pedal to the floor and shifted the truck into a grinding fifth gear. The vehicle lurched and took off, throwing up a spray of cold gravel in its wake.

In the back of the moving van, Breathred and Jessica were being thrown around. He had long become tired of Jessica's constant griping. If he were her, he'd be glad to ride in back. Breathred might like D'brea, but the idea of sitting beside her mummified corpse while it rode shotgun in the front gave him the willies.

Breathred took the tumbles in stride. With his hands tied behind his back, there was little he could do to stop it, anyway. He eased into a corner and watched Easily. Even in the gloomy light of the shaking box, Breathred could tell she was upset.

He tried to look on the bright side. True, it was hard to find a bright side when you were about to be sacrificed to a dead vampire queen, but Breathred was doing his best. That wasn't exactly true. He was still bothered by the fact Jessica was trying to kill him. She was his friend. Friends didn't try to kill you. They got mad at you and didn't talk to you for a week, but killing you seemed a little harsh.

He had brooded over the fact ever since they threw him in here. Breathred had been trying to find the right time to broach the subject with her, but her constant grumbling had told him to wait. Considering he didn't have much time left, Breathred wondered how much longer he could afford to sit here being patient. He might not be growing any younger, but it didn't look like he would be getting any older either. So, he might as well try.

"Jessica, I think we need to talk," he said, tentatively.

"About what?"

"Well, we could start with why you want to kill me and go on from there." Breathred really didn't think she'd talk to him, but he had to try.

"Breathred, you are truly clueless," she said.

"I might be, but I'd still like to know why you betrayed us to Leopold." When it came to women, he was clueless. Maybe, he could get a book that would explain it all to him.

"Because, you thick Gomer, you jilted me," she shouted into his face.

"I did?"

"Damn, right you did. Not once, but twice," Jessica spat.

"Are you sure? I don't remember doing it." Breathred was sure he had never jilted anyone. You had to have a girlfriend to do that. So, unless he forgot having one besides Luna, he couldn't have.

"Thirteen years ago we were dating, and just when I thought we might have a future together, you up and disappear. Does that jog your memory?" Jessica demanded.

"We never dated. Sure, we had some classes together, studied together and went on a couple field trips, but never during the entire time did we date." Breathred was more than a little shocked she would read so much into those innocent things.

"That was dating, you moron. We passed notes in class. You told me I was the best after I helped you pass the Ancient Civilizations final. We held hands on the bus trip to Alexandria. If that's not dating, I don't know what dating is."

"It's not dating. We were friends and that was all. The only reason we held hands on the trip was because I was throwing up the whole way, and you didn't want any on your shoes, so you made sure I was an arm's length away from you in case of over-spray."

"Hey, you're right. You ruined a brand new pair of loafers. Man, the things you forget. I loved those shoes. They were pink with yellow striping across the toe. I don't know what you ate, but it burned the protective coating off those shoes."

"Uh, Jessica can we get back to the killing me part of this conversation?" Breathred finally asked, after having to listen to a ten-minute flashback about parachute pants and fishnet vests.

"Oh, yeah. So, we really didn't date. Why did I think we did?"

"It might have been the fact you did date my roommate, Carl, for three months until he graduated and went to Prague."

"That's right, we did. Man, talk about being wrong about a guy. He was such a butt," Jessica said, thoughtfully.

"So, does it mean we're friends again, and you'll help me get away?"

"Of course you silly man, we're friends," Jessica reached over and ruffling his hair.

Breathred breathed a sigh of relief. "Good, I was afraid you were going to go through with this."

"But I am going through with it."

"How can you?"

"Be reasonable. I'm almost forty. Things are beginning to sag. This could be the only chance I have to stop the ravages of aging without having to spend a fortune on plastic surgery. You have to see this from my point of view."

"Jessica, they're going to kill me!"

"Don't be a buzz-kill. Look on the bright side. I won't feel a thing." She smiled.

"There is no bright side. I'll be too dead to see the bright side!" Breathred shouted, trying to break through to her how serious this situation was. He didn't mind dying for a good 'cause, but dying for her vanity was not his idea of a good 'cause.

Jessica jabbed her finger into his face. "You are such a man. Do you know that? A real man would be more than willing to die so I could be beautiful forever."

Before Breathred could come back with a snappy retort—not that he had one, but he might have—the truck skidded to a stop, slamming them both into the side of the van. Breathred looked up, his consciousness wavering. A thin ribbon of blood ran into his eye from a deep gash ran the length of his forehead. He struggled to rise, only to fall back, groaning, to the hard metal floor. Blinking the blood from his eyes, he lifted his head to see if Jessica was all right. She might be crazy and trying to kill him, but it was the proper thing to do. His head throbbed from the effort. It took a minute for his vision to clear enough for him to make out anything in the flickering gloom. When the darkness cleared, Jessica was staring back at him a few feet away.

Her body rested in a huddled mass against the wall adjacent to where he was lying. She was close enough for him to reach out and touch. Breathred thought it strange she could be comfortable with her head twisted around in such an unnatural position. Darkness swept over him, as his vision blurred again. Ah, well it must be a woman thing. Maybe, when he woke up, Jessica could explain to him how she did it. The U-Haul's back door rattled up and he knew no more. By then, it was too late to wonder. Something else was in control.

Fifty Two

If you have a minute, it's time we talked about using protection.

  The helicopter skirted the tree line as it headed south toward America. Luna looked down at the racing landscape, wondering if by some remote chance she might spot Breathred below her. Knowing it was a stupid idea, she kept her eyes glued to the patchwork landscape. The first pink light of false dawn broke through the tinted window. Luna wrapped a blanket around her, as her body returned to its human form. Stud gave her a smug smile and handed her a bag of her clothes they had gathered before leaving the camp.

  Luna sat back in her chair, thoughts of changing the last thing on her mind. Reluctantly turning her face away from the narrow glass of the window, she had to face the fact Leopold must have reached Seattle by now. Despite all Brogan's assurances, they'd lost them. Her poor Breathred could be dead. No, she couldn't think like along those lines. It would have taken Leopold this long to even reach Seattle. He couldn't have done anything yet. If he had, D'brea would have felt something.

  Luna looked over to make sure the possessed chimp wasn't acting funny. The humor of the thought did not escape her, nor did it make her stop looking. She wasn't sure which of the two was in control, but if she had to guess, it had to be D'brea.

  Luna wondered what the woman thought about this new world she had wakened into. She could only imagine what was going through D'brea's mind. All these thoughts accomplished were to unsuccessfully distract her from worrying about Breathred. She didn't delude herself. The fears were still there.

  The door to the helicopter's cockpit whooshed open. Brogan stomped into the back, a hard grimace masking his face. Luna had hoped he would bring back some good news. From the set of his, face her hope had been in vain. She caught him looking her way. He shot her a half-hearted grin, but she didn't read anything into it.

  "Any news?" she asked, when he sat beside her.

  "Yeah, and none of it good. The Mounties found the U-haul abandoned at a small airstrip not far from the dig site. The tower said a plane filed a flight plan for a straight trip to Seattle. CACA contacted all the Seattle airports and, thirty minutes ago, the plane landed at another small airstrip on the outskirts of the city."

"So, they made just before dawn?" she asked, not really expecting an answer, just trying to work it out in her head.

"They wouldn't have had time to do anything, Kid. He's safe," Brogan put his arm around her neck.

"For the moment. In a little over eight hours though, he's dead meat."

"Don't think like that. We'll get to him in time." He swiped a tear from her cheek. "Luna, there's something else, but I don't want to upset you any more than you already are."

Her heart ran cold. In spite of his assurances Breathred was all right, something in his tone said it wasn't.

"Shoot," she said, steeling herself for the worst.

"They found Easily's body in the back of the van. Her neck had been snapped."

"Couldn't have happened to a nicer bitch."

"Luna!"

"Well, what the hell did you expect me to say? Oh, the poor dear? Nobody deserves to have something so horrible happen to them? Well, screw her! She betrayed us to Leopold and handed Breathred over to him without a second thought. God knows what she did to Doctor Grayson and Truehart, or did you fail to notice they never came out of the tomb?"

"Uh, are you talking about those two tightwads that came in with Breathred?" D'brea asked, walking over to them.

"Do you know what happened to them?" Luna had felt bad for not checking on them earlier, but so much had been happening she had forgotten about them until just now.

"Well, I might have zombified them, but they're basically all right. To tell you the truth I forgot all about them," she said.

"Don't you think you should un-zombie them?" Stud grumbled. "Truehart might be an ass, but Grayson doesn't deserve to be a zombie. If you can't do them both, feel free to leave Truehart."

"Wait a minute…Okay, they're awake, but you might want to send somebody to pick them up. The one you call Truehart is freaking out," D'brea told Brogan.

"On it." Brogan hit a button beside his seat, and relayed the message to the cockpit. "They've contained the tomb but somebody will retrieve them as soon as they show."

"I feel sorry for Doctor Grayson. She thought this would legitimize her research. Not only does she sleep through it, but nobody'll ever find out about it. Will they, Brogan?" Luna asked.

"Probably not, darling. CAPP SAT will clamp a lid over the whole thing. Once we deal with Leopold, this fiasco will be black-filed. If the doctor tries to publish any of her findings, she'll be painted to look like a loon, if not outright locked away."

"They can't do that to her!" Luna shouted.

"They can and they will. What do you think the public would say if they were to find out there really were vampires running around? They'd go nuts and see them behind every shadow. The world functions because the governments have agencies to keep the dark secrets locked away," he explained. "I might not like it, but I can't change how the game's played."

~ * ~

It was a somber group that stepped off the helicopter. Brogan's words had set a depressing tone for the rest of the flight home. Brogan instructed the pilot to take them to the same airfield as the one Leopold's plane set down at earlier. A team of investigators were already giving the vampire's plane a thorough going-over.

Luna barely noticed. Her thoughts were on Breathred. Brogan had told them, as they neared Seattle that CAPP SAT hadn't been able to track Leopold after he left the airport. Apparently, the vampire used a string of dummy accounts to charter the airplane and was met by a waiting limo. The same string of accounts had rented the limo. An interrogation of the driver revealed nothing. The man had a blank spot in his memory from the minute he got to work until he returned to the garage. Even a database search on any of Leopold's purchases in the Seattle area turned up nothing.

Since Brogan had told them about Easily, Luna had been searching her feelings for a trace of Breathred. The connection they shared because of the talisman should have let her sense him. She wouldn't have been able to track him to where he was hidden, but would have at least been able to tell if he was still alive. Whenever Luna concentrated on him, all she could get was a void where he should have been.

It wasn't until they were ushered from the airport's lobby Luna realized they were even on the ground. The knowledge did her little good. The hole where Breathred should have been was too big to ignore.

"Luna! Luna Walking Batch, over here," a voice yelled across the parking lot.

Luna looked up, startled anyone would know she was here. Except for the three of them, no one knew she was even back in Seattle. Her guard went instantly up. Over the past few days it had stayed up, not that pumping it up a few extra notches would hurt anything.

She had to smile though. Brogan went instantly into macho-nacho mode. Apparently, Stud was back in control of his body because the chimp was skulking behind her.

The voice called out again. This time Luna made out the voice's owner. It was Uncle Joan. What was she doing here? Better yet, how did her uncle know Luna would be here?

"Uncle Joan, what are you doing here?" Luna asked, as the woman crossed the street to join them.

"Runs Like Frightened Girl told me you were in trouble," Joan smiled.

"It still doesn't explain how you knew I'd be here."

Joan gave her a wink. "He told me that, too."

"Who the hell is this?" Stud demanded.

"This is Joan Prancing Elk, my uncle," Luna's look told him not to push it.

"So, who is this Runs Like Frightened Girl, your Aunt?"

Joan stuck her hand out. "No, he's my spirit guide. You must be Stud."

"What tipped you off? My hairy ass?" Stud drew back his hand quickly. "I'm not judgmental, but you're one scary whatever-you-are."

"He's just as you described him," Joan said, turning away from the chimpanzee. "But what I have to say is important. Perhaps, it would be best if we were to get out of here first. I have my mini-van in the lot."

"Best offer I've had all week. Lead on," Brogan said for them all.

~ * ~

Nobody spoke, as the aging Astro van tooled down the street. By unspoken agreement, they had decided to wait for Joan to explain his earlier statement, Stud hadn't agreed but went along with it, seeing as how the vamp was twisting his cerebral cortex. After ten minutes of driving, it didn't look like the whatsit would spill anything but a medley of Ambrosia hits, which he'd been singing non-stop since they took off. Stud saw only one option to end the awkward karaoke—he had to be the one to open his big mouth. "Look, Papa Smurf. We've had a shitty coupla days, so could you cut the claptrap and tell us what you meant back there?"

"Oh, I'm sorry. I thought it best to wait till we got back to my place," Joan reached over to turn off the radio.

"Thank God! One more minute of that crud and I was gonna spew," Brogan mumbled, as he uncorked his fingers from his ears. "Not to offend you, Guy, but the seventies are best left to AM radio."

"This is really freaking me out. I know you mean well, but," Luna said, breaking into tears.

"There, there, Luna. I know," Joan said. "Your man's alright. Stop all your crying. Your Uncle Joan is going to help."

"Oh, Uncle Joan. I wish I could believe you, but you have no idea what we've been through."

"Yeah man, we talking bout some crazy shit. I'm talking about some shit that'd make your curlies go straight for life," Stud said, poking his head through the seats.

"Hey, Stud. Where's D'brea? She hasn't been talking," Brogan asked.

"Oh, she's talking a nap. She accidentally took a peek into my Bea Arthur fantasy and said she needed to rest after seeing it."

"Look, if you feel she's slipping away, let us know. Just to be on the safe side."

Stud gave him a thumbs up. "Will do."

"Can we get back to Breathred?" Luna snapped.

"He's fine, Luna. Runs Like told me to make sure I told you that," Joan said, patting her on the knee.

"You know where he's at?" Luna cried.

"I don't, but Runs Like does."

"Then, what the hell are we waiting for? Let's go smash some heads," Stud said before Luna could get a word out. She was too distraught to think straight, so he would take charge.

"Hold your horses. Runs Like says we can't rush into this. He sees danger in haste. We must make plans and think this through," Joan advised.

"We don't have time to twiddle our thumbs. If we can get to Breathred before the sun sets, we can do this without having to face the vampires," Stud snarled.

"The vampires are the least of your worries. The vampires have awakened something in your friend—something not exactly bad but something that should've stayed asleep," Joan said.

"I'm not calling you crazy, but get real. Breathred is as gentle as a lamb. The only thing inside the geek is more geek," Brogan interjected.

Joan pulled the van over and came to a stop. "You're wrong. Breathred is more dangerous than you know."

"And you know this for a fact?" Luna asked.

"Not me, but Runs Like says it's so, so it is."

"What could have happened to make the goob go all Anakin?" Stud asked, though he had his suspicions Breathred wasn't firing on all six cylinders.

"Runs Like saw death surrounding Breathred last night. He saw darkness, then felt Breathred give himself over to this power. The only way to stop the vampires is to stop Breathred before he gives himself over to this power completely," Joan explained.

"Then, what are we supposed to do?" Luna asked.

Stud saw the tears were threatening to return. "Come, Luna. You have to be strong for Breathred's sake." He put his arm around her shoulder.

"We get ready, because unless I'm wrong, you are the only one who can save him now," Joan said, as he pulled back into traffic.

Fifty Three

What good is the stake, if you forget to bring the hammer?

Breathred awoke to darkness. He strained to make some sense of where he was. The whole room was a black blur in his eyes and his discomfort didn't end there. His wrists chafed under the none-too-tender embrace of the manacles Leopold had relished in imprisoning him in, before leaving at the first signs of dawn. His head ached, but it was to be expected. The coppery taste in his mouth served to remind him of the accident that had given him the bump he was sure was the source of his pain. Breathred guessed he should consider himself lucky.

After some befuddled thinking he was now sure Jessica was dead. A sad voice in the back of his brain kept telling him so. Sometimes the voice told him other things, things that scared him. Breathred tried to block it out, but the longer he ignored it, the louder it became, until finally it was the only thing he could hear.

Breathred pushed past the evil thoughts that populated his brain, remembering hearing the voice once before. It had been softer then, but he could recall it was the same voice. Reginald, Truehart's brother had been with him then. In the darkness the elder Truehart had heard it as well. He was just as certain it had driven the man mad. Breathred remembered it all too well.

With not even a window light the sparse room, Breathred tried for the hundredth time to make out something in his prison. In the end he had to give up trying. His comfort was the least of Leopold's concerns, it would seem. Breathred hadn't expected to be put up in a Five-star hotel, but a bathroom would have been nice.

Breathred knew he was going to die. The voice had told him so, repeatedly. He just hoped he would not have to meet his maker with soiled underwear. Somehow unclean undies and heaven seemed just plain wrong.

You don't have to die, a voice whispered in his mind.

"Everyone has to die," Breathred informed the voice, knowing he was simply talking to himself. Nobody was here with him. He was all alone. Then again, he was trapped in a vampire's dungeon. It wasn't like anybody was going to be listening in and saying, "Look at Petrifunck; he's finally lost it." Why not go ahead and talk to himself? Breathred knew he was losing what was left of his mind. Why not have somebody to enjoy it with?

But not tonight. Let me out and I will save you, the voice grew impatient with Breathred's delay in responding.

"Who are you?" Breathred asked. It didn't hurt to make sure there wasn't anybody in here with him.

You know who I am, the voiced laughed.

"Elvis' alien love child," Breathred offered with a shy smirk. He always wanted to say something like that, but Stud always beat him to it.

No, the voice answered in exasperation. *All right, it doesn't matter who I am. All that matters is I can help you, if you'll let me.*

Breathred shook his head. "I don't think accepting help from an imaginary voice would be a good idea."

Why? Because you're afraid of what I can do? Long ago you let me in. It's time to finish what we started on that fateful day. The days of quiet submission are over. The two of us can vanquish the evil that holds you. Let me take control, and I will show you the true power that resides within you, the voice said, its tone smooth as freshly woven silk in Breathred's ear.

Breathred didn't answer, aloud or in his mind. He didn't know what to say. After repressing these thoughts and memories for so long, he couldn't even be sure what was real anymore. The voice made sense of the holes in his memory.

Something had happened at the Shrine of Seven Veils. If Breathred gave into the voice's offer, he could find out what. Did he want to find out? This could be nothing more than his mind still playing tricks on him. He was under a great deal of stress and when you added his active imagination, it was no wonder little voices were yapping in his head. Well, he had better just wait and see. Until Breathred knew for sure, he wouldn't do anything. If that meant being a virgin sacrifice for a vampire queen, he could live with the decision. Giving in to the voice was too scary to think about when you were alone in the dark, talking to yourself.

~ * ~

The Java Jumper might not have been the best place to go, but Luna couldn't think of anywhere else for Uncle Joan to take them. Her place was too small. Heaven help her, she didn't think Brogan and Stud were quite ready for the Delicious One, or if they ever would be.

Luckily, the Jumper was empty, which was strange for this time of the morning. Luna chalked it up to the horrible weather. Even for Seattle, the weather was bad. Thunder and lightning flashed and raced across the sky. Rain came down in rivers, so hard you couldn't even see the end of your nose. Luna had a sinking suspicion D'brea was the 'cause of it, but kept the opinion to herself. The lack of customers, while not great for business, afforded them the privacy they needed.

Luna looked up to see Edith heading toward them with a tray of coffees and pastries. Her stomach rumbled. It had been a long time since they last ate. The smell of coffee was almost enough to push her over the edge. She had forgotten how good the Jumper's lattes were.

"So, are you like Luna?" Brogan asked Joan, once Edith had gone back to the counter.

"Don't worry, Unc. They know all about my other self," Luna confided, through a mouthful of cream cheese and blueberry.

"If you mean, am I one of Coyote's chosen? No," he answered, his voice doing little to conceal his regret over the fact. "Her lineage can be traced all the way back to Coyote himself."

"He's the Indian trickster god, right?" Brogan asked before taking a bite from his own pastry.

"That is but one of his many faces. He is also the god who brought fire to the world's people. That too was a trick, but one his children appreciate."

"Look, you can sit here and talk this poo poo all day long if you want, but I want to know about Breathred," Stud grumbled. Luna knew he meant business. He hadn't even touched his food.

"Your short friend is right. Luna's mate is who we should be focusing on," Joan said. He reached over and patted her hand.

"What was all that mumbo jumbo about in the van about?" Stud demanded.

"Your friend is not what you think he is. Runs Like senses a darkness in him, a darkness he's fighting at this very moment."

"Bullshit!"

"Hey! This is a family place, monkey. If you can't keep that dirty mouth of yours shut, you can get out," Edith shouted from the counter.

"He's right, Stud. I, myself, have sensed this darkness," D'brea said. It was the first time she had spoken since they left the airport. She sounded tired. Her voice was barely a whisper from Stud's mouth.

"I still don't believe it," Stud groaned.

"Your choice, but it doesn't change the fact," Joan assured him.

"You said you know where Breathred is, Uncle Joan," Luna interrupted.

"He is in a townhouse on the other side of town. Runs Like sees him cloaked in darkness," Joan answered.

Brogan set down his coffee cup. "What about the vampires? Does your spirit guide have anything to say about them?"

"They slumber," Joan replied.

"So, we can get past them," Luna said.

"Yes, but it will not be easy. The place is warded against such an intrusion. The vampires expect you to try to stop them."

"I'm not expecting it to be a cake walk. All I need to know is, can we do it?" Brogan said, bluntly.

"Yes, but Runs Like advises against it," Joan answered.

"What does he say, Uncle Joan?" Luna asked, taking him more seriously than the others.

"He says we should wait until dusk."

"You're crazy! The vampires will be awake then," Stud exclaimed.

"Nevertheless," Joan folded his arms over his chest, "he says moonrise is the time to strike."

"Luna, this is up to you. I'm willing to do whatever you want to do," Brogan said.

"I don't know what to do," she answered.

"What does your heart tell you to do?" Joan asked her.

"It tells me to run to him, but my head tells me you're right." Tears were streaming from her eyes.

Brogan reached over to take her hand. "What's it gonna be, Kid?"

"We do like Uncle Joan said. Runs Like wouldn't deceive us. If he thinks we should wait, we wait," she said, finally.

"Then, it's settled. We go in at dusk." Brogan stood. "I've got to go arrange some things. Joan, can you look after these two?"

"There's three of us, Beef Cake," D'brea interrupted.

"Excuse me. Joan can you look after these three until I get back?" Brogan corrected himself.

"Sure. They can come home with me and catch some z's. Here's the address." Joan handed over a business card.

"The Delicious One?" Brogan smiled, in spite of his grim exterior.

"It's my shop. I have an apartment over the store. Just go around back and ring the bell. I'll buzz you up."

"Okay, I'll be there around five. That should give us enough time to get to Breathred," Brogan said.

"If you're going to be late, just call the number on the bottom of the card. The girl on the counter will transfer the call to my apartment," Joan told him before he left for the door.

Brogan waved but didn't answer. The rain was still blowing when he stepped out onto the sidewalk and pulled the collar of his jacket up to protect his ears against the biting cold. He trudged through the ankle-high water that was backing up from the street and overflowing onto the deserted sidewalk.

In spite of the rain and cold the man was glad to be free of his companions. Brogan was tired of words. He'd spoken more in the past week than he had in the past ten years. It was beginning to wear on him. Truthfully, he needed some time to himself.

This whole situation was getting out of hand. Brogan needed to get some perspective. He was used to acting on his own. Most of his assignments were one man in, one man out and liked it like that. He didn't enjoy having people depending on him for backup, or having to depend on somebody else, for that matter. This time, it was a different game altogether. For the first time in ages Brogan needed some help and it left him uneasy.

He knew his bosses well enough to know they weren't about to offer any. CAPP SAT wasn't about to stick their necks out any further than they already had. They were putting a tight lid on things as it was. He hadn't wanted to say anything to Luna, but was sure this whole episode would be swept under the rug, Black Ops all the way.

Who was he trying to fool? They were going to be so black even he wouldn't know about them. His superiors hadn't come out and said so, but Brogan knew how to read between the lines.

He was on his own. The PTBs—powers that be—wouldn't be contacting the US authorities, either. CAPP SAT didn't want this getting out. Brogan was used to such things when it came to his job, but he had to wonder how far they would go to keep things quiet. More importantly, how far they wanted him to go to make it stay quiet.

Fifty Four

Vampires are the most dangerous when cornered in their homes, so don't do that.

D'brea was nervous. She felt the coming dusk and was afraid. All afternoon, she sensed herself slowly slipping away. She had thought hiding in Stud's body would be enough to keep her spirit together. She was wrong. Her last hope was nightfall would give her the strength to hold it together until her companions returned her to her body.

She had watched them deal with Breathred's loss and still found their reactions strange. He was just one man, yet they acted like he was the entire world. The girl had been trying to sleep throughout the day, but had yet to find the rest her spirit needed. D'brea's heart went out to her. She wondered what it felt like to love someone that much.

Her host was not immune to these feelings. She caught glimpses of his emotions when his mental shields were down. He cared for the man as much as the girl, if not more. The chimp's bluster hid the fears that consumed his every waking thought.

Finally, she induced the sleep he so badly needed. D'brea wished she could do the same for Luna. She had tried, but her powers were just too weak to do more than send a calming wave throughout the room. It took the edge off the tension but did little else. The girl had stopped pacing, so it achieved the desired effect to a certain degree. Nothing short of an elephant tranquilizer would put the girl down, but every little bit helped.

D'brea shifted Stud's head toward the little window overlooking the storefront. Her gaze had constantly been turned toward the street. It was strange to see the things for herself that her mind had glimpsed during her slumber. The plane ride had only been the start of the marvels she witnessed. It made her thirst for the feel of her own body.

It also made her wonder if she was willing to return to the sleep she had enjoyed. No, she would not return to her old half-life again. D'brea wouldn't be a slave to her vampiric children either. She was ready to live. Would Breathred and his friends feel the same way?

The opening of the door tore her from her thoughts. Joan waved as he tiptoed into the room, trying to be quiet so Luna could rest. She could have told him not to bother, but held her tongue. The girl was pretending to be asleep. D'brea saw her lift an eyelid when the door opened. The girl shut it as soon as she caught sight of the big man.

"Brogan just called. He's on his way up," Joan announced in a hushed whisper.

Luna sat up. "Is it time to go, already?"

D'brea felt the excitement uncoil from where it sat in the girl's gut.

"Not yet. We still have a little time left. Try and get some rest before you strain something important." Joan laughed and flicked her fingers at the girl.

"I couldn't, if I wanted to." Luna threw the quilt off, swung her legs around and pouted.

"Don't give me that face. It didn't work when you were a kid and it ain't working now." Joan reached down and pulled Luna's cheeks up until a forced smile plastered the girl's face.

Luna batted away the man's hands. "Stop it! I'm not five years old, anymore."

"Touchy. Touchy." Joan shook her finger at Luna. "Then, stop acting like it."

Before Joan could say another word, Brogan walked through the door. Luna nearly leapt for joy to see him. D'brea believed the girl would have been grateful to see the devil himself walk through the door, if it meant stopping one of her uncle's tirades.

"So, what did you find out?" Luna turned to Brogan once he sat down, hoping it was enough to distract Joan from any more mothering.

"Not much. I thought I might score some intel, but nothing." Brogan slumped into an open seat with a loud sigh. "Nobody knows anything. Or they won't talk."

"Well, I've got a plan." Luna's gaze swept across the group to see if she was the only one.

"Shoot, this is your show, as far as I'm concerned." Brogan rocked back in the chair. "The closest thing I got to a plan is buying fake vamp teeth and knocking on the front door posing as Avon ladies."

"All right. The way I see it, Leopold will be expecting Stud and me. He'll figure Brogan will stay in Canada, and has no idea at all about Joan." She paused long enough to see if they were following her. "So, I think me and Stud should just walk up to the front door and knock. While we distract Leopold, Brogan, you and Joan find a back way in."

"And we get Breathred and D'brea, while he's busy killing you two. Nice plan, but I don't think so." Brogan eyes went wide. "I've heard some crazy shit in my life but that tops it all. That's not a plan. It's a recipe for suicide."

"I hate to say it but she's right. If we come at them head on, he won't be expecting you. Come on, Brogan. You know us. This is so crazy Leopold'll buy it." Stud said. "I hated to say anything, especially when it might involve me getting killed, but I can't think of anything else that'll work."

"You're forgetting something. D'brea'll be along with us. She's our ace in the hole." Luna said. Brogan had to see that with D'brea along, they'd have all the protection they needed.

"Joan, what do you think?" Brogan asked.

"I'm like you. Luna's mama would skin me alive for putting her in danger, but I can't see any other way." Joan stared blankly into the air for a moment. Just as quick, the moment passed. "Runs Like agrees with Luna. He sees no other way. This is the path we must follow."

"See, Brogan? You have to go along with my plan." Luna sat forward with a smug look on her face.

"Count me in." Brogan sighed, as he turned from the window. "In for a penny, in for a pounding, as my dad used to say before the whippings started."

D'brea listened to the friends, but didn't speak. She had her own thoughts about the plan and Luna's dependence upon her and saw no reason to disabuse the girl's notions. Perhaps when her spirit was again close to her body, her powers would return to their full strength. Yeah, and unicorns would dance a jig out of this monkey's butt. Only blood would strengthen her. The only hope D'brea had was her body would be reawakened. Then, she could return to it.

At least that was her hope. It was a slim one at best, and not one she wished to voice. D'brea didn't want to talk at all, afraid her feeble voice would betray her weakness to the others. Pride was an old sin she had cultivated to the extreme, and one she wasn't about to throw it away now.

The first threads of dusk were hidden behind the mounting stormheads. Through her connection with Stud, D'brea heard the others rising from their seats. Soon, they would leave. Already, she sensed the urgency in Stud's thoughts to be gone from this place. She wondered how ready he would be, if the chimp truly understood what he was about to face. Probably, he was stupid enough to ignore the obvious.

~ * ~

Leopold was so giddy with anticipation he hadn't been able to sleep. He simply stared at the satin lining all day, counting a thousand individual threads before growing bored with the project. Lewis had been thoughtful enough to put the mail in before retiring for the day. Most of it was worthless, like all mail tended to be. But, sweet nirvana greeted him at the bottom of the pile. So, he spent the remainder of the afternoon reading his new issue of Vogue by flashlight.

The vampire was thinking about getting one of those refrigerator lights installed in the coffin. That would save him a fortune in batteries. The clerk at the Buy-U-More was constantly giving him the strangest of looks, when he pushed the rattling death trap of a cart through the checkout. The first few times, Leopold chalked it up to unrequited feelings of a purely sexual nature and nothing more. He tended to have a powerful effect on the weaker willed.

Then, the abuse became highly vocal and of a personal nature that Leopold could not dismiss. It was most unsettling to be harangued by a blue-frocked, prepubescent, closet masturbator. Finally, he had decided to avoid the subject altogether by being especially snippy to the pimply-faced buffoon. It seemed to work, except for the fact the clerk wiggled his finger and made an annoying buzzing sound every time he went through his checkout.

But, that was not important now. The dark was coming and with it the greatest achievement of his long life. The resurrection of the Mother would show Marcus and the rest of those old women he had the balls to do what they were too afraid to do. After tonight they would be the ones bowing and scraping to his will. No more putting up with the high and mighty council and their womanish ways.

They were the vampiric lords created by the hand of the Mother herself. For countless ages they enforced the law that no vampire should reveal him- or herself to the human world. Some of their laws were simply ridiculous. Why should they hide? They were the ones with the power, not the humans. When he and the Mother were finished, everyone—vampires and humans—would know who held the true power.

Oh, Leopold knew he wouldn't be the one in power, but he knew behind every woman was a man who did the dirty work. He would be that man, as long as he didn't get dirty doing it. He planned to buy a whole new wardrobe befitting a man of his vaulted position. Leopold must order new catalogues from the finest shops. No more would he be forced to wear chain department store knock-offs and bootleg seconds from Thailand sweatshops that still smelled of forced child labor. No, he would dress like the king he was born to be.

But, what of Lewis? There would be no room for two right-hand men. The younger vampire deserved some sort of remuneration for his years of semi-loyal service. A Duchy in a far off locale. It would have to be somewhere garish to fit his personality. Las Vegas, Rio, and Brooklyn sprang to mind. Perhaps, it would be best to leave such decisions to a later date. The Mother would have ideas of her own. She might even want to keep Lewis as a pet. Deities were known for such dark humors.

All these fanciful notions were nothing more than that—notions to wile away the time. For Leopold had no more time to waste. Night had fallen. Outside the confines of his slumber-less coffin storm clouds masked the night, but it was there nonetheless, like a patient lover.

Leopold rose to greet his lover. He had done so for over three hundred years, but tonight it was different. Tonight, he would be its master. And, heaven help those who got in his way. He may even take the time to go to Buy-U-More and find out just what that wiggly finger meant before shoving it up... Well, you know the rest.

Fifty Five

Don't blame us if you get your butt killed. And don't come back and bite us on the neck, either.

The rain lessened with the coming night. It had not disappeared, but it moved toward the north at a slow, meandering gait. Luna thanked God for even a short respite.

She and Stud stood in the drizzling rain for fifteen minutes, trying to work up the courage to cross the street. Leopold's townhouse mocked them with its darkened silence. Blank windows glared, telling them only despair awaited within its confines.

Luna couldn't accept that. Breathred was in there. She stared at the huge house, looking for some indication he was still alive—like Leopold would have signs put up saying, "Virgin Hostage Inside." It was stupid of her, but she had to look. It was the principle of the matter.

Lightning crackled above them, sending her flailing back into the shadows. The idea of revealing herself to the vampires made her skittish. It shouldn't have. That was what they were here for, wasn't it? To be perfectly honest with herself—her bravado back at Uncle Joan's had played itself out.

Stud's hand closed over hers. Luna gave him a weak smile. His returned smile looked as strained as her own must have to him. In spite of his pained look, it was nice to know she wasn't alone. Brogan and Joan were close by, but weren't here with her. For tonight, at least, Stud was her knight in shining armor. Together, they would be Breathred's.

"Luna, they should be in position by now." Stud looked across the street.

"I know. Stud, I'm glad you're here with me at the end." She smiled down at him, feeling a little better for his comforting hand.

"What is this the fricking last movie in a trilogy? They're just vampires, not some dark lord bent on world domination."

"You're an ass. Do you know that?"

"I try, but it's hard being this hairy and not Greek." Stud started to laugh, but she gave him a look to say now wasn't the time.

"What does that have to do with anything?"

"Nothing. I just want it made perfectly clear—in case the subject comes up—I'm not Greek." He made a disgusted face at the thought and spat on the murky sidewalk. "So, are you ready, or what?"

"As much as you are." She bit her lip to hold back laughter, and looked back to the townhouse. Reality set in, drying her laughter into a cold lump that clogged the middle of her throat.

Before Luna could think herself out of it, she stepped off the curb. Her ankles were instantly surrounded by a rushing torrent. She chose to ignore it. After all it was just water. The way things looked she would be wading through a lot worse than this before this night was done.

~ * ~

Breathred was thrown roughly into the room, his arms cuffed behind his back. His knees skidded across the cold, stone slabs that made up the floor. He let out an involuntary whoosh, as he came to a jarring halt somewhere in the middle of the room. Breathred wanted to open his eyes to see where the vampire had taken him, but when he did, the voice would come back.

As long as he kept them good and crunched up, Breathred could convince himself the voice wasn't real. He was getting good at it, might even have succeeded if the vampire hadn't come to get him. It was too late to worry about imaginary voices now.

Breathred could smell the cloying scent of jasmine incense burning around him. It made him want to sneeze. Which he did. He bit his tongue in the process, drawing a thin river of blood into his mouth. His first impulse was to spit, but considering his companions, he decided against it. Soon enough, they would be seeing more than he liked without giving them a free preview.

"God bless, you." Leopold tittered.

"Thank you." Breathred answered back. They may be able to kill him, but that was no reason for bad manners.

"See, Lewis. I told you we should have turned up the heat. That was very rude of us. The virgin is catching a cold." Leopold continued to laugh.

"A cold'll be the least of his worries in a few minutes, Boss," Lewis snorted.

"Come, come, Lewis. There is no reason to remind Mr. Petrifunck of his impeding doom. I want this to be a pleasant experience for him." Leopold shot the vampire a harsh look.

"Dammit, Leo! We're not taking this guy to a day spa. We're gonna take a really long knife and..." Lewis made a chopping motion toward his chest, but Leopold interrupted him.

"Hush, not in front of the irgin-vay," Leopold hissed.

"That's okay. I kind of figured out what was going on back in the van," Breathred broke in.

"See what you've done? Now, he's all upset about being sacrificed." Leopold chided his fellow vampire.

"Can you blame him?" Lewis snorted.

"Well, no, but that's beside the point. I won't have a skittish virgin bringing bad karma down on all my Feng Shui. I paid a lot of money to have Bowen make this room cosmically balanced. I won't have it thrown away because you can't keep your mouth shut." Leopold shook his finger in the other vampire's face.

Breathred ignored the rest of the tirade. He figured as long as this would be the last room he ever saw, he might as well see it. It wasn't like he had anything better to do.

The room was decorated in cool pastels—greens and blues, with a dark, forest green border running across the top of the walls. Breathred's eyes followed the border to two French doors that opened out onto a garden that looked over-grown and unkempt. The doors were thrown open and a light dusting of rain filtered through them.

He turned his attention back to the room itself. A raised dais had been constructed in front of the French doors. Atop it rested D'brea's body. Leopold had unwrapped her and dressed her in a flowing white gown. A braided gold belt served as her only adornment, other than the diamond-encrusted tiara that rested in the folds of her strawberry-blonde hair.

Breathred had to admit Leopold had outdone himself. The room was fabulous. He couldn't think of a nicer place to die, though the angel-shaped candleholders were a bit over the top.

The two vampires had finished their fight and were looking directly at him. Not a good sign. It meant they had decided it was time to get the show on the road.

"So, guys. It looks like you have a lot to work through. What say I step outside for a few minutes while you do that?" Breathred grinned.

"Thank you, but no. This farce has reached its end, Mr. Petrifunck. My long wait is over. The Mother is ready to be born again. Your time has come." The excitement bubbled out of the vampire's voice.

Leopold motioned for Lewis to come forward. The younger vampire held an intricately carved wooden box. He shot Breathred a snotty look before handing the box to Leopold.

Breathred let out a gulp as Leopold opened the box. The vampire winked over the top of the lid and pulled out a wicked-looking gold knife. Breathred squinted. He couldn't be sure, but it looked like there was an etching of Vivian Leigh on the blade.

"I see you admire the fine workmanship. Only the finest for the Mother. I ordered this from the Franklin Mint for three monthly payments of $39.95. It's from their 'Gone with the Wind' collection. I was hoping the Rhett Butler one would come in before the sacrifice, but alas—Scarlet will have to do," Leopold mused, more to himself than Breathred.

"I can wait, if you want," Breathred offered.

"No, Ms. Leigh is more than up to the job," Leopold laughed, running his finger over the blade's razor edge. A thin red line appeared on his fingertip.

"Boss, can we get this over with?" Lewis snorted.

"An excellent idea, Lewis. Tie him to the altar," Leopold ordered, as his blood dripped down the knife blade.

Lewis reached down and jerked Breathred from the floor. It was like he was weightless in the vampire's hands. Breathred grunted, as Lewis jammed his arms back. He felt his shoulders pop from the strength of it.

Without an ounce of compassion, the vampire dragged him toward the altar. Breathred didn't even struggle. With his hands bound behind his back there was nothing he could do, anyway.

In the back of his mind the voice said different. Its promises reawakened in Breathred's mind. Breathred saw everything slipping away. He was a failure as a vampire slayer. Heck, he was a failure at everything. Luna, Stud and D'brea were depending on him to save them, and what was he doing? He was about to become a pincushion. That's what he was doing. Breathred was just grateful Luna wasn't here to see this.

If only there was some way to get out of this.

But, there is, the voice said stronger than ever. *Give in to me and you can save them all—Luna, the monkey, everyone. All you have to do is let me out and all this will be over.*

"What do you want from me?" Breathred screamed.

Lewis stopped dragging him and looked down at him like he was crazy. At this point Breathred couldn't be sure he wasn't totally bonkers. He'd ask the voice. It seemed to know everything, anyway.

"All right, put the virgin down and nobody gets hurt!" Stud yelled, stepping into the room.

Breathred couldn't believe his eyes. Luna and Stud had come to the rescue. He might just make it out of here after all. That wellspring of hope died when he saw Leopold slip around behind them. Breathred screamed out as the vampire grabbed Luna and pulled her back to him. Stud jerked his head toward them, but it was too late. The golden knife was at her throat.

It's not too late. I can save her, the voice cooed in his ear.

"What do I have to do?" The question a near silent breeze from his lips.

Just let me take care of everything. That's all, the voice promised.

Breathred held his breath, not sure he could trust the voice, but he couldn't let Luna die, either. He watched Leopold play the knife across her throat. No, she wouldn't die, if there was anything he could do about it. He'd bargain with the Devil, himself, to save her.

"Do it," Breathred said to the voice, and in the darkness of his mind the voice smiled.

Fifty Six

Just when you think you got vampires figured out, they go off and do something really throws you for a loop.

Seeing Leopold in action, Lewis regretted telling him not to wear the Gary Oldman Dracula wig. It would have looked good with his red Kimono with the black dragons copulating on the back. The young vampire was so distracted by the sight of his master and the girl he didn't even notice Breathred had slipped away.

"Let her go," Stud demanded.

"I don't think so, monkey boy." Leopold stuck his tongue out at the chimp. "See, I have the big knife, so I get to do what I want."

"Well, I've got the big hairy monkey, Wormy Mc Worm. So, you can suck it, Asshole," Stud shouted back.

"Stud, shut up. You're not helping matters." Luna screamed. Even Lewis winced as Leopold jerked the knife tight against her throat, pulling the flesh tight enough to make a pink indention in the skin.

"Yeah, back off before I slit doggie girl's throat. Now, shoo." Leopold shook his toe at Stud as he backed away from the chimp.

"You hurt her and I'll—" Stud warned.

"And you'll do what? Rub your dirty monkey butt on me? Go away. I will not have monkeys at the Mother's rebirth," Leopold snapped.

Stud made a move toward the vampire. His legs felt like lead weights as he moved to take a second step. He knew instantly D'brea had taken control of his body again.

What are you doing, you crazy bitch? he thought at her.

If you try to help her, all you'll do is get the both of you killed. D'brea answered, her voice a pale whisper in his head.

The chimp could tell the vamp was using too much of her already-depleted energy to keep him in check, and it showed. Even holding him in place was taxing her. If D'brea didn't get back to her body soon, he wondered what would happen. Would she find herself roaming around for all eternity without a body—or worse—be trapped in his body? Stud felt her doing the same as she shared his thought.

D'brea's trick had given Leopold enough time to get Luna closer to the altar, and out of his way. With a sigh of relief Stud felt her let control of his body go back to him. From their contact he felt her thoughts and knew if D'brea had a body, she would have been covered in sweat from the effort. As it was, even her spectral body shook from the effort, and he could feel her drifting away. Then the connection was gone and he couldn't feel anything from the woman.

Stud let out a strangled gasp as he felt D'brea exit his body and instantly felt the empty place inside himself where she had been. His feelings weren't hurt by it, either. He just knew she had planted flowers or something equally girly in his Super Id. He knew for a fact the ghost had been painting clothes on all his dirty dreams, so she was liable to do just about anything.

Whatever D'brea had on her freak-on-a-leash mind was not important now. He had to get to that floor-flushing vampire who had Luna. Stud didn't know what D'brea was up to, but it had better not screw up them saving Breathred. Dead or not, he'd go to hell and kill her ass for a second time, if she did.

Leopold's shouting brought Stud out of his musing. "Lewis, what the hell did you do with my virgin?"

Stud looked around and saw Breathred was nowhere in sight. The big goob must have gotten away in the confusion. At least something was going right.

"Damned, if I know! He must have slipped away when you and the monkey were yelling at each other," Lewis answered back, roughly.

"Don't take that tone with me, Playah. I don't care when he got away. Just find him!" Leopold screamed.

"Looking for me, hellspawn?" Breathred asked from the shadows that lay beyond the altar. His voice was cold and hard, sounding like a shadow rasping on the edge of the sun.

He stepped into the light. His hands were no longer cuffed behind his back, but were clinched into fists at his side. Stud barely recognized him. Breathred looked the same as always, but there was something different about him. Even his voice didn't sound like him. The chimp wasn't sure what was going on, but he sure as hell planned to find out.

"Breathred, are you okay?" Stud shouted to be heard over the quarreling vampires.

"Sub-creature, I am fine." Breathred stated.

"Sub-creature! Who the hell, are you calling a sub-creature?"

"Breathy, what's happened to you?" Luna sobbed.

Breathred swung his head around until his dead eyes fixed on her weeping face. "Woman, Breathred is gone."

"What do you mean Breathred is gone?"

"He sacrificed himself to save you from the abomination. He is no longer here. Only I exist in this body," the voice-made-flesh answered.

"Lewis, you broke my virgin!" Leopold pouted, letting Luna slip from his grip.

"And just who the fuck are you?" Stud shouted.

"I am the Antipaste, the fallen one." Breathred/Not Breathred answered.

Time stood still as they all looked at each other. Vampire stared at primate. Primate stared at human—well not human, but we're not going to go into semantics. Needless to say they were all confused.

"Did he just say he was a pile of linguini that just fell on the floor?" Leopold leaned back and asked Luna.

"I don't think so, but at this point anything is possible." Luna whispered back.

"What a crock of horseshit! Breathred, I don't know what these assholes did to you, but snap out of it." Stud told his friend. He had to have to have a serious talk to the goob when this was over. All those comic books were going to his head. Antipaste indeed! Next thing you know, he'd want to be called Darth Breathred again.

"Sub-creature, be quiet, lest I deal with you as harshly as I will with the abominations," the Not-Breathred snapped.

Stud shook his fist at him. "Friend or no friend, if you don't cut that sub-creature crap out, I'm going to slug you."

"So be it," Breathred said, a slow evil grin slashing his face.

Lightning blazed from Breathred's hands and engulfed the chimpanzee. Energy crackled around his diminutive form. The smell of burning hair filled the air, as he writhed in the center of the ball of electrical hell Breathred created around him.

Okay this shit hurts, Stud thought.

Feel free to jump to another point of view now. I think I'm going to cuss my ass off then pass out. Thank you very much for ignoring the fact I may soil myself somewhere in the middle of all the cussing.

"Breathred, stop it! You're killing him," Luna screamed.

Non-Breathred looked at her. For one brief second Luna swore she saw a flicker of the old Breathred. She bit her bottom lip, waiting for her words to break through to him. They had to. On some level he must know they were his friends. Somewhere in there, the Breathred she loved still existed.

"Please, let him go," she begged, as Stud's anguished howls filled the room.

Breathred blinked. Without a word, he lowered his hand. Instantly, the energy surrounding Stud disappeared, sending the chimp shooting through the air. He came down in a cussing, smoking lump against the far wall.

"Thank you," Luna said, weakly.

"Milady," Breathred said with a nod of his head.

"Look! I don't know what's going on here, but I will not have it. We are here for a simple virgin sacrifice. Is that too much to ask for?" Leopold shouted.

"Leo, chill out. You're kind of losing it and beginning to look like a total dweeb," Lewis advised him.

"Dweeb! I am over three hundred years old. People my age do not—I repeat—do not look like dweebs!"

"Well, a jackass, then." Lewis mumbled under his breath.

Leopold gave him a harsh look. "I heard that."

"I meant you to."

"I'm so sure you did, you mutha," Leopold snarled.

"Shut yo mouth." Lewis grinned.

"This is no time for your retro clichés. Get my virgin!"

"Silence!" Not-Breathred yelled.

Luna's mouth fell open at the sound of his voice echoing through the room. She wasn't one bit surprised to see the entire room fall silent or when every eye turned to the possessed Breathred. Luna knew shock was the least of the things running through any of their minds at the moment.

"There he is. Go get him." Leopold whispered to Lewis, drawing a weak chuckle from her.

"You go get him." Lewis told him. "I'm no fool. That whatever-it-is ain't the same nerd. You risk yo' lily-white ass if you want to, but I ain't."

"This farce is at an end. Demon spawn, it is time to pay for your unnatural existence," Not-Breathred said in his cold, empty voice.

Luna couldn't move. This was all wrong. She was torn between her love for Breathred and the realization he may no longer exist. What was she going to do, if he was truly gone like this Antipaste character said? Luna couldn't accept that. Uncle Joan had said she could save him. How to do that was what had her stymied.

Luna heard the sound of Stud moaning from where he lay against the wall. She had forgotten all about him. With everything that had been going on, she couldn't be expected to remember everything. The chimp was moving, so he couldn't have been hurt that badly. Besides, she always thought he needed shock therapy, anyway. As much as she would have liked to check on him, Breathred needed her more.

The world behind her exploded with the sounds of battle. Well, it really wasn't a battle. Maybe a one-sided ass-whooping would be closer to the truth. In any case, however you want to describe it, it didn't sound good.

She turned around just in time to see Breathred unleash a hail of lightning after the fleeing vampires. They barely dodged the bolts by jumping behind the altar. The lightning tore holes in the marble altar. Luna was happy to see, thankfully, D'brea's body missed a direct hit during the barrage. Luna would hate to see the vampire queen come to any harm. Aside from being a shameless hussy, D'brea was good people.

Everything was happening so quickly, she didn't know what to do. This sounded so simple back at Uncle Joan's apartment. Now, it was all going to hell in a hand-basket. Where were Uncle Joan and Brogan? Luna wasn't sure how much help they were going to be, but at this point anything was better than nothing.

"Fiends, there is no sense hiding. Your judgment is upon you." Breathred's voiced boomed.

"Can't we talk this over? I might have been a little hasty about sacrificing you," Leopold yelled, waving a lace hanky above the altar. "Perhaps, we could work something out."

Luna watched in horror as a lightning bolt shredded the hanky.

Leopold drew back the smoldering handkerchief. "Well, that was just rude. A polite no would have been enough."

"Breathred, stop this! This isn't you." Luna pleaded.

"Woman, I said be quiet! If you cannot control yourself, I will do so for you," Not-Breathred said.

Before Luna could say another word, Breathred flicked his hand, sending her sailing into the air. She looked around to see the far wall rushing toward her. Luna twisted her body at the last minute, but that didn't save her from the skull jarring impact that shot through her, as she connected with the wall.

Luna had five seconds of lucidity before everything went black. Disbelief splashed through her mind, as her consciousness faded. Her last thought was that Breathred wouldn't hurt her.

Stud smacked the smoke from his eyes at the sound of Luna's impact. He turned around just in time to see Luna's body crumple next to him. He slapped out the last of the embers from his head and shuffled over to her side.

Lightly moving the hair from her face, the chimp saw a thin line of blood ran from Luna's mouth and cascaded down her cheek. Stud held his breath, fearing the worst. The sound of his beating heart drowned out the fighting going on in the room around him. She had to be all right. He couldn't lose Breathred and her all in the same day. Who would pick up his dry cleaning? R.J. sure as hell wouldn't.

Stud wasn't even sure what had happened to her. One minute he was lit up like a Christmas tree, then the next he was doing his impression of a cigarette butt, which wasn't his idea of a fun night out on the town. He couldn't see Breathred, even if he wasn't possessed, hurting Luna, so that left the vamps. Dirty-ass bloodsuckers were bound to have done it.

A sound escaped Luna. Stud's eyes instantly fell to her. She still looked like hell, but some of the color was coming back to her face. Her chest moved with the slow rhythm of steady breathing. Stud let out a sigh, although he didn't want to let her see he was worried.

Her eyes snapped open to Stud's relief. She tried to get up, but he pushed her back down. "Don't even think about it. Now lay there and tell me what happened." He placed his hand on her shoulder.

"He's gone," she started sobbing.

"Who's gone, Sweetie?" Stud was confused, but a thousand volts tended to do that to you.

"Breathred," she whispered; tears swelled from her swollen eyes. "He hurt me, Studie."

Stud's heart went cold. He could understand Breathred taking a swipe at him. You could only repress anger for so long, but Luna? Breathred would never hurt Luna. The idea was so insane Stud had problems even processing it. He would have still been sitting there with his mouth hanging open if she hadn't reached up and grabbed his neck. "He's not in there anymore. Th-that whatever it is, has taken him over." Stud could barely hear her words through the sobs tearing through her.

He didn't know what to say. She wouldn't lie to him. The thought sent a wave of anger boiling through him. His Gilligan was gone. The asshole in his place had hurt the only other person in the whole flaming world he cared about—besides Estelle Getty—who wasn't returning his e-mails anymore, so she didn't count.

Stud wasn't about to accept that. One way or another, he would get his damn Gilligan back and, if any way possible, a Ginger. He knew just how to do it. The same way dear old mom would do it. He'd sneak up behind him and hit with something big and heavy, like a statue of a big naked guy with a little weenie. Which Stud grabbed as he put phase one of his plan into action.

Fifty Seven

Don't go to the bathroom yet, this is the part you've been waiting for.

Slinking around the edges of the room, Stud kept his eyes on Breathred and the two vamps. So far, he had been able to get close without any of them noticing. Maybe they had forgotten all about him. Dodging lightning bolts and trying to electrocute your enemies kind of blocked everything else out, or at least Stud hoped so.

A stray bolt of lightning raked down the room directly in front of him. Stud ducked and hit the ground. The slick statue shifted in his hand and he had to scramble to catch it before the thing went ballistic. Stud let out a mumbled curse. The last thing he wanted was to lose his only weapon.

From his floor-eye view, Stud could see Breathred was making mincemeat of the two vampires' hiding place. A full-on blast rocked the altar from the floor up, cleaving the block of marble into two uneven pieces with the vampire mother's body thrown haphazardly between them. Somehow, either by blind luck or poor marksmanship, D'brea's body had missed any damage from the goob's barrage. If Breathred kept it up, that wouldn't last too much longer. The only other thing working in their favor was that Breathred was so intent on the two vamps he'd forgotten all about anyone else being in the room.

Chimps have a saying: *He who turns his back on the baboon, has a shitty hairdo to show for it.* Well, Breathred was about to get a pompadour from hell.

The chimp was about to make his move, when two shadows moved in the darkened doorway behind the fighting. Hunkering back down, a flash of scarlet lipgloss about six and a half feet in the air told him reinforcements had shown up. 'Bout damn time too! Chimps were thinkers, not fighters.

He caught a glimpse of Brogan slipping away from the other man. Joan angled to the right. It was a classic flanking move Stud had learned from hours of video games.

The chimp scooted back. Why should he risk himself, when there were two humans more than willing to do it for him? The fact they had no idea what had happened to Breathred didn't even occur to him. The way Stud saw it, they'd find out soon enough. Well, he was just a little monkey. The minute he popped his head up to say, "Hey, the big human with lightning bolts shooting out his fingers is possessed," he'd be a fire-grilled chimp. The safest thing to do was sit back until the two heroes were the ones getting their asses kicked, then sneak up and whomp Breathred upside the head. If he were lucky, the two vamps would be out of the picture before that happened.

It was a good plan. Too bad Luna didn't get the memo.

She rose on shaky legs. Blood caked her face. It did little to mar the determination that called her face home. Her first step threatened to send her back to the marble floor. Luna shook away the pain, coiled it around the beast that begged to be called to freedom. Breathred was her only concern. Her only thought.

Luna vaguely noticed the fact Brogan and Uncle Joan had finally arrived. Her centered mind did not even acknowledge the existence of the two vampires, who sat huddled behind the shattered altar. Her footsteps were muted echoes under the screaming power of Breathred's attack.

Her stealth mattered little. Luna wanted the bastard who had put the hoodoo on Breathred to know she was coming. It had taken the only man she would ever love from her. He was going to pay for that. Even if she had to kick Breathred's ass to do it, that sucker was going back to hell where he belonged.

"Breathred!" Luna howled above the ungodly din. Every head stopped what they were doing and turned toward her.

"Woman, your would-be lover is gone. Only I remain." Smoke curled from Not-Breathred's fingertips.

"I figured it out on my own, Dipshit," she spat.

"I have ignored your aberrations because of the misplaced emotions of my host, but no longer." Breathred stepped around the broken altar, placing himself but feet away from it.

D'brea's desiccated body was nestled between the altar's two halves. Leopold and Lewis peeked warily over the mummified remains of their queen. Neither made a move to flee. Like everyone else, they were rooted in place by the tableau playing out before them.

Antipaste's attack came so fast Luna didn't have time to react. A blue fireball shot from his outstretched hand and engulfed her. The spinning orb threw her into the air, the eldritch energy holding her at the ball's center. Stray offshoots of energy crackled and sparked over the ball's surface. Luna screamed as the energy spiked into her.

Stud did something that, if you knew him, would have surprised the shit* out of you.

*Excuse my French.

He leapt from his warm, safe hidey-hole and ran for Breathred. His short, stumpy legs propelled him past his cowardliness—no mean feat. With the marble naked guy high overhead, Stud closed the distance between them and swung.

Stud had less than a second to think how crazy he was acting. Sure, Breathred needed a good knock upside the head, but preferably not when he was a ghost-poxed nutcase. The thought hung there for the span of one heartbeat. Then the smack to Breathred's head got in the way of any doubts he might have had.

The sound of the impact of the statue wasn't the gunshot you've read about. It wasn't even as loud as a pop-fart in a library. It was more like the sound of a wet noodle slapping a plate, only it wasn't marinara shooting off that plate.

Breathred's head rocked forward, his eyes wide with surprise. The power ebbed and sputtered from his hands, sending Luna crashing to the floor. Her body let out a weak whimper as she hit.

Breathred staggered back. His face was a clear map to the confusion that played across his mind. Blood trickled down his forehead from a cut high above his right eye. He stumbled backwards, giving Stud a hurt look before collapsing into the shattered altar.

"Stud! What the hell's going on?" Brogan rushed into the room.

"What's it look like? Everything went FUBAR while you and Joan were tiptoeing through the tulips," Stud snarled, as he ran to Luna's side.

The chimp ignored the rest of the man's comments as he dropped beside Luna. Except for a perm from hell, she looked okay. Her breathing was steady. Stud let out a sigh. Now he could check on Breathred.

Stud turned around to see Leopold and Lewis heading for the door and sprinted to catch them, yelling, "Brogan, the vamps are making a break for it!"

The two vamps stopped like deer in headlights. It was more than a reactionary move. You have a chimp, a hairy Canadian, and seven-foot-tall transvestite running at you, and see if you don't freeze up like Frosty in a Dairy Queen. The vamps never had a chance.

"Where do you think you're going?" Brogan growled, grabbing for Leopold.

Leopold slapped at his hand. "Don't touch the silk, you ruffian. I will not have rough hands stroking me in such a manner." His voice was a high-pitched squeal.

"Let me do it." Joan stated with a sly wink.

"Yes, move Hairy Man." Leopold pushed Brogan out of the way and planted himself firmly in Joan's arms. "I am your prisoner. Do with me what you will!"

Joan staggered back as the vampire swooned into his arms.

"Hold him tight, while I deal with the other one." Brogan turned to

Lewis, who immediately threw his hands up.

"No worries here, Chief. It was all the honky's idea." Lewis grinned sheepishly. Stud would have laughed if something else hadn't caught his attention. "Uh, guys. I think we have a problem."

The broken altar was glowing. High above it, D'brea floated. The dried husk of her body was gone; in its place rose the glorious Vampire Mother, come to life. Her face was a stone cold mockery of humanity.

"You can unhand me now," Leopold said smugly. "But don't go anywhere. I may keep you as a pet." The vampire sighed before striding toward his queen.

Stud gave Brogan a shove. "Are you just planning on standing there, or are you going to stop his ass?"

"Nope." Brogan grunted.

"Why the hell not?"

"Do you really think D'brea's going to give that dufus the time of day, let alone the power he's expecting?"

"What about him?" Stud jerked his thumb toward Lewis.

"You ain't got to worry about me. That is one freaky-lookin' white chick." Lewis had backed up against the wall.

"Mother, I bow before Your Majesty and offer myself to Your service." Leopold executed a perfect courtly bow before the vampire queen.

"Rise, My Son. Your Mother is pleased with your subjugation." Stud began to worry until he caught a sly wink from D'brea. "You will be my right hand in my plan to bring the Vampiric Nation back to its former glory."

"What is Thy bidding, My Mother?" he asked. Stud almost gagged on the pitiful Sith reference.

"We must repopulate the world with true vampires. None of this biting that has become the rage of the newer generation." An evil smile plastered D'brea's face.

"No biting? But how do you make a vampire without biting?" Leopold lifted his head confused.

"Surely you've heard of copulation." She faced toward Stud, showing him the wide smile she had plastered on it.

"With women?" Leopold squealed.

"But of course. I myself will handpick your first harem. Nothing big, a hundred or so nubile vampires to begin with should do it." Stud could see D'brea pinching herself to stop from laughing.

"Couldn't we begin with artificial insemination first? This is too important to trust to blind chance. What if they don't catch the first time?" Leopold was actually backstepping toward the door.

"Then you'll have to keep banging away until we have the invincible vampire army we need to take over the world." D'brea pumped her hips at the fleeing vampire.

"Thanks for the offer My Mother, but I forgot I am a prisoner of this gentleman. It would be unfair of me to forgo a previous obligation and embark on something of this magnitude," Leopold sputtered as he climbed back into Joan's arms.

"Is this true, human? Does this one owe you an obligation?" D'brea asked Joan.

"Yes, ma'am. Not more than five minutes ago he surrendered to me."

"And how long does his imprisonment last?" D'brea turned her steely glare on Leopold.

"No less than a hundred years My Queen," Leopold squeaked. "It would not be right to serve less than that for the horrific crimes I've committed. I will understand if you wish to find another vampire to fulfill your dreams."

"That will not be necessary. I can wait."

"It could be longer than a hundred years. I am quite nefarious and will undoubtedly do something dastardly to earn added time to my sentence."

"I am patient and will wait until the end of time if need be." D'brea answered in mock resignation. She turned her attention to Joan. "Sir, do you accept guardianship for this man until such time as his sentence is completed? Even if it calls for him to be treated most grievously, possibly even chained or beaten unmercifully while you are dressed as a schoolgirl?"

"I think I can manage that." Joan grinned.

"Then hie him from my sight until such time as I have need of him," She waved them toward the door.

Leopold nearly dislocated Joan's arm pulling him through the door. The sound of their retreating footsteps echoed through the opening.

"I thought he'd never leave," D'brea said after they'd left.

"Uh, could somebody tell me what just happened?" Lewis asked.

"None of your damn business. Shut up before I lose my good mood," Brogan gave him a shove toward the vampire queen.

"Stud, get over here and help me lift him up." D'brea ordered, as she bent down beside Breathred.

"What about Luna?" Stud was torn between his two friends. Despite his earlier examination of the girl, she still hadn't wakened.

"She is fine. I hear her pulse from here. It is strong. We need to get Breathred awake. He is the key to breaking her slumber," D'brea shouted.

Stud shrugged and went over to the pair. D'brea put her arm behind Breathred's neck and motioned for Stud to get on the other side. He still wasn't sure she was right about Luna, as together they pulled him up into a seated position. A low groan escaped him as he settled back against the ruined altar.

"Before Breathred wakes I think it best we do not mention what happened to him. I sense it would only bring the creature back into control," D'brea warned.

"How can you say that? Whatever the thing inside him is, it nearly killed Luna. We need to do something about it." Stud countered, even though he wasn't all too sure what was going on himself.

"No. It is something that must stay buried until he is strong enough to defeat it himself. The being is ancient, older than even me. If there was anyway to excise it from him, it was forgotten long ago. He must be watched, but beyond that I don't know. I just know if Breathred becomes aware of its existence, the knowledge could very well tear him apart." She looked right into Stud's eyes as she spoke.

"Okay." Stud didn't like it but for now he would go along with it.

"What happened?" Breathred sputtered, as he slipped back into consciousness.

D'brea shot Stud a warning glare. "You did it, Sweetie. The vampires are gone. You ran them off and brought me back to life."

Breathred blinked and looked around. "I did?"

"Yep." Stud said through gritted teeth.

"I had this weird dream and in it I hurt Luna. Where is she?" Breathred sat up, only to fall back in Stud's arms.

"She's hurt, Breathred, but it wasn't you." Stud tried not to flinch at D'brea's lie. He'd go along with it for now, but he would get to the bottom of this Antipaste thing, so help him.

"Take me to her. I need to see her." Breathred thrashed to get to his feet.

"Calm down, Dweeb." Stud pushed him back. "Brogan, leave the dead wood and get over here."

Breathred felt two pair of hands lift him to his feet. He tilted his head to see Brogan and one of the vamps behind him. He gave the Canadian a weak smile, and wondered why the man gave him such a weird look. Chalking it up to all the excitement, Breathred quickly forgot about it. He needed to see that Luna was all right. They half dragged him over to Luna's sleeping body.

Seeing her lying there, Breathred drew away from them, staggering the last few feet on his ow

He collapsed beside her. She looked so small. Her face was a blank slate. There was nothing there to indicate the lively girl he… The thought choked in his throat. What if she was dying? He couldn't live without her. He'd tried for so long, and all he had was an empty existence. Ever since she'd come into his life, he'd come to know what being alive was truly about. He couldn't lose her now. She had to be all right.

"Luna," he let the words fall like a prayer from his lips. "It's me Breathred."

Her face remained a placid, limp mask.

"Come on, wake up. I need you to be all right," he cried, his tears flowing down his cheeks to waterfall onto her. "I love you, gosh darn it."

Luna's eyelashes fluttered and popped open. "Breathred, is that really you?"

"Uh huh," he sobbed. His hand worked furiously to dry the tears from his face. The last thing he wanted was for her to see him crying.

"Did you just say you loved me?" She smiled weakly.

"I-I th-thought you c-couldn't hear me."

"Did you mean it?" She frowned, but a playful gleam was in her eyes.

"If I say yes, will you try to kiss me?"

"Yep." She beamed.

"Then you better kiss me."

And she did.

Epilogue

Breathred looked across the Java Jumper looking for Luna. She was late. It had been a week since the vampire thing. In spite of that, he still found himself looking over his shoulder expecting an all-out vampire assault at any moment. He would feel better if he could remember anything of what had happened.

It was a big blur. As much as he'd like to accept Stud's berserker rage amnesia as an explanation, he couldn't. These weird snatches of memories kept hitting him at the oddest times. In them he was doing things to Luna. The bad things in these nightmares were totally different from the nasty things he'd been doing to Luna in the other dreams. Breathred wished the dreams would just go away so he could go back to dreaming about important things like comic books.

The door opened for the hundred and fiftieth time, drawing his gaze. He smiled as, this time, Luna walked through the door. The fact that Stud, D'brea, and Brogan followed her in didn't detract from the joy he got from seeing her. Besides, in a few hours, the last were leaving for parts unknown. It wasn't that Breathred was glad to see them going, but he missed all the peace and quiet. Not to say Stud allowed for much peace and quiet.

"Hey, Sweetie." Luna plopped down beside him and threw her arm around his shoulders.

"You're late," he said nervously.

"Don't nag her, Big Boy. She and the monkey were helping us pack," D'brea chided him.

Stud slid in opposite them. "Yeah, Breathred. She had me to watch out for her. There was nothing to worry about."

Breathred thought it best to ignore him, so turned to Brogan. "Aren't you going to sit down?"

"No can do, Bub. We got a flight out in thirty minutes. We just stopped by to let you know we were gone." Brogan slipped his arm around D'brea's slender waist and pulled the vampire queen toward him.

"Stop it, Badger Britches." D'brea protested—but not much, Breathred noted.

Out of everything that happened he still found it hard to believe the Canadian mountain man and D'brea had hit it off. The twelve hour nookie-fest, as Stud put it, might have had something to do with it, but Breathred wasn't up to asking what a nookie-fest was, so took Stud's word for it.

Whatever the case, it solved one of his big problems—what to do with the vampire mother. As much as he liked being a vampire slayer, he couldn't bring himself to slay any of the ones he'd met. Leopold and Luna's Uncle Joan had headed off to Rio at Leopold's urging. The vampire thought it best to serve out his hundred-year sentence somewhere far away from

D'brea, and Rio was the furthest place he could think of that offered indoor plumbing and nipple painting.

Lewis had slipped away before anyone could think to stop him.

Breathred's big chance to be a vampire slayer had ended with no slaying, unless you counted the ones at the mall. So, guessed he did slay some after all. A couple was better than none. It wasn't the best way to start his career, but he had gotten a good bit of publicity out of it. Somehow or another a reporter had gotten wind of the debacle up in Canada, put two and two together and come up with five. His article had very little truth in it, but Breathred's name had been mentioned as well as *Petrifunck Paranormal*. The end result was the phone had been ringing off the hook with jobs.

"Breathred, I want to thank you." D'brea said, drawing him from his thoughts.

"You're welcome," he answered automatically then thought he had better find out what for. He might have agreed to something totally icky. It wouldn't be the first time either. "What for?"

"Bringing me out of my boring prison. Hon, this whole thing has been a blast. I can't wait to get out there and see how much trouble me and old Iron Bottom, here, can get into." D'brea laughed.

A horrible thought echoed through Breathred's mind. "Uh, you won't be sucking the blood out of anyone will you?"

"Darling, I'm old enough I can go years without a nip. Plus, your blood should keep me in dutch for centuries. We didn't have blood that pure back in my day. And then we had vestal virgins." She cackled.

"I'll keep an eye on her." Brogan gave Breathred's shoulder a friendly punch. "If she steps out of line, I got just the thing to stake her with."

"Oh, Brogan. Let's get out of here before you make me blush." D'brea cooed, as she dragged the man away from the table.

"See ya later, guys." Brogan waved as they headed for the door.

"Now, tell me more about this Mile-High Club," D'brea's voice shouted over the din of diners, bringing the entire coffee shop to a silent pause.

"Don't even think about asking," Stud said to Breathred, who promptly shut his mouth.

"So, what do we do now?" Luna interrupted.

"Well, I did have an interesting phone call today about a demonic goldfish that was taking control of this poor woman's cat and making it eat lasagna." Breathred answered with a childlike wonder in his eye.

"Sounds good to me." Stud jumped up on the table and yelled. "Edith, my love. Three Banana Choca Lattes to go. We got demonic fish-ass to kick."

~ * ~

A note from the Author

I told you it would be hard to believe, but you went ahead and read it anyway. This ends the tale of how the idiot—with my help—saved the world from vampiric domination. This is in no way the end of Breathred's adventures. Unfortunately, they just won't seem to stop.

I know some of you are pissed off because you didn't find out about the Antipaste, or if Luna ever convinced Breathred to jump in the sack. Well, you aren't finding out here either. You'll have to buy the next book. I've got my eye on a set of pornographic dolphin figurines on E-bay, so you better get to saving them nickels and dimes.

Stud L. Monkey, Esquire.

About J.

J. Morgan grew up in a small town in northern Louisiana. A Fine Arts major in college J. dreamed of becoming the next Michelangelo or a comic book artist, whichever came first. It was only later in life that dreams of writing tore him away from the easel to buy a laptop and start writing.

He is happily married to fellow author Jenna Leigh. J. can be found in front of the TV pretending to write while really watching endless hours of drivel and laughing at the voices in his head who feed him plotlines. While the voices may not be in control yet, one day they hope to have a book deal of their own, 'til then J. Morgan will get to spend the royalty checks.

Visit our website for our growing catalogue of quality books.
www.champagnebooks.com